TomKat:

Double Impact

A novel by

Lance Winchester & Michael Crane

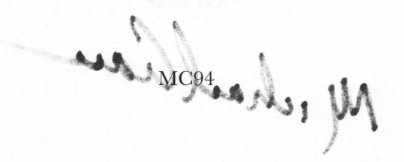

MC94

Dedicated to the men and women who fought and died fighting our country's enemies for the last 250 years of our country's history.

PROLOGUE

Tom Ford recently turned twenty-one and took a well-earned break from his studies and work. He found himself fifteen miles northeast of his home in Orford, New Hampshire, on the Connecticut River twenty miles north of Hanover, NH, Dartmouth College's home. He always enjoyed his escape to hike the Mt. Moosilauke region, a graceful landscape of rolling hills, forests and fields. However, Tom was not hiking on this day. He was hunting, hunting woodchucks, a despised varmint of farmers.

Tom was enjoying a splendid early July day: hot, dry, deep blue skies and no cloud cover. Except for distant rising heat waves, the conditions were perfect for shooting: superb visibility, a bright sun, and best of all, he would be free from that adversary of long-range riflemen -- wind.

For varmint hunting, Tom preferred a Remington Model 700 Varmint Special in .308 caliber. He determined the .308 round the best choice for extreme-distance shooting, his passion. The Remington features a heavy barrel which, though more rigid than is a lighter or sportier barrel, gives exceptional accuracy. He swapped the stock trigger for an adjustable Timney and lightened the trigger pull from four pounds to one. He now exerted one pound trigger force for his shot -- the lighter and smoother the trigger-pull, the more accurate the shot. It's often called a "hair trigger."

Tom had set his sights on a tiny brown rodent weighing between five and ten pounds. Woodchucks burrow homes in the middle of sweeping pastures and fields where they can spot danger from a great distance. This gives the chuck enough time to safely descend into his burrow. These creatures spend the day eating clover and grass, sunning themselves on the mound of earth surrounding a dug burrow. Chucks have incredible vision and detect coyotes, foxes, hawks and other predators long before they become a tasty meal. The fertilized pastures offer an abundant food supply, and woodchucks are exceptionally prolific. Their population growth never seems to be checked. Dairy farmers hate woodchucks because their valuable cows sometimes step into the chuckholes breaking their legs and dislocating shoulders. Farmers heartily give chuck hunters permission to shoot to their hearts' content.

Tom had a productive morning. From his excellent vantage point behind the steep crags overlooking a chain of hay fields, he targeted five chucks and killed three. Tom's latest kill was an impressive four hundred and fifty yards shot.

Tom was pleased that his marksmanship had improved in recent years. His first of two misses was a 550-yard shot that appeared to hit the ground six inches to the right. Considering his rifle could shoot a one-inch group at 100 yards, (which means the rifle could shoot a bullet within a one-inch circle at 100 yards, and a five-inch circle, (which under perfect conditions, at 500 yards) it was a good shot. To maximize the probability of consistently hitting a woodchuck-sized critter (six to eight inches wide standing) at 500 plus yards, he would need a far more expensive military-grade rifle. Perhaps one day.

Tom sited another chuck through the scope. As he pulled the trigger, the second critter dove into his hole. The bullet whizzed above the woodchuck's head as he ducked. Tom smiled to himself, "*Lucky guy.*"

Suddenly, a police siren broke the valley's silence. Tom swung his rifle with its thirty-power Bushnell spotting scope towards the blare and watched where the highway curved around the edge of the farthest field. He observed a state police cruiser, red lights flashing, behind a pickup truck. Jim Hutton, emerged from the vehicle, a second trooper remained in the car, and Tom assumed he was checking the pickup's registration over the radio.

Sam Lattimore, the pickup's driver, was on probation. He and his brothers bought three kilos of cocaine in Lawrence, Massachusetts that morning and Sam faced a long stretch in prison if these troopers searched his truck and found the drugs.

"We are fucked if those cops find the three keys behind this seat. I'm not going back to the can." Larry Lattimore opened the glove compartment revealing three revolvers. Sam Lattimore gave the order to his brothers while he passed around the guns: "Let's get these two."

Two doors slammed open as the officer approached the truck. The three armed brothers bounded out. Sam Lattimore pointed his ancient Colt 45 at the trooper and fired. The trooper collapsed to the ground from the center chest hit. Seconds later, Tom heard the dim echo of the shot.

Sam moved toward the fallen officer. He kicked the cop, believing him dead. He anxiously approached the patrol car for the downed trooper's partner. Astounded by the scene, Tom realized, *"My God, I've just seen a trooper murdered in cold blood. "*

Sam Lattimore, joined by his two brothers, turned their attention to the second trooper who was now hiding behind his patrol car. The trooper drew his pistol from the holster, waiting for the shooters. Tom sensed a bitter chill coursing through his body as the brothers approached the patrol car.

At that moment a rage he had never experienced swept through him. Everything became crystal clear—another side of him had awakened. Tom understood his duty to protect the troopers who were under attack. He pointed his rifle at the distant target. He estimated the distance to be six-hundred yards and adjusted his Unertl Ultra Varmint sixteen-power telescopic sight, referencing the bullet-drop table taped to the rifle stock. These adjustments seemed to take an eternity, although they took only a couple of seconds.

Tom heard another shot. Through the scope he saw the second officer now propped against his car holding his leg – his vehicle provided only partial cover. The Lattimore brothers cautiously approached him from two sides of the squad car with their handguns extended toward Bill Layton, the remaining trooper.

Tom spotted the crosshairs high on the first man, the brother who had shot the officer. He breathed out then squeezed the trigger. The rifle kicked but the gun's mass minimized recoil. The 168-grain Sierra MatchKing bullet covered 600 yards in a second. The bullet had left the rifle's muzzle at 2600 feet per second and found its mark -- it struck the right side of Sam Lattimore's back at 1400 feet per second. The bullet's impact splattered blood, flesh, and bone on the patrol car. Sam Lattimore experienced incredible pain as he collapsed to the ground. Moments from death, the darkness enveloped him.

After the muzzle smoke cleared Tom saw that his shot found its intended target. He worked the bolt, ejecting the spent cartridge, and chambering a fresh round. He centered the crosshairs on the second brother. In seconds, the bullet pierced Larry Lattimore's lower chest, breaking into three fragments, any one of which would have killed him. Larry gave a shuddering low moan and died.

Earl, the third brother, terrified by the fate of his brothers, ran towards the pickup truck. He jumped into the driver's seat, simultaneously starting the motor and slamming the door. Tom Ford had one chance before the man drove beyond range. He pointed the rifle at the pickup, aimed at the driver's side window and pulled the trigger.

Still sheltering behind the patrol car, Bill Layton heard the glass shatter followed by a terrible thud as Earl's head exploded like a ripe melon, leaving a thick scarlet coating on the windshield. A soft rumble echoed in the distance; the pickup's idle marred the silence that usually characterized the valley.

Layton slid inside his cruiser, his fingers firmly grasping his injured leg. Tom assumed the trooper was requesting assistance. Aware that he must evacuate the area, he scrambled down the knoll with his sandbag, ammo, three empty shell casings and rifle. Tom had parked his WWII Willys Jeep in a deep hollow behind the hill - out of view from the road. He climbed into the jeep and navigated the rutted dirt road to the paved town road that led west to Route 10. Tom then headed home, 10 miles south.

His adrenalin slowed during his drive, the action euphoria abated. At first, the experience distressed him, but a sense of gratification soon raised his spirits. He recognized he had fired three shots within fifteen-seconds at six-hundred yards and hit three killers. When he considered the three, he regarded them not as human but as varmints. Tom never thought of reporting to the authorities. Although a young man, inexperienced in many ways, he was, as the cliché goes, wise beyond his age.

He realized the judicial and law enforcement systems have been politicized and corrupted. Some ambitious and aggressive prosecutor would salivate at the prospect of working this case. The publicity would give any young lawyer an excellent start for a successful political career.

Tom asked himself, can anything be gained by surrendering? At the very least he would be subject to lengthy interrogations, a grand jury inquiry and doubtless, numerous additional aggravating legal practices he hadn't even envisioned.

Nobody would question the three perps' guilt and that justice was served. Moreover, he knew he saved taxpayers substantial costs. The state would have given the killers an expensive trial. The Lattimores would have lived their remaining lives at government expense in a comfortable prison. His shooting not only saved a state trooper's life but also rid society of true vermin, much as he helped the dairy farmers by hunting their woodchucks.

After a little thought, he recognized that it would be difficult to link him to the shooting. Tom never met the brothers. They did not know Tom. A motive would be nearly impossible to establish. That he was no closer than a third mile to the scene from the shooting made implicating him even more difficult. Tom concluded that had someone witnessed the shooting and he subsequently arrested, no grand jury would indict him for saving a police officer's life.

Nevertheless, Tom became concerned about the implications of his shootings. Looking through a telescopic sight at men six-hundred yards away resembled the tiny targets seen at a shooting range. Shooting them was somewhat the same -- it didn't seem real. He was aware of the damage a high-powered rifle inflicts on living creatures, but he preferred to overlook the issue at this time. Nonetheless, another trooper would have died if he hadn't acted. He relaxed as he drove home.

He arrived in Orford thirty minutes later. Tom, raised to be open and honest with his parents, felt compelled to tell them about the shootings. As he entered the door, his father, Dr. Robert Ford, far more excited than was his usual composed serene self, exclaimed, "You won't believe this, Tom, someone shot and killed the three Lattimore brothers as they ambushed two troopers on Moosilauke Highway. The news just came over the police scanner. I guess they'll need the coroner's services and not mine."

Tom replied, "I know. I shot them." The doctor looked curiously at his son but was hardly surprised. Tom sat with his father and told him the full story. "I simply couldn't watch those troopers die without doing something," he said to finish his account.

Dr. Ford smiled a proud father smile, "Well, you did well son. Both troopers will be OK. They are now on their way to Dartmouth-Hitchcock – one with a bullet lodged in his thigh. Fortunately, the bullet missed the femoral artery and the bone. The other trooper suffered broken ribs from the shot he took. Fortunately, he wore a kevlar vest but the bullet slammed him hard enough to break his ribs and temporarily knocked him out." The doctor added, "It's ironic that Bill Layton, one of the wounded troopers, arrested Sam Lattimore twice for felonies. I remember the news reports. Sam should have been locked away for two or three more years but a judge freed him on an early release program. Well, that decision cost three lives...you saved the troopers' lives, you'll be considered a hero."

"Perhaps, but I prefer we keep this our secret."

"Are you sure, Tom?"

"Yes, I am."

"Well, I will keep this between us, of course, but I must tell your mother."

Tom mindful of the pledge they took when they married -- no secrets -- realized his mother must be told.

"Let me tell her," said Tom taking his father's shoulder.

Dr. Ford nodded affirmatively.

The shootings created considerable stir in the media and the investigation lasted for several months. Investigators found scant evidence, beyond some shards of .30 caliber bullets, the most common high-powered rifle caliber in the world. Sure, they realized they were dealing with a skilled marksman and reviewed military records for locals having sniper or other special training, but the few leads led the investigation nowhere.

Police investigators questioned farmers who had granted hunters permission to shoot woodchucks on their land, but none took names and no one had heard or seen anything odd the day of the shooting. Everyone in the valley thought their community improved by the Lattimore brothers' elimination As heartless as that may appear, only their mother mourned her sons' deaths.

The state police, notably the barracks of troopers Hutton and Layton, were pleased the mystery sniper saved their two brethrens' lives. Justice had been swiftly served by the quick death of the Lattimore brothers. New Hampshire State Police crossed a few T's and dotted a some I's, satisfying administrative requirements, but nobody had the heart to find the shooter. The subsequent perfunctory investigation, as expected, yielded nothing. Several local media reporters gave cursory effort to investigate the case, but they, too, soon lost interest by the little public concern for finding the shooter. Additionally, they experienced no cooperation from the locals for giving any leads. Nobody divulged anything to the investigators.

Tom, following the news coverage of the investigation, recalled the shooting of the town bully of Skidmore, Missouri decades earlier.

A Tom McElroy, arrested dozens of times, with infrequent convictions and little jail time, was shot by at least two men in plain view of 30 to 40 witnesses. The police never arrested anyone for the murder. The entire town adopted the code of omertà, the mafia's code that demands silence and prohibited anyone from ratting to the authorities. Neither the police nor the prosecutors ever convinced any of the witnesses to tell them anything they knew about the shooting. Tom suspected all the area's farmers he shoots chucks for adopted the code of omertà when speaking to investigators.

All investigations were conveniently buried in numerous file cabinets, likely never to be resurrected. As time passed, the troopers hoisted many an off-duty beer to the "ghost sniper" with genuine affection and admiration rarely expressed by law enforcement officers for such a "criminal."

Tom continued his life, unconcerned with detection of his shooting. He suffered no anguish, remorse or guilt for killing the Lattimore brothers. Instead, his marksmanship that day provided him with a deep gratification of saving two good men's lives. Tom, a highly moral and principled young man, fully understood his achievement. He recognized the Lattimores were solely responsible for their deaths.

CHAPTER 1: *The Fords*

Tomkat's story began twenty-one years earlier at the home of Dr. and Mrs. Robert Ford of Orford, New Hampshire.

Amelia Briggs Ford heard a car stop on the circular gravel driveway; seconds later she heard a door slam and a car accelerate from the house, a barrage of pebbles launched against the massive wood Gothic front door.

She opened the door to investigate and watched a car race down the driveway before turning left onto the town road. Looking down, Amelia noticed an old Budweiser beer box on the porch floor. Inside the box, she saw a blue blanket...and the blanket was moving. She raised the blanket...revealing a baby!

Amelia took the baby inside. It was a cool, crisp late autumn day, but the baby wore only hospital-issued pajamas. The baby wasn't crying. She hoped it wasn't ill or suffering from trauma. Amelia lifted the baby from the box, exposing a note underneath. She placed the box on a nearby table and read the handwritten note.

Dear Dr. and Mrs. Ford,

I am sorry to do this to you, but you have the best reputation in the Dartmouth community. I believe I can trust you to do the best for Thomas (Tom is not his father's name, but my father's).

I am a Dartmouth student and have struggled the last few months of whether to terminate the pregnancy or to have the baby. The father, a Dartmouth professor, lobbied hard to abort -- he was concerned about discovery of having an affair with a student. I walked into the women's clinic several times but couldn't kill my baby.

If you keep him or give him for adoption please be sure he will be well taken care of. I am leaving Dartmouth and transferring to a school near my home in California. I am aware that you could easily identify me, but I beg you to protect my privacy. In return, I promise never to contact you. Perhaps, one day you will tell Tom that his mother loved him but couldn't properly care of him. You can't imagine how hard it is to abandon my baby but I have no other choice. Thank you for the love and care I know you will give him.

Sincerely, Tom's Mother

Amelia placed the note in the box and scrutinized the baby. What a beautiful boy, she observed; his piercing blue eyes, wispy blond hair, a determined demeanor, and a regal bearing impressed her. She thought he gave her a n expression stating, "I am yours now, and you better do an adept job raising me."

Amelia called her husband, who had just concluded his rounds at Dartmouth Hitchcock.

Dr. Ford looked at his pager: Amelia. He called home from the hall desk. "Amelia, so good hearing from you. Why a call at this time of day?"

"Robert, someone left a baby on our front porch. Please come home as quickly as you can and stop at maternity to pick up a couple bottles of milk. Tom must be famished."

"Tom?" the doctor asked.

"Yes, Tom. The note said his name is Thomas."

"I'll hurry home."

"...and don't forget the milk!"

The doctor drove home after first stopping at the maternity ward for milk. Amelia, he assumed, was considering adoption. They have been married for twenty years and had had frequent serious discussions about adoption.

Amelia suffered a tragic car accident when she was twelve. Besides a couple of broken legs, she suffered severe abdominal trauma, including uterine rupture resulting in hemorrhage and a necrotic uterus. She had an emergency hysterectomy to stop the bleeding and as she later expressed, simply and stoically, "...and that was that."

Robert Ford understood he had no convincing arguments against adoption. Money presented no problem. Neither did they have mortgage payments or any other debt. Besides his Dartmouth-Hitchcock salary and earnings from his private practice, Amelia Briggs inherited half of the sizable Briggs family estate when her mother died. The estate included the house where they now live. For more than a century, it served as the family's summer retreat, with ample room for additional beds. Only their ages could preclude an adoption. He recently turned forty-six, Amelia forty-two; however, the two enjoyed excellent health and a superb physical condition. They hiked the area's hills each week and skied the nearby slopes every Sunday during winter. Dr. Ford could still run a sub-six-minute mile. Age will not dissuade him.

Amelia would be an exceptional mother. She possessed a sterling character; many considered her a saint. She volunteered twenty hours a week for the Junior League teaching disadvantaged pre-school children of West Lebanon, NH. The children, all from dysfunctional families, adored her. She saw their disappointment at class end knowing they will soon return to their cheerless broken homes.

Each year, at the conclusion of the school year in June, Amelia hosted a picnic for the kids, parents and teachers at their Orford home. The animals in the barns of a neighboring farmer fascinated the children. Jim Scott, the neighboring farmer, gave the kids rides on his Shetland ponies.

Robert Ford turned his thoughts to himself. Does he want to be a father at 46 years of age? Can he be a capable father? Does he have the energy for such a challenging task -- he thought about raising a child as he drove up the driveway to the house. The doctor ambled to the door thinking of his options.

His decision made, he opened the door.

He spotted Amelia rocking the baby as she sat on the couch in the living room. Robert Ford approached Amelia Briggs Ford, looked at her, then the baby. She said nothing.

"Yes, Amelia, we'll adopt Tom as our son."

Amelia, the now proud mother, introduced Tom Ford to his father.

"Oh, Robert, he is beautiful!"

She handed him the baby. When Robert looked into Tom's steely blue eyes -- a bearing he will never forget. Being a physician, he had held countless babies in his arms, but he immediately sensed Tom Ford was special. He looked forward to becoming Tom's father and raising him with Amelia.

"Here are the milk bottles. You may want to warm them before you feed him. I'll give him a quick examination to check his heart and lungs and be sure he has all his parts."

****

The Fords were an impressive couple. Mrs. Amelia Briggs Ford descended from a long line of successful industrial entrepreneurs. The Briggs, fine old-line New England entrepreneurs with Mayflower heritage, manufactured their products by the Claremont watermills since the War of 1812. Briggs and Raymond, for example, machined musket barrels used by the Union army during the Civil War.

The Briggs never presented themselves to high society status, preferring instead to maintain their traditional Yankee values of thrift, self-reliance and living the simple life. All Brigg family members throughout the years volunteered to work the factory floor during emergencies, of which they often experienced. No one ever complained about the hard, squalid labor required for the work.

Amelia's sibling, an older brother, lived in Alexandria, Virginia. A physicist for NASA – the National Aeronautics and Space Administration, he told her that he worked on spy satellites. He couldn't reveal more. "I would have to kill you if I did." He has been saying that to anyone who asked for the twenty years he's been on that project. Funny man.

Amelia attended the Spence School in New York City. Her parents realized that sending their daughter to such a girl's prep school may help augment her experience outside New Hampshire's bucolic and isolating country setting. Early 1960s Spence was very genteel, with tea served in the dorms each afternoon after classes; a contrast to her later years at Wellesley College when the social upheaval precipitated by Vietnam War protests upended many traditional mores and accepted behavior.

Amelia ignored the tumult surrounding her as best she could, concentrating on her studies and the burgeoning relationship with a young medical student named Robert Ford.

In the late spring of her sophomore year, she met Robert Ford at a ZA (a Wellesley College literary organization that hosted parties) event.

Robert stood out alongside the younger Harvard and Yale undergraduates at the party. She looked askance when he broke the ice by asking her if any-

15

one had asked her whether she believed she resembled the actress Maureen O'Sullivan -- Jane, from the classic Tarzan films. She regarded him with suspicion but she said, "They had." She gave him a faux look of annoyance adding, "Well at least you didn't say that I looked like Cheetah!"

Robert laughed. Thus, with the ice broken, they spoke for hours in a corner of the room, away from the party's din. Amelia never admitted their relationship had grown into love until he asked her hand in marriage after her graduation party two years later. Her Yankee breeding wouldn't allow her to indulge in such notions. However, she unhesitatingly accepted her feelings for Robert Ford. Amelia had no doubts about her prospective spouse. It was love at first sight and grew stronger over time.

Robert Ford appeared initially an average man — average height, average weight and average looks. Since childhood his need for glasses added to his undistinguished countenance. – he certainly wouldn't stand out in a crowd. Yet, no one would describe Robert Ford as an average young man.

His parents were second-generation Irish – shanty Irish at that, his father proudly told him. Dad, a factory worker, and his mother a traditional homemaker. The Ford household of two parents and four children was a veritable beehive of learning.

Their children were well educated. They attended the Harrison, NY Catholic schools which at the time were populated by Irish, Italian and Polish working-class families; the parents, of whom, also believed in the importance of a comprehensive education for their children. The nuns and priests of these schools devoted themselves to a student's traditional education.

Robert, the high school track team's top miler, set numerous county and state records. His impeccable academic record, near perfect SATs and a National Merit Scholarship added weight to his college applications. Many colleges and universities offered him athletic scholarships. He chose Yale University.

He continued running at Yale and was offered a chance to train for the Olympic team and the 1964 Summer Olympics in Tokyo, Japan. He declined, preferring to focus on his pre-med studies and his applications to med schools...a full-time task.

Robert Ford was accepted by his favored choice: Columbia University College of Physicians and Surgeons – Columbia Med School. He desired to be near to Harrison as he planned to live at home, at least for the first year.

The four years of medical school passed swiftly. His daily run around Central Park, after he moved to Morningside Heights, and his courting Amelia that included a fortnightly road trip to Wellesley College, provided the few breaks from his rigorous studies.

Dr. Robert Ford accepted residency at The Veterans Affairs Medical Center in White River Junction, VT, across the river from the antiquated Briggs family summer cottage in Orford, NH that Amelia inherited when her grandmother died the previous year.

The doctor chose well. The hospital later expanded into the massive Dartmouth–Hitchcock Medical Center in Lebanon, NH where he maintained employment and privileges with the hospital for the remaining years of his practice.

Following their graduations, Robert and Amelia married that summer. They moved into the antique but rundown cottage surrounded by more than six hundred acres of forest and farmland in a private valley. Renovations took three years and they restored the house to its original appearance of an 18th Century Cotswold-styled stone cottage – the model that Anglophile great-great-grandfather Tristram Briggs originally adapted for the house.

Life was good with little hardship for the Fords. That is, until they found a baby named Tom in a dilapidated Budweiser beer box on the front steps of their home.

As expected, the Fords had no trouble adopting Tom. They were a respected couple in the Hanover community. Besides, most who worked for the local Health and Human Services office were Dr. Ford 's patients — they experienced, firsthand, the fine gentle care he provided.

Robert and Amelia had definite ideas in mind about how they will raise Tom.

Robert knew from his medical education and practice that an organism quickly atrophies and dies unless it continually develops all its faculties. Life must be nourished and carefully cultivated, much like a garden or field, whether it is to produce flowers or crops. A thorough and rigorous education is needed to develop mind, body and spirit. No single element of this triad will reach maximum potential in an individual unless all three are thoroughly strengthened and developed.

Robert and Amelia agreed Robert would be responsible for Tom's physical development; Amelia, his spiritual guidance, and both be engaged in his intellectual schooling. They raised Tom a Christian – not as a member of any specific church or denomination – but as a member of the Judeo-Christian civilization they believed had bestowed mankind the spiritual backbone to emerge from its barbaric past.

Tom later appreciated his parents' judgment here; notably when he drove by local churches flaunting rainbow flags. Tom could not understand what pride in one's sexuality had to do with religion. He believed churches had abandoned their mission of assisting their flock in nurturing their spiritual life; choosing instead to join the suspect diversity bandwagon.

The new parents had a few differences regarding their young son's education, but they agreed that under no circumstances their son would attend a public school. Amelia commented during their discussion about Tom's education. "Robert, you see these kids coming from these schools – they are mental and moral midgets. We owe Tom an effort to avoid these propaganda mills called schools. Besides, public schools seem to be giving considerable effort to feminize the boys -- to confuse and humiliate boys regarding their masculinity."

Dr. Ford agreed. "I see these kids every day and you won't believe their language and behavior." Should Tom attend public school for twelve years, the Fords believed he risked graduating a mind-numbed social justice warrior who valued inclusiveness and cultural Marxism far more than the merit-based principles, reasoning skills, knowledge, wisdom and patriotism they sought to instill in him.

Amelia commented that replacing Western Civilization's great books with *Heather Has Two Mommies* was scarcely the direction the Fords desired to take Tom's education. She asserted, "We'll trust the traditional and remain skeptical of these dubious experimental educational theories."

Dr. Ford, an H. L. Mencken devotee, often quoted Mencken's aphorism, "The aim of public education is to reduce as many individuals as possible to the same safe level, to breed and train a standardized citizenry, to put down dissent and originality."

Namely, public schools favored mediocrity. Dr. and Mrs. Ford will spurn mediocrity for Tom. He deserved more and the Fords wouldn't abdicate their sacred parental obligation to provide Tom with the best education possible.

The Fords home-schooled Tom for the next eighteen years. Fortunately, Amelia had the time, skills and education to home school Tom. They converted a guest bedroom to a classroom that included a large desk, blackboard, AV equipment and bookcases. Amelia purchased a computer when Tom grew older, giving him hundreds of online courses to master.

Robert augmented the lessons, not only with his lectures, but with professors of Dartmouth and other nearby colleges. The doctor later specialized in orthopedics and had no trouble persuading enough teachers to tutor Tom in exchange for a new knee or hip -- an option made fiscally possible by an independently wealthy wife.

The Fords didn't need to pressure Tom to study. He was an avid learner.

His parents carefully structured his day. Academic studies began in the morning, usually taught by Amelia, followed by physical activity, either outdoors or in the basement gym. At 5:00 PM virtually every day, Robert gave his son lectures on History, Geography, Politics, Current Events, Physics, Chemistry, Biology and several other subjects. On Friday, the aforementioned professors tutored Tom. Tom audited classes at Dartmouth during his later teen years. He experienced a most unique educational experience.

His education did include some hitches. Tom was always amused when he recalled one of these. His father believed that when Tom turned ten he could improve his hand-eye coordination by playing computer games. Dr. Ford bought several popular games to give Tom an opportunity to play them for an hour every couple of days. Tom, however, spent too much time on the games, distracting him from his studies. Dr. Ford noticed Tom sneaking into the classroom to play the games. He was becoming addicted to gaming and the doctor knew too well about addiction. Dr. Ford witnessed the devastation addiction wrought working at the hospital. Though not posing the physical threat as drug addiction, excessive gaming can be detrimental to other aspects of Tom's growth.

He read the academic literature regarding gaming. "Playing video games cause a precipitous dopamine increase in the brain -- about 75%. Although adults use their reasoning power to overcome this rush, children's prefrontal cortex has not developed enough to move on to more critical tasks. Children are at far greater risk for developing a complication called 'gaming disorder.'"

One evening after dinner Robert said, "Tom, let's go outside for a little target practice." Tom readily agreed. They took their guns to the 100-yard range. To Tom's surprise, the gaming console sat on the target table. Tom said nothing. His father drolly asked, "Do you want the first shot?"

Tom never played another computer game. Dr. Ford's simple cure for gaming addiction was very effective.

Dr. Ford later explained people achieve far more without spending time on such frivolity. Tom found playing computer games a waste of time compared to the alternative activities available: his education, for self-improvement and, of course, for his marksmanship. Tom didn't resent his father's prescription. He laughs at the incident today – it makes a great story.

Dr. Ford managed Tom's physical development. Robert wanted to expose Tom to a broad range of sports and other physical activities. Running was an important, virtually daily, activity. Tom ran with his father a mile around the sizable 10-acre field's perimeter on the property -- it took four laps to complete the mile. They ran for time, competing against the clock to break the six-minute barrier. Tom didn't beat his well-conditioned father until he turned fifteen – his father was sixty.

Tom was not raised isolated from other children. He joined the Cub Scouts, graduated to the Boy Scouts and achieved the rank of Eagle Scout. Scouting taught him valuable lessons and skills he carried with him for the rest of his life. Tom frequently recalled the merit badges he earned when he applied the skill to a particular job.

He developed many great friendships with the boys in scouting and the various sports teams he joined. He participated in organized sports including Little League, Babe Ruth League and Pop Warner football. Tom was frequently promoted a level in consideration of his larger stature and strength in comparison to youngsters his age.

Tom immersed himself in wrestling, boxing and judo. He eagerly trained in MMA when the no-holds-barred fighting became the rage. Tom enjoyed all the sports he practiced, but shooting remained his passion. The Fords created a shooting range on the spacious, isolated Ford property to provide Tom easy access for practice at various distances.

He understood his lifelong training with weights, martial arts and running gave him a dangerous advantage over the other kids. He feared he could seriously hurt someone if he used all his strength against an opponent. Playing middle linebacker, for example, he would wrap a runner and tackle him as gently as possible – effective, but often the runner gained an additional yard or two. Tom never reached his maximum potential on the football field. The coaches didn't appreciate his coddling of opponents but Tom was satisfied with his play.

Then there was Butch.

The appropriately named Butch, the league's largest and brawniest player, was also its leading bully. Butch enjoyed punishing opposing players, primarily the smaller ones. He ended perhaps a half dozen players' seasons with various injuries, including a few severe concussions. Several parents kept their child from playing when their son's team played Butch's team.

Tom decided Butch needed a sportsmanship lesson. Youth Football wasn't the NFL -- a vast difference in size, talent and strength was common among the players. Tom recognized that the bigger and stronger players had a responsibility to protect, or at least not injure, the smaller players. Butch didn't comprehend or even think of so a simple concept.

Tom looked forward to playing against Butch — his team's stat running back. On the first play from scrimmage, Butch took the handoff from the quarterback and hit the hole between the center and right guard. One yard from scrimmage Tom fought off a block and met Butch with a crushing tackle. Tom smashed his shoulder pads into Butch's gut and heard cracked ribs reverberating through his helmet. As he stood, he observed Butch gasping for air from his deflated lungs -- his football season ended.

Tom received an outpouring of kudos and thanks after the game from his teammates and their parents. Even a few of his opponents thanked him. His coach, patting him on the back, praised his hit. "That's a Division 1 hit — hardest I've ever seen in this league." Tom smiled to himself and thought, *"Like Robert Kennedy, he saw wrong and tried to right it."*

Butch learned a painful lesson from that hit, and the encounter with Tom Ford turned his life around as he entered adulthood. Years later, Butch joined the West Lebanon Police Department. He once stopped Tom who often drove his vintage Jaguar on the country roads well over the posted speed limit. Butch laughed when he looked at the driver's license. Handing back the license he told Tom, "Here, I owe you one. If it wasn't for that hit you gave me on the football field I'd still be an arrogant asshole everyone hated. I learned a little humility that day. Take it easy on these back roads around here."

The cop's words initially bewildered Tom, but he thankfully emerged from the incident without a speeding ticket. Tom realized a few minutes later that "Joe Libby," the name on the cop's badge, was Butch, the guy he crushed on a football field twelve years previously.

****

Amelia Briggs Ford had to fight hard for Tom's spiritual and character development. Yes, his academic studies and athletic pursuits were essential to Tom's development, but she could hardly neglect the third important factor: becoming a mature, civilized gentleman in an increasingly vulgar, crass and impolite culture. She was raised a Briggs -- no son of hers would become a man without learning all it takes to be a gentleman. Robert and Amelia often discussed this aspect of Tom's growth. They both agreed Amelia lead the effort to assure Tom becomes a "polished man of honor and gentility" - as Amelia labeled the endeavor.

She first introduced Tom to Emily Post's Etiquette, the 1923 edition, when he turned eight.

One day, as he studied an American history textbook his mother walked into the classroom, "Here is a book my mother gave me, and which her mother gave her. Now, you may find these lessons a touch too quaint or outdated, but regard them as an excellent guideline for the proper treatment of others. Emily Post provides wonderful advice for boys becoming gentleman."

Tom did, indeed, read the book and repeatedly referenced it to answer certain questions regarding manners and propriety. He also found Emily Post entertaining. He doubted he would ever need to instruct a butler where to stand at a dinner party or how to behave at formal teas. Despite this, the etiquette rules given in the book served him well in later business and social settings.

He particularly remembered Emily Post's warning about misbehavior at a party, "The extreme reverse of a smart party is one which has a roomful of people who deport themselves abominably, who greet each other by waving their arms aloft, who dance like Apaches or jiggling music-box figures, and who scarcely suggest an assemblage of even decent – let alone, well-bred people. Tom always behaved himself at parties. The vision expressed by the book's passage constrained Tom from any scurrilous behavior that later could prove embarrassing or damaging to his reputation.

He also learned to control his language -- no swearing, especially at home. His mother instilled in him to be exact with his words, "Swearing and cursing reveal verbal laziness. Think about what you want to say and use the most appropriate word to describe it." For respect of his mother, Tom seldom swore during his life, and then in extraordinary circumstances.

Robert and Amelia added hard physical labor to Tom's daily regimen. Robert's blue-collar background together with Amelia's Yankee sensibilities gave the Fords more than enough reason to find jobs for Tom outside the house. Neighbors or patients of the doctor who owned businesses needed casual help. Tom never denied a job offer from them.

Tom first worked for the neighboring Jim Scott farm. He cleaned the horse stalls or shoveled the endless supply of manure. Tom was ecstatic when Jim promoted him to cut the hayfields. He enjoyed driving the tractor for hours, back and forth across the fields. He was 13 when promoted, leaving the manure piles to a younger neighbor.

Tom also worked for a local logger cutting limbs off downed trees, but eventually graduated to faller on the logging operation. He spent a summer as a mechanic for the local garage renovating 1950s sports cars and another summer separating metal at a Wilder, Vermont scrap metal yard.

The latter was his favorite. He worked for Wilder Scrap Metal Co. across the river in Vermont. Tom, now sixteen, could legally drive instead of bicycling to work. Arturo Rossellini, the proprietor, a first-generation immigrant from Italy, changed his name to Art Rossi when he became a US citizen. "It sounds a little more American," he proudly proclaimed.

Art taught Tom about recycling, not the green fantasies peddled by the media and academia, but recycling material of real value. Art was fond to say, "We work to recycle valuable metals and not waste our time on worthless crap like plastic bottles."

Tom also learned common sense principles of business from Art: It takes ounces to make pounds, pennies to make dollars." Art drilled this aphorism whenever Tom ignored a small piece of copper on the ground. In other words, little things are needed to create big things. Art, a talented businessman, became affluent from his hard work and skills. His sizable mountaintop home overlooking the Connecticut River Valley evidenced his business skills. Quite an accomplishment for a man who, 20 years ago, walked down a tramp steamer's gangplank with less than $100 remaining in his pocket.

Tom enjoyed his first beer at the junkyard. The entire crew celebrated Happy Hour every late Friday afternoon. All gathered to receive their weekly checks. Art handed a beer with the check. The guys sat on the plentiful barrels strewn around the grounds to banter about the week's work. Tom, being the low man on the totem pole, was often their target of good-natured ribbing. He didn't mind the banter, even when they offered to introduce him to Martha, the tired-looking prostitute who walked by the yard each day.

Life was outstanding for the Ford family in Orford, New Hampshire. The Fords, however, once encountered a significant problem homeschooling Tom.

New Hampshire elected a new governor when Tom was twelve. The determined governor proposed abolishing homeschooling in the state and enroll those students into public schools. She alleged homeschooled students were receiving an inferior education and parents who kept their children from attending public schools were practicing child abuse. The teachers union that financed her campaign savored hiring additional teachers, doubtlessly encouraged the governor. The Fords, outraged at the governor's plans, were determined to stop her.

They created a simple strategy to gain publicity and embarrass the governor into abandoning her scheme to end homeschooling. The Fords challenged the Hanover, NH Middle School to a College Bowl-type contest: Tom Ford vs. the school's top 10 students.

The rules were simple. One hundred questions about math, science, history, geography and other topics would be asked of the competitors. The competitor with the answer stands to answer. A correct answer earned one point, an incorrect answer minus one. After 100 questions, the team with the highest score wins. A neutral but entertaining Dartmouth College professor from the Education Department volunteered to be Master of Ceremony for the event. He also generated the secret question list.

The middle school principal remarkably accepted the challenge that would take place on a Saturday afternoon in late winter. Initially, only the local public access channel planned to cover the event. However, the Ford's and their friends' hard work and persuasiveness expanded the media to include statewide coverage on public television. As word of the competition spread, local and state newspapers and radio stations covered it extensively. Boston's top-rated talk show host Gary Gilliam interviewed Tom and his parents on his show and created an additional buzz in the region. This fascinating encounter soon captivated the entire state, along with nearly all of New England.

The questions were fair – answers every well-educated middle-schooler should know. Questions like:

"What is the equation of a straight line?"
"What do the initials D.N.A. represent?"
"What was the Compromise of 1850?"
"Which mountain range separates Europe from Asia?"

Amelia was confident Tom would crush the opposition, which he did, 80 to 17.

The contest would have been more of a route had the professor not added a few contemporary culture questions. Questions like "Which hip-hop group hit the top of the record chart with songs titled 'Cap a Cop' and 'My Ho's a Ho?'" and "Which actress plays Hannah Montana on the Disney Channel?" Tom had no idea, but his opponents correctly answered these questions.

Amelia Ford, appalled by the results, felt sorry for the remarkable ignorance these students displayed, purportedly the best and brightest from an affluent academic community. However, she was not surprised after reading the school's mission statement: "The school prepares the student to understand the world as a global village and appreciate its interdependence and diversity." She realized from these words their students couldn't compete against the rigorous, fact-based education Tom received. Nor in the world, where well-prepared and educated Asian students, for example, unburdened by Utopian constructs, secured entrance to top colleges and universities with a far greater rate than did their numbers suggested.

The results embarrassed the governor. She quietly dropped her plans. However, her decision outraged her union backers and liberal supporters. They had lost an opportunity to control thousands of students plus the money that accompanied them.

Tom learned an important lesson from the experience. He realized that many people sought to make the lives of others miserable and to promote themselves or their agenda. They must be crushed in some way, like his parent's efforts stopped the governor's objective to destroy homeschooling in the state. Tom recalled his old football coach's command for aggressiveness,

"You never see the hammer broken, but you always see the nail bent. Be the hammer, not the nail"

Tom and his parents thwarted the will of Moloch, the pagan god of child sacrifice. He realized the power of goodness and truth CAN thwart the countervailing corruption and treachery of evil intent. He incorporated this experience into his character that influenced all life decisions he encountered from that day.

The entire family recognized that Tom when eighteen had received an education equivalent to numerous undergraduate degrees – and, perhaps, a master's degree or two. Tom had no desire to attend college. He audited a number of classes at Dartmouth, but the students' knowledge and acumen didn't impress him -- even the seniors.

Many had trouble grasping simple concepts he learned years ago. Colleges had developed into intellectual wastelands – ideological boot camps for eager social warriors.

Dr. Ford told a story at the dinner table about the experience of one of his patients -- a Dartmouth College teacher. The story's absurdity generated considerable laughter that evening. Dr. Ford told of his conversation, "It appeared the college taught a required class that endeavored to de-masculinize the male students – to eliminate their 'toxic masculinity.' The goal is to curtail traditional attitudes and change beliefs concerning gender. The male students are encouraged to examine their own biases and behaviors to eliminate their misogyny and gender-based violence."

Tom looked at his parents after Dr. Ford ended his narrative."They could have saved all the effort in class and asked dad to cut it off. Gelding men is their real goal. Lefties fear real men. They are an obstacle to their Cause."

Diversity, multiculturalism, social justice, white shaming and virtue signaling have taken its toll on American universities. The Fords wanted no part of the intersectionality movement. They concluded there wasn't much he would learn in college that he couldn't learn at home. Nevertheless, Tom had difficulties deciding his future. Tom assuredly wasn't a Peace Corps or VISTA kind of guy. Changing the world, as they viewed it, was not his thing.

Perhaps he should enlist in the Army? No, he disapproved of the recent direction in which the Pentagon and politicians were transforming the military. The obtuseness of Pentagon bureaucratic officers had damaged the troops' morale. The strict Rules of Engagement the brass had developed for combat zones also concerned Tom. He could never delay returning fire when fired on, but the new ROEs required permission from a JAG for such action. Tom believed he'd be court-martialed if assigned into a combat zone.

No, he must find a more fitting way to serve his country. He will find it. Meanwhile, he would continue his studies, his marksmanship and his jobs.

Tom had been studying Spanish and French recently, often speaking French with Amelia at dinner when Dr. Ford, who didn't speak the language, was on his rounds. Tom expended substantial efforts to master Mandarin Chinese and Classic Arabic. He had soon abandoned his study of the Chinese logograms and abjad script, content to learn these languages with conversational fluency.

Most importantly, Tom's unique educational experience created strong, well-thought-out principles that developed his character for life.

Tom developed these principles from Edmund Burke's concepts of social and political development. Adopting the traditions of civilization and culture, developed over the millennia, are crucial to living the good life. He trusted that traditions could hold a person together much as it glues a country into a solid entity. Traditions form the foundation of stability, stability necessary for individuals to fully develop their character, skills and talents. Why disregard the frequent mistakes man had committed throughout history, risking ruination and destruction?

Tom distrusted the alternative view, especially Jean Jacques Rousseau's theories as adopted by the Left. He understood that Rousseau's Social Contract invariably leads to an arrogance of individualism, which destroys the family and other elements of the established order. Tom read about the late 1960s turmoil that engulfed the country. The public passions for change emerged from this arrogance -- "If it feels good, do it" and "if you want it, take it" -- a sure recipe for the misery that can only be avoided, ironically, by submission to the collective, the General Will. The growth of the state facilitates the destruction of civilization and culture and the greatest corruptor of individualism.

Tom Ford objected to this dogma. He believed tradition and stability must be protected if civilization and human liberty were to survive. Each individual is responsible for its maintenance and security. Stories from his parents, who lived through the Sixties anarchy, confirmed his convictions. News stories from the Middle East gave him additional evidence by which anarchy could devastate a region.

****

The next two years were uneventful. Tom continued his near-daily long-range rifle target practice, but he never competed formally, except for one occasion. On his drive back from a date at a nearby college, he noticed a sign at the entrance to a local gun club. It read: TURKEY SHOOT SATURDAY 10:00 AM, VISITORS WELCOME.

Tom drove to the club to register for the shoot on Saturday. Thirty competitors, each sporting impressive rifles and scopes, competed that afternoon. Tom, the lone college-aged competitor, garnered curious looks from the shooters and the sizable member audience.

An older man sporting a worn but nice Bob Allen shooting jacket walked over to introduce himself as the club president. "We don't get anywhere nearly enough young fellows as I'd like to see. Welcome." he said shaking Tom's hand with a firm grip.

"What's the contest?" Tom asked.

"Three shots at three hundred yards at a two-inch circle in a four-inch X ring," the president answered.

Tom asked, "Do we shoot prone or from a rest?"

Jim, the club president, retorted, "Well, if these fellows didn't fire from a rest, hardly any could shoot any holes in that circle at any distance. You can't use sandbags, but you can rest your rifle on the log over there. We prefer to give the competition a natural setup, you know, like you were hunting and you took a long shot at a turkey or a deer."

Tom smiled, "Sounds interesting."

"As a guest, you may shoot last if you like," Jim said.

"Good, I appreciate that," Tom replied.

The club members moved to the log for three shots at the distant white circle.

After each shooter fired, a fresh paper target replaced the spent target and the score announced over a loudspeaker. Some members were good, others were poor, and as Tom expected, most were average. Few placed all three shots into the four-inch circle, but only two shooters hit the two-inch circle twice.

The club champion shot before Tom. He took a position behind the log. Joe Blake employed a Remington 40-X in .243 caliber with a 25 power Lyman scope. Tom liked the 40-X, but it was a relatively expensive semi-custom gun.

He regarded the .243 a good choice for this event: low recoil, accurate and flat shooting.

Joe Blake moved to the log and took his three shots. All quieted as they waited for the score. Through the speaker, the scorer announced, "Three X's, by Joe Blake." Applause broke out and the members surrounded Joe.

After congratulating Blake, Jim said, "O.K., everyone clear the line, we have another shooter, a young man named Tom Ford." Tom set his rifle on a folded sweatshirt covering the log. He comfortably assumed his woodchuck hunting position. The circle target appeared minuscule through his scope, like a chuck at 500 yds. He took several deep breaths to relax and steadied the crosshairs on the distant circle's center. He waited as he entered the "zone," a state of mind where solely the target, the trigger and crosshairs existed. When he sensed all aligned, he fired his three shots. Nobody gave much attention until the scorer announced, "Three X's, Ford."

A moment of stunned silence overwhelmed the crowd as a hundred faces turned to Tom. The crowd erupted, giving Tom warm, appreciative applause for the remarkable achievement they witnessed. Jim reached out to shake Tom's hand. Soon, the members crushed together to offer their congratulations. After conferring with two members, Jim walked over, "Tiebreaker will be three more shots at the same target, but we'll move it farther out but not divulge the distance. OK with you?"

"That's fair," said Tom.

Jim nodded to Blake, "You're turn, Joe."

Joe lifted his rifle from the rack and walked to the log for his shots.

Tom estimated the target to be four hundred yards. Accurate long-range shooting relies on skillful distance estimation and Tom knew from experience that bullets started descending around four hundred yards. His .308, zeroed for two hundred yards, shot nine inches low at three hundred yards, but, when you shot to four hundred yards, the round dropped another sixteen inches. To hit a long-range target, you had to accurately estimate the distance to the target, adjust the scope's elevation, and trust the distance correct. Any error would result in a shot too high or too low.

Shooters compensate for bullet drop by holding high or low on the target, but Tom maintained he needed to keep dead center to hit a minuscule object at such long range. He adjusted his scope for four hundred yards.

In the meantime, Blake fired his three shots and waited for the announcement.

"Three hits, One X, Blake," from the P.A. system. Blake's shots elicited a solid round of applause from the members.

Tom took hold of his Remington and walked to the log. He observed no wind as he evaluated the shot he was about to take. His first shot felt adequate, but he thought he may have slightly pulled the second. The third shot, doubtless, was his best -- he believed he won the contest if his range estimate accurate.

The club members watched him as he awaited the score.

Jim approached Tom and asked, "How did you do?"

"Two shots were OK, but I may have pulled one a bit, assuming a four-hundred yard range."

"Three hits, three X's, Ford," came through the speaker. Joe Blake shook his hand, "You are a hell of a shot."

"Thank you, Mr. Blake," Tom said. "I enjoyed the competition."

Jim presented Tom with a gold medal. As the members gathered around Tom Jim shouted loudly enough for all to hear, "Congratulations to Tom Ford. I haven't seen shooting like that in many a moon. You are always welcome here. We'd be pleased to have you back as our guest."

The crowd applauded to express their appreciation of the feat they had witnessed.

Tom, warmed by the warmth and friendliness, joined them for a delicious venison stew. He thanked everyone for their kindness as he left. Tom returned home, proudly wearing his Gold Medal.

Hunting season approached. Tom and Doctor Ford often hunted together -- deer in season or birds that populated the property. Varmints were always in season and Tom usually hunted this game by himself.

A few weeks later, when barely twenty-one, Tom hunted woodchucks, his favorite game. He didn't expect to shoot and kill the varmints he shot that eventful day -- the Lattimore brothers.

Chapter 2: *Kat and Mike St. John*

William Bishop, the foreman of St. John's Orange Groves, an 800-acre farm owned by Mike St. John that specialized in growing Temple oranges and tangerines, took new hires to the local roadside barbecue bar. Locals frequented the tavern, as did the Palm Beach and Wellington swells for what is regarded as the best Southern BBQ in the county.

Bishop intended to learn some more about the grove's new employee, but he also planned to tell a story. The pair sat on the stools they found in the middle of the bar. Bill, as everyone called him, ordered two beers.

It was the conclusion of Ken Strong's first week working at the grove. Bill was impressed with the recently discharged eight-year Navy veteran. Bishop, who served in the Navy for eight years himself, believed veterans were more reliable and trustworthy employees.

Ken spent virtually all his career aboard the aircraft carrier USS George Washington as a catapult launch team member -- the Navy's most dangerous job. Bill believed any member of so an elite team must be responsible enough to arrive for work on time and do the job assigned for the day. St. John paid well, and Ken considered the job an excellent transition while mulling career possibilities. After eight years in the Navy, he wanted nothing too serious. He needed a break, especially after wearing the yellow jersey on the flight deck all those years. The hard work demanded at the St. John orange grove provided the needed respite.

Bill and Ken discussed the grove, the Navy and the Miami Dolphins when Bill pointed to a vintage framed black and white photo behind the bar. It showed a soldier sitting on a Blackhorse track armored vehicle carrying an M-14.

"Bill asked, You see that guy in the photo to the right of the register?"

Ken nodded affirmatively.

"That's your boss, Mike St. John. He is considered a hero around this part of Florida -- given the Congressional Medal of Honor."

"Mr. St. John was awarded the Congressional Medal of Honor?" Ken asked, astonished.

"Yep!"

"What did he do?"

Bill took a long sip from his beer and told Ken a story he had told to countless new hires through the years.

"A crack group of North Vietnamese regulars threatened Lt. Michael St. John and his concealed Ranger platoon in the Highlands. Mike's platoon waited for further orders which gave them a little spare time. Mike had climbed a massive tree and sat in it for three days to scout the terrain. He could see a small village, a half-mile away, from the treetop. He surveyed the area for enemy penetration, everything appeared normal.

"On the third day, he climbed the tree before dawn. The village had helped a downed American pilot, and rumors circulated that the Vietcong planned to make an example of the village. They hit the defenseless village before dawn. The Vietcong assembled the entire village, tortured the village chief to death and followed those crimes by gang raping his thirteen-year-old daughter and wife. St. John heard the screams, but the murky early morning light prevented him from determining the source of the screams.

"With daylight, he noticed that the young girl was dead, but her mother was alive, but barely. St. John was shocked to see a full colonel, and several majors and captains, sipping tea as they watched their men raping the village chief's wife.

"St. John took a sniper rifle to a tree approximately 400 yards from the village. He had a clear shot of the Vietcong. He enjoyed sufficient cover which concealed him from his target. Within several minutes, he shot the colonel through the gut. He added two majors and three captains to the casualties. Several huts had been set on fire by the Vietcong, and the noise, smoke, and extreme distance of his shots created considerable disarray among the North Vietnamese troops.

"St. John killed eight men, mostly officers, before the shooting stopped. A captain, the ranking officer unscathed by Mike's bullets furiously ordered his men to locate and destroy the source of the shots. He knew if he failed, their defeat would spread to the surrounding villages jeopardizing their control of the region. St. John prepared his forty men for the imminent attack.

"Within the hour, the North Vietnamese had found St John's camp location and initiated efforts to wipe it out. Confident of their superior numbers, they hit the camp with more than two hundred men. St. John was beyond the range of artillery support and not willing to risk civilian casualties by air support he had another solution to save the village and his men.

"A jeep armed with an M-55 Quad 50 had hit a land mine the previous day and sat inoperable, but the quad fifty, an anti-aircraft weapon comprising four .50 caliber machine guns bolted together in a four-foot square, still worked. It was a helluva weapon for spraying massive quantities of lead at the enemy. Mike had salvaged the Quad 50 and installed the gun on a steep rise, a hundred and fifty-hundred yards away from the enemy line. He camouflaged the emplacement well enough to render detection impossible from a distance.

"The platoon occupied a series of foxholes joined by trenches. St. John ordered the men to duck when the enemy approached. He waited until the enemy had breached the last strands of barbed wire, fifty yards into the compound and ten yards from the front line of foxholes. Mike sat in the gunner's seat. Four men stood alongside him, feeding the long cartridge belts into the machine gun.

"St. John's initial burst struck the largest concentration of the North Vietnamese soldiers dead center. He blasted their entire front line. Mike's 750-grain armor-piercing bullets traveled at three thousand feet a second through heads, legs, arms, and other body parts. His platoon joined in the carnage after Mike expended his ammo. In two minutes, St. John and his platoon killed more than one hundred and twenty-five men by the first volley. Some commies dropped their weapons and tried to surrender. St. John didn't hesitate. He picked up his M-16 and continued shooting until he and his platoon had killed them all. His platoon suffered four dead and eleven wounded.

"They killed more than two hundred of North Vietnam's best soldiers that day. After his wounded were cared for, Mike returned to the village with his medical corpsman and a several riflemen. As I said, the young daughter died, but the mother was alive and the medic treated her. The North Vietnamese colonel was also alive, though critically injured.

"The villagers were so terrified they were frightened to go near him.

St. John had the mother and colonel placed on stretchers. He took them, along with the entire village, to the battleground. The villagers experienced shock and then total joy when they observed what had happened. He had the colonel carried around the battleground and forced him to see his dead soldiers."

"He told the mother through his South Vietnamese interpreter that he was sorry about her daughter and husband but four of his American friends gave their lives to avenge her loved ones, that nothing could bring them back, but two hundred communist scum had paid with their lives. It won't replace the loss of her loved ones, but the carnage would give her a sense that justice was meted out to her tormentors.

"Mike gently lifted her off the stretcher and held her. Hardly a dry eye could be found in the village, including St. John's. The translator, who thought he had seen everything during the years of war, was crying so hard he couldn't talk for the next minutes. When everyone had calmed down, St. John pointed to the wounded North Vietnamese Colonel. 'He is yours. Be sure his passing is suitable for a rapist of young girls and murderer of honorable men.'"

Bill continued after another sip of his beer, "The villagers took the colonel back to the village and dropped him into the outdoor privy. They securely tied him and planted him directly under an outhouse hole. The colonel was shortly covered entirely in shit. Although shot in the gut, he lasted the entire day. The villagers took great pleasure in defecating on the colonel's head. It was a long time before any commie passed through the region without being mocked.

"St. John spent another six months in the region. No commies approached within twenty miles of the village until his tour was over and he returned stateside."

A moment of silence ended when an impressed Ken exclaimed, "My God, Mr. St. John is a big-time hero. That's the best war story I ever heard."

Thinking a minute, he asked, "How do you know so much about this story?"

"When first hired at the grove twenty-five years ago, the foreman bought me a beer in this bar, on these exact bar stools, to tell me the same story. I later looked up the transcript of his recommendation for the medal and found everything to be true. Mike was quite the soldier."

Bill told another story touching their boss. "Mike despised hippies. He considered them nothing but communist scumbags. They repeatedly taunted him when he wore his uniform to ROTC class at the University of Miami. Mike, of course, would confront them and had to slap a few around to put them in their place, but it wasn't until he returned from Vietnam that he had his chance to give real punishment for their behavior.

"Everyone knows the story of the lefty hippies spitting on the soldiers when they returned from their Vietnam tour. With St. John's tour over, he flew back to San Francisco. He arrived early in the morning. On his way to the baggage carousel, three anti-war protestors, long-haired, Berkeley-types, ran to him screamed "Baby Killer" and threw blood and feces on St. John's uniform. Unfortunately, this was a common protest in San Francisco during the Vietnam War. Usually, the soldiers froze as the protestors ran away. But not this time.

"The two men and the woman who attacked Mike ran, but Mike immediately knew what had happened and pursued the hippies. He was outraged by their defilement of the uniform he proudly wore. He caught the nearest male. The guy turned, swung at Mike, and hit his shoulder but caused no damage.

"Mike grabbed the man's long hair with two hands, lifted and swung him 360 degrees before letting go. The guy spun across the floor, smashing his face on a steel baggage cart. The impact knocked half his teeth and shattered his jaw. His friends had stopped and watched all that happened to their friend with utter disbelief. They had attacked returning soldiers dozens of times but usually evaded apprehension.

"The second man called St. John a murdering bastard and attacked him with a half-ass karate kick. Our lieutenant grabbed the outstretched leg, breaking it by quickly twisting the hippy's foot. For insult, he delivered a swift kick to the balls. The girl called our man a baby killer. Mike, an equal opportunity enforcer of acceptable manners, grasped and pulled her hair, forcing her to lick the feces and blood off his uniform. She choked, became enraged, and tried to kick him. He viciously kneed her chest and broke three ribs. I found this all in the official report I read after I heard the story.

"At this point, twenty soldiers from St. John's flight watched Mike, cheering him on. Eight MPs from the airport contingent arrived, saw the battered civilians, and moved to subdue our man. An M.P. Captain, familiar with the protesters' routine, led the crew. However, he regarded it far easier to control military personnel than civilians, especially Berkeley protesters He wanted to avoid the criticism he would surely receive from the press and local pols had he dared detain a protesting civilian hippy.

"St. John explained to the Captain that they attacked him first. The officer ignored the explanation, ordering his men to handcuff Mike -- another terrible mistake. An MP reached for our man's arm; a struggle ensued and he struck St. John with a blow with a billy club.

"Blood flowed from a cut above Mike's eye. The twenty combat veterans, half of whom were Special Forces, witnessed one of their own attacked simply for defending himself. The MPs, picked for their size and strength, were, nevertheless, no match for combat-hardened Special Forces men. The brawl lasted barely a minute. Several MPs had broken bones, but no one was seriously injured. St. John had personally taken care of the MP Captain, who sat moaning, hands cupped a broken, bleeding nose."

Ken, incredulous, said, "Someone should make a movie about Mr. St. John. He was a wild man."

Bill resumed his story, "Naturally, all hell broke loose. The MP's wanted to arrest everyone and throw Mike into the slammer for twenty years. A call from a two-star general, St. John's division commander, clamped the lid on the problem. Once the JAGs investigated, they understood the twenty soldiers would be witnesses for the defense and testify that St. John had been attacked first. Prosecuting a Medal of Honor recipient had scant appeal to anyone at a time when heroes were rare. All charges were quickly and quietly dropped."

"That's a helluva story, Bill."

Bill continued, "Mike St. John is likely to be the best boss you'll ever have; all you do is observe two simple rules. Give him an honest day's work and stay away from his daughter. "

"He has a daughter?" asked Ken.

"Yes, Kat. She recently graduated from college and intends to work at the grove this summer. Mike is very, and I mean very, protective of her, though she can well take care of herself."

Bill responded, "Yes, it is quite a story and will help you understand the environment in which Mike raised Kat. Mike and his daughter are extremely close; she also inherited many of his traits. "

Bill ordered another round and continued his local history lesson.

"I have another story for you. Kat St. John had just turned twelve but enjoyed working with her father's farmhands. Among her chores, she cared for the scores of polo ponies boarded at her father's orange grove. Everyone at the grove was aware Kat received the utmost respect and she usually gets it. Mike expected no less from anyone working at the grove.

"The farmhands treated Kat like their baby sister. One day, a new hire, Wes, who didn't fully understand the message, got a bit weird with Kat in the barn. Mike dashed to the barn after hearing her scream. The lone question about the incident was whether Kat's assailant survives the beating he will soon receive. Though not a lightweight, Wes had scant chance of defending himself against Mike. Wes emerged from the barn a bleeding pulp. After the well-deserved beating, Mike dragged him to the manure pile and body-slammed the poor soul into the muck. By beating the guy to a pulp, Mike wanted to show the staff the consequences of any aggression toward his daughter.

"The guy later pleaded for the police to press charges against Mike, but the police, having respect and even fear of Mike, told Wes as he recovered in the hospital to leave town or they would arrest HIM! A week later, he did exactly that. Wes left Florida, never to return. He believed Mike would have killed him if he remained.

"Mike St. John treated Wes rather kindly compared with an intruder who broke into the St. John home on a midsummer night a couple of years ago. Mike awoke to an alarm he had rigged to sound only in his bedroom. He took care not to scare any perp away -- he had different plans for them. Mike checked the CCTV screens in the walk-in closet. Astounded to see a man sitting at the counter drinking his beer Mike decided the man's fate. He nodded to himself, *'And it's beating time.'*

"Mike crept down the steps as stealthily as he did decades ago in the Vietnam jungle pursuing Vietcong snipers. He peeked around the corner and observed the man bent over the open refrigerator looking for a free meal.

He also noticed the man's gun planted on the counter next to the beer. In a second, Mike bolted from the doorway. He slammed the refrigerator door against the intruder. Stunned by the impact, the man collapsed to the floor. However, he remained conscious. Mike yanked him by his shirt collar for the prospective beating. A minute later, he dropped the man, satisfied his lesson had been effectively rendered. The perp, lay crumpled on the floor, bleeding and nearly unconscious.

"Mike rummaged the man's pockets. He pulled out his wallet to inventory the contents: driver's license, more than $300 in cash, a few credit cards with names not matching his driver's license and a couple of food stamp cards. Mike pulled out a bag of pot and a glassine bag of white powder from another pocket. He thought, '*We have a potty and a hoppy all rolled into one piece of crap.*' He jammed the drugs back into the pocket, '*This guy will need a little something to relieve the pain he'll feel in the morning.*'

"Mike called me. I was living in the nearby garage apartment. I gave Mike assistance to prepare the perp for proper disposal. He asked me to find a roll of shrink wrap which I did. Mike inspected the man's gun as he waited — it was a new Smith & Wesson Model 500, a.50 caliber cannon that had recently arrived at gun stores. Mike had planned to purchase one but this gun fell into his hands. He wondered where the intruder stole the gun.

"I found a roll of 24" shrink wrap and we cocooned the unconscious perp with layers of plastic, covering his entire body but his head. After we finished, Mike poured the remaining beer onto the man's head, instantly waking him. He grabbed the man's gun, cocked the hammer and jammed the barrel against the guy's temple. With his other hand he opened the wallet and scrutinized the driver's license. 'Is David Herbert your real name?'

"The now terror-stricken man shook his head yes.

"Let me give you a simple warning, David. I will kill you if you ever approach my property again. I'll then dig a deep hole and drop you in it. You'll never be seen again. Do you understand?'

"The man, now panicked, vigorously nodded, 'Ye-Ye-Yes!'

"With that, Mike gave the man's head a hard smack with his fist, rendering him again unconscious.

"Mike and I carried David Herbert to the car, depositing him into the back of Mike's pickup.

"We drove a half hour to the Everglades edge and dumped him on the side of a remote service road.

"Mike looked at me, 'He should be OK by morning, unless the gators get to him.' I laughed. Mike took the intruder's cash from his pocket. He gave me the money. I refused to accept it. Mike coaxed him, 'Bill, it's his money, not mine.' I took the money.

"Kat slept through the entire incident, and she didn't find out about it until her 18th birthday party, years later. Mike and I were laughing over a couple of beers. Curious, she approached us and asked what was so funny. Mike pondered, placed his hand on Kat's shoulder, 'Kat, did I ever tell you the story of how I got that Smith and Wesson 500 I have?'

"That is the home Kat grew up in."

With that, Bill took one last swig of his beer. "I got to go. The horses need feeding."

****

Mike St. John wanted a son and was disappointed his firstborn was a girl. He didn't reveal his disappointment to his wife, Eve, but she sensed his let-down from day one. How else could anyone explain Mike's efforts to raise Kat as a boy with sparse concern for her feminine side? Her circumstances worsened when Kat at five lost her primary feminine influence, her mother, who died of leukemia.

Eve's death devastated Kat. Her father believed that to compensate for her loss he would lavish her even more love and attention than he had previous-ly – which was considerable. To the ex-Ranger, this meant more sports, more shooting, more work around the farm, and generally, Kat's continued treatment as a boy.

As she grew older, Kat accepted the problem and played along with his ef-forts…but not always. When a ten-year-old, she knocked on her father's office door, sat in front of him and demanded, "You will take me to Worth Avenue to buy some nice dresses. The other girls at school look so pretty in their dresses. All I wear are the pants and work shirts you bought me. Those days are over, daddy. Take me shopping!"

Her father neither frightened nor intimidated her. Kat knew he loved her and wanted the best for her, but sometimes he needed a little guidance. Strong guidance. She often gave to him -- in her own unique way.

Impressed by her order, Mike readily acquiesced and took her on a shopping spree that weekend. Later, reflecting on the incident, Mike appreciated Kat's boldness and audacity. Although she loved her father, Kat wouldn't let him rule her life to the extent he intended. She enjoyed the hunting, fishing, scuba diving along with the other sports her father introduced her to. Nevertheless, she resisted some of his dictates -- primarily when they countered her femininity and burgeoning womanhood.

Kat reciprocated her father's protectiveness with some of her own. She looked out for her father -- even as a ten-year-old.

Palm Beach is a target of gold diggers, men and women who seek a wealthy spouse strictly for the money. Mike St. John found himself a prime target of these lowlifes -- his property alone was worth a fortune as development encroached on his orange grove. Mike, a good-looking man, maintained his fitness throughout the years. He dated many women, but, he didn't have any serious relationships following Eve's death.

Kat noticed a woman who repeatedly appeared during a certain two-week period. Kat immediately hated her. The artificial breasts, too blonde big hair and hard appearance were in harsh contrast to her beautiful mother's elegance and grace. Kat decided to rid her father of this nuisance.

One morning, Kat found the woman sitting in the kitchen drinking coffee and reading a newspaper. "I know what you're doing," she said as she circled the woman.

The woman coolly set her coffee on the counter, "...and what is that?"

"You want my father's money. Period. I heard about women like you."

"What do you know about women like me?"

"I heard Daddy's friends talk about this woman, that lady, all who want to marry some rich guy for their money."

"Oh really? Do you think I am one of those women?"

"No two ways about it! You are a gold digger and I intend to stop you."

"Oh really?" The woman's curt dismissal angered Kat. She stormed from the kitchen to devise a plan to rid her father of this tramp.

Kat spent the next week urging her father to drop this blonde bombshell. She told him forthrightly, "Daddy, you are embarrassing yourself with that woman. Drop her now." Kat stunned Mike by her harangue. Mike cannot be easily shocked, but Kat surprised him.

Mike assumed Kat feared this woman would compete for his affections, but, as he learned more about his new girlfriend and her acquaintances, the majority of whom were well-known in town, he realized Kat was correct. He soon dropped the woman. Kat quietly celebrated her victory -- she helped her father with this issue, reciprocating his years of support and protection. She hoped his next romance will be more suited for a man of his stature.

Mike treated Kat like one of the guys. Kat, stood slightly over five feet tall and weighed ninety pounds. Mike had her help loading trucks of the thousands of 32-pound orange crates despite her size. She kept pace with the men. She didn't complain and resented any special privileges her father gave her.

Kat enjoyed the hard work and found her strength increased a little each day during the harvest season. The work also toughened her with the sports she played.

She played Little League baseball with the boys for two years until the puberty hormones kicked in and gave the boys an overwhelming advantage on the field. She switched to the school's girl softball team and excelled, leading the team in home runs for the two seasons she played.

Although baptized a Presbyterian, Mike's aversion to large groups kept him from regular church attendance. His wife's death, though, forced him to ask the church for assistance with Kat's moral and spiritual development. He was discouraged by all he heard from the churches, but a Rev. Campbell Stewart of the Palm Beach Presbyterian Church impressed Mike with his traditional approach to religion and values.

That Rev. Stewart was an Army chaplain for twenty-five years gave a major plus from Mike. Stewart, a no-nonsense but kindly man, was deemed perfect for teaching Kat the words and wisdom of the Bible.

He sent Kat to Sunday school every week for eight years until the Rev. Stewart died and was replaced by a far younger and more progressive pastor. Mike promptly took Kat from Sunday school classes after he read the handouts she took home. Instead of exhorting all to behave like a good Christian and follow Jesus' words and the Ten Commandments, these handouts gave diversity special emphasis, suggesting the malevolence of America's patriarchal capitalist system.

They urged the children to think green before they die from global warming. Mike had no interest in wasting Kat's time or filling her mind with such nonsense. He took her from the classes without protest from Kat. She, too, knew the babble she heard from the callow reverend sounded extremely foolish.

Mike realized early in Kat's life that she differed from other young women her age, and now, in her teens, he knew her beauty would doubtlessly attract legions of suitors vying for her attention. Her stunning looks were matched by her intelligence, physicality, fearlessness...and her marksmanship.

He recalled an incident when Kat, who had been standing in the doorway socializing with the employees, observed a coyote slinking toward the chicken coop. A chicken had been rendered a coyote dinner two days ago and placed the crew on high alert for more such incursions. A cook grabbed his Ruger mini-14, a small semi-automatic rifle chambered in 223 to deal with coyotes and other varmints. The escaping animal was now thirty or forty yards away in the orange grove when he fired three shots at the speedy critter. They all hit the trees but missed the coyote.

The coyote would soon be out of range. Kat asked whether she could take a shot. With rifle in hand, she took aim at the animal, now sixty yards away. She spotted the coyote between the trees and fired two shots, both finding the target's heart, causing the animal to crash heavily to the ground. All eyes went from the downed coyote to the young woman. Kat took a bow as the men gave her a hearty round of applause.

Mike remembered another example of Kat's shooting skills. Last year, at his shooting club, a dozen men competed shooting a running faux deer target at one hundred yards. Shooters were given twenty-seconds to take as many shots they could, the victory awarded to the shooter with the most hits. The club champion shot last, hitting the deer four times. When the men were getting ready to congratulate the winner, Mike approached the men and asked them whether Kat could shoot.

The men laughed -- Kat was only fourteen and her Browning BAR Mark III Semi-Auto rifle dwarfed her skinny teenage girl frame. Despite this, they offered her a chance to compete. All moved back as Kat approached the line. Twenty-seconds later, she hit the deer seven times and Kat had not only won the event but set a new club record. Mike smiled to himself as he watched the men's amazement when they announced the score. He thought to himself, "*Who needs a son when I have my Kat.*"

Kat had a traditional education; besides the weapons, martial arts, sports, and farm work she was engaged. She attended the local grade school for six years but had to leave after beating a boy who tried to bully her. The principal and teacher judged a broken nose and cheekbone suffered by the bully as too great a punishment for a little bullying. Mike and Kat didn't agree, forcing Mike to transfer her to private schools through high school.

However, Mike did criticize Kat for the incident. He asked her about the moves she exerted on the boy. She told him a roundhouse kick. Mike shook his head, "A bit of overkill there, Kat. You should have given him a simple Double Leg Takedown. He wouldn't have expected it, plus the maneuver would have saved his nose and cheek from that readjustment you gave him…maybe next time."

Kat's grades and SAT scores were impressive enough to secure an acceptance from Williams College in Western Massachusetts. She enjoyed her four years at Williams, found the academics challenging, and not too PC. Kat also enjoyed a far more than adequate social life.

Kat's unusual good looks, athletic figure and acerbic wit developed from working alongside her father's bantering workers at the grove, attracted considerable attention from the boys on campus. They quickly learned that Kat was no easy conquest. She developed a reputation of "Miss Tight Ass" -- a reputation for which she proudly nurtured during her college years. The opposite sex was intrigued and challenged by her chaste behavior. Kat later proclaimed, "Many have tried, but few have succeeded, and those only on my terms."

Kat never had a problem with the men of Williams College. Perhaps it was her choice of male friends, her reputation as a girl demanding respect, or her well-known skills in the Williams Washu Club -- the college judo club -- but the Williams College boys treated Kat St. John with the highest respect.

However, not so with the girls. Not all, but only a few of them. Kat recalled an incident from her sophomore year. She had repeatedly been outspoken in the classroom, snarkily challenging the liberal orthodoxy that dominates Williams' classrooms.

One day she joked about Molly Yard, a celebrated feminist icon -- the joke concerned a beauty tip. Several members of the campus group, The Daughters of Sappho, took umbrage of the joke and confronted her in the hall after class. They demanded she apologize to Molly Yard (long dead by this time) and all the women at the next class ...or else. "Or else" wasn't defined, but Kat assumed she wouldn't be receiving a dozen red roses from The Daughters of Sappho.

Kat never intended to apologize, nor did she during the next class. As she walked out after class, the same coterie of feminists confronted her, but this time Gladys Kelsey, a quintessential Stone Butch, accompanied them. Kat recognized her as the women's basketball team center. Gladys stood six feet three inches tall. She tipped the scales around two hundred fifty pounds. Although hardly a skilled basketball player, they recruited her to play the team's "enforcer." Her size, clipped hair and nasty demeanor magnified the intimidation, especially in the more confining surroundings of a school hallway. Clearly, the Daughters expected Gladys to inflict a lesson on sister-hood to Kat.

Gladys was dressed all in black: black sneakers...black socks...black sweat-pants...a black sweatshirt displaying white Gothic lettering stating, "Wic-cans for Gaia." Her black hat caught Kat's attention: a black pointy top ski hat displaying a white embroidered pentangle. Gladys confronted Kat, blocking her movement.

Kat looked up at Gladys, "Who are you? The Blair Witch?"

Gladys growled at Kat, "I heard you had some mouth. You are a threat to liberated women everywhere. I'm here to give you a thorough behavioral adjustment."

Kat laughed, "Well, it looks like you OD'd on your man pills this morning. Those hormones can make life miserable for any girl. Now I understand why you're a little prickly this morning."

Infuriated, Gladys charged Kat. Before she knew it Kat grabbed her arm and aided by the attack's considerable momentum executed a successful Uki-Otoshi on Gladys' hefty bulk. Kat slammed Gladys hard with a loud thud on the solid wood floor — knocking the air from Gladys' lungs. She followed by thrusting her fingers deep behind her attacker's windpipe (a trick her father taught her).

The girls moved in. Kat hollered to the girls, "Back off, unless you want your friend's voice box pulled out!" Kat knew she couldn't pull out a person's voice box, but she also knew her opponents weren't aware of this inconvenient fact. Besides, they were stunned that Kat easily tossed their massive thug to the floor. Gladys frantically waved her free arm, a desperate signal exhorting her friends to retreat.

They did. But Kat wasn't finished schooling her attacker. Before releasing Gladys, she gave the girl a firm backhand slap across her face, not hard enough to hurt the girl, but hard enough to send a message. The Daughters gasped as the slap reverberated through the hall. Kat warned Gladys and her friends, "The next time I won't be so magnanimous. I hope there won't be a next time. Will there?" Kat looked at her attacker and relaxed the pressure on her throat. Gladys vigorously shook her head no.

Satisfied, Kat released her, stood and walked defiantly through the crowd that separated as Kat passed through -- she had another class to attend.

Kat recalled something her father told her years ago, "Usually, a firm backhand to the chops can be more effective than compassion, dialogue or a modicum of understanding." Kat found how right he was.

Ironically, Kat developed a little respect for The Daughters of Sappho by the incident. They didn't report the incident to security or the administration, nor did they ever harass her again during her remaining years at Williams. Gladys even managed a smile for Kat whenever their paths crossed on campus. Kat invariably reciprocated.

Kat majored in art history to pursue her dream of opening a wildlife art gallery. Florida's fauna particularly interested Kat. She proudly displayed her photographs at a student show featuring a black panther brood she found in the Everglades. Kat employed the skills to wildlife photography her father taught her of hunting -- including tracking, concealment, tree stands and simply waiting.

She spent considerable time photographing animals in their natural habitat and also engaged in underwater photography. Her father promised not to shoot the animals she photographed. He usually kept his word, but a 12-point buck Kat found grazing in Alaska a few years ago became his one transgression. Kat understood when he asked her permission for the shot. The buck's massive taxidermied head now adorns Mike's office.

After college, Kat worked for an upscale Palm Beach gallery as an assistant manager. It was the ideal job for her and gave her the opportunity to learn the business of operating a gallery. Rachel Lewis, her mother's old friend, developed the gallery from a modest second-hand store in Boca Raton to a highly respected art gallery on Florida's Gold Coast. Kat couldn't have found a more suitable source to learn the business.

One day, Cindy Hannah, a college friend, had sent Kat an invitation to her wedding in New York City. Kat and Cindy were close friends at Williams, but their friendship suffered somewhat by distance and time. Cindy lived in New York and Kat had seen her only twice since their graduation three years ago. Kat will, by all means, attend the wedding.

CHAPTER 3: *Tom's Great Escape*

Tom, Amelia and Dr. Ford gathered that evening after the Lattimore's shooting in the rarely used drawing room. The room had a long colorful history where the Briggs clan met to reach important decisions that involved the family's future. Formal gilded-framed oil paintings portraying the grey-bearded Briggs patriarchs adorned the walls; each man sternly gazed at their progeny, demanding the proper decision to serve the family.

Tom explained the shooting to his mother. He added his justifications for not reporting the shooting to the police. Although most would regard him a hero for saving the two state troopers' lives, he feared an aggressive, and liberal, prosecutor may view Tom's case ideal for career enhancement -- perhaps a springboard for governor.

"Think of it," Tom said, "Some rich kid shooting three poor locals. Normally this would mean little in court, but it is a perfect headline grabber."

Tom was well aware of the risks he assumed for taking the law into his own hands. America has a mixed history with vigilantism – the Boston Tea Party highly celebrated, and the Ku Klux Klan's foul violence the most condemned.

Tom was hardly a vigilante; his encounter with the Larrimore brothers was not premeditated. He merely mitigated a critical situation he witnessed by his skills and the available weapon. He never had an internal debate touching the morality of shooting the brothers -- he took careful aim at them eliminating the danger that threatened the troopers. Saving innocent lives is indisputably moral.

Amelia said, "Tom, we are proud that you did the right thing. You acted exactly as we taught you all these years."

Dr. Ford concurred, "I can't conceive of any argument that would warrant legal scrutiny."

He looked at Amelia and added after considerable deliberation, "We have been talking about a world trip for your 21st birthday. Perhaps this is a fitting time. The old mobsters sent their hitmen out of town after a whack until the heat cooled."

"Robert," Amelia exclaimed indignantly, "Thomas isn't a hitman!"

"Of course Tom's not a hitman, but it wouldn't hurt to send him away for a while."

Tom enjoyed the exchange.

He interjected, "Let's do it. I always wanted to go on the lam."

Nonetheless, Tom had been planning the trip for years when one evening, last month at dinner, his father surprised him by an offer, "Your mother and I have discussed your round-the-world trip for your 21st birthday. We know you haven't been away from this house too often and this trip would befit the education we have given you. You need to experience the world."

Tom, pleased his parents shared his objective, gave them his best smile. Although he had had a few experiences outside Orford, NH -- including a 90-day summer internship with his uncle at NASA, a grueling 30-day Outward Bound expedition in the Rocky Mountains and several Boy Scout and family trips -- his life has been mainly confined to a 25-mile radius from his home.

"To be honest, I already prepared an itinerary. Do you want to hear my plans?"

"Yes, please continue," replied the doctor.

"Well, I plan to take an east-west direction, first stop California."

Tom resumed his description, "I plan to attend a sixty-day program that mirrors the actual Ranger training – except for the live grenades and explosives. It's in California. Next, I will travel to China for three months at a Shaolin Monastery martial arts academy. Shaolin is a Buddhist temple that offers instruction in ancient shaolin qi gong for personal defense. I also want to improve my Mandarin Chinese. I just hope they don't give me anything to read."

The doctor asked, "Where did you ever hear about the Shaolin Monastery?"

"A few civilian monks are decent kickboxers. Some even competed well in MMA, so their fighting style attracted my attention," replied Tom. "After five months of training, I plan to relax and sightsee: Nepal and the Himalayas, followed by a couple of weeks in India then on to Israel and Europe."

The doctor interjected, "Before you leave I'll introduce you to my patient, Ariel Fishel. He is a Jewish Studies professor at Dartmouth and ex-Mossad agent. Even at 60, and with two bum knees he is still one tough guy. Perhaps he could arrange introductions in Israel – give you some company and show you around."

"Thanks, dad. That would be great."

"From Israel, I want to determine which Middle East countries are safe for an American to visit."

Amelia quipped, "I will tell you right now which MiddleEast countries are safe: none. I don't want you to take any unnecessary chances when you travel there, Tom. "

"I've heard Jordan, Bahrain, Oman, and Kuwait are all safe. Oman offers the best scuba diving in the world. I have been certified for two years now and have dived only Nantucket Bay, Long Island Sound and our backyard pond. You will agree that our pond isn't too interesting for diving."

Tom added, "From the Middle East, I'll go to Italy, rent a car to drive throughout Europe for a month or so. I'll conclude my trip in the Scottish Highlands and a single-malt scotch distillery tour. How does that sound?"

"Grandpa Briggs would be content we spent his money for such constructive activities," Amelia replied as she subconsciously looked about the room at her ancestors.

"I am sure you'll have a few good stories to tell after the trip Tom," commented Dr. Ford.

****

Twenty-one year old Tom Ford was ruggedly handsome, blue-eyed with light brown, short slightly wavy hair. He appeared years older than did his chronological age and his body, sculpted by weightlifting, wrestling and the many other sports he participated in, was spectacular. He grew to a height of 6'3" and now weighed 225 lbs., possessing a perfect NFL safety physique: his muscular arms, chest and shoulders, tapered to his slim hips and waist. He could bench 315 pounds – the triple nickel- and 225 pounds for more than 30 reps – NFL linebacker territory. The speed required by wrestling, and now karate, stopped him from excessively bulking up creating a catlike combination of speed and power. He appeared to be a different breed compared to the average athlete.

Thus, on January 2nd, and a very warm day for winter desert weather, Tom Ford found himself on the first day of "Mad" Anthony Wayne's Ranger Academy.

Located in a remote valley, surrounded by the rolling hills between Apple Valley and Lucerne Valley, the academy was approximately 150 miles northwest of Los Angeles. Tom regarded the site perfectly suitable for such a facility. The buffer given by the desert and hills muted the noise from gun-shots and obscured the camp from prying eyes.

Mad Anthony Wayne claimed to be a descendant of the same-named Rev-olutionary War hero. No one in the class of forty believed him, but, doubt-less, the man was possibly mad. Tom couldn't recall whether Anthony Wayne ever spoke at a volume below a loud scream. Tom estimated his standard volume approaching 120 decibels. His hands and arms jerked in constant rapid motion as he instructed a class, and he never cracked a smile — at least not when teaching. Nevertheless, Tom grew to respect him when he discovered his combat experience along with the man's mastery of com-bat tactics and weapons of war.

Wayne, a 20-year Army Ranger was recipient of a Silver and Bronze Star plus a Purple Heart. His right arm displayed scars from the two rounds he took in combat during the first Gulf War – Operation Desert Storm. Everyone assumed the wounds resulted from fragging -- the deliberate killing or attempted killing of a despised soldier by a fellow soldier – until they dug a 7.62 slug from his arm, likely from an AK-47 -- the Iraqi enemy in the region were armed with AK-47s.

"Mad" Anthony Wayne's Ranger Academy attracted a diverse group of men: predominantly average guys desiring to improve their physical fitness, a handful of older men seeking a challenge and a few younger men planning to join the army after the two months believing the training could enhance their chances of acceptance into the US Army Ranger School.

Others hoped to prove to themselves that they could handle the 60 days of challenges.

Forty men were listening to a welcoming lecture by Wayne.

"Welcome everyone to our Ranger school. We will simulate Ranger training for the next eight weeks, except for the explosives -- I couldn't get any insurance. So no live grenades. We'll work with dummy grenades. We will focus on fitness, combat tactics and firearms. I see nearly all of you are in fairly decent shape but after our training you will all pass the Ranger Fitness Test. You better. I won't give you a certificate of completion unless you pass the test. The Army Ranger School divides training into three phases: Benning, Mountain, and Swamp. We'll combine these phases into one, but you won't be shortchanged on your training.

"I have three assistants. Guys, please stand when I say your name.

"Derrick Welles is a 12-year Ranger. He had tours in Iraq and Africa and earned a Bronze Medal for his combat in Iraq. Derrick will train you in small unit tactics and functional skills related to missions that engage the enemy in close combat and direct-fire battles.

"John Otis wasn't a Ranger but a SEAL for eight years. SEALS work cheap so I decided to hire him. Otis will work with you on the fitness phase and obstacle course training. You are bound to soon hate him, but he really is a good guy.

"Last, but not least, we have Carlos Rodriguez. Carlos, a decorated sniper with thirty-six confirmed kills in Iraq and other Middle Eastern countries, will train you on shooting. He'll introduce you to many firearms -- from the Beretta 9 mm sidearm to the Barrett M82. We also give you some experience with the M1919 Browning machine gun if you pay for the expensive ammo.

Any questions? None? Dismissed!"

As the men exited the building, Tom approached Anthony. "Mr. Wayne, I decided to come here for instruction and practice on the Barrett M82. I'm extremely competent at shooting up to 500 yards, but I want to improve my range, which can only be done with a more powerful rifle like the Barrett. Is it possible for me to take extra Barrett lessons if I pay you extra money?"

"You want to pay extra for lessons on the Barrett?"

"Yes sir."

Anthony Wayne yelled across the room, "Carlos. Please come here for a minute.

Carlos, talking to a recruit, excused himself and walked to Tom Ford and Anthony Wayne.

"Would you be interested in tutoring this young man with the Barrett 50 for some extra cash?"

"Of course. I can give the lessons after the regular training a few times a week."

Tom thanked Anthony Wayne and Carlos Rodriguez.

The days were challenging, but Tom found them thoroughly enjoyable. The physical conditioning exercises, the runs and marches, obstacle courses and combat drills presented no problems for Tom. Weapons training ranked highest in his interest and satisfaction. They introduced him to a variety of weaponry he had never experienced, including the fearsome Barrett M82, a .50 caliber sniper rifle. He had scant experience with targets beyond five-hundred yards, but this rifle had a two-thousand yard effective range. Such long-distance shooting presented new dimensions and complexities.

Tom practiced twice weekly with the Barrett on the thousand-yard range after the standard daily class ended. He had little trouble hitting the target of a thousand yards with the Barrett. The target consisted of a large half-inch steel plate cut to a silhouette of a full-sized buck. The bull's eye repre-sented the deer's "boiler room" – a six inch diameter circle painted red be-hind the shoulder and representing the deer's heart and lungs. Tom con-stantly missed this bull's eye.

Carlos tweaked Tom's technique that improved his aim, but Tom continued to miss the bull's eye. "It is only a matter of practice," he said. "Let's try again tomorrow, I'll give you my sniper manual I have in the office. You should read the manual tonight." Tom thanked him for his advice as they walked to the office for the book.

Tom spent the evening reading the book. He looked forward to applying the information in the manual to the range. The next day he did, indeed, improve, as he did for every day he practiced the following weeks.

Carlos spent considerable time coaching Tom about the sniper craft. He explained the triad of sniping: tactics, marksmanship and fieldcraft. Tom, though an excellent marksman, possessed little tactical knowledge or fieldcraft. Carlos drilled them into Tom. He also introduced Tom to the Ballistic Data Card and the Whiz Wheel. The Ballistic Data Card is an invaluable tool to long-range shooters. The shooter tracks a database of the shots taken by a sniper on the range. Weather, wind, type of ammo, muzzle velocity, yardage, milliradians, bullet drop and other important information affecting the shot are all recorded on a Ballistic Data Card for reference of future shots.

The Whiz Wheel is a simple rotational device that solves complicated problems regarding ballistics and trajectory. The wheel was developed from the old E6B Flight Computer, employed by bombardiers during WWII to calculate air conditions, wind correction, time en route and other variables needed to plot a flight course. It calculated as rapidly as a computer, but was far lighter and needed no power -- essential properties in the field.

Several days before the 60-day academy ended, Tom hit the steel buck's boiler room with ten straight shots from the Barrett, Carlos on the binoculars shouting "BULL'S-EYE" after each shot. He heard someone behind him yell, "Good shooting, son." He turned around. It was Mad Anthony Wayne. Did Tom detect a glimmer of a smile from the grumpy gray soldier?

Tom didn't attend the academy to foster friendships. Though not unfriendly and naturally social, he attended the camp to acquire the skills of war every Army Ranger must master. Instead of hanging out at the local bars with the guys at night he spent each evening studying the instructor's many handouts.

However, a particular recruit (as they were called) caught Tom's attention. He seemed out of place at the school – not for of any ineptness on his part, but his military knowledge matched the instructors and he looked comfortable executing the exercises. Tom conjectured he could be an ex-Ranger or SEAL reliving his military experience. He looked like a vet -- roughly 5' 9" tall, crew-cut hair, a lean, wiry build, perhaps forty-five years old. He even walked military.

Tom sat across from him at lunch one day to initiate a conversation. He introduced himself. The man replied, "I'm Jackie Brandt."

"Jackie, you appear unfazed by anything they throw at us — physical conditioning, hand-to-hand fighting, the obstacle course, weapons handling...you seamlessly assumed leadership of your platoon during last week's paintball contest when the designated leader demonstrated he didn't have a clue of what to do."

"Well, thanks for the kind words, but I'm simply an accountant from San Bernardino who just wants to stay in shape."

Although skeptical, Tom nominally took him at his word. He changed the subject to their experiences at the academy – shoptalk.

He and Jackie became friends, customarily driving to the nearby restaurant for dinner. He learned much about the man, but his skepticism of Jackie Brandt remained.

Tom particularly enjoyed the Paint Ball Wars, as they were known by the recruits, which provided simulated battle every Friday afternoon. Mad Anthony split the class in half, with one side playing defense and the other playing offense. Team Offense was tasked with capturing an abandoned barn halfway up a hill. Team Defense was ordered to defend it.

Virtually everyone preferred to play offense. Tom favored defense. Defense allowed him to pick off the attackers as they wended their way up the hill. Yes, the paintball guns weren't as accurate as his Remington Model 700 .308 caliber nor had much range but he valued the experience of shooting a moving target in more pressured circumstances.

The sixty days became a blur, but before Tom knew, it was time to leave. Mad Anthony Wayne Academy completely satisfied Tom. Ranger training provided an excellent first stop on his world tour.

Mad Anthony and the instructors ordered pizza and beer for a casual goodbye party. Tom gave his farewells to the guys and thanks to the instructors. He also generously tipped the staff, courtesy of Grandpa Briggs. Yes, even Mad Anthony smiled when Tom handed him a check.

Jackie Brandt approached Tom, "You complimented me about my leadership here, but you were the standout here. You may have been among the youngest, but certainly proved the most talented. How do you intend to use your skills?"

"I'm not sure, but I have nine months to think about it. My next stop is a Chinese monastery. Maybe the monks will give me some good ideas."

He liked Jackie and gave him his New Hampshire address to maintain contact. Jackie gave him a business card that listed his phone number and address in San Bernardino. Tom remained skeptical -- something about him made no sense.

****

Tom found himself in another country, on his own, for the first time in his life. Yes, he took overseas trips with the family through the years. Europe, Bermuda, Mexico and Brazil were destinations of the family vacations, but this was different. He will live outside the US for an extended period and not as a tourist.

Besides improving his Mandarin, spoken at the Shaolin Monastery, Tom anticipated learning a new, well, new to him, martial arts style and discipline. He was interested in Xiao Hong-quan (roughly translated: Little Flood Red Boxing), the monastery's signature martial art. Tom intended to learn as much as he could in three months to become proficient in a discipline that usually took five to six years to master.

The monastery continuously solicited funds for the expensive maintenance that the ancient buildings on the compound require. Tom thought giving a generous donation from his future inheritance (thank you, Amelia) would be wise since he expected to request a few favors during his stay at the monastery.

After the long flight, a seemingly endless bus trip and a short taxi ride, Tom arrived at Mountain Gate, the Shaolin Temple's main gate. Before he left California he had his hair buzz cut to adapt to the monastery's prevailing grooming customs.

Tom was more interested in learning their martial art system than in Buddhism. Nonetheless, he will respect their religion and adhere to its rules and procedures when at the monastery.

On the first day, after orientation, the monks tested the 30 students in the class for their relative skills. Tom looked around the class, aware he was the only student of European background. The monks paired the students by approximate age and size for a strictly non-contact contest. Any full contact would be cause for immediate expulsion from the Temple. The monks graded the match by points. Each hit netted a point, but the hit had to be pulled — no contact allowed. A bell sounded after a "hit," which stopped the action. The first to receive five points was declared the winner. The entire class watched each match and the instructors presented their advice and instruction to the fighters after each point.

Tom fought a confident young Japanese man named Kenichi Shishido, who he later learned had recently earned a second-degree black belt in a martial arts discipline called shoot boxing – a combination of Judo and Kickboxing. Although slightly smaller than Tom, Kenichi stood six feet tall, but was well-muscled and looked in tremendous physical condition.

Tom had never opposed anyone so quick as Kenichi. Yes, he marveled by the speed Bruce Lee exhibited in the many YouTube videos he watched. The competition at the local clubs and gyms in New Hampshire or Mad Anthony's Ranger school didn't match Kenichi's skills. Tom was grateful for the non-contact rule after losing the first points.

Kenichi defeated Tom 5 to 1, with Tom's only point resulting from a spinning hook kick that Kenichi failed to parry. Tom quickly realized he was up against a more capable and well-prepared opponent. The Temple placed a premium on speed over strength. Tom looked forward to the challenge.

The primary training element of Shaolin-Do is the form, or kata. Forms are scripted motions and combat sequences used to teach proper technique, speed, timing, and execution. Forms training builds strength, cardiovascular efficiency, flexibility, balance and memory. Tom trained hard and was satisfied with his progress. He lost 10 pounds on a lean diet and seemingly endless exercise.

More than fifteen hundred years ago, the Shaolin Temple monks developed a training tools carved from granite that resembled kettlebells. They are called stone locks and are primarily a strength-building tool. Various exercises are performed with the stone lock but theThe ultimate routine with the stone lock is tossing the padlock high in the air, letting the stone flip over a several times, catching it on your clinched fist, and finally, raising the stone above your head. An extremely dangerous exercise, style, balance and timing are as important as strength. Tom initiated this training handling a 10 kg stone lock but worked his way to 60 kg on the last day competition, a feat only the more advanced students accomplished.

The Shaolin experience included extensive weapons training. Tom practiced daily with The Dao (a broadsword), Kwan Dao (heavy blade), Quiang (a spear), and the Shaolin Jiu Jie Bian (Nine Sections Whip), but he especially enjoyed the "Double Daggers" and the "Flying Knife" – knife throwing. He became adept with throwing knives, regularly hitting the target and sometimes the small bulls-eye at nine meters.

After three months, Tom completed his grueling experience at the monastery. Although not a convert to Buddhism, he respected the calmness and confidence their principles instilled in the individual. He left the monastery an improved athlete after the countless disciplined drills. Moreover, he found himself considerably quicker, far more flexible and more proficient in the martial arts and other weaponry.

His final spar was a rematch against Kenichi Shishido. He reversed the results of their previous match and won the match by a score of 5 to 1. Kenichi thanked him for the bout, "I am a much better fighter since our first match, but you far exceeded my progress. I wish you success."

He had been training intensely for five months – two in California at the Ranger Academy and three at the monastery. He needed a vacation and hoped his next few months would give him a little R & R.

Tom visited Nepal and India before he arrived in Jerusalem. These two countries are marked by incredible beauty and poverty, as he never saw in America. He took time to climb a smaller Himalayan mountain – Island Peak in Nepal -- a two-day climb presenting moderate challenges for a climber of Tom's experience.

When in India he visited the Taj Mahal. As he withdrew cash from a nearby ATM he noticed three local men were watching him. They followed him as he walked the next half-mile to his destination. He didn't believe they would attempt something in such a crowded street...it was mid-day and hundreds of people were shopping the local bazaar -- a miscalculation by Tom.

These were gangbangers who "owned" the street. The locals learned by vandalism and vicious beatings to be blind to the gang's crimes, especially when rich Westerners were the mark. The merchants paid the gang protection money to be left alone and wouldn't help a stranger likely to be the gang's next victim. The three men closed the distance to their prey. Tom turned to confront them.

They formed a semi-circle around him. The largest of the three, a dark-skinned Indian in his early 20's with rotten teeth, pulled a knife from his jacket and prodded Tom's chest. "Give me your wallet, your phone and your watch, asshole. Fast or I'm gonna stick you, faggot," he sneered in heavily accented English. Tom thought, "*I could replace the phone. I have only $100 cash in my wallet, but my watch is a Marvin Chronograph Vollkalender my grandfather took off a German soldier he shot in the Ardennes in WWII. I will kill the banger should he try to take it from me.*"

Tom assessed the threat in order to devise a strategy to defeat the three attackers.

The lead banger noted Tom's hesitation to comply with his orders. Tom bewildered him. Western tourists invariably obeyed his commands. He took a step forward, touched Tom's jacket with the point of the knife. At that moment, as though signaled, the others took a step forward. Without hesitation, Tom grabbed the gangbanger's hand that held the knife, violently twisting the hand to the right and downward. The knife fell and the man screamed in pain; the crack of tendons ripped from bone filled the neighborhood with a sickening sound.

The gangbanger crashed to the sidewalk. Tom pulled the perp towards him then drove his foot into his assailant's lower jaw. He heard bones and teeth break as he forced the jaw into the head. The man collapsed on his back to the sidewalk, his legs stiff -- indicating decorticate rigidity and brain damage. Tom recognized the symptom observing his attacker lying on the ground.

The second man reached into his pocket. Tom dropped to his knees, simultaneously grasping the man's legs and driving his shoulder into his midsection. It was a basic wrestling moves, but nearly impossible to stop unless you were a trained wrestler. Instead of releasing him, as custom in a match, Tom held on, smashing the man's head to the sidewalk. A soft "thunk" of the crashing skull signaled the success of his maneuver. A vision of tackling Butch on the football field years ago crossed his mind, though he was sure these thugs wouldn't learn the lesson Butch acquired that day. The third man panicked, having no interest in suffering his two friend's fates. He turned and ran down the street.

Besides a splash of blood on his blue blazer – their blood – Tom emerged from the experience unharmed and satisfied that he defended himself from the attempted mugging. He suffered no panic or fear, and surprised himself by which he quickly, almost intuitively, planned his tactics for a counterattack. His exhaustive training served him well.

He left the scene of the attack without attracting too much attention. The apparent apathy of the merchants and shoppers was palpable, but he did notice smiles on a few of the street vendors.. Tom didn't know whether any of the muggers' friends were in the neighborhood, but he believed they would soon be seeking revenge for their bloodied and injured compadres.

Tom hastened to the Taj Mahal and blended into the enormous crowds the popular tourist attraction draws. He never again spotted his attackers.

Dr. Ford will be thrilled to hear about his son's intriguing adventure during the next weekly telephone call to his parents. However, Tom planned to withhold this experience from his mother. Instead, he intended to focus on describing the beauty and history of the Taj Mahal.

Tom continued his trip with no further such criminal incidents. He dove the wrecks around Oman, viewed the pyramids and other archeological sights of Egypt and joined a camel caravan through the Sahara Desert. Before long, Tom Ford found himself landing at Ben Gurion Airport outside of Tel Aviv, Israel.

He registered at the Crown Plaza on Tel Aviv Beach, close to the US Embassy. Tom had an appointment to meet Reuven Berman, a government official and friend of his father's patient, Professor Ariel Fisher. Reuven loved Americans and Israel. He especially enjoyed showing his country to American tourists, in particular, friends of Ariel Fisher.

Tom walked off the elevator and headed to the beachside bar to meet Reuven Berman. Ariel had emailed him a photo of Berman. Tom knew who to search for.

He entered the bar, scanning the tables to find his guide. Reuven sat at the corner table facing another man who had his back turned to Tom. Tom greeted Reuvan, extending his right hand as he approached.

Reuven reciprocated Tom's handshake. He said, "Tom, I believe you have met Major Jackson M. Brandt of the Defense Intelligence Agency."

Jackie Brandt stood and turned around.

Tom laughed, "No, but I know a Jackie Brandt, CPA from San Bernardino, California."

Jackie gave Tom a snappy salute. He offered his hand that Tom eagerly accepted.

Jackie laughed, "That's not totally bogus, I do have an accounting degree and was born, and continue to own a family house, in San Bernardino."

"I was always skeptical of your quiet accountant from San Bernardino act," Tom stated.

"I understand, but I had no reason to tell you the truth at the time. I intended to give you the real story should I ever met you again."

"So, what is this about?" asked Tom.

"Let me explain Tom," said Major Brandt.

"We have kept an eye on you since we heard of those three brothers you shot in New Hampshire."

This revelation shocked Tom more than he had ever been shocked in his life. Outwardly, however, he remained calm.

"What are you talking about?" he asked Jackie.

A waitress stopped to take their drink order. Reuven Berman spoke, "May I suggest we sample an Israeli beer called "Dancing Camel Goliath?"

Tom and Jackie laughed at the name, but concurred with the suggestion.

The conversation resumed after they ordered the drink. "Don't worry, we aren't interested in any criminal aspects of your vigilante adventure. On the contrary, we marveled at the skill required to hit three moving targets in less than fifteen-seconds at such a distance -- as divulged in the reports."

Tom looked perplexed but didn't want to admit any criminal activity, "Who do you mean by 'we'?"

"I'll let Reuven explain later."

Berman nodded affirmatively.

Jackie continued, "The local police and state troopers had leads that you were among the dozen or so suspects but their hearts weren't into the investigation. They buried the file under a pile of other cases. Frankly, they didn't want to find the shooter. Nevertheless, we procured a copy of the extensive file and hired a private investigator on the case. He went undercover, as witnesses were more likely to be open to his questions. A few of the farmers mentioned to our investigator that they periodically permitted you to hunt their land as you lived relatively close to the shooting. However, we found the puzzle's final piece from the shooting contest you entered at the local rod and gun club. Everyone raved about this kid coming from nowhere to beat the club champion at 400 yards."

Jackie Brandt stopped his monologue when the waitress delivered their beers.

He resumed the conversation after she left, "We were 90% confident you were the sharpshooter, but we had to be 100% sure. We discovered you enrolled in Mad Anthony Wayne's Ranger school. I decided to investigate myself, since I also needed to get back in shape and had a little vacation time. You and I became friendly. I watched you on the range shooting the Barrett 50. You soon erased all doubt. You were clearly our man."

Tom admitted nothing but his skill with a rifle. He didn't know these two. For all he knew Brandt and Berman were police investigators wired to record the entire conversation. He didn't want the conversation to turn into a confession. Tom sipped his beer then asked, "So who are 'we'?"

Jackie Brandt looked at Reuven Berman to answer Tom's question.

Reuven gazed at his nearly empty stein, "Do you like our beer?"

Tom and Jackie hoisted their steins in assent.

Reuven spoke, "I am a Mossad agent and worked with Ariel Fisher. Your father probably informed you that Ariel was a Mossad agent. We were partners for eight years. We worked for Mossad's secret assassination unit called Kidon. Kidon's existence is no longer a secret, but its targets and methods remain murky to the public, as it should. Ariel personally killed two Munich Olympic murderers. He was especially gruesome dealing with his last target. Good man, that Ariel."

Tom, mildly surprised, heard Ariel worked for the Mossad, but he couldn't visualize the mild-mannered professor killing anyone.

Reuven added, "You probably didn't know that Ariel's parents were Jewish Avengers, the Nokmim, after the war. Ariel was a young boy when his parents hunted at night to kill ex-SS troopers responsible for atrocities against local Jews. Vengeance is in his blood.

"Kidon's main task, on the other hand, was to assess targets and decide the best method to eliminate the threat. After 9/11 the government scrutinized the entire Western intelligence apparatus for this apparent intelligence failure. They introduced certain changes like sharing intelligence among agencies, but surprisingly, many changes involved appeasing the jihadis.

"Academics suggested that if we discover their goals to understand their savage behavior we could mollify the terrorist mind and coexist in peace. It's all a fantasy. Others, like Ariel and myself, believe the terrorists irrational.

"They crave Western Civilization's destruction and replace it with their dreary and oppressive Caliphate, a world ruled by Sharia Law. These two factions, I call the Appeasers and the Realists, developed within the many intelligence agencies around the world. The Realists and the Appeasers in the CIA, FBI, DIA and the NSA developed their own policies – unknown to the others. They also collaborated with foreign intelligence organizations, such as those of France, the United Kingdom, and, of course, Israel. We're right in the heart of everything."

Tom, amazed by these revelations, asked Reuven, "How can a country develop a cogent anti-terrorist policy with so many competing factions sniping at one another?"

Reuven Berman responded, "The US president presented a united front after 9/11 to the country and the world. They occasionally succeeded to improve intelligence, but tribalism rules the federal bureaucracy and progress is slow."

Reuven continued, "Many disparate factions are involved in developing these policies. Some are rogue players, yet their operations are decentralized from idea to implementation. Fewer than a half dozen government agents know of their operations."

"Reuven and I belong to a faction we call The Martels," Jackie Brandt said as he finished his beer. "We named ourselves to honor Charles Martel, a Frankish military leader who dedicated his life to stopping the Muslims from invading Europe. He defeated them at the famous Battle of Tours in 732 A.D. Too many Westerners are unaware that we have been battling Islam since 622 A.D. We would be worshipping Allah and living under Sharia Law if it weren't for Charles Martel's skill and courage and later King John Sobieski in Vienna. That war continues today. We have lost nearly seven thousand Americans fighting jihad around the world since 9/11."

He added, "Some call today's efforts by the Islamists 'The Third Jihad' However, their goal is the same: a complete takeover of the West and destruction of Western values."

Reuven commented, "The Martels is composed of many private individuals, all volunteers, representing several countries acting collectively for a common cause against a common enemy. Our leaders have lost the will to defend civilization. We assume a hard line against the jihadists and are convinced we will only win this war by killing them before they kill us. Their Holy Grail is to detonate a suitcase nuclear bomb in Times Square, Piccadilly Circle or Tel Aviv. We want to prevent that. Right now, the West fears them more than they fear the West. We plan to change that."

Tom asked, "So the Martels is a response to Western governments' complacent response to jihad?"

"Exactly," replied Reuven. He added, "The West has lost its will to survive. We 'll give The West a backbone."

Reminded of Gibbon's *The History Of The Decline And Fall Of The Roman Empire* Tom deliberated, "The Roman Empire eventually fell because the Romans didn't properly address the threat of invasion. Failing to act against these threats ultimately crippled Rome. A weakened Rome motivated the invasions a few centuries later. Toynbee asserted civilizations die from suicide, not by murder. Rome committed suicide much as we contemplate collective suicide today by our recent inexplicable defense policies."

Reuven commented, "And we, The Martels, endeavor to pull the West off that suicide bridge."

Jackie added, "History is replete with many examples, but too many leaders refuse to accept these implicit warnings."

"Our new historic president disclosed he intends to conduct Middle East foreign policy under the supervision of two studies, *'The Doha Compact'* and *'Changing Course,'* the first of which was funded by one-worlder George Soros and the other by the liberal Brookings Institute," Brandt stated.

Both suggest that we, the United States of America, bear the bulk of the responsibility for peace in the region. The Muslim countries are exhorted to go easy on the anti-Israel rhetoric, but are asked to do little more. The studies were very biased, but the president followed their prescriptions closely for the last two years. Consequently, we have seen a vast increase in groups' power like the Muslim Brotherhood and ISIS. The president withdrew American troops from Iraq, long before it became advisable. The resultant vacuum allowed the Islamic State to grow its power. The historic president allowed a perfect storm to develop for increased the terrorism we have witnessed in many countries. The Left, of which our current president is a member, is a close Islamic ally. They ignore the history of Muslim atrocities and conquest, but include the religion in their rainbow of multiculturalism. They believe that the Muslim oppressors are the oppressed. Oppressed by The Big Satan and The Little Satan. As such, they ally with the struggle against Western hegemony, if I may borrow their rhetoric."

"Jackie is being kind," Reuven interjected. "Muslim outreach, the kind your president practices approaches dhimmitude in its application. You saw him bow to Muslim leaders. It's not the America I know. Your historic president is more interested in finding why the Muslim world is angry at us than he is of protecting the country from their aggression. It isn't generally known that fifteen Muslim countries prohibit Israelis from entering their countries. And they label us the oppressors! We overuse the term "existential threat" nowadays, but not when applied to Israel. Israel must rely on extraordinary strategies to survive as a nation and a people. Remember these venerable Talmud words, 'Those who are kind to the cruel are cruel to the kind.' Being nice to terrorists -- jihadis -- is a betrayal of those we are enlisted to protect. The good people of the world are in great danger of being killed. Some of us in Israel believe that allying with the Martels cause is critical to achieving our anti-terrorism goals."

Tom answered, "The Muslims know that our president is ignorant of their simple tactic, 'By means of your democracy we shall invade you. By means of our religion we shall dominate you.'"

Reuven replied, "That boils it down to their core strategy. Jihadists live by the words 'al-wala' wa al-bara' -- loosely translated, 'We love and hate for the sake of Allah.' They hate us because we are disbelievers. Infidels. The West is naïve to believe the notion we can work with these terrorists. The Koran orders all Muslims to hate infidels. Koran 60: 4 -- 'We hate you, first and foremost, because you are disbelievers.' The radicals will never change. They will never surrender."

"So how would I fit in?" Tom asked.

Jackie Brandt responded, "You are a civilian, anonymous, a trustworthy patriot and, most critically, possess certain skills we can use."

"You refer to my shooting skills?"

"Exactly!" Berman slapped the table. "We want you to shoot the bastards! Good guys rarely fight evil until it's too late. We didn't fight the Nazis until they invaded Poland. That was September 1939, long after we discovered they clearly intended to kill millions. Instead, we got 'Peace in Our Time.' Similarly, we discussed détente with the communists after they had killed millions. We were negligent until President Reagan got tough with the commies in the early 1980s. We now face a determined enemy exhibiting a unique style of fighting. We must push them back with equally cryptic tactics. The savage only understands death."

Jackie Brandt concurred, "To state it not so simply, we must do to them before they have a chance to do what they want to do to us." Tom took another sip of his beer. The offer didn't shock him, and it had a certain appeal, but he needed to know more about the Martels and their goals. How can I be certain you are legitimate?"

Reuven Berman, "Well, we aren't legal, but we are legitimate. Moreover, I assure you of our dedication to this cause. "

Tom sat back to absorb these revelations. His initial impressions were not only daunting but somewhat overwhelming. *Assassinations? Defender of Western Culture? Vigilantism? Why would I ever want to involve myself with something like this?*

Jackie Brandt stood, paid the table's bill and added, "I appreciate you have much to contemplate. We aren't asking you to accept a mundane job like writing an essay on coexistence for the local alternative newspaper. I won't lie to you. Our work is serious and could be dangerous. Please think about it, Tom. I'll call you when you return to the states. I'll give you a tour of the

DIA facility and introduce you to friends at the CIA. By the way, what will you do after the trip?"

"I plan to move to New York City and start a career in finance."

"That would be a perfect cover!" Jackie exclaimed walking away.

Tom left astonished by the conversation with Brandt and Berman, but not by the motivation for their objectives. The Muslim attacks on 9/11 angered Tom; three thousand Americans were murdered simply because they didn't share the same beliefs as the terrorists. He also understood these deaths didn't placate their madness: the jihadis will seek more blood and carnage during the coming years. They are certain to never stop until the entire world worships Allah.

On the one hand, Tom appreciated the appeal of using his skills to stop potential slaughter; however, the assignments would be bold, dangerous and life threatening. At the very least, he should expect to serve an extended stretch at a federal Super Max prison if caught, but he had been examining several options to employ the extraordinary skills he has developed. This offer seems to satisfy his ambitions.

Regardless, Tom Ford decided to delay any decision until he returned from his trip. He spent the next days sightseeing the Land of the Bible under Reuven's guidance and his occasional company. Reuven did not express another word concerning the offer given to Tom. He took Tom to the Western Wall, commonly called the "Wailing Wall," a surviving remnant of the Temple Mount in Jerusalem, the center of the Hebrew religion. The emotion Reuven and the other visitors exhibited at the Wall impressed Tom. Many visitors to the Western Wall have commented, "You don't need religion to be moved by this structure's mystical powers."

Tom understood Reuven's passion for the Martels. His country, his people and his religion have all been jihad targets for centuries, Tom's country for only twenty-five years. He realized it time to stop jihad before the terror grew cataclysmic. He admitted to himself that radical Muslims could never compromise their ultimate goal: total Islamist supremacy over the human race.

Within a few days, Tom landed in Rome, rented a car for travel around Europe during the next months. Much of Europe was a Fantasyland: Magnificent cities, historical sites, tremendous museums and endless panoramic agricultural landscapes. He enjoyed this aspect of his trans-continental journey.

Tom found a darkside to this paradise - the No-Go Zones. These were ghettos of Muslim migrants so dangerous that non-Muslims were warned not to visit. Although denied by the media Tom had to find the truth about them for himself. He toured the "zones urbaines sensibles," referred to as ZUS in France, and found an atmosphere like his visits to Muslim counties like Oman and Kuwait. The majority of the people were cordial and friendly and the food was excellent. Tom enjoyed the excellent Kofta and Shish Tawook in the restaurants. Yes, he received looks of absolute hatred from a segment of the population, but he also received such looks from a few Parisians over his American accented French.

Tom searched the Tours and Poitiers area for information on the Battle of Tours. He was shocked to find so little of this significant battle in civilization's history. The two forces waged battle on farmland between the Vienne and Le Clain Rivers. Here is the location where Charles Martel halted the Muslim conquest and ensured the West's survival, but a disappointed Tom Ford found only a small battlefield memorial overlooking a field.

Tom continued his European travel throwing stones in Germany (Steinstossen). He competed tossing the caber in Scotland. Invariably, the locals, noting Tom's size, recruited him into these various competitions. His trip ended in Edinburgh, Scotland after a ten-day trip with Olga, Jackie Brandt's friend.

Olga, unknown to Tom at the time, was a special Martel operative. Jackie Brandt described her thusly, "Jay Bailey Morgan III had rescued her from starvation in the mid-1990s Moscow. Seven or eight-years old when she walked the streets searching for food, a real Dickens character. Morgan, the Martels founder, took her from Russia, brought her to London and gave her to friends who raised her. He supported her financially and she graduated from the London School of Economics. Olga sells for a Morgan business that exports the highest quality Russian furs to American and European furriers. She speaks perfect English, Russian, French and Spanish, all with a seductive Russian-accented voice. Olga seldom fails to complete a sale."

Jackie added, "May I add she is brilliant, determined, loyal and, by the way, beautiful?" Tom didn't need more convincing. He met her in a London pub off King's Road. Initially, Tom assumed the Martels recruited her to persuade him to join their efforts, but Tom and Olga seldom discussed the

Martels during their time together. They discussed little politics, except for her personal experience with socialism.

Tom hadn't enjoyed a woman's company as he did Olga's. Olga proved herself a perfect guide to show London -- she was well acquainted with the city. Later, she joined him for castle and pub hopping in Northern England and Scotland. They also enjoyed the Single–malt Scotch distillery tour – Tom sent several cases to his father for later consumption.

Tom and Olga became great friends and occasional lovers, but he realized their relationship could not develop further. Olga was not immune to the cultural pessimism that so many Europeans suffer. Tom believed her Russian experience scarred her psyche and presented an impenetrable barrier to a deeper relationship. Tom preferred American women, at least those uncorrupted by the feminists, who don't share such pessimism. He liked the cheerfulness, confidence and enthusiasm of many American women he had met during his short dating life. Neither Tom nor Olga seemed to mind the dismal prospects of any future relationship, but they thoroughly enjoyed their time together during Tom's last leg of his trip.

Tom and Olga were soon to meet again under decidedly different, and far more serious circumstances.

CHAPTER 4: *Tom's New York Adventure*

Tom arrived at Kennedy Airport in mid-January. He had been traveling for nearly a year and was elated to return. His parents greeted him and were surprised by his growth, not necessarily in height and weight, but in his appearance. No longer the callow boy they last saw; he was now a man.

They booked a room at the Waldorf and reserved another for Tom across the hall from them. As dinnertime approached, they dropped off Tom's two bags at the hotel, parked the car and walked to the restaurant. Dr. Ford never missed a trip to New York without a dinner at the 21 Club, so 21 it will be.

During dinner, Tom detailed his trip to his parents. They had communicated with him during the year via weekly phone calls and the occasional letter or postcard. Tom spoke about Jackie Brandt and the cryptic meeting with Jackie and Reuven Berman.

Reuven Berman piqued his father's interest.

Tom replied, "Yes, Reuven Berman was a partner of your patient Ariel Fisher who, I guess, arranged the meeting. At first, I was shocked to see Jackie with Reuven, and then it all made sense."

"What do you mean by 'It all made sense,' Tom," asked his mother.

"I believe they want to recruit me into their group. Exactly what group, I'm not sure."

"… the CIA or FBI?"

"I don't believe so. They seem to be a splinter group from the intelligence agencies. It appeared very mysterious."

His father changed the subject to discuss the primary purpose of the dinner.

He asked Tom, "Well, son, have you determined what you want to do with your life, now that you are an adult?"

"I want a career in finance," Tom replied.

He added somewhat facetiously, "…just like Gordon Gecko – greed is good and all those great 1980s principles. I met a girl in London who called me a Randian hero — tall, intelligent, ruggedly handsome and well-built.' I took it as a compliment, though she probably didn't intend it as one. She was a communist." His parents laughed at their son's experience with a Red.

"You would do well in finance," Dr. Ford said. But you must get your foot in the door. That's bound to be difficult. You have no degrees and they worship their credentials."

"You're right, but I understand more about economics and finance than does virtually all who apply for jobs in that industry. You know that."

Dr. Ford nodded his head agreeing, "Yes, all you must do is convince THEM of your knowledge and skills."

Amelia interjected, "Perhaps we could speak to Professor Gaffney, your old economics tutor, to provide some leads and a possible recommendation. He praised your understanding and knowledge and urged you to enroll in the college."

"That would be great, Mom."

Dr. Ford added, "I am sure son, once you progress past the gatekeepers you will convince them to hire you."

Tom and his father spent the remainder of dinnertime sampling the many single malt scotches under the countless toys of capitalism hung from the 21 ceiling. Tom recounted a few adventures he experienced on his world tour.

Amelia watched the spectacle while she sipped her champagne cocktail, knowing full well the task before her: leading her two men to a taxi and into their hotel beds.

Before the Fords returned to Orford Dr. Ford thought Tom should be fitted for several business suits. He will need them for his interviews and, ideally, his job. Gordon Carey, a Paul Stuart salesman, immediately came to mind.

The doctor purchased his first suit from Gordon and every other suit he had since worn.

Amelia went shopping on 57th St. and the doctor and Tom trekked to Paul Stuart on Madison Avenue. As Robert ascended the second-floor steps, he immediately spotted Gordon, a tall but slight and impeccably dressed black man in his early 60s.

"Gordon, it has been a long time," exclaimed the doctor.

Gordon turned around to the familiar voice. He smiled and extended his hand to the doctor, "Dr. Ford, indeed, it has been a long time. How is Amelia?"

"She is fine, Gordon. This is my son, Tom. He needs a few suits."

Gordon shook Tom's hand. "I've been dressing your father since he was a medical student at Columbia. He may have been my first customer."

"Has it been that long?" Dr. Ford looked quizzically at Gordon.

Gordon Carey nodded his head, "Time passes quickly."

Gordon stepped back, changing his attention to Tom; evaluating his suit size. "You're a 46 long and a 31 waist. That requires made-to-measure suits." Gordon knew how to size a customer.

Tom explained he will be interviewing for a job in finance and needed an appropriate wardrobe.

"I know exactly all you will need. Can I sell you a raincoat and overcoat along with the suits?"

"Gordon, you are still the consummate salesman," the doctor laughed.

"…and don't forget the shoes. We sell those downstairs."

Gordon walked them to the array of gray and blue suits at the 46 Long rack. He took one off the hanger to evaluate his initial impression of Tom's suit size. The 46 Long fit almost perfectly; the suit jacket simply needed minor alterations around the arms and waist.

An hour later, a tailor had measured him for five suits, all appropriate for the Wall Street club he planned to join. He also bought the raincoat and overcoat both, of which, needed alteration. To the shopping spree they added a couple of Blue blazers (summer and winter weight) and a dozen matching shirts and ties.

Dr. Ford reviewed the bill, "Gordon, it appears we paid your rent for the month."

Gordon gave his biggest smile for Dr. Ford. He worked for commissions.

They gave Gordon their goodbyes, thanking him for his help.

"I'll ship everything to you in two weeks. I'll place a rush on it," yelled Gordon as they left.

Dr. Ford and Tom exited the store and headed to the Waldorf's Peacock Alley for lunch with Amelia at noon. After lunch they drove home, Tom returned home after a year away to chart his future.

****

Professor Lucas Gaffney gave enthusiastic support to Tom's job search. "I'll call my ex-students on Wall Street who have done well and can give you an interview. You realize, that without a college degree you face extreme prejudice from these Wall Street firms."

"So I understand," Tom admitted during the phone call.

Professor Gaffney, true to his word, arranged three New York City interviews. The first: Jameson Lorimer of the old-line uber-WASP firm Spence, Brownell and Townsend, now known as SBT Worldwide. Tom scheduled the Lorimer interview for February 22, two weeks away.

Tom called Prof. Gaffney to thank him for his efforts. He also wanted to learn about his interviewer. He read all he could find about SBT and other investment banking firms. The company soon became his preference.

"Jameson was among my best students, highly intelligent and invariably rather arrogant. He took economics passionately and scored 4.0 at Dartmouth. We have kept in touch. I occasionally see him in the city and invited him to speak at the economic conferences I hosted. He is brilliant and perhaps even more imperious than he was as an undergraduate."

Tom reflected on this new information, "It appears I have considerable work to do to impress Mr. Jameson Lorimer."

"Yes you do. But Jameson doesn't impress easily."

"What else can you tell me about Jameson Lorimer?"

He has two interests besides his job and family: The New York Giants and Rubik's Cubes."

Tom, a Patriot's fan, thought it best to avoid discussing football with Jameson.

"Rubik's Cubes?"

"Yes, he loves Rubik's Cubes…he believes they provide excellent exercise for the mind. He always keeps one on his desk."

"…very interesting, professor. Thanks for the information."

"Good luck. Keep me informed on how it goes."

"Will do and thanks again, professor."

Tom had an idea. He played with Rubik's cubes after his father had him shoot his computer games. He became fairly proficient in solving them. He worked his way to solving a 5 X 5 cube. Tom hit the internet looking for the appropriate algorithms to refresh his memory. He memorized them all.

Computer-driven robots can solve the 3 X 3 cube in less than a second -- The human record is about four seconds. Tom didn't need to solve the cube that speedily, but he believed twenty seconds was possible. He practiced two to three hours a day, lowering his time for the standard 3 X 3 to a bit more than forty seconds. Not bad, but hardly an eye-opener. Tom needed eye-opening to impress. He had five days remaining until his interview.

Tom took out his 5 X 5. He believed solving a far more complex cube would render a 3 X 3 to child's play. He was right. After a few days working the 5 X 5 he hit his twenty-second goal with the 3 X 3, actually eighteen seconds.

Tom also realized he had to converse with Jameson Lorimer while he worked the cube, appearing natural and unmindful of that cube in his hands. He practiced as he recited Hamlet's soliloquy. He practiced reciting Tennyson's "Charge of the Light Brigade." And he practiced reciting Abraham Lincoln's Gettysburg Address. His parents must have thought him losing his mind. He took his time to less than twenty seconds. Tom tested himself by speaking to his parents: 16 seconds. He was now fully prepared for the interview.

Tom's scheduled his first interview for Monday. He decided to relax and socialize for the weekend. He had packed two suits that Gordon sent him and headed south – to Greenwich, Ct. and a visit to an old friend. He arranged to leave his car at his friend's driveway and take the train into the city. Tom arrived in New York Sunday afternoon and walked to the Waldorf from Grand Central to prepare for the three interviews -- the first with Jameson Lorimer at 10:00 A.M. Monday.

Tom spent the evening googling and reading everything he could find regarding SBT. He had researched news stories about SBT. Within a few hours, he knew more about the company than did nearly all SBT's employees. He discovered that many weapons makers and other defense companies are among SBT's clientele. Should the conversation devolves into a discussion of weapons, he could certainly hold his own.

Tom woke early, showered and shaved his stubble. He wore a narrow-lapeled, pinstriped three-button, traditional charcoal grey suit Gordon recommended for the interview. Looking ever the youthful Wall Streeter, he again solved the Rubik's cube. Satisfied, he left to meet Mr. Lorimer.

Tom arrived at Mr. Lorimer's office on the Spence building's 45th floor. Dark walnut wood-paneled walls, Oriental rugs, and burgundy leather upholstered club chairs reflected the firm's conservatism and traditions. A very attractive young receptionist completed the image.

Tom approached the desk. He addressed the very attractive smiling young receptionist, "Good morning. I am Tom Ford and have an appointment with Mr. Lorimer."

"Yes, Mr. Ford. Mr. Lorimer is expecting you. Please have a seat; he'll be with you shortly. Mr. Lorimer is on an emergency conference call. Would you like a cup of coffee while you wait?"

"No, thank you." Tom thought the receptionist must have read Emily Post, her manners so impeccable.

Jameson Lorimer finished his call and remembered an interview scheduled with someone Prof. Gaffney recommended. He considered the meeting strictly a courtesy. SBT hired no one without a BA. Most hires were MBAs, usually from prestigious schools like Harvard, Columbia, Wharton or Stanford, but Prof. Gaffney had been generous to him and he owed his old teacher a favor.

Lorimer leaned over and pressed the intercom button, "Miss Wilson, please send in Mr. Ford."

"Yes, Mr. Lorimer," came back through the intercom.

Tom entered the office. Jameson Lorimer, an early middle-aged clean-shaven man of average height, but with ramrod straight posture and a full head of black hair, stood to greet him. Lorimer smiled a perfect professional smile as he firmly shook Tom's hand. Tom spotted the Rubik's cube on the corner of the desk and planned the turns he had to execute to solve it quickly.

"Are you a cuber?" Tom asked.

"Why, yes. I play to relieve the many tensions found at this job. Working the cube also keeps the mind sharp."

Tom replied, "That it does. Do you mind?"

"Of course not." The request surprised Lorimer. He thought, "...*what is this...who is this guy who wants to play with a Rubik's cube at a job interview?*"

Tom took the cube and rapidly turned the cube's layers, thanking Lorimer for the interview. He focused on Lorimer while working the cube, only occasionally glancing at the rapidly rotating cube. "I understand I am an unusual job interview, coming here without the requisite school credentials, but I believe SBT Worldwide could benefit from my skills."

Tom placed the solved cube back to the desk in front of a stunned Lorimer. Never had he seen anyone solve the cube in under five minutes; roughly his time. Tom Ford solved just over fifteen-seconds, almost as an afterthought as he seamlessly maintained his conversation.

"Please take a seat, Mr. Ford." Tom Ford had piqued Lorimer's interest.

Lorimer and Tom conversed for more than an hour. Lorimer employed all the tricks he learned from twenty years of interviewing prospective employees, many of whom, were hotshot MBAs, to baffle Tom. He tested all applicants' mettle under fire. If they couldn't endure his withering rapid-fire questioning, they wouldn't hack it in negotiations with the many questions prospective clients, government regulators and a myriad of other agents who can block a deal with a wrong answer.

Tom never faltered, further impressing Lorimer.

Lorimer raised his old standby, the Slutsky Theorem. Besides doctorates in statistics or econometrics, few could explain much, if anything, about the Slutsky Theorem. Many laughed when asked -- they assumed he was joking. Jameson Lorimer never hired the laughers. However, Tom confidently replied, "The Slutsky Theorem states that continuous functions of random variables form cyclical patterns. Statisticians often apply the theorem to business cycles but it also has many other applications."

Jameson was astonished, but also pleased. He rated Tom extremely high as applicants go and wished to hire him, despite his lack of academic credentials. Prof. Gaffney told him Tom Ford was special but this was absurd.

"Tom, I want to send you to Prescott Brownell, our senior partner," Lorimer said as he raised his phone. "His grandfather founded the firm."

He called his secretary, "Miss Wilson, please connect me to Prescott Brownell?"

"Yes, Mr. Lorimer."

A minute later, the phone rang. Prescott Brownell.

"Mr. Brownell, I have a young man here I interviewed for a job. I think you should talk to him."

"…and why is that Mr. Lorimer?"

Jameson cupped the phone and asked Tom to wait outside for a minute.

Tom left the office and sat on a leather chair facing Miss Wilson. She smiled at him, "Your interview must have impressed Mr. Lorimer; he rarely sends a prospect to Mr. Brownell."

Tom smiled back. He knew he hit a home run with the interview.

Jameson resumed his call, "I just interviewed this kid. He is only twenty-two, lacks experience in the business and a college degree, but Lucas Gaffney, my economics professor, highly recommended him. Although skeptical, I owed the professor a favor and granted an interview."

"Tom Ford presents an excellent appearance, he's quite articulate, speaks four languages besides English, knows economics and finance more thoroughly than any MBA I have interviewed. He also solved my Rubik's cube in under twenty seconds. I highly recommend him for a position at SBT Worldwide."

After a short pause Brownell spoke, "Mr. Lorimer, for the twenty years you have been with us I have never seen such enthusiasm from you."

"Trust me, Mr. Brownell, you will like Tom Ford. I hate using the term, but he has that 'It Factor.'"

"Well, by all means, send him up Mr. Lorimer."

Lorimer placed the handset to its base. He stared at it awhile then stepped into the reception room. Tom stood and Lorimer spoke, "Mr. Brownell will speak to you and Miss Wilson will escort you to his office. Miss Wilson?"

Thank you, Mr. Lorimer. I appreciate your courtesies."

So far, Tom had been treated fairly by Jameson Lorimer. Jameson offered his hand to Tom. "I gave you a great recommendation to Mr. Brownell. Now go upstairs and impress him. The job is yours if you succeed."

Jameson had to know something before Tom left, "Mr. Ford, I am curious. Why did you believe you could walk into SBT, considered the most prestigious investment banking firm in New York, without experience, without credentials and leave with a job?"

"I let no one define me. Some erect barriers to other's success, others demolish them. I enjoy demolition and look forward to working at SBT."

Lorimer appreciated Tom's response. He survived Tom Ford's wrecking ball. He gave Tom a knowing nod. Jameson couldn't tell whether Tom Ford was an extremely talented, confident young man or merely an arrogant prick. He didn't care. He wanted Tom Ford on his team.

Miss Eliza Wilson motioned for Tom to follow her. They walked to the elevator. Tom had a short time to ask the very attractive Miss Wilson for a date. So he asked her, "Do you care to join me for dinner after work?"

She was astonished by his audacity, surprising from a person seeking a job at the company. Despite this, she found him too interesting and attractive to refuse the invitation.

She said yes.

"Good. Meet me at the Oak Room after work. What time do you finish work?"

"Five o'clock."

"I'll meet you there after five."

"O.K.," she responded, somewhat demurely.

The elevator door opened and he followed her to Brownell's office.

Brownell's secretary announced Tom to her boss and Tom entered the office. It was as sumptuous as Jameson Lorimer's (very men's clubby), but included an impressive battleship model encased in a glass display case behind his desk.

Brownell stood to greet Tom. Tom speculated he was about seventy. He stood close to six feet, lean, possessing a full head of grey closely-cropped hair and a neatly maintained pencil mustache. Brownell strode around the desk to greet Tom.

"Welcome to Spence, Brownell and Townsend, Mr. Ford. I doubt I'll ever get used to SBT Worldwide -- an idea of the marketing crew. They claimed the name sounded more modern and would increase our international business. They were right but old habits die hard.

"Thank you for your time, Mr. Brownell."

"Please call me Press. We are formal in public, but I prefer to relax a bit in the privacy of my office."

"All right Press." Tom and Brownell took their seats. Tom studied the model behind the desk. "That's an Iowa-class battleship, isn't it?

"Yes, The USS Missouri. I served on the Missouri as a fresh First Lieutenant towards the end of WW2. I was fortunate to see the Japs sign the surrender documents on her in Tokyo Harbor. It was an amazing experience."

Tom calculated his age. *"Prescott must be at least 85. He looks incredible for his age!"*

Tom asked, "I imagine so. Did you experience the kamikaze attacks?"

"Yes, they gave us a some rough days. I was in the Deck Four conning tower when a Zero slammed us. Fortunately, those eighteen inches of steel surrounding the tower did its job. Otherwise, I wouldn't be talking to you today. We lost many good men from those attacks."

Prescott's voice trailed off as he looked down to the desk. "So, Tom, I understand you are looking for a job?"

"Yes, the world of finance appeals to me."

"You are aware we rarely hire anyone without, at least, a bachelors degree? In fact, I don't remember whether we hired anyone in the last 30 years without a college degree.

"So I have been told, but, I believe my knowledge, education and skills exceed that of college grads, perhaps most graduate students."

"Well, don't worry too much about it. I didn't graduate from college. I enlisted in the Navy after my freshman year at Harvard. I was nineteen. My father arranged a commission as an officer. I intended to return to school after the war, but school seemed trivial after seeing men die in battle. Besides, I walked into a lucrative position with the family firm. My father was a senior partner in 1946, as I am today."

Tom and Prescott spoke for a half hour when Prescott Brown rose from his chair. "Jameson raved about you. He's a little stiff at times, but a good man. I trust his judgment. I believe in assuming risk. A successful banker takes prudent risks; otherwise, he's doomed to mediocrity. We abhor mediocrity here. You appear to be anything but mediocre. We'll start you as a lowly analyst, but there is no ceiling to your career at Spence."

"Thank you, Press. I won't disappoint you."

Prescott Brownell extended his hand to Tom, "Welcome aboard, son."

He added, "I'll have my secretary call Personnel to give them a head's up."

Prescott's secretary guided Tom to the Personnel Office (Yes, SBT World-wide still calls it the Personnel Office) to fill out the reams of paperwork required from all new employees. He enjoyed this short experience with SBT and concluded he will fit in well and satisfy the faith the company gave him.

Tom returned to his hotel room by 3:00 P.M. He called to give his parents the wonderful news. The Fords were ecstatic for their son. He didn't tell them of the date he also arranged. Tom Ford had a great day.

As a courtesy, Tom kept his other two appointments. Emily Post continued to influence him, but he also hoped to generate industry contacts, pick their brains about the business and develop a perspective for his future competition. Everything went smoothly, and everyone friendly, upfront, and open concerning their profession. He didn't expect any job offers, nor did either firm offer one. "Tom, you are an impressive young man, but we only hire college graduates here." Neither did he prepare for, nor research these two firms as he studied SBT Worldwide.

Besides, there was no Rubik's Cube to break the ice.

****

New York City was a grand, unwieldy, inconvenient, expensive place. The city also offered many fine restaurants, shopping, museums, and art galleries, many of the world's best. Although he was not new to New York, he found the city to be intriguing and constantly engaging. Tom Ford discovered city living far more enjoyable to live there than he had expected.

He especially liked the Museum of Natural History, the Metropolitan Museum of Art a close second. He also enjoyed visiting the Bronx Zoo, a short subway ride away from his Columbus Circle apartment. His apartment was also a pleasant 15-minute walk to his office at 46th and Avenue of the Americas.

Spence, the in-house moniker for SBT Worldwide, exemplifies New York's investment banks. Tom had enough hours in the day to finish his "To Do" list. The days -- impelled by the office's frenetic pace -- flashed by.

The firm had extensive corporate accounts that generated substantial fees, the firm's lifeblood. Once a company became a client, there seemed to be an endless need for more money. Each executive was accountable for keeping the client satisfied with the firm's access to capital.

Spence's business included new business development. This could be a one-time-only deal as an IPO, a large bond offering, or an opportunity to initiate a longer-term relationship. They assigned Tom to new business development.

A young partner, a Harvard Law School graduate named Martin Paxton, took responsibility for Tom's training and integration into the firm. Martin was short, slim, intense, and extremely bright. His father was American, a WASP at that, his mother Japanese. His parents met in Hong Kong when trainees initiating their business careers.

Martin professed to be taken aback by Tom's appearance. He asked Tom, "Is there anything you can do about your looks?"

Tom, stunned for a moment asked, "What do you mean?"

Paxton replied, "We are supposed to look pale, overworked, and exhausted, not like Tarzan on steroids. It is our charade we assume for our clients and assures them they are getting their money's worth." Tom laughed at Martin's comment.

He realized his good fortune. His boss a rare creature, an attorney with a sense of humor. Many of the successful lawyers he had met were serious, too often humorless.. He found them interesting enough when discussing the law, but he found them unimpressive in social situations. He wondered whether they believed that to be a successful lawyer, one needed only think of the law.

Tom said, "Well, I do work out fairly regularly, I guess."

Paxton looked across his desk, "No shit, and here I assumed you had a rare disease."

Martin Paxton and Tom Ford worked well together. They also became close friends.

The first months passed swiftly and the work at SBT Worldwide satisfied him. He worked on several clients' accounts, establishing a solid reputation with each. Tom gave extraordinary attention to detail. He recalled his old boss Art Rossi's dictum, "It takes ounces to make pounds, pennies, dollars." Tom found this applies to investment banking as it does to the scrap metal business. Tom also worked hard to generate new clients for his employer. He learned much in a short time about the company and the Spence accounts.

Martin, an inveterate runner, ran Cross Country in college. He approached Tom with Tom's employee evaluation, "Don't worry, I gave you an A- plus but may I ask you something"

Tom asked, "Sure, what's that?"

"Do you want to join me for my twice-weekly run?"

Tom replied, "Tell me about it."

"I run the six-mile Central Park Loop. I run for time, always trying to keep it under forty minutes."

"Sounds good. When do we start?"

"Tomorrow after work."

"Let's do it."

Tom enjoyed their twice-weekly run around Central Park. Usually, they run the route in 38 to 40 minutes, but occasionally run for dinner and lower the time to between 35 to 37 minutes. Paxton would win those races, usually by less than ten yards. He had a competitive streak about him and tracked their times on an Excel chart. After a year, he performed all sorts of statistical gymnastics with the data and passed his analysis throughout the office. The charts showed his slight edge over Tom. Martin's efforts amused Tom.

Tom's social life mirrored his career. He found New York's women interesting, entertaining, and attractive. Despite having no long-term relationships he enjoyed the city's social scene. His typical date typically included dinner, movies, a Broadway show, museums, and walks in the park.

Every other weekend he left the city for the country. Usually, he headed north to visit his parents -- often with the girl de jour, but sometimes he traveled alone. Tom hiked the Adirondacks, canoed the Delaware River or hunted deer in the Catskills. He needed to be in the country, a respite from the crowds he found in the city.

New York women were urbanized and had a strong aversion to leaving the city; unless taking a trip to the Hamptons on a summer weekend was in the offing. After a few months of dating, he decided a trip to the country was in order. He hoped his current girlfriend would join him, but her absence wouldn't prevent his enjoyment of the weekend.

Tom returned to his long-distance target practice when visiting his parents in Orford. He and his father placed empty wine bottles on the 500 yard table. Tom seldom missed. He also practiced filling out his ballistic data cards. He now had thousands points of data which helps to more accurately gauges a long-distant shot.

He converted a few of his oh-so-sophisticated weekend dates to shooting. Nearly all had never previously handled a gun and were reluctant to pick one up. At Tom's insistence, they gave it a try. He usually gave them his old Marlin 39-A to shoot. The Marlin is a reliable, safe gun with no kick -- perfect for a beginner. His dates started their lesson by shooting bottles at 100 feet, a challenging, but not impossible shot for a beginner. Tom enjoyed teaching these Seven Sisters graduates about the joy of shooting. Many later boasted to their friends about their skill blasting bottles in New Hampshire.

Tom further improved his martial arts skills by adding karate to his hand-to-hand weaponry. After years of training, Tom developed proficiency in judo, boxing, wrestling, MMA and after his three months at the Buddhist temple, kung-fu. He heard Yong-sun Kim was the best karate tutor in the city and Tom impressed Kim by his mastery of other martial arts disciplines he was proficient.

He appreciated the way Kim had taught him karate. Tom's karate blows developed impressively in accuracy and power aided by his serious strength and speed. Kim realized Tom had become highly effective with karate and moved him into his most experienced and proficient practice group. In five short weeks, Ford not only held his own, but dominated the karate school's best students. Even Kim was surprised by his progress. Kim predicted that in a year's time, only the best could survive against Ford's karate skills. Overall, life was splendid and Tom enjoyed his New York experience.

Tom's pleasant routine was soon to be interrupted. While entertaining new clients at 21 Jackie Brandt walked to his table. He asked, "Tom Ford, how is the old Ranger doing these days?"

Tom, stood to greet his Ranger friend, "Why am I not surprised to see you, Jackie?"

"I'm not sure I can answer that, Tom. Please give me your business card and I'll call you. Let's do lunch. We have much to talk about."

Tom immediately realized what he wanted to discuss. He recalled the meeting in Israel with Reuven and Jackie Brandt, but his work was demanding and their offer receded into the background. He reached into his suit pocket and handed Jackie a card. "Yes, please call me."

Jackie left and Tom sat. A client asked, "Were you an Army Ranger?"

"No stolen valor here. I wasn't a Ranger -- never in the military. However, Jackie and I participated in a fantasy Ranger training camp a couple of years ago in California, but he is a major in Army Intelligence."

Chapter 5: *Tom's First Hit*

Tom didn't wait long for Jackie's phone call – he called the following day.

"Can you do lunch today?"

"Late lunch, say, about two."

"Good. Let's meet at the Landmark Tavern on 11th Avenue and 44th."

"I know it. See you there."

Tom finished the phone call wondering what adventure Jackie had planned for him.

Remembering his last meeting with Jackie and Reuven Berman, he could only imagine it would be confounding. Although he often deliberated about the quasi-offer given in Israel, their schemes' danger and illegality gave him considerable reluctance to join their efforts. He needed more information to convince him — much more.

Tom finished his work earlier than expected and walked to the restaurant. A delightful spring day helped give him the needed tone to clear his mind of business concerns before meeting Jackie.

Tom arrived precisely at 2:00 P.M. He looked around and spotted Jackie Brandt (in civilian clothing) sitting at a corner table by the window. Jackie rose to greet Tom, they sat and Jackie started the conversation, "So, how is life at SBT?"

"Great! I enjoy the experience far more than I could ever have imagined – certainly as a kid from the country who didn't graduate from college. I have developed a strong client base and business thus far is excellent."

Jackie gave his approval, "Never in doubt."

"So Jackie, where are you now?"

"Still with DIA, but I am Lieutenant Colonel Brandt today."

"Congratulations!"

"Thank you." Jackie added facetiously, "…and I won't retire until I have four stars sewn on my epaulets."

The beers they ordered arrived and the waitress set the beers on the table. They gave her their simple food order – two hamburgers, medium rare, with fries.

Jackie continued, "I want to be serious now. Do you recall our Tel Aviv conversation? Our country has been under attack for nearly twenty years. This is the same enemy Judeo Christian Western Civilization has fought since 622 A.D. The same enemy the great King John Sobieski defeated at Vienna in 1683 as they threatened the entire European continent. Of course, I refer to militant Islam, a sizable slice of the Muslim religion that waged war to install the 12th Imam.

"They call him the Hidden Imam, also the Imam of Time and believe he will save the world by establishing the Allah's words as spoken by Mo-hammed. These jihadists prepare their world for his Coming by violence and murder. Jews and Christians refused to accept Mohammed as their prophet. They were considered Islam's enemies, fitting only for conquest. Islamists are engaged in an aggressive jihad against all unbelievers. Jihad is the Koran's teaching that is currently in vogue and has inspired much re-cent terrorism."

Tom added, "Fight those from among the people of the Book, who believe not in Allah, nor in the Last Day, nor hold as unlawful what Allah and His Messenger have declared to be unlawful, nor follow the true religion…Surah 9:29."

"I forgot you studied their language and culture."

"I visited a few Muslim countries on my trip. Although I was treated well by the majority of the population I detected an undercurrent of hatred to-wards Westerners by a few."

Jackie agreed, "Yes, Muslims are like all people. They want to live comfortably, raise a family in a safe environment. Above all, they want to be left alone. However, at least 10% of Muslims have been radicalized and pose a threat to non-believers and Muslims who don't share their zeal for the religion. Since 9/11, there have been more than 30,000 Islamist terrorist attacks, the greatest violence has been directed to these Muslims. Shiites murder Sunnis. Iraqis kill Iranians. Iranians kill Iraqis. Wahhabis kill everyone. It's a plight that has been an element of the religion since founded. All we can do is protect ourselves when they expand their murderous impulses. And this is where our problems begin."

Tom asked, "What do you mean? "

"Well, thanks to our historic president guiding our foreign policy we have taken a 'See No Sharia' approach to the terrorist threat. Consequently, we curtailed surveillance and monitoring of radicals at certain mosques. Civil Rights and Civil Liberties guidelines issued by DHS, DOD, FBI, CIA and other federal agencies deemed returning vets, gun-owners and patriot groups as the greatest terrorist threats.

"Their policies are nonsense. The government seems more interested in Muslim outreach than protecting our country from the subversive influences of groups like the Muslim Brotherhood. Call to mind the president changed NASA's central mission from space exploration to 'Muslim outreach.' The historic president had those words written into NASA's mission statement…amazing…but certainly a wake-up call."

"As the jihadists accelerated their pursuit of a global Islamist state – a Caliphate – our federal government receded into a weak defensive position vis-à-vis jihad. The federal bureaucracy granted a Muslim group called CAIR extraordinary influence on U.S. policy. Have you ever heard of them?"

"Yes, the Council on American-Islamic Relations, advertised as a moderate Muslim organization, but they are, in fact, closely related to the Muslim Brotherhood."

"Correct! CAIR, the ACLU, the National Lawyers Guild and many other groups have worked hard to stop many of our more successful anti-terrorist policies in court. Consequently, they have crippled our front lines of defense for the last few years. Our country's efforts to defend itself against the Islamist assault have been hampered."

Jackie continued, "For every action there is an equal and opposite reaction. Newtonian physics can also apply to politics. We have seen appreciable repercussions from the military, intelligence, law enforcement and business communities to these capitulation policies. Some officers outright ignore the more egregious orders. Interest groups take the government to court.

"However, another group, a confederation of patriots that I am a member, is determined to counter these new policies they assert will inevitably lead to a massive terrorist attack on our homeland."

Tom asked, "Do you refer to the Martels you spoke of in Israel?"

"Yes."

"Tell me more. Do you consider yourselves vigilantes?"

"Hardly. We're not a rabble with pitchforks attacking the king. On the other hand, we aren't allied with any centralized organization. We only know the persons in our cell -- like the 1950s commies. These cells act independently but all profess the same goal. I understand we have dozens of cells in many countries. There may be an overlap of tactics, but we have a single objective: protect the country from a terrorist attack. Our country is under attack from terrorists, within and outside our borders. Human lives mean nothing to them – they operate without scruples. They despise the United States because it hasn't accepted Allah's oneness. Islam's holy warriors have only one goal: to destroy us. It's that simple."

Tom had to ask the question he suspected he knew the answer to, "Jackie, what is your cell's specialty?

"We have a simple mission -- we assassinate the bad guys. When we receive well-founded intelligence reports concerning a prospective terrorist or someone planning an attack, we go on the offensive to kill him."

"How long have you been killing the bad guys?"

"…more than three years."

"…let me guess. You still want to recruit me into your cell?"

"Yes."

"Why not recruit a military sniper? Someone retired?"

"We already have a few on our team, but you are ideal. Ex-military snipers are the first suspects after an assassination. You're a well-respected businessman. Who'd think of looking at you? Besides, you may be a better marksman than most snipers."

"Well, you found me by the New Hampshire shooting."

"Yes, but we had those records expunged."

"How did you manage that?"

"Let me say it this way: We have friends everywhere who want to help. The Deep State works both ways."

Tom took a deep breath and took a sustained chug of his beer. He wasn't surprised by the offer; they had pitched it to him in Israel, but he was enjoying his trip and didn't want to think about it then. Despite this, he was well aware of the enormous danger he would encounter.

"I'd like to think it over."

"Of course, but keep in mind that we need your talents. I witnessed your marksmanship at the Ranger school. You have already did the dirty by shooting those thugs in New Hampshire. You are a natural for the job. I don't want to sound too jingoistic, but you can serve your country. The government won't acknowledge your efforts. They may also hunt you like a common criminal, but remember your reaction after shooting those three thugs. Pretty good, huh?"

"I felt great. When I realized they wouldn't ever find me, I remembered those two troopers, their families, and the lives I had saved. I discussed this with my father, a doctor. He told me that this is the same feeling he gets when he saves a life. It's what his profession is about."

"You will save thousands, perhaps millions, of lives by your efforts. Consider Bill Clinton and the lives he could have saved by assassinating Osama bin Laden when he had the chance."

"I guess he had other things on his mind. When do you need to know?"

"In about a week? Let's meet here, same time next week."

"Plenty of time. I'll see you next week." Tom stood to leave.

"Naturally, our conversation remains between us."

Tom sat again, "I must tell my parents. They have been extremely good to me since a Dartmouth student dropped me on their steps in a beer box. I owe them my utmost loyalty. I told them about the Lattimore brothers shooting an hour afterward. They have kept it quiet all these years. I must tell them or I won't do this."

Jackie laughed, "You win. Talk to your parents about our offer, but make sure to emphasize the importance of keeping the details within the family. Your life, and theirs, may depend on it."

"Thanks, Jackie. See you next week."

Jackie added, "Tom, here is something else to think about: Never forget the terror and tragedy we all suffered on 9/11. We must actively prevent another such attack on our country."

Tom knew he was right.

Tom drove home for the weekend to discuss Jackie Brandt's offer with his parents. He had decided to work for Jackie. He remembered a quote from a Middle Age history lesson: "The primal Teutonic duty of free men is to bear arms in defense of home and nation."

Furthermore, the memory of 9/11 still rankled him. The three thousand murders must never be repeated. Any risk will be worth taking if he can stop another such atrocity. And he would have no moral question about shooting terrorists. The US has killed terrorists by airstrikes and drones since 2002. Not enough in Tom's mind. Besides, he had developed a great life and did not want some crazy jihadist to destroy it. He had to act.

A courier delivered a package to the office the day after he met with Jackie. The package held secret documents that explained the legal justifications for assassinations. A note from Jackie read, "Here's some reference material to help with your decision. Destroy all after you read them...Jackie."

The documents gave evidence these killings are justified and legal when "a target's activities threatened national security and against whom the use of deadly force could be justified." Nevertheless, these killings need authorization from the executive branch, something Tom was sure Jackie and his group didn't receive. Additionally, Executive Order 12333 signed by Gerald Ford prohibits the act of state-sponsored killing of foreign officials outside the U.S. boundaries. What if the target isn't a "foreign official?" Tom didn't expect they would ask him to shoot government officials. His targets would likely be freelancers who worked outside of any government authorization.

That weekend Tom's parents wholehearted supported Tom's decision to join Jackie Brandt's covert efforts to fight terrorism. Dr. Ford remembered delivering Bill Layton's baby after the shooting. He appreciated that Layton's son wouldn't have been born had not Tom's excellent marksmanship and initiative saved the trooper from a Lattimore bullet and certain death. The Fords understood Tom could save many more lives with his skills. Yes, the missions would be dangerous, but millions of parents through the years sent their sons to war knowing the risks. The Fords were no different. They won't stand in his way.

Nonetheless, they requested Tom investigate Jackie Brandt and the Martels before committing to their recruiting efforts.

His mother raised an important point, "You are trusting his word regarding his identity. You once mentioned he invited you to his office when you met him in Israel -- you should accept his offer."

Tom agreed and asked Jackie at his next Landmark Tavern meeting.

"Sure!" Jackie responded. "I'd be disappointed if you didn't ask. When would you like to visit?"

"Can you do this weekend?" Tom asked.

"No problem. We are open 24/7/52."

DIA headquarters was located in southern Washington, DC. Tom took the Acela Express from Penn Station at 8:00 AM Saturday and arrived at Union Station by 11:00 AM. He had a noon appointment with Jackie.

Tom enjoyed a leisurely cup of coffee at a local Starbucks, read the Washington Times and admired the downtown DC street scene. At 11:45 he took a taxi to the DIA headquarters, a few miles from Union Station, across the Anacostia River. He arrived at noon and paged Lt. Col. Jackie Brandt. Jackie met him attired in an impressive full dress uniform, a fruit salad overflowed with ribbons and medals.

"You give quite a show, Jackie. "

"Remember, I am here to impress. I have already registered you. Here is your badge."

Tom placed the badge around his neck, wondering whether he was now on someone's watch list. He asked Jackie.

"No. Check the badge."

Tom looked and noticed the name on the badge read "Thomas Brandt."

"Who is Thomas Brandt?" Tom asked.

"Thomas Brandt is my nephew. I assumed signing him in would be easier than signing a stranger. Besides, I don't want your name on any records in this office."

Jackie pointed to a wide double door. He opened it with his ID card.

"Ready for the grand tour? It's Saturday. We have a skeleton staff but I have much to explain. I work for a division called the Defense Clandestine Service. DCS that works with the CIA and Joint Special Operations Command. We are the former HUMINT but we were recently expanded and assigned new responsibilities. After the intelligence failure that led to the 9/11 disaster, the military and politicians recognized the dangers of relying too heavily on satellites and other technological assets. They expanded human intelligence sources – the old spy about the streets – to improve our intelligence gathering. James Bond and all that."

Tom entered a DIA's watch center. The scene overwhelmed his senses. The room, 20,000 square feet, accommodated more than a hundred enormous flat-panel TVs that lined the walls. Dozens of cubicles, each manned by personnel, operated an array of computers on their desks. The room impressed Tom.

"We keep an eye on the happenings around the world," Jackie explained, "and monitor nearly all news shows in scores of languages. You'd be surprised by everything you could learn from a simple interview of a Third World dictator."

Jackie gave Tom a tour of the facility for the next hour. The number of rooms and corridors which even a Lt. Colonel in the DIA had no access surprised Tom.

Jackie explained, "Most rooms you don't want access. You wouldn't want be a suspect should anything go wrong in that department. I have access to a third of the building."

The tour ended at Jackie Brandt's station. His station, a mini watch center, held an expansive World Mercator Projection displaying hundreds of various colored lights clustered on the far wall. The ceiling rose thirty feet and the room was a quarter of the first watch center's size. Jackie's office was perched on a mezzanine opposite the map. Large screens covered three walls and more than two-dozen cubicles, each manned by a casually dressed civilian, filled the floor.

"We keep tabs on our overseas assets from this room. Those lights indicate the status and location of a team or individual on duty." An analyst strode to Brandt, a young man not too much older than Tom, "Colonel, will you take a look at something on my screen?"

"Sure, Bob." Jackie walked to Bob's cubicle where they discussed the anomaly displayed on the screen. It appeared routine to Tom; neither looked concerned.

Jackie patted Bob's shoulder and walked back to Tom. "Nothing earth-shattering there. Let's go to my office for a talk."

Tom followed Jackie to the office. The office, built on steel I-beans, overlooked the expansive room. Tom sat on a worn Steelcase office chair alongside Lt. Colonel Brandt's desk.

"Tom, I hope you enjoyed the tour. I trust your concern is mitigated by my bona fides as an officer in the DIA."

"Jackie, I am certain you are who you say you are."

"Good! May I assume you accept my offer?"

"I do have a concern. My parents may be in danger if I am captured or my name is disclosed. These jihadists are lunatics and may take revenge on them."

"I admit that's a possibility, but remote at this point. Your name, mission and association with the Martels will never be written down -- nothing on paper or electronic bytes. Your name will never appear on anyone's records. We will conduct our correspondence by a secure phone I will give you...or at face-to-face meetings like this – no emails, memos or letters will be utilized. Should the government catch you we will do our best to have you released or find a way to otherwise free you. As I said, we developed many contacts with allies who will help us."

Tom laughed, "All right, I accept your offer. I gave this considerable thought and I remembered sitting with my parents watching vintage Davey Crocket movies starring Fess Parker, "Be sure you're right and then go ahead." Well, I believe this is right and necessary. I'm all in if my talents with a rifle can save innocent lives."

Tom continued, "The great snipers -- Simo Häyhä, Lyudmila Pavlichenko, Carlos Hathcock and Chris Kyle, have always impressed me. Their bravery and skills were an inspiration for my decision. Jihadists declared war on America -- I want to fight back. When do I start?"

"I am glad you asked. The answer is: immediately."

Jackie gathered some files on the shelf behind him and handed them to Tom.

The name Zayan Hussein splashed the top file's cover. "Your target."

"Zayan Hussein is a top computer engineer for the Islamic state. He worked as a hacker and became a leading jihadist recruiter on social media. He recruited many lone wolves, most of whom operate in our country. The Brits convicted him of leading a hacking group called Team Poison. Team Poison hacked into the Iraqi military computers that led to the assassinations of more than a dozen officials, including two American civilians working for us. However, in their brilliant evaluation of Hussein, British prosecutors regarded him simply as a bored youth, merely hacking for fun.

They asked for and he received a six-month term for his hacking. The fact is that Hussein is a talented but dangerous jihadist. Our intelligence determined they will smuggle him to Syria after he is released from prison next month to expand his recruitment and hacking efforts. Zayan Hussein's freedom will lead to many more deaths. We must stop him. "

Tom browsed the file as Jackie spoke. "His file indicates he's a British citizen. Are we authorized to kill Brits?"

"We aren't officially authorized to kill anyone, but unofficially all who threaten us are targets."

Jackie explained, "Robert Conquest's *Third Law of Politics:* "The simplest way to explain the behavior of any bureaucratic organization is to assume it is controlled by a cabal of its enemies."

Tom replied, "I am familiar with his argument. Politics perverts an institution's mission statement. The politicians gain control of the organization and write the rules for its operation."

"Exactly!" Jackie was getting to the point. "A left-wing cabal has hijacked much of our intelligence organizations. They believe that forcing diversity and gender equality into the bureaucracy is far more important than fulfilling its actual goals. Many in the DIA, however, continue to believe that the agency's primary job is to find the bad actors and stop them before they destroy the country."

Tom asked, "Well, how serious is this problem?"

"So serious, that the Martels, which you are now a member, must secretly work to assure the mission legislated to these agencies by Congress is carried out. Some hold that pursuing the bad guys is racist. Instead of stopping terrorism, they would inexplicably file charges against a good agent for hate crimes because he too aggressively investigated Muslims."

Tom shook his head, "Is it that grim of a situation?"

Jackie nodded affirmatively, "It's that grim."

Tom asked, "What are the details of the hit?"

"The Brits intend to release Hussein from prison in five weeks. They will take him to Old Bailey to face additional charges. We have found the hearing to be merely a formality. The prosecutor will drop all charges. Zayan Hussein will walk out a free man. You can shoot him from a building 450 yards away as he emerges from Old Bailey. The shot won't be uncommonly long for you. The problem: his followers will closely surround him, but fortunately he is 6' 3" -- five or six inches taller than his friends. Go for a head-shot. The building is slated for demolition and is empty. At eleven stories high, the 11th floor should give you a clear sightline to the target. The file I gave you includes area maps and photos...also a few photos of the building, including interior shots and a telescopic photo of the door Hussein will exit. Our MI-5 friends did a thorough job. Any questions, Tom?"

"Not now. I'll analyze the information you gave me and calculate the rifle, ammo and any other supplies I'll need for the assignment."

"Great! May I buy you dinner?"

It was now close to 4:00 P.M. and Tom missed lunch. He had an open ticket back to NY. Dinner sounded perfect to him.

"I'll take you to my favorite DC restaurant, the Old Ebbitt Grill. You will appreciate the place."

"I'm familiar with the Old Ebbitt. It's the favorite of the SBT people when they have business in Washington."

Tom and Jackie arrived at the restaurant at 4:30 P.M. Before dinner, Jackie bought a bottle of Cristal champagne. "Drug lords celebrate a big score with Cristal. You're my big score."

Tom proposed a toast: "Here's to making Zayan an honored shahid in his community."

After the spirited toast, Jackie explained to Tom that he will also score a little business in London to provide cover. Jackie clarified, "An ally of our cause, the eccentric billionaire J. Bailey Morgan III, helps finance the Martels. One of his subsidiaries needs financing for an upcoming expansion and their representative will call your office on Monday."

"I've heard of Morgan. He is among the world's richest men and has his hands in virtually everything."

Tom considered his mission an unusual way to attract clients but he never turns away any business opportunities – especially from J. Bailey Morgan III.

****

Tom returned to New York that evening and the next morning studied the file Jackie gave him. He googled the name Zayan Hussein and found dozens of results. The guy even had a Facebook page. Hussein had a couple of websites in Arabic. He sent links of these sites to his former Dartmouth Arabic tutor for translation. He suspected the rhetoric was considerably more inflammatory in his native language than the English translation. His fears were confirmed a few hours later. Professor Abayan replied to his email, "Who is this guy? He is a pure radical jihadist who writes about slaying and beheading infidels. Here is a typical passage from a radical site he uses for recruiting:

"If you wish to know the way to glory and power, to goodness, security and joy, you must learn that there are no rights without jihad, no justice without jihad, no dignity without jihad, no security without jihad, no future without jihad, no life without jihad. No life without jihad! ."

The professor added his opinion regarding Zayan Hussein, "The failures of past terrorism plans only encourage them to do it right the next time. And they employ the internet to attract more recruits. Zayan Hussein appears dangerous."

Tom decided Mr. Hussein would best serve mankind six feet under, or wherever Muslims stow their dead bodies. Zayan Hussein's rants on multiple websites suggested he won't moderate his opinions after he is released from prison. Prison radicalizes moderate Muslims but unhinges the crazies.

Zayan appeared an excellent choice for Tom's first target. Tom doubted he would suffer remorse for shooting this jihadist. Zayan's death will slow ISIS's efforts around the globe. He could not be easily replaced.

Tom spent the next few days compiling a supply list for the hit. After exhaustive research, he chose the CheyTac M-310 SS .408 sniper rifle. The CheyTac is a heavy gun, weighing more than thirty pounds. However, that's not a concern as he won't be required to lug the gun any great distance. The rifle has a range exceeding, two thousand yards and is also among the world's most accurate rifles. Any sub-MOA rifle would be insufficient for the job.

Under ideal testing conditions, the CheyTac had shown its accuracy in group shots exceeding all available sniper rifles. The rifle set a world record for best grouping at two thousand yards. Tom evaluated the shot – a headshot of close to five hundred yards at a target surrounded by a sizable crowd. The parameters gave him a margin of error of less than two inches, little leeway when innocent lives are in the vicinity.

He also ordered the Leupold Mark 8 3.5-25x56mm M5B2 Front Focal scope. He may possibly be shooting from bright sunlight to the dark shadow cast by the building. The Leupold brightens the shadows and eliminates a possible depth perception problem.

He added an M408 suppressor to reduce the noise from 160db unsuppressed to 127db suppressed. Still noisy but the reinforced concrete room and the din of an urban setting should drown the report of the shot. The crowd's confusion about the direction of the shot could mean the difference between the mission's success or failure.

Tom chose a Harris HBRMS bipod with rubber-tipped legs; ideal for the concrete floor from which he will shoot. Tom added two hundred-round boxes of .408/419 grain ammunition. He planned to shoot one-hundred and ninety rounds for practice, leaving ten for the London shot. He preferred to use ammo from the same batch to ensure consistency.

Tom visited the NY Public Library to email the list to Jackie's special encrypted account for this mission. He planned to avoid using his personal or business accounts for any contact with Jackie during the entire mission. Jackie also gave him a burner phone that only contacts Jackie's burner phone. The phone had no screen or keyboard – only a green button to call and a red button to end the call. Welcome to the intelligence community!

Jackie called three days later.

He asked, "So when can we deliver the stash?"

Tom replied, "I'll be in New Hampshire this weekend. Perhaps I could pick it up on Friday."

"No, I'll have someone deliver it to you."

"Where is it coming from?"

"Boston."

Yes, please deliver the package to the house."

"Good. Todd will deliver it to you this Saturday morning."

"Todd? Do you trust Todd?"

"Yes. He's my 23-year-old son, a Coast Guard ensign, a recent Coast Guard Academy grad. He is aware of the Martels and supports its cause."

"I didn't even know you were married."

"Divorced," Jackie replied.

Tom realized he didn't know much about the guy who will lead him to this adventure that could lead to personal ruin...or worse.

Todd arrived Saturday noon carrying the gun. Tom was eager to shoot it. A gunsmith had assembled the gun, adjusted the trigger pull pressure and sighted the scope at five-hundred yards. He lifted the rifle from the hard Halliburton case.

The gun's long length and bulk, finished in matte black that minimized reflected sunlight, gave it a distinct, formidable appearance. The rifle's manufacturers assert, "the primary intent of the .408 is as an extreme range anti-personnel system."

Good enough for Tom.

Tom looked at Todd. "Do you want the first shot?"

"No. I'll give you the honor." Todd said. He followed Tom to the five-hundred yard range. Tom's parents shortly joined them. After the introductions, Tom settled on taking his shot. He took it from the prone position as he will in London.

He hit the steel target. A solid metal clang assured him he hit the target. He looked back to his audience who cheered him on.

"What a great gun! It's perfectly smooth and stable -- like driving a Mercedes after a Yugo. I'll take a few more shots before passing it around."

Amelia commented, "I like that gun. It's quieter than your other guns."

Tom pointed to the suppressor at the end of the barrel, "This suppresses the noise a bit."

Tom took another shot – a bull's eye. He led the crew to the 100-yard range and handed the gun to Todd. Todd had experience with handling a rifle like the CheyTac. His father gave him his first B-B gun when seven. He eventually graduated to shooting a twin-50 deck gun at the Academy. He was unfamiliar with the scope, thus placed his first three shots too high on the target. Tom gave him a quick lesson regarding the Leupold scope. Todd improved his aim by hitting the 6-inch bullseye with the following three shots, the familiar loud clang from the steel target indicating success.

Dr. Ford hit three of six and was satisfied with his marksmanship, considering he was shooting an unfamiliar gun. Amelia, as customary, politely refused the gun when offered by Tom.

She did, however, invite Todd to join them for lunch. He accepted. Tom directed Todd to the back barn where they stored the guns. They built a safe-like room in the corner of the barn over three weekends ten years ago.

They realized the increasing value of their burgeoning inventory and determined the need for more security. The walls, floor and ceiling were of six-inch thick poured reinforced concrete. A steel door secured by a combination lock provided added security to their homemade gun safe. A dehumidifier and heater maintained a perfect climate for the inventory. Tom and Todd hauled the gear to the storeroom where Tom gave Todd a quick tour of the Ford's impressive gun collection.

Amelia and the doctor walked to the house to prepare lunch. Tom and Todd soon followed, sat at the table where the conversation naturally drifted to guns.

Todd, an affable, voluble young man, devoted himself to the Coast Guard. He described his Coast Guard experience, "I patrol Boston Harbor on a 45-foot Response Boat. It's a great assignment. We interdict drugs, illegal aliens, potential terrorists, child sex slaves and all kinds of contraband. The children we see are heartbreaking. We know they were sent to the US for auction to some pervert who'd exploit them as sex slaves until they become too old. They are then cast out onto the streets and replaced by a younger victim."

Dr. Ford replied, "Yes, we see few around here, but my colleagues from the big cities tell me about the pathologies suffered by these children. They are malnourished, uneducated and suffer from countless disorders including STDs. Many suffer from poorly-healed broken bones from incredible abuse. Human trafficking is a serious problem that not many in our country know much about."

Tom, curious about Jackie Brandt, took the opportunity to quiz his son, Todd. "What was Jackie like as a father? "

"I had great parents. Unfortunately, they had different ideas about raising children. I have a younger brother at Antioch College."

"Antioch? Tom asked. "Antioch is among the most liberal colleges in the country. Why is it that you graduated from the Coast Guard Academy and your younger brother attends Antioch?"

"Well, my parents divorced. My father influenced me more than my mother, my brother by my mother. My father professed conservative, traditional and patriotic principles. Mom was liberal, free-spirited but suspicious of American ideals. I am not sure why they married."

Amelia interjected, "I believe that 20 to 25 years ago politics didn't matter as much as it does today. Women were more attracted to strong men -- men they could trust to keep their end of the promise that marriage requires. The liberal men I have known tend to the beta range – they may offer finer poetry, but poetry won't sustain a marriage. Women need an anchor, a solid foundation, to raise a family. A weak-willed, anything-goes husband is unacceptable. Robert stood out at the party where I met him. We had an immediate attraction."

Dr. Ford responded, "So that was the secret of my success? I behaved like a man!

"Yes, Robert, but I doubt that would impress today's modern women. I saw it first at Wellesley. Those students were the most pampered and privileged women the world has ever seen, except, perhaps, for England's queens. Amazingly, they were collectively angry at the system that gave them all they had. They asserted they could do it all on their own. 'I am woman hear me roar.' Time has proven them wrong. Too many of them need various pharmaceuticals to survive the day."

Todd commented, "That's describes my mother. She changed during the marriage. Although a long-time liberal, she became increasingly feminist and bitter. My brother became a victim of her transformation. She resented my father's extended absences because of his military commitments. She was lonely and embraced feminism as a weapon against my father. The marriage wasn't pretty and ended in divorce. She retained custody of Michael and me but my father remained an important part of my life. Michael rejected him, believing him the cause of the breakup. I don't blame him, he was four years younger and was closer to mom than dad."

"What a sad end to a marriage," Amelia said. She added, "I warn you two young men – don't marry a feminist. Marry a traditional, old-fashioned woman. A real woman is a nice, soft, feminine person who respects everyone, including men. She has character and a strong moral fiber. For her, marriage and family come first. Work is important, too, but work must be subordinate to family responsibilities. The feminist believes everything revolves around her; she rejects the nuclear family which requires considerable sacrifice by women."

Tom looked at Todd, "There you go Todd, Mom has spoken. Ignore her at your risk."

Amelia gave Tom her stern expression that he had often seen, "Tom, you know I'm right!"

Tom did. She had many generations of Yankee sensibilities to back her.

The lunch finished on a more relaxed note but, curiously, Todd didn't inquire about the rifle he delivered. Tom imagined Todd thought the less he knew the better.

The next day Tom and his father took the gear to a terrain of rocky outcrops and hay fields, ironically near the location of the Lattimore shootings. Tom needed practice for the shot he will take in London. He had two weeks to prepare.

They set a 12" diameter round iron target of quarter-inch steel mounted bolted to a stand 485 yards away and found a perfect spot to recreate the shot's height and distance, a rocky hill 100 feet high adjacent to the field where they placed the target.

Dr. Ford called the field's owner that morning, a patient who had never received a bill from the doctor. The patient gladly consented to use of the field. The hayfield had the second cutting of hay and the farmer had already carted away the bales. It was perfect for target practice.

Tom spray painted the target black but added a small oval of white paint to represent the area of the brain called the medulla oblongata -- the lowest portion of the brainstem that controls heart and lungs functions. A hit to the medulla guarantees a one-shot kill.

Fortunately, a dirt road led to the hill's top negating the need to lug the gun and gear up the steep hill. The doctor stood in as Tom's spotter using the Vortex Razor Spotting Scope. He also filled out the Ballistic Data Card after each shot. They positioned the rifle on a sandbag and Tom began calibrations for the shot, announcing each step to his father.

His first shot hit the target, a little low and to the right from the two-inch white dot painted on the target. "Not good enough," observed Tom. The moderate but steady wind, left to right, made compensation a somewhat easier.

His next shots crept closer to the white dot after he adjusted the scope. Finally, his sixth shot found the target. He hit the next twelve. The bullets chipped away all the white paint that represented the medulla. His father posted all the data of each shot.

After fifteen shots Tom had his father reset the scope to force Tom to restart the entire exercise. They repeated the process until they depleted the box of 100. All eighty-five shots hit the head. He hit the smaller faux medulla target with 75% accuracy. Although satisfied, he needed to come back for 90 more practice shots the following week. Tom intended to save ten rounds for London...more than enough for the job.

****

Tom had an interesting work week. He received a call from a J. Bailey Morgan III subsidiary company in London. Michael Livingston Keenan asked to meet in London next week to discuss a $100 million bond offering that Tom Ford and SBT Worldwide would underwrite. Tom immediately accepted, knowing Martin Paxton will approve any new business from among the wealthiest men in the world. Although this deal wasn't an exceptionally lucrative bond offering, it would be the most lucrative of Tom's short career.

Tom doubted Keenan knew of the plans but speculated what Michael Livingston Keenan, who sounded strictly business and very British, would think if he found he was now character in the secret War on Terrorism.

The week and the weekend flew by. Tom again practiced the shot in New Hampshire. He clustered his shots on the target; none had strayed more than three inches from dead center. He was confident of his ability to hit his target when he took the shot in London.

He left the gear with his parents. A Jackie ally would later collect the gun, deliver it to London and deposit the piece to the sniper blind on the 11th floor of a London building that overlooked the famous courthouse, Old Bailey.

However, Tom foresaw a problem. They scheduled Zayan Hussein's hearing for 10:00 A.M. Thursday. Tom will be traveling and working with Martin Paxton. Martin was his friend and colleague but Tom didn't want to involve him with the mission. Tom, aware he couldn't schedule any meetings that morning, must find a reason to be AWOL. He called Jackie for advice.

Jackie acknowledged Martin could pose a problem. "Let me think about it and I'll get back to you."

Tom received a call that afternoon on the burner phone from Jackie. "It's all set."

"What's all set?"

"Your alibi for Paxton. He's married, isn't he?"

"Yes."

"Perfect. He will understand, appreciate and envy our solution."

"What's that?" Tom asked.

"...your old friend Olga!" exclaimed Jackie.

"Olga?" Tom remembered his terrific time with her in England and Scotland.

"So, what's the plan?"

"You take Paxton that Wednesday evening to the Savoy Grill for dinner. After dinner insist on a visit to the American Bar at the Savoy. How can an American visit London without sipping a Gilbert Rumbold at the Savoy

Bar? Take a seat at the bar. Olga will sit next to you and initiate a conversation. She'll explain that she is a Russian fashion executive on business. Pretend you don't know her. Doubtless, Martin Paxton will be impressed with her. After another drink, you tell Paxton that you will take Olga to her room. You apologize to Paxton and tell him not to wait, you will meet him the next morning. He will understand."

"Jackie, that should work. I will need a small gym bag packed with toiletries, a sweatshirt and sweatpants for sleeping in Olga's room. I will also need a navy blue work coverall I will wear over my suit, a long bill black baseball cap and a collapsible Tote's umbrella – it's London where rain is always a possibility. Oh, and add a pair of Brooks Brothers white formal gloves, extra large, to the bag. Please deliver everything to Olga's room."

"I understand why you want the gloves, but why Brooks Brothers formal gloves?"

"The gloves are fabricated with sheer lambskin that provides an excellent grip and feel of the gun – perfect for shooting."

"You got it."

Tom flew from Bradley in Hartford, CT, early Monday morning, comfortable with his London plans. He arrived in London at 5:00 P.M. London time.

Tom took a taxi to the May Fair, a five-star hotel, compliments of J. Bailey Morgan III. Although SBT is generous with its expense accounts, a five-star hotel stay is not fully reimbursed. SBT pays for the average cost of a three-star of any city visited; the higher costs of more expensive hotels must be personally funded. Tom usually stayed at the three stars.

Tom scheduled a 7:00 P.M meeting with Martin Paxton for dinner at Galvin at Windows, a restaurant giving great London views, the dinner again courtesy of Mr. J. Bailey Morgan III.

He arrived at seven. The maître d escorted him to the corner window table where Martin sat enjoying his cocktail. Martin dressed in his customary charcoal-grey suit. Tom wore his blue blazer, khaki pants, blue button-down shirt and a Dartmouth College repp tie – a going away gift from Amelia. This ensemble formed his uniform, except for the suits he wore for business meetings.

Martin stood and greeted Tom. "Have a good flight?"

No problems...and yours?"

"Very smooth."

They sat and Martin asked Tom a question that intrigued him, "How did you ever arrange this deal with a Morgan company? We've been trying to access Morgan Industries for decades. Goldman is their usual partner on these deals."

Tom reflected, *"Well Martin, I'll be shooting a murderous jihadist as a member of a shadow group, that J. Bailey Morgan III supports. This business deal is cover to send me without suspicion to London, where the assassination will occur."*

Tom, expecting the question, had prepared an answer during the flight that sounded plausible, present an element of truth and mitigate Martin's curiosity about landing a potentially lucrative account.

Tom couldn't reveal the truth, but he created an explanation that should suffice. He told Martin, "My mother is a Briggs. The Briggs and the Morgans had been doing business for generations. The Briggs factories were subcontractors to Morgan industries. My uncle John Briggs, is a scientist for NASA but occasionally consults for Morgan Industries (all true). I believe he mentioned my name to executives at Morgan (probably not true but plausible), who passed my name around. It somehow ended on Michael Livingston Keenan's desk. We'll ask him when we meet tomorrow."

Martin seemed satisfied by the explanation. They resumed their dinner conversation, shifting the subject to the strategy for securing the business at the next day's meeting.

The Wednesday morning meeting revealed much. The Morgan reps' eagerness to do business with SBT Worldwide astounded Martin. New clients were wary of bankers they hadn't worked with previously. They seemed to like Tom and directed their inquiries to him. Martin was fine with Tom's popularity and content to answer the finer legal and regulatory points of which he was an expert.

By 3:00 P.M. they had completed the contract. Approvals had to be secured from the home office, the final documents drawn and signed by the respective parties. This may take a week and could be completed by courier. Tom and Martin's job was finished but for a quick document review meeting tomorrow at 2:00 P.M.

Tom invited Martin, Keenan and his two assistants to a celebratory Savoy Grill dinner. All accepted and Tom made dinner reservations for 7:00 P.M. Two bottles of a superb Château Ausone 2000 accompanied the excellent dinner. The conversation focused on business, working for J. Bailey Morgan III (apparently quite the character) and living in London. Soon the talk veered to the July, 2005 Underground suicide bombings in London. Jihadists killed fifty-two and injured more than seven hundred by that terrorist attack.

The Brits became irate. "We don't take these terrorists seriously. They intend to kill more of us, but all we do is invite more into our country. It's crazy!"

Tom gave a slight nod of agreement, contemplating his appointment with the ongoing Crusade the next morning.

The Brits left after the excellent meal and Tom invited Martin to the American Bar for an after-dinner drink. Martin didn't need much persuasion and readily agreed. Jackie Brandt's plan was launched. Tom looked forward to his reunion with Olga.

They entered the bar down the hall and took a seat at center bar. It was after nine and the tables and bar were only half filled, a relief to Tom. He wanted to save a seat for Olga.

Tom ordered two snifters of Lagavulin 14-year Scotch for their nightcap. Martin offered a toast to the success of their London trip.

"Tom, you have been employed by SBT for a year but landed a potentially enormous customer for us. No one has racked such a score in such a short time. You realize our bonuses will reflect these new deals?"

"I guess I got lucky with this deal. You know how those old WASP families like to keep the money circulated among themselves. Besides, I had a great mentor." Tom offered his glass for another toast when a provocative woman's voice interrupted him, "Hello, my name is Olga, may I join you?"

Tom turned around, stood and took her extended hand, "Of course. I am Tom Ford ... this is my colleague Martin Paxton."

Martin stood to shake her hand, but her beauty temporarily paralyzed him. Here the brilliant attorney, a moot court winner of Harvard Law and someone accustomed to clearly explaining a few arcane points of law in front of demanding judges and clients, now stood stunned to silence by the beautiful Russian.

Olga towered above his 5' 8" frame – she had to be six feet tall – her flowing dark brunette hair framing a, flawless face. She wore a short silver silk dress that intimately conformed to every curve of her well-toned body. He had never seen a more beautiful woman…in the movies, in fashion magazines, anywhere.

Martin regained his composure, "Yes, Olga, please take a seat." He moved over a seat and offered the chair between them.

Tom asked Olga if she wanted a drink. She smiled, "Thank you, I'd like that. Lagavulin neat." She gave Tom a knowing smile.

Martin asked, "Judging by your accent, are you Russian?"

"Yes, Moscow. I am here to sell fashion fur to London furriers."

"Isn't that a hard sell these days considering the animal activists objecting to wearing fur?"

"They do present marketing problems, but we have a great deal of demand for fine fur and we sell the best."

Tom commented about her excellent command of English. She replied, "I was born in Moscow but moved to London when eight. I graduated from the London School of Economics up the road from here. I live in Moscow and London these days, depending the season."

The conversation continued for another twenty minutes, but Martin soon recognized that Olga was paying Tom increasingly more attention. Not wanting to become the archetypal third wheel, Martin stood and excused himself, "Olga, Tom, it has been a long day. I'm still a little jet-lagged so I think I'll retire for the evening. See you tomorrow. Tom, don't forget, we have a 2:00 P.M. meeting to finish the deal."

"O.K. Martin. I'll see you tomorrow. It's been a great day."

"Yes it was, and apparently your day isn't over yet."

"Martin, you know I'm a gentleman!"

"Tell me that tomorrow. See ya!"

Tom turned to Olga. "Olga, it is so good to see you again."

Olga stood, wrapped her arms around him and kissed him. "I missed you. I know your plans tomorrow. Jackie gave me the abridged version and my role to assure its success. I am all with you. Being Russian, I understand history and the danger of ignoring it. I admire all you and the group are doing and want to help in any way I can. Let's go upstairs. I have a room all set."

****

Tom understood this will strictly be a business relationship that night. Although Tom and Olga had their history together, he knew he couldn't afford any distractions. Olga could be a distraction.

And she had the same opinion. "I couldn't book a two-bedroom suite. The Savoy doesn't offer one, but I found a room with two double beds. We'll share a room, but not a bed. I assume this arrangement meets your approval?"

"Absolutely. I'll need a full night's sleep for tomorrow."

"You can sleep knowing what tomorrow holds?"

"Like a baby. A good night's rest is mandatory to maximize the mission's success."

Tom intrigued Olga. She never saw this side of him in the past. She thought nobody could be this composed knowing the nature of his mission.

Tom spoke, "I'll set the alarm for seven. I want to arrive at the shooting gallery by nine. The hearing is at ten. The target will be out of the hearing between 10:30 and 11:00. Do you have the gym bag?"

"Yes, it's in the closet." Olga walked to the closet and handed the bag to Tom.

He placed the bag on the table and inventoried the contents. A package of condoms lay on top. He picked it up to show Olga. She turned a deep red, which surprised him.

He placed the condom on the table, "Jackie Brandt's idea of a joke."

Tom inventoried the contents: toothbrush, toothpaste, comb, sweatpants, sweatshirt (for sleeping), long bill baseball cap, navy blue overalls, an umbrella, the Brooks Brothers gloves and a note: *Best of luck. Call me when you finish your work. Jackie.*

Tom and Olga conversed for ten minutes before they retired. They exchanged a summary of their lives since Scotland, including their respective love lives. The conversation turned to Jay Bailey Morgan III. She commented, "You'd like Mr. Morgan."

Tom replied, "So I heard. He seems to be quite the character." He added, "I won't wake you in the morning and will head home after my meeting tomorrow afternoon. Here's my card. Please call me when you find yourself in New York City with nothing to do. And thanks for your help – you were perfect. I doubt Martin will question my whereabouts tomorrow morning."

Olga took the card, intending to do precisely that.

Tom's head hit the luxurious Savoy pillows by 11:00 P.M. He fell quickly asleep.

He woke at 6:45 A.M. and turned off the alarm so it wouldn't ring and wake Olga. He took a shower and donned his suit and coveralls. Tom would rejoin Martin at the Mayfair after the mission and present an appearance that he spent an evening with a beautiful Russian girl – which he did -- but not the way he hoped to impress on Martin Paxton.

Tom looked out the window and noted the light, misty rain. He observed the flags on the buildings surrounding the hotel and noticed they hung limp: no wind. He thought, *"A perfect day for a shooting."*

Tom brewed a coffee replaying his plans for the next few hours in his mind as he had dozens of times previously — each time tweaking small points to ensure success and lack of detection. He took his last sip of coffee, slipped on his baseball cap when Olga walked in from the bedroom. She approached and enclosed him with her arms, "Tom, I'll be devastated if you are caught. Be careful. I next want to see you in New York a free man, not on television in handcuffs." They kissed, more passionately than Tom expected. Tom left the room after giving Olga a goodbye hug.

He avoided the elevator, took the stairway down the eight flights of steps and took the service exit, looking appropriate in his coveralls. Umbrella opened, he walked towards the Shooting Gallery, a 20-minute trip away.
Tom took side streets to avoid as many eyes as possible. He hoped the coveralls, long bill cap and umbrella would conceal his face from any potential witnesses or security cameras. Tom Ford looked like any guy walking to his blue-collar job at eight in the morning. He effortlessly blended into the London cityscape.

Tom arrived at the building, a 1960s era concrete and steel monstrosity. The building will be demolished in a few months, but was presently vacant. Empty, that is, except for Jackie's man who broke in that morning and posed as a security guard and watchman for the assignment.

He walked to the door and spotted the guard, wearing the same coveralls as his, sitting at the reception desk. He slipped on the gloves and looked inside. The guard saw him and walked to the door.

The guard asked, "Can I help you?"

Tom replied with the passwords, "Charles Martel sent me."

The guard opened the door and Tom entered the building.

"How did you break in?" Tom asked.

"MI-5 teaches its agents many skills."

"*So he's a Brit*," Tom wondered the extent of Jackie's network.

"I took your gear to the 11th floor. You'll have a nice clear view of Old Bailey. Pick up your cartridge when you are finished, close the windows, that I opened for you, pack the gear and bring the gun case with you. I see you are wearing gloves so fingerprints shouldn't be a problem. Keep your hat on, you don't want to shed your hair. Wipe any of your sweat – just in case. Don't forget anything. I will take you to the garage below and drive you back to the Mayfair. I want to be out of here within two minutes after the shot."

"Will do. Little of the report will reach Old Bailey's considering the thick concrete walls, street noise, the distance and the suppressor on the rifle. I expect considerable chaos for minutes afterward. We should have no trouble with our escape."

Tom turned to the stairwell. The Brit said, "Here, take this." He handed Tom a flashlight.

Tom climbed the ten flights and reached his destination -- the flashlight illuminating the darkness. He found the room and opened the aluminum Halliburton case on the desk and took out the spotting scope. The scope magnified Old Bailey down the street. Tom noticed the enormous black Gothic doors that gave a great background for the shot. He looked at the flag atop the building across the street. It lay motionless. Tom expected the wind to remain calm.

He noticed the two large windows were louvered on the bottom and sides. Tom shut the left side louvers. The right side window provided a preferable sightline. He closed the bottom louver window -- enough to allow his shot without the rifle barrel extending outside. *"Excellent, the closed windows should keep much of the noise from the shot inside the building."*

He took out the rifle and Data Card that his father filled during his practice shots to prepare the shot. This wasn't a difficult shot – relatively short, with no sun or shadows and little or no wind. Jackie's intelligence reports found that Zayan Hussein's entourage will be waiting for him as he exited the door.

Tom expected the crowd to slow or stop Hussein when he greeted his adherents in celebration, giving Tom a stationary target.

A modest crowd had already gathered by 9:30 A.M. Tom evaluated the scene, *"...so far the intelligence has proven correct."*

Tom had an hour until the time for the shot. They scheduled Hussein's hearing for ten, but who knew how long the British wheels of justice takes?

He thought he could relax until ten when he would man the rifle. He sat on a desk near the wall, cleaning off a layer of dust that had settled on it since the building was abandoned. Tom kept an eye on Old Bailey's door, watching the growing crowd that eagerly awaited the appearance of their jihadic hero.

Keep coming, the more the merrier." He wondered if any of his future targets may be lurking within the crowd.

Tom surveyed the decrepit office. He wondered how a kid from New Hampshire could find himself in such circumstances. He recalled his emotions as a fourteen-year-old watching replays of the planes crashing into the World Trade Center.

Then there were the jumpers. They chose to jump to their deaths from 100 stories rather than dying by fire. What a choice! He remembered seeing the jumpers only during the early hours after the attack. The media deleted these horrid scenes from subsequent reports. Two hundred and thirty-four people decided to jump than burn to death. The New York mayor called them rose blossoms for the extensive blood splatter they left on the sidewalk.

Those jumpers created an indelible mark on Tom's psyche. He craved revenge for their attack on his country.

Tom reflected, *"Well, it's revenge time!"*

The 9/11 attack impelled Tom to study the history of Islam since 622. He discovered that the 1400 years of Mohammed's religion marked a protracted, intermittent war against Western Civilization. Muslims, or Moslems, as they were called through much of their history, observed the Koran dictum of convert or kill all non-believers – the Kafirs or infidels. They also prized the booty that supplements conquest.

Muslims conquered Spain, Portugal and virtually the entire Europe in the Eighth Century. The popes organized the Crusades to protect the Catholic pilgrims and churches in Jerusalem from Muslim atrocities. It devolved into incredible barbarism by all sides.

Later, Thomas Jefferson sent our navy to stop the Barbary pirates from their murder and plunder. The war endured throughout the world to this day.

Tom now found himself a volunteer in a secret army to defend his country from jihad. Here he waited in London to fire his first shot for the cause.

By 10 A.M. the crowd numbered close to two hundred. *"Popular guy,"* Tom thought. *"Little do they realize that they will soon witness the execution of their favorite killer."*

Tom turned his baseball cap around, positioned the headphones over his ears and assumed a prone position behind the CheyTac. He adjusted the scope according to the conditions presented for the shot. The light rain continued -- the famous London mist -- the flag remained limp. He hoped a group of six-footers didn't surround Hussein. The gathering horde would make an easy shot more difficult; increasing the odds of an innocent bystander becoming a victim.

By 10:20 A.M. the populous crowd stirred. Tom assumed Hussein was approaching Two uniformed guards opened the doors. Hussein's entourage poured from the building and, finally, Zayan Hussein appeared. Tom centered Hussein through his scope. He observed, "Thank God this guy is tall." He reminded Tom of Howard Stern – tall, skinny, glasses, with long black stringy hair.

Hussein waved to the throng and clasped his hands above his head in victory and defiance. His gaze shifted to the right, his left temple now visible. Through the scope, Tom viewed his objective and the ideal approach to Hussein's medulla oblongata. The now hundred strong passionate mob that had spilled into the street had reached a crescendo of cheers for their released hero.

It was time. Tom heard the cheers, even from his distance from Old Bailey. Hating to end the party, Tom gave the rifle its final guidance to the target. He concentrated the chosen reticles on Zayan's temple.

All his practice, study of weapons and shooting, and experience shooting targets had now led to this mission. Convinced his aim was true, Tom Ford pulled the trigger. The explosion in the chamber launched the .408 full metal jacket bullet to its target. A split second later the bullet penetrated the skull, exited and ricocheting harmlessly off Old Bailey's massive stone walls. Hussein's blood and brain followed the bullet and splashed a vivid scarlet and gray on the wall. Hussein collapsed onto the sidewalk, dead before his head bounced off the pavement. Very dead!

Strangely, an old movie line entered Tom's mind, "*May the power of Christ compel you.*"

Tom didn't hesitate to savor his success. He closed the window, packed his gun, gave a final check of the premises and dashed towards the stairwell. He hurried down the steps to the ground floor where he caught the MI-5 agent motioning to him. The guard opened the door to the garage and they bound down a flight of steps and found the black SUV. The agent opened the tailgate and Tom threw the case into the back, covering it with a black blanket. They hopped into the front seat and the vehicle found its way up the ramp onto the London streets. Tom looked back to Old Bailey. He observed an expanding crowd gathering around Zayan Hussein's body.

"Mission accomplished!"

The agent said nothing but nodded his approval.
Tom took off the coveralls, gloves and cap to effectuate his transformation back to a reserved businessman. He stuffed the items into a plastic garbage bag and tossed it in the back seat. He assumed the Brit would properly dispose of the evidence.

"What will you do with the rifle?"

The Brit responded, "We'll remove the barrel, melt it and fit a new barrel to the gun's body.

The rifle will likely be used elsewhere in the world. These are costly rifles."

Tom asked, "What about the bullet? Can they trace it by Instrumental Neutron Activation Analysis or Chromatography and Mass Spectrometry? The .408 isn't a common round?"

"Not to worry, we hand load our own ammunition. Each batch is given a slightly different alloy mix. Even the powder has minuscule chemical variations to confound any investigator. The Martels have a Wyoming man doing their gun and ammo work. He is a retired metallurgist from one of Morgan's businesses and does peerless work. We never had a problem with investigators -- all leads lure them to dead ends."

Within minutes they arrived at the Mayfair. Tom asked the agent to drop him off a block away so he could walk to the hotel from the opposite direction of Old Bailey. After giving his thanks to the Brit he calmly walked to the hotel.

His first stop was the hotel room he shared with Martin. Martin finished eating his room-service breakfast and had the television turned on to the BBC.

"Tom, you won't believe this but someone shot an Arab leader not too far from here -- in front of Old Bailey, no less. Amazing!"

"Who was shot?"

"They haven't mentioned a name," replied an unconcerned Martin.

"Hey, how did it go with Olga last night?"

"All went well. Olga is quite the woman."

"You're telling me," said Martin, "I have never seen a more beautiful woman. Will you see her again?"

"I believe so. We exchanged cards and I invited her to call me should she find herself in New York. She was positive of that happening. She occasionally conducts business in the city."

Martin opened his laptop and noticed he had received an email from the legal department. "Well, it looks like we have a little work before our meeting this afternoon. I received the contract. Let's review the documents in an hour."

Tom nodded as he walked to the bedroom, "I'll join you after a shower and a change of clothes. I had a long night…and morning."

Chapter 7: *Tom and Kat*

Bill Griffin enjoyed the high spirits his crack pipe gave him; its idle potency gave him a sense of power and invincibility. He glanced at his watch. It was nearly 9:00 P.M. He boarded the subway heading south to midtown. Being a sizable, extremely strong man, little frightened him, especially when armed with his Raven Arms MP-25 handgun, the notorious Saturday Night Special. He also carried a switchblade that he wielded as his persuader. His physical size, the crack swagger, and new expensive black leather jacket presented a formidable and intimidating menace as he walked through the subway car. An old black man and two young white men looked away when his gaze swept them when he entered the train. *"They better look away,"* thought Griffin.

Griffin planned to repeat his exploits this night as he had the previous month. His last target, Rebecca Rosenberg, expressed terror when he forced her into the narrow alley on the Eastside. The thought still excited him. All he had done to her during the next ten minutes excited him even more. With his knife to her throat, he had forced her on her back, tore off her blouse and underwear and brutally raped her. She was so terrified she couldn't even scream. He finished his rape of the woman then stabbed her a dozen times. She managed a final deafening scream during his killing rage, but Griffin silenced her as the blade pierced the soft spot of her neck, slashing her windpipe and the carotid artery. Her gold watch and a three-carat diamond ring gave him his best night ever. He enjoyed reading about his exploits in the papers for several weeks. Mrs. Rebecca Rosenberg, a thirty-seven-year-old mother of two, was of no concern to Bill Griffin.

Griffin had served three years of a six-year sentence for rape and assault. He met with a psychologist monthly and his fellow inmates advised him to be respectful and discuss his depraved and dysfunctional childhood. Hell, no problem. Griffin's childhood had been one long nightmare. Convicted of two felonies, Griffin had to convince the parole board that he no longer presented a danger to society. They quickly released him, so he must have said the right things.

He had raped and murdered three women since freed a year ago. Griffin smiled as the train exited the 59th Street station: *"It's time for another."*

****

Kathryn St. John slowly walked along 5th Avenue towards the Plaza Hotel where she usually stayed during her NYC visits. She was pleased to be alone after the week's frenzy of social engagements and a dinner party that night. Cindy Hannah's wedding was scheduled for late Saturday afternoon; she will have time to relax before then.

At twenty-five, she and Cindy were the only two of the eight close college friends who were unmarried. Kat had looked forward to the wedding and seeing her old friends again. She enjoyed living in West Palm Beach, Florida, especially since her father's orange grove was only thirty minutes away. Nevertheless, Kat was excited to be back in the Northeast.

As she walked, her stunning beauty caused many heads to turn, even in a jaded city like New York accustomed to many models, dancers and actresses adorning the city streets and sidewalks. Five-ten, a magnificent athletic figure, a narrow waist, and long, slim legs garnered considerable attention wherever she appeared in public. Her long mane of light brown, nearly blonde, hair framed a virtually perfect face that further added to the impact. But her large blue, almost violet-blue eyes, were her most striking feature. Doubtless, Kat had an immediate and powerful impact on men.

Kat crossed 5th Avenue after 9:30 P.M. and approached the Plaza Hotel. About to enter the lobby, she decided the night was too alluring to go inside. Kat continued her walk. Crossing the street, she strode west along the southern edge of Central Park, a street lined with Hansom Carriages awaiting riders.

It was an early summer weekend night and the city pleasantly quiet for a change. She passed the park's entrance across from the New York Athletic Club when she felt a slight burning sensation on her back. A powerful hand grabbed her arm and pulled her around the stone wall into the park.

A gruff voice in her ear growled, "I got my blade on you, bitch. One sound and you are dead." He roughly pulled her into a darker patch behind the shrubs. *"My, my, I'm getting mighty lucky these days,"* thought Bill Griffin.

He continued holding her arm, but now forced the knife against her throat. Kat realized she must not challenge her attacker at this time -- his knife too

119

close to her jugular for any defensive moves. In a deep thickening voice he ordered, "Do as I say or you as dead as that Rosenberg bitch."

Griffin enjoyed seeing the total terror on the white pasty faces of the women he was about to rape and kill, but this bitch was different -- her look expressed more surprise than fear. Her demeanor angered him and he hit her on the back of her head, knocking her to the ground. As she lay stunned he tore open her blouse. His excitement escalated. He reached for his pants to free himself and caught the woman's eyes. For a second he thought he noticed her face expressing outrage. It was, but Kat saw that he dropped the knife into his jacket pocket.

Her assailant was brawny and intimidating. She assumed the man intended to kill her after the rape. Kat knew she had one chance to live. As he lowered his pants Kat seized her opportunity. With his testicles exposed Kat bolted to one knee and sharply struck them hard with her fist. He let out a low groan. Griffin grabbed his balls and his gun tumbled from his pants pocket to the pavement. Kat rolled away onto the nearby path then forced her hand into her handbag -- a special bag her father had custom made for her by John Bianchi, a famous holster maker. She had practiced this maneuver a hundred times, pulling the gun from the handbag, rolling away from an imaginary perp, standing and shooting the target.

This time she was up against a real and dangerous adversary, and her movements had to be flawless. She instinctively reached for her Ruger LCR .38 Special Double-Action Revolver. The heavy spring in the handbag pushed the pistol upward, instantly freeing the gun. Kat rolled back three feet, jumped up, holding the .38 in a two-handed combat stance, aiming at Griffin's chest.

Griffin's pistol had dropped from his pocket in his excitement, landing on the ground to his right. He grappled for his pants, that were now humiliatingly halfway below his knees. Kat stared at him, her gun steady. He could tell by her assured stance she was adept with guns. The threatening hole in the barrel he faced told him she meant business.

"Don't move," she ordered.

"Jesus, let me pull up my pants."

"I said, don't move."

Griffin's crack high, now history, was rapidly being replaced with panic -- a new experience for Bill Griffin.

"On your knees and move away from your gun," commanded Kat.

Something about the bitch's voice caused a chill to run down Griffin's spine. She differed from his previous victims. They buckled at the sight of his knife or gun.

None fought back.

He meekly and awkwardly knelt, a foot from his gun.

"Why do you want me...?"

Interrupting, she ordered him again, "Move away from the gun!"

Griffin considered grabbing his gun, but he suspected this woman wasn't a person to fuck with.

Kat re-aligned the sights to his head.

"Oh, God! Oh, God!"

"Is that what you said to Rebecca Rosenberg when you raped and killed her? I read about that poor Rosenberg woman. I won't be your next victim."

"She wanted it," snarled Griffin.

The reignited memory of his latest conquest boosted his confidence while exacerbating his already intense hatred for the woman in front of him.

No cracka whore can order him around.

His courage thus bolstered Griffin lunged for his gun: he believed his only chance to defeat the bitch. It was also his last moment of life. Kat shot him in the left temple, instantly killing him. The Hydra-Shok did its job spraying the Central Park grass with Griffin's blood and brains as the bullet exited from his right temple. She stood triumphant over the crumpled body of rapist and killer Bill Griffin.

Kat glared down to address Griffin, "The feared hunter is now the defeated prey. Burn in hell." She lowered the gun to her side.

****

Tom and Martin emerged into a dynamic team for SBT Worldwide during the next years. They even impressed Prescott Browning, who uncharacteristically gave Tom and Martin a high five to express his gratitude for the unprecedented new business they brought in. No one in the firm knew the secret to their success but Tom.

During the three years, Jackie Brandt assigned Tom four new targets: London, Paris, Berlin, and Detroit, with each job rewarded with a lucrative deal. Surprisingly, the Detroit mission proved rather difficult and nearly ended in disaster. Tom barely escaped without detection…and his life.

Tom learned a lesson from the Detroit mission. He agreed to do the Detroit mission as a favor for Jackie Brandt, who, in turn, repaid a favor to a DEA contact. The target was the leader of the Shabazz League, a Black Muslim front that specialized in illegal drug imports to the Detroit metropolitan region. Nasheed X, its leader, profited $millions from his venture, law enforcement says $billions, but the torture and murder of three DEA undercover agents scored him a visit from Tom Ford.

The regional DEA director was furious the DOJ gave little concern to the deaths of his agents. He believed the administration didn't want to upset his Detroit constituency by prosecuting Nasheed X who gave 25% of his drug profits to local charities and politicians. Nashhed's generosity netted him many influential friends in the community…and in government.

Jackie tasked Tom to remove Nasheed X from the drug trade and exact some revenge and justice for the local DEA. Unlike his earlier hits, Tom had no input into the actual planning of the shoot. He met a DEA agent at the airport who briefed him of the plans. Tom, although skeptical, assented to the arrangement from respect for Jackie.

The plans required Tom to hide overnight under a debris pile -- broken skids, wooden boxes, old machine parts and the like. This heap of discarded remnants of Detoit's more productive history provided ample cover in an abandoned auto plant on the city's outskirts. Nasheed X was scheduled to speak that morning to a hundred or so of his followers at the far end of the seemingly endless third floor of the crumbling Packard factory. For Tom, hidden 600 feet from the podium this was not a difficult shot. After the shot

Tom planned to rappel out a nearby window down the building, run more than 100 feet and scale an eight-foot fence to a parking lot where an awaiting DEA agent would drive him to Willow Run airport for a private Lear Jet flight back to New York City. He should be back in New York before the police launched an investigation of the shoot. Simple!

Unfortunately, Tom faced a problem unforeseen by the planning. He had no problem shooting Nasheed X. Nasheed X met his Maker by a well-placed shot to center chest, but Tom's troubles had only begun. Instead of ducking for cover as Tom expected, Six well-armed bodyguards ran, weapons drawn, directly towards him. The guards wildly shot in his direction but Tom expected their aim to quickly improve.

He assumed they must have been hopped-up on Nasheed's products to run to a shooter. Tom also believed they would probably shoot him in the back if he attempted an escape. He had to take out the six attackers before exiting the building.

He quickly raised his M-4 and fired well-aimed shots at the bodyguards. Tom shot the rear-most men first. Tom's defense took only seconds and resulted in six wounded bodyguards. He shot them below their knees. Painful, yes, but Tom believed they didn't deserved to die for their actions. They were only doing a job.

None approached to within fifty feet of his hideout. The moaning, writhing bodies, aided by the pandemonium and commotion in the expansive room, signaled to Tom that he could leave. He exited through the window, rappelled down the building and made his escape. All turned out well, but the complications left Tom dissatisfied. A better plan could have avoided his shooting six men.

Each assignment gave him new business from the numerous subsidiaries of Morgan Holdings. Tom grew affluent from his success. He purchased a roomy Central Park West co-op overlooking the park. He also paid for the renovations of his parent's Orford house, which, after 30 years, needed considerable repair. Tom added an architecturally complementary cottage for his weekend getaways. He also gave his parents a three-month Holland Lines Grand World Voyage to express his gratitude for all they had given him. When Dr. Ford retired from the hospital Tom judged the time favorable for the voyage. Both enjoyed excellent health and now had the time. Tom's parents didn't need much persuasion to accept the gift.

Tom enjoyed his now active social life. He developed a fine, long-distance relationship with Olga and occasionally dated Eliza Wilson, now an analyst for another shop in town. New York City also gave many opportunities for a bachelor to thrive and Tom took advantage. However, he engaged in no serious relationships during these years. Perhaps he was distracted by his work as a hitman for Jackie Brandt, J. Bailey Morgan and the Martels, but more likely he simply didn't meet the right woman.

Tom and Martin continued their twice-weekly jogs around Central Park, Martin maintaining his assiduous tabulations on Excel, but Tom now typically beat his boss, compelling the frustrated Martin to keep the Excel data private, away from any prying eyes.

One of these Central Park runs inexorably transformed Tom's life. It happened during a late Friday evening run Tom and Martin took after an arduous week's work.

They had passed the Tavern on the Green restaurant approaching their finish line near the Columbus Circle corner when they heard a gunshot to their right. Tom instinctively paused and dashed towards the sound. Martin screamed, "Where are you going?"

Tom looked back, "Someone is in trouble. Let's go."

Against his better judgment, Martin followed Tom along the path off the jogging track in the direction of the shot. Moments later, they encountered a woman holding a gun, standing over an obviously dead body.

"What happened?" Tom asked.

Kat turned to Tom, "Mr. Rapist just received his due."

Tom looked at the body, the gaping hole in the head continued to seep blood onto the ground. "I'll say...are you all right?"

"I am now," Kat St. John replied.

"You must get away from here," said Tom.

"Why? I did nothing wrong."

Martin replied, "Irrelevant in New York. You're holding a gun – that's illegal."

He added, "This city doesn't recognize self-defense as a defense for a carry violation."

Kat said, "I did nothing wrong. I simply shot the piece of crap who intended to rape and kill me." Tom admired her haughty demeanor in the aftermath of the incident.

A curious crowd flooded through the narrow trails surrounding the shrubs. Among them were the cops. Tom realized escape was no longer possible.

A cop approached Kat and took her gun. "What happened here?"

Kat explained the attack she suffered from Griffin. "Do you have a license for this gun?"

"Yes, a Florida license."

"We don't recognize other states' carry licenses here. You could be in trouble here, young lady."

Kat showed no surprise, fully expecting such treatment from an "enlightened" city.

Another cop approached the body and covered it with a blanket.

Minutes later, a plain-clothed detective approached Kat. Her investigation of a mugging nearby the shooting ceased when she heard the shot.

"Hi, I am Detective Denise Brown. What's your name?"

"Kathryn St. John. Kathryn with a K."

"What happened here," the detective scrutinized her.

Kat explained why there happened to be a stiff with a massive hole in his head sprawled out on a remote Central Park path.

The detective lifted the blanket that covered Griffin. "Jesus, that's a nasty wound. You did a helluva job to his head. You're either damn good or pretty damned lucky with that revolver." Brown bent over for a closer inspection of the body. "Did you use a .45?"

Kat looked at the detective, "No a .38 with Hydra-Shoks. I'm skilled with a gun."

"Oh good Lordie, Annie Oakley has arrived. Perhaps we should turn you loose to clean up the town."

"Detective, this town needs a little disinfectant if this is an example of what you have walking around." Kat gestured to the blanket-covered heap a few feet away.

Brown asked, "He's the perp who killed Rebecca Rosenberg you say?"

"That's what he said."

Kat recounted the shooting ending her statement, "When I drew on him, he lunged for his gun and I shot him."

"Let's continue the questioning at the precinct. The officer will take you to the car. Kat looked at the cop who placed the blanket on Griffin's body. He looked back, "Follow me ma'am."

Detective Brown turned to Tom and Martin, "You two are witnesses?"

Martin said, "We were jogging and heard a shot. We thought someone needed help and rushed to investigate."

"Investigate?" the detective asked. "Who are you? Columbo?"

Tom interjected, "I believe he meant we wanted to help someone who may have been in trouble."

"I see. So, what did YOU see?"

"We arrived ten, fifteen-seconds after we heard the shot and saw the girl standing over a dead body."

"She was just standing there?" asked Brown.

"Yes, she was just standing there, calm as could be, still holding the gun."

She looked at Martin, "Do you agree with him?"

"Yes, detective."

Brown asked Tom and Martin a few more questions. She took their names, addresses and phone numbers. She asked them to remain in the city for possible additional questioning. The detective believed the two were by-standers of the shooting but were also important witnesses as they were first to the crime scene.

Tom walked to the car and detected Kat sitting in the back seat. He said, "Martin and I will see you at the station -- you may need help."

Kat looked at Tom, and despite the defiance glowing in her eyes, she gave a half smile to Tom, "Thank you."

With that, the patrol car wend its way through the swelling crowd of on-lookers, entered Columbus Circle heading to the precinct. Tom watched the car exiting the park profoundly impressed by its passenger -- a woman who shot and killed her would-be murderer and proud of her successful defense. He wondered whether the city, its laws and the police will regard her en-counter as heroic or criminal.

Tom asked Martin to change and meet him at the precinct. She will surely need a lawyer by her side during questioning.

Martin concurred, "I'll bring my NY State Bar Card. It will allow me to sit in the interrogation room."

"Good. See you there."

Tom rushed home, took a quick shower, donned his blue blazer uniform, and hopped in a taxi to the 20th Precinct on West 82nd St. He asked the desk officer about the woman who shot the rapist in Central Park.

She informed him Detective Brown was interrogating her. Tom realized she needed a lawyer and waited for Martin. Martin arrived in five minutes. Tom explained the situation to him. Martin showed his card stating he was the lawyer for the woman now in the interrogation room. The desk officer asked them to sit for a minute while she called Detective Brown.

The detective walked out surprised to see the two witnesses. Martin ex-plained he'd be acting as counsel for the woman she will question.

"Do you mean Kathryn St. John?"

"Is that her name?"

That's her name," replied the detective. "I will ask her whether she accepts your counsel."

She left, returning a minute later, "O.K. Perry Mason. She is all yours." Martin asked if Tom could join.

"Why not? She's not under arrest and he's a witness. Perhaps he could fill in some missing info."

The trio entered the interrogation room. Tom saw Kathryn St. John sitting at the table. He looked at her under a bright light, but despite the unflattering fluorescents her beauty astonished him. She didn't have Olga's exotic, Eastern European beauty, rather more of a girl-next-door, All-American look.

Martin asked for a few minutes with his client. Detective Brown granted him a quick consultation.

Martin spoke after the detective left the room. "Kathryn..." She interrupted him, "Please call me Kat."

"All right Kat. I'm not a criminal lawyer but I know enough of the law to help you here. Should the case go any further my old friend, perhaps the best criminal lawyer in the city, can help.

Martin added, "You should have no problem with the shooting, it was clearly self-defense. Nevertheless, they may arrest you on gun possession charges."

"So I understand."

"This city thinks the Sullivan Law, a very restrictive gun control law, to be the greatest legal document since the Magna Carta. They strictly enforce gun laws. The city values gun control far above a person's right of self-defense."

Kat rolled her eyes and commented, "Lucky me. I would be a hero in Florida."

"...and nearly all other parts of the country," Tom added.

Detective Brown returned to the room with an audiovisual man who carried a video camera on a tripod and a recorder. Do you mind if we tape the interview? It's for your protection."

Martin spoke into her ear. Kat replied, "I have no problem."

"Okay, let's go through all that happened again."

Kat again explained the attack and the subsequent shooting — the detective listened carefully, jotting a note here and there.

"So, he had hit you, knocked you to the ground, and had dropped his pants to rape you. You punched him in the testicles, rolled away, and pulled your gun from your handbag. Is that the way it happened?"

"Yes. He then dove for his pistol, that had fallen from his pants, and I shot him." Kat finished her testimony.

Brown addressed Kat, "You don't appear too upset by your experience tonight. I mean, most women would be mildly hysterical after nearly getting raped and then killing someone."

Kat's deep blue eyes scowled, "Detective, I'm far more upset about what could have happened than what did happen. Without luck, and my gun, I would be the corpse lying on a slab in that morgue today and not the rapist awaiting an autopsy. As for shooting that piece of crap, I have no remorse whatsoever. I performed a service for every woman in this city."

Detective Sergeant Denise Brown thought to herself, "*I like her. She has guts...a regular Wonder Woman.*"

"Ms. St. John, listen carefully to me. Be sure you tell investigators everything that happened in that park tonight, exactly as you've told me, specifically the shooting details. The Manhattan District Attorney will ask you a few questions, but he comes from a different perspective. He may indict you for carrying a pistol without a permit.

You should be aware this is the same man who convened three separate grand juries to indict that subway shooter guy...what's his name..uh...Bernie Goetz. Goetz shot five thugs who attacked him. Among them they had forty-seven arrests. Three were arrested even as the grand juries were being convened. Seventy-seven percent of New York City residents considered the shootings justified and the guy should walk. The first and second grand juries agreed and wouldn't indict. The D.A. eventually persuaded the third to indict. At the trial, they acquitted the shooter of all charges except illegal handgun possession. He served six months in jail."

The detective continued, "We have the same D.A. who prosecuted Goetz. Our gun laws are unlike Florida's. New York is a strange place and the more time you spend here, the more bizarre it seems. You should act like killing Griffin was upsetting, even though he was a murderer and rapist. The typical New York woman doesn't carry a gun in her handbag. Nor do they have the skill or the grit to use it. They were raised to be victims."

Detective Brown stood to continue her monologue, "Two and a half, possibly three, million illegal handguns threaten the city. It is difficult to obtain a legal carry permit. Only the police, bad guys, or good guys breaking the law, have handguns. And any time a good guy uses that gun, even to save his life, our D.A. makes the guy serve time. So, don't look too proud and fierce, look scared and sorry."

The policewoman's statements rung true to Kat. It was kind of her to give this information. She liked her and appreciated the help, but Kat would have a hard time hiding pride in her shot. And looking scared? Forget that!

"Okay. I have your gun and will store it in the station lock-until this thing is settled. The desk sergeant will give you a receipt when you leave. Here's my card, get some rest, and call me tomorrow afternoon. I'll give you any updates about the case." Kat agreed and they filed from the interrogation room.

The following days would be grueling and irritating, but she had been lucky in a number of ways. The first was having Detective Sergeant Denise Brown assigned as the investigating officer. Denise, a bright, tough black woman, was an outstanding police officer. And despite Kat's initial impressions she believed Detective Brown had real compassion for Kat's predicament. Kat also appreciated her blessings to meet Tom and Martin, whose support she greatly appreciated. They were truly kind to her, a welcome contrast to the brutality she received from Griffin.

She called her father to tell him everything that transpired earlier, that she was unharmed and could handle her plight. She didn't ask him to come to New York and explained that his efforts to protect her would likely backfire and cause even greater problems. Kat envisioned her father beating an Assistant DA should the questioning become aggressive. Mike acknowledged her concern and agreed to stay away...for now. He told her to find a lawyer and have the lawyer call him when possible. She told him she would and she loved him.

The media remarkably discovered her Williams College yearbook and the tabloids plastered her formal photo on their front pages the next morning. One headline read, "BERNICE GOETZ." She admired the paper's rapid research.

Kat decided she couldn't attend the wedding. Her presence would divert attention away from the bride. She couldn't do that to a friend. Kat called Cindy early that morning. Cindy understood the situation and wished her the best.

Later, she called Detective Brown who informed Kat, "We found a valuable diamond ring in the stiff's room. It belonged to Rebecca Rosenberg. Griffin is unquestionably the rapist and killer we were looking for."

Brown added, "You did the city a service; I hope the DA's office appreciates your bravery. They want to interview you Monday morning."

Kat was not surprised by all she heard about this DA. She decided she must attend the meeting with an attorney. She took out the card Martin gave her and called his cell phone. "Martin, thank you for your help last night. I spoke to the detective. She informed me the D.A. requested I appear downtown Monday morning for an interview."

Martin expressed concern, "He must have seen the tabloids. He probably believes he needs to assert his legal authority over any vigilantes daring to defend themselves in the city. Let me call my friend and get back to you."

"You may call my cell number, which you now have."

Martin hung up and called his friend Paul Bernard. He and Paul were close friends at Harvard Law -- the only law students in the class with a Japanese background. Martin's parents were Japanese and English, Paul's were Japanese and Jewish. The two had Japanese mothers.

Martin and Paul developed a healthy competition with Paul taking the top class ranking, before Martin's number two. They found their first jobs in New York City, Paul specialized in criminal law and Martin in banking and financial law. Both acknowledged Martin earned far more money, but Paul had far more fun. His clients included mobsters, corrupt politicians, crooked executives and common street thugs. Paul Bernard seldom experienced a dull moment, neither in the office or the courthouse.

Martin phoned Paul who decided to work a few hours at the office on a Saturday afternoon. After some pleasantries, Martin initiated his serious concerns. "Paul, did you read the story about the girl who shot the thug in Central Park last night?"

"Sure did. Front page of the tabloids. Some story. Great-looking girl!"

"Yes she is, but I was there last night. Tom and I were jogging after work, when we heard a shot and ran to check out the scene. We were later with her at the station and sat in as her attorney for the interrogation."

"You did? And they didn't condemn her for life last night?"

"Very funny. However, I'm not a criminal lawyer, but she needs one. The DA wants to talk to her."

"You're right. That prick will grab on to this case for all its worth. She's in trouble with O'Grady. I participated in frequent run-ins with him and his office through the years."

"I know. Which is the reason I called. Can you represent her?"

"I hoped you'd ask. I love these high-profile cases. They pad the CV."

"Please call her. She's staying at the Plaza Hotel."

"...be glad to. What's her number?"

Paul finished his work and called Kathryn St. John. Martin warned him to call her Kat.

"Hello Kat, this is Paul Bernard, I am a friend of Martin Paxton. He asked me to call you. Let's talk to determine whether I can take the case."

"Thank you for calling, Paul."

Kat spoke to Paul of her ordeal. He immediately told her he would take the case. He explained the problem she confronted, "Unfortunately, the city's district attorney, John O'Grady, has the law on his side. You brought an unlicensed gun into the city and shot someone. New York City's firearm laws don't recognize carry licenses from other states, nor does it give much consideration to the circumstances of how you used your gun. Nevertheless, the law presents a loophole: prison sentences are mandatory except where the 'interests of justice dictate otherwise."

"You'd be dead today if you didn't own a gun. This means nothing to the D.A., but a great deal to New Yorkers. I likely can't keep you out of jail if we treat this as strictly a legal case, but as a cause célèbre, creating a political football, we have a decent chance of avoiding a prison sentence."

"And what does that entail?" Kat appeared concerned.

"Make a lot of noise about your predicament. Never refuse a media interview. Start a campaign to inform their audience of the adversity you face. Fortunately, you are attractive and articulate, they will beg for your time.

Remember Amanda Knox?" Paul continued without waiting for an answer. "Amanda Knox was convicted of murder in Italy and sentenced to twenty-six years in prison. For most defendants, their case ends there. Sure, you receive the requisite appeals but chances are the defendant faces long incarceration."

Paul Bernard shifted in his seat and took a deep breath. He continued, "Amanda Knox was also attractive and sexy. The tabloids wouldn't let go of her story. They even gave her a pet name: Foxy Knoxy. The staggering publicity about her case led to another trial in which they exonerated her. Trust me, we cannot keep your plight quiet. We may be getting ahead of ourselves here, the D.A. could drop all charges, but I know this guy, he is an inveterate gun controller. He hates guns and the people who own them."

Kat was dismayed but hopeful. She realized the process wouldn't be so simple if, say, she shot the bastard in Florida or Texas. Yet she was confident New Yorkers would not send her to prison for defending herself from a murderer. Kat asked, "Should we meet beforehand? They scheduled the meeting for nine at the D.A.'s office."

I have a bail hearing across the street at eight. It shouldn't take long. I can meet you around 8:30. We'll find a conference room to talk."

"Great! Can you do me a favor and call my father? He'd like to speak to you about the case and your compensation."

"I'll call your father, but there will be no charge, unless we go to trial. The publicity is worth far more than anything I could earn from your case."

"Thanks very much, Paul."

Kat then dialed her father's number. She told him about her new lawyer and the Monday morning appointment with the district attorney. Kat was surprised by her father's calm reaction to the news, she had expected him to be enraged. He had seen the photos on the internet and commented about her calm demeanor in the photographs, some, of which, were taken minutes after the incident. Kat knew he wanted to assist her, but he couldn't just now.

She spent the remainder of the day reading the newspapers and avoiding reporters. When and if the time came to talk to the media she wanted to do it on her terms. Satisfied with the coverage thus far, she could add little to the story until after tomorrow's meeting. She asked the hotel to block any phone calls to her room. They complied and did their job.

Tom Ford called that night on her cellphone. They discussed recent events, including hiring criminal attorney Paul Bernard. "It's funny," Kat told him, "I don't feel like a criminal!"

"You'll like Paul Bernard, he's a good man. Very bright, but won't rub it in your face as do some New York City lawyers. He has won many eminently notable cases."

Tom asked her out for dinner the next evening, which Kat accepted.

"I'll need some entertainment after the last 24 hours," she said.

"I'll do all I can to entertain and inspire," he assured her with a laugh.

Kat was pleased that Tom called. He intrigued her and she looked forward to spending time alone with him. Kat's prospective suitors of recent years never impressed. They possessed little of the qualities she expected from a man, traits she observed in her father that made him, in her opinion, the great man he was. Tom differed from the others and something about him reminded her of her father, Mike St. John.

She was thinking of Tom when she heard a knock on the door — her friends from Williams College. They were quite tipsy and carried numerous champagne bottles they stole from the bar. They greeted her with a merry, "We thought you could use some company and bubbly."

She let them in and they partied until midnight, reminiscing about their years at Williams, discussing a little sleazy gossip and recapping the wedding. Kat loved it. She was pleased everyone avoided, except for occasional offhand quips, any discussion of the shooting. She erased the shooting from her mind for that evening.

A few stories of the shooting appeared in the media the next morning; mainly a listing of Bill Griffin's arrest sheet and interviews with his family members. No family members expressed any grief over his death.

Ronald Trumbull, the billionaire New York City real estate developer and his model fiancé Melody replaced Kat's on the newspaper's front pages. The happy couple wed on Saturday.

Kat ironically had met Melody. Trumbull had a home in Palm Beach and Melody purchased a painting from the gallery where Kat worked. She liked her and thought Trumbull was a lucky man to find her.

Tom arrived for dinner promptly at six. Kat asked that he take her to a quiet restaurant, preferably candlelit, where she wouldn't be seen. She wore sunglasses and arranged her hair to mask her identity. She didn't want to ruin their evening by aggressive reporters or others who may accost her. Tom knew the perfect spot.

They took a taxi to Café DuPont, a restaurant in the West Village. It was perfect – cozy dark and romantic.

Tom pulled her chair and she sat. He remarked, "I only bring my hot dates here."

"Well, I'll do my best to cool this one," she replied.

Tom laughed, "I promise to remain a gentleman."

"You better. You know what happened to the last guy who wasn't?"

Tom laughed again and they sat down.

They proceeded to a conversation which Kat thought insightful, engaging, and hypnotic. Tom's knowledge of even her specialty – fine art amazed her. More importantly, he did not monopolize the dinner talk with incessant discourse about himself as too many men do. Kat considered such egotistical behavior a strike three. She would never contemplate a second date with such a man.

Tom artfully picked her brain concerning various aspects of her life. Her childhood and her father interested him. She chronicled the events that earned him the Medal of Honor. Tom was fascinated by the ongoing tug-of-war between father and daughter. "My father is very protective. Sometimes, I must take extra-ordinary measures to maintain a trace of independence; however, he is a great man, a wonderful father and I love him dearly. I'll have him no other way."

Tom asked, "What does your father think of your recent adventure?"

"He's proud of all I did. He thinks the city is out of their collective minds to pursue this. He wanted to come here to help me, but I wouldn't let him. My father is a wonderful man, but he can intimidate people he doesn't like. He would be furious should anyone mistreat me, there's no telling what he may do." Tom understood exactly the means her father would deal with his daughter's assailants.

Both learned they had a common interest: guns. Tom and Kat had learned to shoot since either was strong enough to handle a gun. Their fathers encouraged and instructed them about the correct, safe handling of firearms.

"Yes, a gun saved my life two days ago," Kat quipped, "and I'll thank that gun every day for the rest of my life. I will give that gun the most loving cleaning and oiling since my father gave it to me."

The conversation turned to the inevitable questions of her upcoming conference with the D.A.

Well, Tom, what do you suppose I'll be facing tomorrow?"

He paused for a moment, "I'm not sure. You're getting considerable publicity across the country for shooting Griffin. The public supports your self-defense against a murderer, but 2016 New York is a different ball game. The New York Globe ran an editorial on your case yesterday."

"I read it," Kat said.

"They wrote that 'an individual does retain the right to defend oneself, but added 'there are far too many illegal guns in New York, and the last thing we need are more.'"

"But, Tom, there's no way I could have acquired a permit here and there is no way that I will walk around this city without a little protection."

Kat, I know that, and the Globe knows that, but the story doesn't suit their agenda, so they characterize your gun as illegal, but they don't acknowledge there was no way for you to carry legally. The average person is defenseless in the city."

Tom continued, "There are more than two million illegal handguns in this city, and the smallest number of legal handguns by far of any major city. New York politicians ignore the fact that criminals are armed but make it harder for ordinary folks to possess a gun.

"I've lived here for five years and I still have no a clue why. I believe it was Ernest Hemingway, who said, 'New York is a city where a person whose entire family was butchered in front of them the week before can walk into a cocktail party and everyone will go to him offering consolation and solace. Another person, who killed three murderers and saved his family from being killed will stand alone at the same party and be lucky if anyone even speaks to him.' The people here are bright, well educated, and positively ferocious when it comes to business and commerce, but when it comes to using deadly force to defend themselves, they won't do it. And they vilify anyone who does. It's a strange place."

Tom asked, "What time is your meeting with the D.A. tomorrow?"

"Nine in the morning."

"Please give me a call tomorrow after the meeting," Tom pulled out his card, handing it to Kat. She looked at the card and placed it into her bag.

She reached out, tenderly touching his arm, serious for a moment. "I appreciate your assistance," Their eyes met and Kat said, "This experience has been tolerable because of you."

He turned, looked into her face, and smiled.

Instinctively, he said, "You're an incredibly beautiful woman."

"I know," she said, giving him a sweet, innocent wide-eyed look and a captivating smile.

He laughed, "Oh God, what have I signed up for here?"

"More than you can handle, buster."

They taxied back to the Plaza, the couple increasingly excited with the other's company.

Tom walked her into the hotel. At the elevator she turned and thanked Tom for dinner. She then kissed him on the cheek.

"Tom, thank you for a wonderful evening. I enjoyed the food, the wine, and the company was even bearable." Tom gave her a faux hostile stare.

She noticed the hesitancy on his face but it pleased her. This episode was like a first date in high school. Kat was excited, even flustered, about this new man in her life. Gazing at him, she impulsively asked, "Can I buy you dinner tomorrow night?"

His expression of genuine pleasure touched her.

"I'd like that. Let's talk tomorrow," he said.

Tom took a step forward, wrapped his arms around her and hugged her tightly -- only a hug of friendship, but with the promise of far more.

He took a step back, "Good Luck tomorrow."

Their eyes met. Tom turned and walked through the lobby to the street.

****

Kat arrived at the D.A.'s office at 8:30 A.M. Paul Bernard was waiting for her. "My hearing was quick and easy -- $10,000 bail. He paid cash."
Paul asked her to follow him to a conference room. They sat and Paul gave her the scoop. "I talked to a friend in O'Grady's office, an assistant D.A. He told me O'Grady won't charge you if you apologize for breaking New York law by bringing in your gun."

"Apologize for what? Saving my life? New York should apologize to me for giving that thug early release. He should have been in prison for another decade, considering his criminal record. Rebecca Rosenberg would now be alive and I would be home in Florida today after enjoying a weekend wedding with my friends. As it is, I face a year in jail for exercising my God-given right to defend myself."

Paul nodded in agreement, "I know it sounds crazy and is unfair but I believe that will be the offer. I can't tell you to do anything; all I can do is present the facts and the legal ramifications. This is your decision."

"Why is an apology that important to O'Grady?"

Paul thought for a second, "He realizes the poor, the gang members, the drug dealers, organized crime, don't give a damn about the law. On the other hand, the middle class is arming itself. For some reason, people defending themselves drive him crazy. I don't know why. Perhaps he sees a race war brewing."

"So, he's frightened that more women may carry guns for protection, unless I admit I was wrong."

Paul answered, "Something like that."

"… of all the dumbest things I've ever heard."

Paul said, "Kat, I may be wrong, but the police say if you're robbed, give the perp your money, jewelry, anything, but don't resist, your life is far more important than your property. The problem is, these days, even if you don't resist, there's a reasonable chance of being hurt or killed anyway. Most are hopped-up on street dust and care little for human life or too much else. The legal system, at least New York's, has yet to adjust to this unequivocal fact. Many states are liberalizing handgun laws because they acknowledge the data that more guns mean less crime. They recognize the law doesn't protect decent citizens anymore. It's time to give people their right to defend themselves."

At nine o'clock an assistant D.A. knocked on the door and asked Kat and Paul to follow him to the Manhattan District Attorney's office. Attending the meeting with them were the two assistant D.A.s and John O'Grady.

John O'Grady: A tall, gaunt man, late fifties, an almost cadaverous appearance. He reminded Kat of the old horror film actor John Carradine.

O'Grady had graduated from Brooklyn Law School and spent his entire career in New York City. Initially, O'Grady earned the respect of everyone involved with the justice system. However, he lost considerable credibility and support of the law enforcement community by his steady opposition to capital punishment.

For example, the arresting cops were outraged when the D.A. refused to seek the death penalty for a drug dealer who had tortured and killed his rival's entire family -- father, mother and children -- to protect his turf. There were far too many of these incidents, and the police were frustrated by the O'Grady office's casual attitude toward the criminals.

The police believed the penalty should fit the crime. They placed their lives on the line to arrest a perp and maintained that the O'Grady D.A.'s office didn't have their back – the D.A. wasn't doing his job as the police were doing theirs.

O'Grady started the meeting by stating, "I'm pleased you weren't harmed by your encounter with Mr. Griffin. Unfortunately, a death resulted, but these things happen. You are aware, we have strict laws against carrying handguns without a permit. Though your Florida permit is current and in order, you violated the Sullivan Act, section 400.00 of the New York Penal Law. You knowingly violated the law by taking your gun into the city, but because of mitigating circumstances we won't fully prosecute if you cooperate."

"What do you mean by cooperate?" Kat asked knowing the answer.

"We ask you to apologize for breaking our handgun laws and swear you will never again carry a gun into New York. We'll lower your charge from a Class D Felony to a Class C Misdemeanor. You will be given a year's probation and a $2,500 fine, but no jail time."

Paul Bernard leaned over and whispered in her ear.

"Why is this so important to you?" Kat asked.

O'Grady looked at her, "Because I don't want the inhabitants of this city arming themselves like a bunch of vigilantes."

Kat's anger intensified, "My father told me before he gave me a firearms lesson, 'When Seconds Count The Police Are Only Minutes Away.' He drummed that gospel into my head. And do you know what? My experience in Central Park last week proved him correct."

O'Grady gave her his dirtiest look.

Kat continued, "Why did you ask me to avoid the media until we had our meeting?"

"I didn't want you coming across like an ad for the NRA, misleading people into thinking they should all carry guns and kill criminals."

Kat shook her head, "This is the weirdest conversation I've ever had. I carry a valid permit to carry a pistol in Florida. I'm an expert shot. I came to your city and was attacked by a serial rapist and murderer. I killed him, did your city a service, and your one concern is that no other woman follows my example and possibly saves her life if attacked. What am I missing?"

Everyone in the room could see the color rising on O'Grady's otherwise gray countenance.

"Listen to me, young lady. This is not the Western frontier and we have far too many guns in this city. There are two and a half million illegal firearms, the majority of which are in criminal hands."

Kat replied, "You won't even give law-abiding citizens their constitutional right to own a gun for defense. You and I know you make it impossible for the typical citizen to own a handgun, let alone carry one. Even after suffering through the lengthy permit process, you must pay a lawyer a thousand dollars to compel your police precinct captain to give them anything that is legally yours."

A moment of silence tempered the room. Kat broke the silence, "Everyone knew that the police precinct captains had been under orders for years to withhold any permits unless a lawsuit was imminent, which the city realized it would lose. A lawyer charges a thousand dollars and within three days your permit appears."

An angry O'Grady blurted, "You seem well informed about our city."

Kat replied, "I spoke with several New Yorkers who were kind enough to fill me in on how things are done in this city."

O'Grady immediately changed the subject."What's your decision, Ms. St. John?"

"Mr. O'Grady, I'd be dead now if I didn't carry a gun. It is beyond my comprehension why you want me to apologize and promise never to carry again in NYC the weapon that saved my life. Unless you present one valid, rational reason, I won't apologize to you."

Paul Bernard stifled a smile behind his cupped hand.

Another moment of stunned silence overwhelmed the room. O'Grady and his staff believed St. John would roll over and apologize, but here she is defying the chief attorney of New York City's legal system.

The trembling O'Grady grew enraged. The D.A. may be behind the times, but remained a formidable foe, not accustomed to such challenges.

"You will live to regret your decision, Ms. St. John," he barked.

Paul Bernard said to O'Grady, "You can't believe a grand jury will indict her for killing a multiple murderer and rapist. How could you even consider wasting the taxpayer's money on this case?"

O'Grady knew it to be true, but his anger veered close to losing control. "I won't have New Yorkers shooting one another. I'm confident the Globe and much of the media support my position. The fact is, Ms. St. John broke the law, and she is liable for punishment."

Kat's anger mounted; her voice crackled with indignation. "You are totally insane. You have lost control of this city. Criminals don't give a damn about the laws and do as they want. More than 2.5 million illegal handguns are in their possession. Teenagers are arrested every day for bringing guns to school and often shoot each other in gang fights. Most serve no hard time. You've given up on a sizable portion of the population. You spend too much of your resources prosecuting people like the subway shooter and me -- law-abiding citizens who merely protected themselves."

At that moment an assistant D.A.s interrupted, "Everyone, please calm down and discuss this rationally. Let's try to conclude an agreement here."
He gently guided the shaken O'Grady back to his desk. The other assistant D. A., a young woman in her early thirties, angrily defended her boss, "You have no right speaking to the Manhattan District Attorney so rudely. Mr. O'Grady is an attorney held in the highest regard by the legal community. I understand you aren't an attorney and only a visitor to this city, but you don't understand who he is."

Paul noticed Kat's amusement by the comment.

Paul's anger also rose but he made an effort to control his temper, "Mr. O'-Grady, you are a public servant. Our tax dollars pay your salary. Your responsibility is to protect the city's citizens from criminals like Griffin by incarcerating these dangerous lawbreakers. You failed to do that in this case. You under prosecuted Griffin. That's on your office. Now you want to spend thousands of taxpayer dollars to prosecute Ms. St. John, the executioner of a man who raped and killed at least three women, and possibly more. She provided the city an incredible service. She corrected your mistake with Griffin. And you want her to apologize or you will send hero to jail? On the contrary, you should apologize to her and the families of Griffin's victims. You and every citizen of the city should be on their knees thanking this woman."

O'Grady, his face an even darker shade of red, abruptly stood, "This meeting is over. You two have decided what you will plead and must live with the consequences."

He left the room; the door slammed behind him.

His assistants looked astonished by the outburst. One assistant spoke to Paul, "We will discuss the case and call you."

Paul and Kat exited the office. In the elevator Paul told Kat he will provide updates on the D.A.'s decision when he received them. "Kat, O'Grady clearly won't compromise his demands. And I realize you won't concede. You should consider my advice to blitz the media and pressure O'Grady to drop the case." Kat agreed, nodding her head.

Kat returned to her room and planned her media blitz, but she knew she would need help. She called Tom Ford.

"Tom, I returned from the meeting with the D.A. He's somewhat unhinged by my case and it doesn't appear he will let it go without a fight."

"Then, let's give him a fight. I have contacts in the media via my clients and will call them this afternoon. How are you doing?"

"The meeting discouraged me a bit, but the more I think of my predicament, the angrier I get. His attitude makes no sense."

"I understand and you have my complete support with your efforts."

"Thank you, Tom. Don't forget I am buying you dinner tonight." Kat reminded him.

"Of course I won't forget. I'll tell you at dinner about the media I found for you."

"Good. Does seven work for you?"

"See you then."

Kat's next call will be more challenging – a call to her father. She feared O'Grady's behavior may anger him and unquestionably he would likely punch him out. Or worse. Nonetheless, he was her father and she needed him by her side during this difficult time. He would be a great teammate.

She dialed his cell and caught him riding a tractor. "How did the meeting go, Kat?"

"Not too well dad, the D.A. is a real prick. He asked me to apologize for bringing a gun into the city. I will under no circumstances apologize. This is lunacy."

"What do you plan to do, Kat?"

I plan to fight the bastard." Mike St. John could never curb Kat's lapse of language -- he taught her the words.

Kat explained to her father the media blitz that Paul Bernard recommended.

"We'll do what Foxy Knoxy did to be released from an Italian prison. The tabloids already gave me a name – Bernice Goetz."

"I'll be there tomorrow. Reserve me a room at the Plaza for the week. Our campaign may last a week or two."

"Are you sure Daddy?"

"Any real parent goes to any length to protect his children. I will throw all my medals over the White House fence like John Kerry before I stay home while my daughter risks jail fighting some lefty D.A."

"Thank you, Daddy. But you must promise not to beat up anyone."

"You have my solemn word on your dear mother's grave."

"Daddy, I want you to meet someone. Tom Ford. He's special and different from the other men I have dated."

"So he isn't a metrosexual wimp like most of your old boyfriends?"

Kat recalled her father's disapproval of the boys she brought home. She pretended not to hear his latest comment. "See you tomorrow, Daddy."

Kat was satisfied with the team she had built around herself. Her father, Tom Ford, Paul Bernard and Martin Paxton gave her an excellent core to beat D.A. O'Grady's efforts to jail her. She despised the man and looked forward to trouncing him in the domain of public opinion.

Dinner that night established Tom's bona fides as a man who delivered his promises. Tom arranged interviews with the two of the city's tabloid newspapers, a segment on cable's top-rated news show —"Ted O'Hara Live!" and the coup de grâce, a full hour interview by Ken Randall, the country's number one radio talk show host.

Tom's immediate production astounded Kat.

Tom had called Jackie Brandt, asking for his help. Jackie immediately contacted Jay Bailey Morgan III who provided the newspaper and O'Hara interviews.

Jackie had helped Ken Randall several years ago regarding a drug charge. Randall had endeavored to illegally import painkillers in his luggage from Jamaica but Customs caught him at the airport. Randall had met Jackie at an on-air interview regarding the Middle East wars and, later, at a few charity golf tournaments in which the two were involved.

Desperate to stop this potential career-ruining arrest from becoming public he called Jackie Brandt for help. Jackie, the master fixer, had the case quietly dropped and the arrest expunged from the records. Jackie's efforts and success amazed Randall and his attorneys. In appreciation, Ken Randall sent Jackie a Gold Rolex Submariner Watch and a promise of any future services should he ever need it. Jackie wears the watch today and he now cashed that chit.

Kat told Tom her father arrives the next day. "Kat, it couldn't hurt to have a Congressional Medal of Honor recipient stand next to you, especially if he is your father. No American could ever accept that the daughter of this brave man be jailed for defending herself."

"I don't know, Tom. You didn't see the O'Grady rage when I didn't accept his offer. He seemed to have taken my rejection of his offer as a personal affront. I doubt he will roll over too easily."

"O'Grady may have no choice should you present your case clearly to the people. He is not a man onto himself, but is a construct of a huge political machine that wields the city's political power. Should other machine pols calculate that O'Grady will become an embarrassment and an eventual liability to their brand they will pressure him to capitulate. He has no choice."

Kat and Mike St. John were the talk of the town, indeed the country for the next three days. Ken Randall started the second hour of his show the next day with an in-studio interview of Kat and her father. He expected his audience looked forward to this segment of his show. Kat and Mike arrived at his Hell's Kitchen studio and were soon on air.

Ken Randall seldom interviewed guests on his show, especially in-studio, but this was different -- he was repaying a favor to someone who helped him save his career. Regardless, Kat St. John's story infuriated him. A lifetime NRA member, he did everything he could to support Second Amendment rights. Moreover, the interview could produce the year's highest ratings.

"I welcome Kat St. John and her father, Mike St. John," said Ken Randall. "You listeners know I rarely do live interviews on my show, but I had to give an exception for the St. Johns. I lost it when I read about Kat St. John's near-rape and murder, her shooting the perpetrator, and the DA O'Grady's ongoing efforts to send her to prison on gun charges.Furthermore, her father is a Medal of Honor recipient for his heroism during the Vietnam War. I am sure he didn't fight for his daughter to be treated so poorly. Mr. St. John, am I correct?"

"Ken, please call me Mike. I shed a little blood for our country, but my experience didn't compare to the soldiers who returned without limbs or sight, not to mention those shipped back in boxes. We volunteered to fight for our country and its freedoms, but when the bullets whizz overhead and the mortar rounds rain around you the attitude changes. You are now fighting for the safe return of you and your buddies. I took an attack on us personally and reacted accordingly."

"I gave no mercy to anyone who threatened my men. I feel the same way regarding attacks on my daughter. This O'Grady character lacks respect for all my daughter accomplished that night in Central Park. She would be dead if he had his way. That isn't acceptable to this old Ranger."

Ken Randall: "Mike, I see your outrage. Kat, what do you want to say to my twenty-million nationwide audience?"

Kat grabbed the microphone, "Picture yourself in the situation I faced that night in Central Park. I believe all of you, had you prepared, as I did for such an attack, would pull the trigger on your attacker. You will also find it outrageous that they prosecute you for saving your life and perhaps many other lives by killing that vermin. I shot a serial rapist and murderer who had a lengthy criminal record. He deserved the consequence of his crimes and the entire city benefitted from his shooting. I eliminated a depraved monster from the city and now the prosecutor intends to send me to prison for a year or two. I strongly disagree with O'Grady and I trust America does as well."

The interview continued for an hour. Kat and Mike were resolute, mesmerizing and persuasive. Ed Randall regarded this the most memorable interview he had conducted since his last interview with Ronald Reagan when he was president.

Randall followed the hour delivering a fierce, biting commentary about public servants out of touch with the duties and responsibilities their offices mandate. Expressing extreme anger, he wondered why any district attorney would lose sight of his major function, which is to protect honest, taxpaying citizens. Randall believed O'Grady coddled abominable career criminals by using suspect interpretations of the law for cover.

He proceeded using all the statistics from the public record Tom Ford had provided Kat: that only twenty percent of repeat criminals serve time for handgun possession alone was a telling fact. Randall stated the mayor's record to date on getting the city back on track had been commendable.

But any mayor who spends thousands of taxpayer dollars to have his D.A. try to jail a true hero like Ms. St. John would force voters to re-evaluate his viability for another term. He ended the segment by describing Griffin's crimes and his victims.

It was powerful, emotional, effective talk radio. Kat and her team were pleased with the show. Twenty-seven million Americans listened to Ken Randall that day. He added millions of new fans from the interview and his subsequent comments.

Kat's other venues were also successful. Two print reporters wrote sympathetic stories of an out-of-towner facing double-edged prospects of either defending herself or violating the law. Kat St. John contended with a classic Catch-22: If you didn't have the means to protect yourself, you could end up raped and/or dead. However, the law was violated and jail was possible for using a gun, or even a knife, to defend yourself. The reporters concluded it was preferable to break a flawed law than be killed. They wrote that Kathryn St. John would certainly be dead hadn't she carried a gun.

In Tom's opinion, scarcely any of the public supported a law that sends someone to jail for defending themselves from a serial rapist and murderer.

However, thanks to Ted O'Hara's television show, Kat became a national celebrity. Her beauty, strong arguments, and abuse by the D.A. swung public opinion in her favor. For the first time, America viewed her face to face. Despite being a sympathetic host, O'Hara posed several probing questions.

"Kat, the police have always said if you are attacked, hand over your money, jewelry, anything, but don't resist, your life is more important than material goods. Yet you resisted. Why?"

Kat, without hesitation answered, "The problem these days is even if you don't resist you have a good chance of getting killed or seriously injured. The cops in this town weren't with me. They didn't see the crazed look in that guy's eyes. He was hopped-up on something and was after more than my jewelry and money. Besides, I learned to defend myself. And I did. Not to defend myself is contrary to whom I am."

O'Hara continued a tough interview...and Kat parried him proficiently. She impressed O'Hara, as were his viewers.

The next day, the entire New York media requested a press conference. Ronald Trumbull, who became a fan of Kat St. John, provided the spacious atrium in his Trumbull Tower for an 11:00 A.M. press conference. Kat, Mike, Tom and Paul would be available for questioning by the media.

The mayor called O'Grady first thing that morning. Their conversation quickly ended. After confirming the twenty percent statistic and the facts surrounding Griffin's shooting, he asked O'Grady what he intended to do. The D.A. explained he will prosecute Ms. St. John should she refuse to re-pent for violating the Sullivan Law. The mayor asked if he had heard the Ken Randall Show that afternoon or watched the O'Hara show last night. O'Grady responded he had read the articles in the newspapers but had not heard Ken Randall or watched Ms. St. John on O'Hara. The mayor said he will messenger a tape to him immediately.

One hour later, a furious, shaken D.A. called the mayor. O'Grady stated his opinion to the mayor, "I listened to that agitating bastard, Randall. He makes everything so damn simple and black and white. He's nothing but a nasty prick."

Interrupting, the mayor burst out, "John, is that twenty percent stat true?"

"Well, yes, but if we confine every felon we apprehend carrying a handgun to jail, we'd fill half of the state's prisons by handgun violators from New York City alone."

"John, for God's sake, listen to me. I heard an articulate, and from every-thing I hear, a very attractive woman, who clearly and succinctly explained how she protected her life by shooting a murderer."

"Mr. Mayor, if we let this woman walk without even an apology, we will send a signal that shooting…"

Now livid, the mayor roared over the phone, "She has the people on her side. You and I will look like fools if you prosecute her. John, you go to that press conference at eleven and tell Katherine St. John, her father and everyone else that you will drop the case and not pursue any further action against her…and you will do it with the best smile you can muster. Fur-thermore, you will apologize for any distress your office gave her and thank her for taking a rapist and murderer off our streets. We must salvage some goodwill from this debacle."

John O'Grady knew his political career was finished without the mayor. A hack he was and a hack he will again become if he didn't work with the mayor. An extremely agitated, but defeated and pale D.A. quietly answered, "Yes, Mr. Mayor. I'll go to grant her complete exoneration."

However, O'Grady didn't appear at the conference. He sent an assistant to the conference to announce a full pardon of Kat that resulted from Griffin's shooting. O'Grady couldn't face the crowd, the media and Kat with his order to exonerate her.

Mike St. John took the team and allies who helped with the campaign for a 21 Club victory celebration. Tom called for a luncheon reservation at the Wine Cellar, a cozy private room in the restaurant's cellar that hid the liquor inventory during Prohibition. It's an exquisite room of brick walls and elegant wine racks. A room that Tom often booked to celebrate a big deal. Now he would celebrate Kat's freedom, the biggest deal — the liberation of someone who has become very important to his life. Tom was too analytical to admit he was falling in love with Kat, but they had grown close during the last few days. Her strength, solid values and courage had impacted him as he had never experienced in his 27 years.

At the 21 Club, the table of twenty-two included Martin Paxton, Paul Bernard, Ken Randall, Ted O'Hara, Detective Brown and the newspaper writers who supported her. Tom invited Jackie Brandt, but Jackie thought he best remain covert with so much press in the room.

No reporters from the New York Globe were invited. However, the mayor entered a welcome crasher. He bought a couple of bottles of champagne for the table and led a toast to the "brave woman to whom the city now gives appreciation and gratitude for her removal of such evil from our city."

Mike led a second toast to honor the mayor "for the courage to come here uncertain of how he'd be received." All around the table gave the mayor a hearty ovation. The mayor invested well by his generous donation of the champagne to the party. Randall, O'Hara, and the newspapers praised the mayor the next day on their venues for his appearance and tribute to Kat St. John.

Ted O'Hara took the seat next to Kat. O'Hara had a reason to sit next to her: He offered her a job as an assistant producer for his show. He suggested the job could develop to an on-air position and praised her for the ease in which she argued her case on the numerous shows she appeared during the last week. He added that you can't teach the obvious talent she had – she was a natural. He asked her to interview at his office Monday morning. Kat honored by his offer, told him she is delighted to meet him on Monday. She couldn't believe her good fortune. She had looked for reasons to relocate to New York. Her motivation for such a move sat across the table – Tom Ford.

Tom developed a friendship with her father. Mike appreciated Tom's efforts to help Kat triumphantly emerge from the sordid pursuit of a misguided district attorney to arrest and imprison his daughter. He asked Tom to take the seat beside him. He wanted to know more about the man Kat had effusively praised and with whom she was clearly enamored.

Mike told Tom anecdotes of war, the family and his father -- Kat's grandfather. He recounted a story that was very familiar to Kat. Mike Sr., a soldier in WWII, was stationed for the last two years of the war in Italy. He experienced no combat near the front lines. On the contrary, he spent his war years as a supply sergeant far from the action. Content with his position, his assignment enabled him to work the black market.

He partnered with the Black Hand from Sicily – the Mafia. Together, they hustled a fortune. He worked alongside Lucky Luciano's cousin who primarily dealt with stolen cigarettes. Cigarettes were the favored medium of exchange in wartime Italy – cigarettes were worth far more than the inflated lira. A carton of cigarettes could buy nearly anything in the country and Mike Sr. handled hundreds of thousands cartons during these years. Mike Sr. was informed when the cigarettes were arriving from the states and he gave word to his partners who then hijacked the truck for their cargo after it left the port.

Cigarettes weren't the only black market item. The war brought considerable other valuables to the black market, including artwork, guns, jewelry, even food and wine. Sgt. Michael St. John worked them all, and no one ever investigated or discovered his enterprise. He became incredibly wealthy by his enterprise.

Mike Sr. purchased an 800-acre Florida orange grove with the money he hustled during the war. He worked hard to build a prosperous business that Mike Jr. took over when he returned from Vietnam. Mike Jr. expanded the business, adding sixty horse stalls in three new barns to house and care for the Palm Beach locale's growing herd of polo ponies. The story impressed Tom. It gave him additional perspective regarding Kat St. John.

After dinner, Tom counted eighteen empty wine and champagne bottles gracing the table. He took a magnum bottle signed by the mayor and other guests at the luncheon – the bottle will be a fine addition to his memorabilia collection.

He invited Kat to spend the weekend in New Hampshire before leaving.

She enthusiastically agreed. "I can't think of a more suitable place to go for a respite from the chaos of the last week," she said. She tightened his hand in hers. They planned to leave early the following morning. Kat informed Tom about the O'Hara offer. Tom noticed Kat was a natural in front of the camera and reporters. He realized why Ted O'Hara wanted to hire her. He also appreciated that Kat would need to relocate to the city.

Chapter 8: *Tom & Kat, Together*

Tom found Kat more attractive than any other woman he had ever met. If her personality, wit, and intelligence even approached her physical appeal, he realized the deep trouble he could find himself. He told himself, relax, take it slowly; you've known her for only a week, and under the extraordinary circumstances. It's far too soon for a serious relationship.

He picked her up Friday morning at the Plaza and parked adjacent to the famous fountain that F. Scott and Zelda sometimes frolicked in during the 1920s. A twenty-dollar bill to the doorman assured him the car remained ticketless for the next ten minutes.

Tom walked through the lobby, taking the elevator to Kat's floor. He knocked on the door and was left breathless when she opened the door. She wore a pair of white linen slacks and a deep blue silk blouse that matched her striking eyes. Unlike her casual and loose-fitting outfits, this outfit was tailored to perfectly fit her figure. The clothes were not unusually tight, but her figure was clearly visible and, to Tom, as with most other healthy man, she was stunning. Kat had expected Tom's reaction, and it greatly pleased her. The mane of shiny, thick hair flowed below her shoulders, her highlights glistened in the morning light.

Kat's merriment was becoming familiar to Tom. She was well aware of the effect she had on men. Kat invited him in.

Smiling, she said, "Wipe that look off your face, Opie, and help me carry the luggage. Daddy left late last night and is back in Florida. He told me to tell you goodbye for him."

Tom took her two larger bags. Kat toted her small carry-on.

Kat checked out of the hotel. Tom helped her carry her bags to the automobile that would carry them to Orford. -- Tom's new toy: a 1974 Jaguar XKE III twelve-cylinder convertible painted British Racing Green. The car mysteriously appeared on his parent's driveway one morning. A note indicated that an anonymous "admirer" gave Tom the Jaguar, a gift for his "special skills." Dr. Ford, in an effort to solve the mystery, checked the registration but found the car listed to an obscure Panamanian trading company. He called Tom about it. Tom assumed a J. Bailey Morgan III connection. Tom contacted Jackie Brandt, but he denied any knowledge about the car. He advised Tom, "Enjoy it for all it's worth. You know enough by now not to ask too many questions."

Tom, indeed, asked no more questions. He decided he earned this lavish gift. Someday, he will thank Mr. Morgan in person.

Tom lowered the canvas top to facilitate enjoying a radiant warm summer day. This generated a loud, rousing drive. The wind, road noise and the twelve resonant cylinders created a too noisy ambiance for a serious conversation. Both knew they had all weekend to talk and were content to enjoy the five-hour ride and engage in a little personal reverie.

Kat reflected on her changed life after the previous week's events. She enjoyed her Palm Beach life and learned a great deal by working for the gallery owned by her mother's old friend. Someday, she will own a gallery.

Kat knew she possessed few required skills needed to become a first-rate wildlife painter, but she did develop into an excellent wildlife photographer.

She was entirely pleased with her professional life and aware there wasn't much money in the field she had chosen, but money wasn't too important to her.

She loved her father and her work at the orange grove, especially tending the horses. For convenience, she maintained a modest apartment in West Palm a ten-minute drive from the gallery. Her fitness club, where she worked out four or five days a week, was a block away from her apartment. She had created a fine life considering her young age of twenty-five.

Kat reviewed her past romantic interests. Her engagement, at twenty-three, had lasted nine months. Dave had been nice enough, but his investment banker life as, Kat realized after six months, didn't suit her. Dave worked long hours, but at age twenty-eight, he earned more money than most men under forty could never have imagined. Many young women would have been excited about dining at the finest restaurants, riding in expensive cars, and looking forward to a prosperous future.

For Kat, the relationship had been fun for three or four months, but certain issues became unacceptable to her as the relationship matured.

Dave had been athletic in his youth, but as he moved deeper into the world of investment banking, his occasional workout was replaced by a weekly business round of golf. Weekends were customarily spent socializing with clients. Golf, dinner, and attending professional sporting events were the usual activities. Dave had no interest in the outdoors, besides golf, and, even if he had, there wouldn't have been time to enjoy it.

However, the tipping point came one night at a dinner celebrating the closing of a substantial financial transaction. Kat became aware that the more successful Dave and his business associates achieved, the more boring they became. She noticed the real big hitters ate, drank, and slept business. Kat understood this single-minded focus was needed to succeed in their competitive world.

Kat also regarded these men as physical zeros, certainly by her standards. Women say they don't value such matters, but this didn't alter Kat's realization: being with an out-of-shape, physical wimp of a man had no appeal to her. If these bankers walked down the street, their net worth unknown, nobody would give them a second look. They weren't a presence.

Her father presented a far more impressive figure. Nearly seventy, but still built like the soldier he was more than forty years ago. His huge shoulders, erect posture, deep tan, and a full head of salt and pepper hair attracted attention. It wasn't the way he looked, it was the way he moved. Confident. Self-assured.

Dave wanted to earn the big bucks, and like other successful businessmen, little else mattered. To Kat, these traits turned them into narrow, unattractive, and ultimately, uninteresting men. Dave gave an energetic effort to keep Kat, but to no avail. She knew he wouldn't change. She broke off the engagement, relieved, without ever looking back.

Meeting Tom changed her life, even more than her shooting Griffin. Here was a man who could compete with Mike St. John. This surprised her. She never imagined another such man existed. She noticed the similarities at the 21 Club dinner while conversing with Ted O'Hara. No, Tom hardly looked like her father but was comparable to him in other ways. Both possessed an inner strength so powerful few could overcome.

Kat was aware she inherited a great deal of that innate strength. But Kat also learned to restrain her father, at least as much as he allowed.
The upcoming weekend with Tom should be interesting.

Tom had dated numerous beautiful women in New York. He had a three-month fling with a stunning model and Vogue cover girl. The problem with the relationship was not the physical, which was initially exciting, but Tom found nothing else to maintain the relationship.

Sabrina had no interests, no knowledge, and committed herself to keep it that way. She took uncommonly good care of her body, but offered little else. She had a large mirror in her bedroom she regularly monitored for any possible defects.

Tom foresaw no future with Sabrina. He was well aware their sporting relationship as fleeting. He hoped he hadn't caused her grief. Sabrina was not an unpleasant person. She simply was seldom compelling enough for a serious relationship.

On the other end of the female spectrum, Tom met an attractive and brilliant young surgeon. They dated for a year. She had graduated from Johns Hopkins Medical School in Baltimore and worked a residency at New York's Columbia Presbyterian. They met at a cocktail party in a downtown New York gallery featuring nature and hunting art. She accompanied her friend, a roommate from Hamilton College in upstate New York.

Dr. Carol Halsey and Tom immediately hit it off. She was witty and bright. He expected the bright, but the wit caught him by surprise. Graduates from medical school were of necessity intelligent, but rarely had the time nor the inclination to develop their wit, and seldom, an engaging personality.

Three or four glasses of wine prompted the conversation from good to excellent to mesmerizing. Carol proved a passionate and committed surgeon. She stated that her patients were the most important concern of her life.

Carol and Tom dated as often as they could, but her full schedule and unexpected emergencies rendered planning difficult. After four months, she told Tom he was the man with whom she wanted to spend her life. Tom surmised he may eventually love her, but he never developed a passion for the relationship. He also understood the difficulties of maintaining the relationship should she accept the job offered in Chicago. Tom urged her to take the position.

The distance caused problems within six months. Carol's schedule required her to work six, sometimes seven days a week. This rarely left her enough time to visit New York or Tom's country home in New Hampshire. Tom understood that even if Carol had two or three straight days off, it would be professionally unacceptable for her to be five or six hours away from her patients.

As time passed, Carol sometimes asked Tom when he planned to move on from his job. She had no respect for investment bankers. He invariably answered the same way: "Carol, I'm quite content with my job and until I believe differently, I won't change a thing."

Her face displayed disappointment. She couldn't comprehend why a person with Tom's education and intelligence be content to live the life he led.

Nevertheless, her visits to Orford shocked her. She spent considerable time on the phone the first day, checking on her patients and dealing with situations requiring her attention. By the end of the second or third day, her entire attitude changed. A night of eating and drinking on the deck, enjoying the spectacular views, followed by hours under the summer night sky, observing the shimmering stars astounded her.

Gazing at Jupiter and its four moons, Saturn and its rings, gave a breathtakingly resplendent experience. Tom aimed his telescope to an empty expanse of sky and a spectacular nebula appeared.

He knew where to search for scores of stellar objects that Carol didn't even know existed. Likewise, the trees, the birds, and the entire natural world Tom opened a new world to the city girl. They spent the days swimming in the crystal clear pond, hiking through magnificently maintained forests, shooting clay pigeons, and many other activities. Carol also enjoyed Tom's parents' company who prepared magnificent dinners in her honor. She particularly reveled in her shared hospital war stories with Dr. Ford. Tom's parents liked Carol and approved the relationship.

After three days, Carol realized Tom wouldn't give up his lifestyle. They spent three of every four weekends apart, he in New Hampshire or New York, she in Chicago. Nothing could change that, short of her abandoning her career or Tom quitting his job. When he gently ended the relationship, she thought she would die. She realized she had been fortunate enough to meet that once-in-a-lifetime mate, but fate had conspired to make it impossible for them to develop the relationship. She understood she must one day overcome the pain and that they were doomed from the beginning to their inevitable fate. But Carol knew she could never again care for a man as she had for Tom Ford. For the next six months, she worked nearly every waking minute to distract herself from the breakup.

Tom's reminiscence ended when he took the Hanover exit off I-91. It was after noon, time for lunch at his favorite restaurant in town, Taddy O'Shea's Pub, at the corner of Main Street near the Dartmouth College campus.

"Let's have lunch here; my parents invited us to a seven o'clock dinner. Well, happy hour is at seven. Who knows when they will serve dinner."

Kat nodded approvingly, "Sounds like a decent plan."

Tom parked the car in front of the restaurant, attracting admiring stares from the male students. He realized they were admiring his passenger even more than the car.

They entered the half-crowded restaurant and took a seat at the bar. Tom waved to the bartender, his friend and occasional shooting buddy, Ian Mc-Keever. Ian walked over and shook Tom's hand. Tom introduced him to Kat St. John. "Wow! So you're the famous vigilante. I can't believe I watched you on the television all week and now here you are. Nice to meet you, Kat. First drink is on me. We were rooting for you."

"Why, thank you, Ian. That's kind of you to say," Kat replied.

They ordered two house whites. Ian delivered the wine. He told Tom, "I need your help."

"What's the problem?" Tom looked concerned.

"I dropped my rifle a few days ago at the range and the scope needs to be realigned and re-sighted. Can you fix it for me?"

Tom smiled, "Sure, no problem. Stop by this weekend and I'll fix it for you. If you can't make it this weekend, my father could repair the scope next week. He's semi-retired now and has plenty of time."

"Thanks, I'll see you this weekend."

Kat turned to Tom, "I look forward to meeting your parents. They sent me a nice telegram to the hotel wishing me the best in my fight against the D.A. I don't remember ever receiving a telegram."

"That must have been my mother. She prefers the old-fashion approach. I believe you will like her."

Tom and Kat finished lunch and resumed their trip to the Ford homestead through the New Hampshire countryside. Tom took the more scenic Route 10 instead of the interstate. He wanted to give Kat a tour of the region where he grew up. He took the back entrance to the Ford property, "We'll see my parents at dinner, I want to show you the property beforehand." Tom continued, "I suggest we take a hike around the property. I've cut paths through the grounds and walking it will give you a sense of the countryside. It is a four-mile loop around our property and the farms surrounding us. Some are fairly rugged, but you'll find it quite a scenic hike."

"Sounds great, when do we go?" she asked.

"We'll take in the luggage and start immediately."

"Great! Let me change into something more appropriate for hiking the woods. I'll be back in a minute."

Ten minutes later, Kat walked out to the deck, "Okay, I'm ready." A pair of Russell Plantation Series Birdshooter boots had replaced her Nike sneakers. The cool country air contrasted favorably to New York's warm temperatures. She decided that her blue, lightweight cotton Pendleton shirt tucked into a well worn-pair of Levis was appropriate for a hike. Her light brown hair looked fabulous pulled in a ponytail through a pink Yankees baseball cap that perfectly complemented the blue shirt.

From the deck Tom pointed out the route they will hike through the woods and hills. Tom led her to a path at the far end of the field. The house, located at a fifteen hundred feet elevation in a high mountain valley, was surrounded by hills ranging from two thousand to three thousand feet. The Ford property didn't include the distant mountains but encompassed the forest and shorter hills that took hikers to a higher elevation. Tom intended to give Kat many glorious and spectacular views during the next hours.

As they hiked the forest, its beauty impressed Kat. Tom, or somebody, had spent considerable effort and hours with a wood chipper and chainsaw to cut and clear the undergrowth and smaller trees to create a splendid park-like effect. Kat had no trouble identifying the trees, like sugar maples. She remembered their stunning yellow, orange and red colors in the fall. Her four years at Williams College had given her an appreciation for colorful fall New England forests that remained with her throughout her life. After fifteen minutes, the path ascended, leaving the thinned woods behind. She noticed rock outcroppings and the more rugged terrain. Conifers, predominantly hemlock, spruce, and pine, became more abundant. She stopped and asked Tom, "What's this tree?"

"American Hornbeam," he answered.

"Kat, do you know the names of the trees in these woods?"

"Nearly all. Actually, everything so far except the hornbeam. Don't forget, Mr. Woodsboy, I went to college not too far from here."

"I am aware of that, Miss Florida wise-ass. But, I assure you few people who attended school in New England, or anywhere else, can walk through the woods and name the trees."

They hiked another thirty minutes, and reached an extensive clearing. From the uppermost side they looked back and gazed at the two Ford houses and fields far below.

"Oh, Tom, what a gorgeous view!" she exclaimed.

"Yes, I'm glad you like it. It's one of my favorites."

"No houses are visible for miles. This is wonderful," she said.

Surveying the modest field, she asked, "Why is this field here? Did you clear it?"

"I had cleared them for the animals to enjoy some sunshine. My friend, Jim Scott, a local farmer and logger, brought his bulldozer to clear six clearings on the property. You can see the deer droppings and other animal signs. They come from the woods to enjoy the sun and escape the biting insects."

Kat's cheeks flushed from the exercise and fresh air, but she didn't appear fatigued.

"How do you feel, Kat?"

"I feel great and enjoy this very much...the perfect prescription for the past week's events."

They reached a fork a half-mile later, turned left, and hiked further up the hill. A few minutes later, they stood by a modest spring that flowed from a milky white quartz wall – a remnant of an old abandoned quarry. Tom picked a stainless steel cup from a nearby limb, filled it, and handed it to Kat.

She drank the water.

"Oh my, this is delicious. Can I have more?"

He handed her another cup, which she promptly drank. Taking the cup from her, he filled it and drank. They watched the sparkling ice-cold water flow into a clear stone pool. The sun gave the white quartz on the stream bed an iridescent quality and the water shimmered as it passed by.

"I had the water tested when I first discovered this spring. The water is uncontaminated by any bacteria and has a high mineral content which gives it a good taste."

Kat flashed a warm smile, "Well, if you're trying to charm me with this incredibly beautiful property, it's working. This is the stuff dreams are made of, at least my dreams. It's similar to our orange groves in that there are no neighbors nearby and you can spend days on your property without seeing another person. Perfect privacy."

Kat continued, "Our grove is in the Florida flatlands and while we don't have a real forest like this, there are plenty of trees – orange trees."

He reached for her and she melted into his arms. They exchanged a passionate kiss, then held each other tightly. They kissed again. The excitement intensified. Kat gently pushed him away.

"Kat, I'm happy you're here with me."

For the briefest moment Kat's face betrayed her heart. She turned away to hide her scarlet cheeks, Tom was well aware that she felt the same way about him as he about her. It was a feeling neither had experienced before. Gaining her composure, she turned to him, "Let's continue our tour. We wouldn't want to be late for dinner."

They hiked for a couple more hours. The path passed through groves of beech trees whose light grey bark contrasted with the dark canopy above. They headed into the lower portion of the Ford's land and arrived at a narrow mountain stream. Although only twelve feet wide, a boisterous eight-foot waterfall blocked their passage. They followed the stream for a few hundred yards and enjoyed how the sun sparkled on the falling water and lighted various colored rocks on the bottom of the crystal clear pools. The flash of lazy brook trout could be seen under the overhangs covering the majestic pools. Tom and Kat held hands, both ecstatic as they delighted in this wonderful setting. A large bird seen through the trees floated high above them. Tom knew it was an eagle from the straight flat wings . About to mention this, Tom was pleasantly surprised when Kat said, "It's nice to have the eagles back, isn't it?"

Squeezing her hand, Tom said, "Yes, it is, Kat."

The couple enjoyed a near-perfect day -- no wind, seventy degrees, and a bright cloudless sky. A warm June sun warmed their faces. He savored his time with someone who cared for him as much as she did for him. No doubt: Tom was rapidly falling in love with Kat.

They completed their hike with two hours to spare before Happy Hour. Entering the house Tom hugged Kat. "I want to show you something."

Tom pulled out a box from the closet's top shelf. He placed the box on the coffee table by the chesterfield sofa. They sat and Tom opened the box. "I told you I was adopted, but there is more to the story. This is the box my mother delivered me in. Not a promising start, is it?"

Kat examined the box, "I didn't take you for a Budweiser kind of guy."

Tom laughed, "I'm not. You'd expect that my mother would have dropped me off in a more appropriate box."

Kat laughed.

He retrieved the box and took out the contents: a blanket and hospital pajamas. He picked up the letter Tom's mother wrote to the Fords and handed it to Kat. She read it and looked at him. "I don't know what to say. I am awfully pleased she decided not to abort you. Did she ever contact you?"

"No, never."

"…any idea who the father is?"

"No idea, no interest."

A silent pause ensued between the two after which Tom looked at Kat, "Let me give you a warning, my parents regard cocktail hour seriously. They dress for the occasion, not black tie, but what I call country urbane. I'll be wearing the uniform."

Kat was familiar with the uniform from their latest dinner date. It helped her choose the dress she will wear to meet Tom's parents.

Kat bounded the stairs to the guest room, took a shower, a short nap and prepared herself to meet Tom's parents. She was more nervous about meeting the parents than her experience last week with Griffin, the police, the district attorney, the media and the prospect of prison. She thought her anxiety irrational, but she wished to favorably impress Tom's parents. She had never met the parents of the man she loved.

At ten to seven she stepped down the stairway. Tom, sitting on the couch reading a magazine, stood dumbfounded as she approached. "Unbelievable!" was all he could say. Kat completed her entrance with a pirouette, followed by a light kiss on his cheek.

She stepped back, "Do you like it?" Kat pirouetted before Tom. She wore a sexy little black dress that ended inches above her knees. A string of pearls complemented the dress and black Dolce & Gabbana medium-heel pumps brought her closer to Tom's height. Her long flowing hair cascaded freely about her shoulders. She felt radiant and confident, excited to meet the parents.

Tom said, "I will need to protect you from my father. He will fall madly in love with you."

"Well, I hope he does!"

They strolled arm and arm along the carefully manicured Belgium block-lined path to the parents' house. Kat admired the orderliness the entire Ford property displayed, the successful fusion of nature coupled with human endeavor. Yes, the Fords created an artwork similar to the Romantic landscapes of the Hudson River painters she studied and appreciated in college. She was at home and drew Tom in closer.

They arrived at the main house where Mrs. Ford greeted the couple. "Welcome to our home Kathryn St. John. You have become a heroine here after we saw you on television and heard Tom's personal accounts."

"Thank you, Mrs. Ford, that's kind of you to say but please call me Kat."

Dr. Ford took her hand, "Yes, of course, Kat. I would also like to congratulate you. You are even prettier in person than you were on the O'Hara show."

Tom interjected, "See Kat, I told you he would fall for you."

Dr. Ford replied, "I confess. Can you blame me? Our guests will arrive in a half-hour but we would like to have you to ourselves for a while. Please come and sit. Care for a drink?"

Kat and Tom spent the next half-hour recounting their confrontations with the DA and the media. Kat retold the Griffin shooting to the Fords. She was welcomed in their home and grateful to experience times like this as a free woman.

"My father insisted I learn to defend myself. He always reminded me that the police couldn't be everywhere. They can only place your body into a bag and hunt for your killer, but there are steps you could take to defend yourself.

Kat added, "…and he was right. I am here today because he gave me a gun and taught me how to shoot it competently."

Mrs. Ford commented, "Kat, we are delighted you survived that ordeal and shared the experience with us tonight."

Dr. Ford asked, "Do you want to shoot tomorrow? We shoot at the range behind the house."

Kat replied, "Great. I look forward to it. I understand Tom is an excellent shot."

"Tom's the best. You will see tomorrow."

The guests soon arrived, two Dartmouth professors and their wives. This group of professors included Ariel Fisher. Tom wondered whether Ariel knew of his extracurricular activities. Ariel Fisher showed no sign of being aware of the Martels despite his close friendship with Reuven Berman, who Tom assumed knew everything.

Travis Potter, the other guest, was the Dartmouth professor of Byzantine and Medieval history.

He said. "Tom, it has been a few years since we had those spirited debates in my classroom. It's good to see you again."

Tom shook his hand and introduced him to Kat.

Tom looked at Kat, "The professor and I had our disagreements, but the discussions were a great learning experience. He piqued my interest in the period, especially the Middle East. Are you still teaching that course?"

"I have been and I will be until they kick my old bones into retirement."

The group sat around the fieldstone fireplace. The burning hardwood logs gave a warm glow to the room.

Kat started the conversation after Dr. Ford served drinks to the guests.

"What did Tom disagree with you about, professor?"

"I gave a lecture on the fall of Rome and discussed the prevalent theory of the time, which held that Germanic barbarians ravaged Rome and destroyed classical civilization. Tom objected, citing the Pirenne thesis. I was astonished that someone cited this theory in an undergraduate course, but familiar enough with it to know its flaws. However, Pirenne presented strong arguments that these barbarians preserved the Roman culture and assimilated into old Rome. Tom supported Pirenne, asserting that Islam caused Roman civilization's destruction and initiated the Dark Ages."

Mrs. Ford spoke, "I recall giving Tom that book for his studies. Was it called *Mohammed and Charlemagne*?"

Tom responded, "It was, and I immediately read the book. I was fascinated by another theory behind the Fall of Rome. Regardless, I wasn't convinced until I toured the archeological sites of Tunis, Akragas and other ancient Mediterranean cities. Each gave more evidence that Perrine's thesis was correct -- the Arabs and later, Islam's rise, thrust the knife into the Roman Empire's back. The 7th-century Arab invaders cut Western Europe from contact and trade with the known world. The Romans looked inward, but it took centuries before the region reorganized into a new society -- the precursor to today's Europe."

Ariel Fisher interjected, "... let's not forget that Charles Martel stopped the Muslim invasion at Poitiers in 732. History would have been far different had The Hammer failed." Ariel glanced at Tom, giving him a knowing smile.

"Fisher knows everything," Tom thought as he returned the smile.

Panie Doubravka entered the room and announced that dinner will be served in the dining room.

Panie Doubravka, the Polish housekeeper/gardener/cook hired last year by the Fords was an excellent cook, having worked in the kitchen of a three-star restaurant in Warsaw. "The only three-star restaurant in Poland," she proudly boasted. The recent house renovation included the construction of a lavish basement maid's quarter. Panie Doubravka, the first resident was quickly adopted into the family. Every Doubravka meal was a delight, and this one no exception.

The dinner offered ingredients from local farms and hunters: Bear meat stroganoff served over homemade lazanki and honey-glazed carrots. Panie Doubravka prepared her own lazanki from her babci's recipe.

The meal and the requisite sampling of single-malt scotches lasted until midnight when Mrs. Ford imposed a curfew to end the evening festivities. Tom and Kat walked back to his cottage, their arms tightly wrapped around each other.

"Thank you Tom, I enjoyed the evening. I love your parents."

"I'm pleased to hear that. You certainly were a hit with them."

"Tom, I noticed how much your parents are still in love. They are amazing together. So many couples who have been together for a long time barely look at each other. Your parents delight at the other's words. It's extraordinary. I want to share such love with my husband one day."

"It's interesting you observed them like that. They haven't lost any devotion to their marriage during their years together."

They talked for another hour and the tension between them became uncomfortable.

He believed he should not proposition Kat until the proper time. Unless she gave him a positive signal, he will defer his desires by respect for her. After 1:00 A.M. he decided the best course would be for them to enjoy a full night's sleep. After all, he had known her for a week -- they must proceed slowly. "Kat, let's call it an evening and have a full night's sleep. I'm up by seven and I always have work to do -- we'll have breakfast, then plan the day."

He noticed the surprised expression on her face, but it wasn't an unpleasant look. She smiled and walked to Tom to kiss him on the cheek.

"See you in the morning, Tom."

"Good night, Kat."

Tom awoke to the smell of bacon. The sun's angle shining through the windows indicated the time long past 7:00 A.M. He checked his watch and was surprised that it read ten minutes past nine. He slept well. A shave and a shower woke him. He changed into a pair of Levis, a medium-weight L.L. Bean flannel shirt, and a pair of lightweight Timberland hiking boots.

He strolled into the kitchen and saw Kat cooking breakfast on the grill.

She glared, feigning anger at Tom. In her best stentorian voice, "At 8:00 A.M. I walked out onto the deck, but I heard no power tools out there, Mr. Up at 7:00 A.M. After ten minutes, I walked around the deck figuring you could see me. Never could I have imagined you were still asleep. I watched the birds for a while and tried some birdcalls. The cuckoo proved appropriate. It took forty-five minutes to figure out Mr. Up at 7:00 should have changed his name to Mr. Up at 9:00."

Laughing, Tom said, "You won't believe me, but this is the latest I've slept in years."

"I don't believe it. You suffered a severe credibility crisis this morning. It'll take days of pravda before I will trust you again. Well, maybe those scotches had an effect."

Is there a quicker way to regain your trust?" he asked.

"I don't know. I'll consider it," she answered.

Smiling, she asked, "How do you like your eggs?"

"Over easy, please."

At the breakfast table the conversation turned to art. "I like your original David Hagerbaumer watercolor of three Ruffed Grouse flushing on a snowy December day. We sold a Hagerbaumer at the gallery where I work. He's fantastic and popular these days. Your prints by Abbott of Grouse hunting and Maase of two Grouse on a snowy tree are spectacular. You have excellent discriminating taste."

"I learned a few things about fine art from my mother. She took me to near-ly every museum on the East Coast. I also took courses at Dartmouth. Why did you become interested?"

"You heard the story of my grandfather's black market ventures," Kat replied. "Well, Grandpa Mike traded for far more than bootleg cigarettes. He marketed stolen paintings, sculptures and other artwork. It was big business and my grandfather was a very successful black marketeer during the war.

"By war's end he possessed dozens of paintings plus a nice collection of marble sculptures. He bribed someone to smuggle them into the U.S. and they found their way to our walls in Florida. We had a Ghirlandaio, a Belli-ni, even a Botticelli. We could have a larger Italian Renaissance collection than the Vatican. I guess living with these paintings all those years piqued my interest in art. I once checked the Art Loss Register and was relieved to find none of our paintings on it, but when dad dies I plan to donate them to a museum or, perhaps Williams College."

"Your grandfather sounds like quite the character," commented Tom.

"Oh, he was. I never knew him. He died before I was born, but the stories endure."

The phone rang...Dr. Ford. "Your friend Ian McKeever called. He is bring-ing some boxes of empty wine bottles. I told him to meet us at noon for an afternoon of shooting. We'll also sight-in his gun."

"Sounds like a plan." Tom hung up the phone.

Tom turned to Kat, "We shoot at noon."

Kat smiled, "Just in time. I don't want to lose my touch."

At noon Tom and Kat met Dr. Ford on the 100-yard range. Ian McKeever shortly joined them. He carried four boxes filled with empty wine and liquor bottles. "It's far more fun to shoot bottles than paper targets -- bottles explode, paper simply hangs there. Shooting bottles is far more dramatic. Let the shooting begin."

Ian brought his Ruger All Weather 77/22, which is an excellent target gun. Tom noticed a small dent on the front edge of the Nikon scope. He peered into the scope, "It doesn't look like you damaged the optics. Let me sight it for one-hundred yards." He secured the gun on a nearby vise and checked the mounts, adjusted the top and side turrets then took a few shots. "Finished. Give it a try."

Ian took the rifle and shot the steel target one-hundred yards away, the unmistakable clang of metal announced a hit.

"Thanks, Tom. It's better than before."

They loaded the bottles on the Polaris Off-Road UTV. Tom and Kat drove the cargo to the target platform -- they covered the twenty-foot-long table, constructed of salvaged 2 X 12's with Ian's bottles.

Tom gave Kat the honor of shooting the first bottle. She chose Tom's venerable lever-action Marlin 39A with iron sights. "My first gun," Tom commented, "It's accurate after all these years and thousands of rounds later."

Kat grabbed the gun, hitting five bottles, missing her last shot. The men nodded their admiration of her marksmanship. Dr. Ford took his six shots and hit three bottles. "Good shooting, dad."

Tom was ready to shoot when Ian screamed, "Hold it, Tom."

Tom lowered the gun and turned around.

"This is child's play for you. Show Kat what you can really do with a rifle." Ian reached deep into his cargo pants to pull out a handful of champagne corks. He drove the Polaris to the table, placing five corks on five bottles.

He drove back and explained to Kat, "Tom had a trick of shooting the cork off a champagne bottle at one-hundred yards without breaking the bottle. Let's see whether he lost the touch."

Tom grabbed the old Marlin. He took careful aim at the first target and hit the cork off the bottle without breaking glass. He hit the remaining four corks in rapid succession, followed by five shots breaking the bottles. His audience gave him an ovation.

Kat approached Tom asking him for all to hear, "Not bad shooting, but a hundred yards is far too easy for a man with your talent. You haven't been much of a man so far this weekend" – everyone laughed at her quip " –Let's see whether you can knock a cork off a bottle at five-hundred yards."

Tom replied, "I can't do it with the .22 Marlin, Its worn barrel and iron sights make for an impossible shot, but I'll try with the scoped Remington."

Kat replied, "That's reasonable."

They walked up the hill to the 500-yard range. Ian took the Polaris to place the target. He returned and looked back, "I barely see the bottle from here. Tom, this will be an amazing shot."

"I'll do my best."

Tom assumed the prone position and placed the gun on a sandbag. He adjusted the scope, checked the wind by the telltales around the target and sighted the cork. Tom applied all he'd learned as a long-distance shooter, making adjustments for wind, distance, barometric pressure, humidity, ambient air temperature, spin drift, bullet weight, and cartridge charge, his mind working like a computer to process the avalanche of information. Satisfied with his analysis, he centered the chosen reticle on the cork and pulled the trigger.

A loud explosion sent the bullet spinning through the barrel. In less than a second the cork flew off the bottle. Tom's shot broke no glass. Ian, looking through binoculars yelled, "Bullseye -- all cork!

Everyone was astounded by what they witnessed. Kat exclaimed, "God! My father couldn't pull off such a shot. Unbelievable."

Tom's next shot blasted the bottle. Everyone looked at Tom in awe as though he was a god who performed an unexplainable miracle. All were shooters who realized the achievement they had just witnessed.

The crew walked back to the 100-yard range and shot for another hour when Panie Doubravka approached. Lunchtime.

****

That evening Tom and Kat enjoyed Sangria on Tom's deck.

Tom's marksmanship intrigued Kat. "Tom, how did you learn to shoot so well?"

"I started shooting when a kid -- wore out three BB guns by the time I was nine. My father's coaching helped enormously. My uncle gave me a .22 for my 10th birthday, the Marlin we shot today. I was an Eagle Scout. Back then, each camp required all scouts to learn gun safety and practice shooting at the rifle range. They placed the targets a hundred feet away but I thoroughly enjoyed the experience and was hooked. Living on this spacious remote property gave me all the opportunities to shoot -- especially long distances. There is a simple secret to accurate long-distance shooting: anyone can place the gun's sight on the target, but it takes considerable practice to keep the barrel on target when you pull the trigger. A skilled shooter doesn't move the barrel's tip when pulling the trigger. A hundredth of an inch movement of the front sight will lead to a foot or greater miss at five hundred feet. Besides all that, I have 20/10 vision, just like Ted Williams had."

"Kat, you're no slouch yourself with a gun. I imagine your father taught you?"

"He sure did. My father had a sizable gun collection. I had to clean and maintain them. I resented the work when young, but I'm glad he forced me to handle guns competently. I'd be dead today if he didn't."

A half-hour later, they were full, relaxed, and mildly intoxicated. Kat said, "I haven't felt this good since I shot the bastard."

"Kat, I want you to be happy here," he said. He filled her glass with more sangria.

"This drink is fantastic...and powerful. Tell me the truth. There is more than wine in it," she said.

"Right you are, my dear. I added a shot of local 200 proof moonshine to the carafe for some extra vigor. White Lightning isn't exclusive to the Appalachians. Jim Scott, our farmer neighbor, diverts a portion of his corn crop to distill the best in the area. He told me his family has been in the moonshine business for more than two centuries. He once showed me the antique copper still he uses. Everyone in town is aware of his operation, yet no one will ever contact the authorities. Even the police chief is a customer."

"I love small-town America. Well, whatever the hell this drink is, it feels awfully potent, and warm" Kat said.

"Let's go into the hot tub." Tom took her hand.

She peered at him knowing the inevitable. The hot tub will only provoke it to happen sooner.

"Okay," she said smiling, "We're not waiting until tonight, are we?"

"I mentioned the hot tub so I can politely remove your clothes."

She kissed him lightly on his cheek and walked around the table to her bedroom. "I can't resist it when a man sweet talks me. I'll be right back." Kat strode upstairs to her room.

Minutes later, she returned and walked across the deck towards the hot tub where Tom had already stretched out against the jets. Her nudity displayed a spectacular body, toned by a lifetime of work, sports and workouts. As she approached, Tom could hardly contain his excitement. She slid into the one hundred and two-degree water next to him. Tom handed her a sangria he had poured.

She took a sip, "Oh, this tastes wonderful!"

She finished her drink and the tension became almost unbearable. Kat had difficulty in catching her breath. She could no longer restrain herself. Looking into his eyes, she leaned forward, wrapping her arms around him. Tom enclosed her with his arms, embracing her for a long passionate kiss.

Tom swept Kat off her feet. She forced her head into his chest as he carried her to his room, each thoroughly savoring the imminent rapturous moment.

Their lives were forever changed when they emerged from Tom's bedroom hours later. Although they didn't discuss their future together, the two were aware they will confront it together...as a team.

They'd only known each other for a week. Even before they made love, Tom sensed something powerful, something neither had ever experienced previously, touched them profoundly. Every hour spent together increased the feeling. But the intensity, the pure white-hot ecstasy, that had taken place in Tom's bed had deeply astounded them.

Tom and Kat had been in relationships with others. They were not starry-eyed, inexperienced teenagers.

It had become patently clear the gods had smiled on them. Most have never approached the intimacy they had reached. Both were awed and thankful for the experience.

They spent the next day making love, talking, hiking, eating, drinking and making love again. Physically, they couldn't get enough of each other. Tom told her he loved her and wanted to be always with her. Her eyes filled with tears of happiness, she held him tightly, whispering in his ears, "Yes, always."

Tom looked forward to sharing his life with Kat. Yet he couldn't, yet, confess his "peculiar avocation" to her. She may understand his motivation and accept his "errands," but he gave a promise to keep the secret and share it only with his parents. One day he will tell her, but not today.

Following Kat's interview on Monday, O'Hara offered her the position. She accepted with the condition that she start could the job in three weeks. She had to arrange two of her clients' art shows for the next couple of weeks. Kat explained she couldn't leave a family friend without giving two weeks notice. Ted O'Hara understood and readily agreed. He appreciated her loyalty to her employer and hoped he will earn such loyalty from her. He wanted to hire her knowing she would be a ratings bonanza when she assumed on-air assignments.

It had been a wonderful, exciting ten days for Tom and Kat. They shared a lifetime of ordeal, adventure and ecstasy. How can they ever surpass their short time together? As they said goodbye at the airport, both looked forward to again in several weeks. They could not have imagined that the previous ten days were only the beginning of a long story filled with many incredible experiences.

Chapter 9: *TomKat*

Tom returned to his apartment and found a note under his door: *Contact Jackie Brandt.*

He called Jackie on the burner phone.

Jackie disclosed his next target: Mohammed Elison. Jackie explained, "Mohammed Elison is a decidedly evil human being. He led the recent bloody bombing campaign against the Coptic Christian Churches in Cairo and was the ringleader of a nefarious group called the Army of Islam. ISIS posted a YouTube video (since deleted) showing Elison decapitating a dozen Christians on a Libyan beach. Ironically, he is a Brit, born in London to a Christian father and a Muslim mother. Apparently, the Muslim half won to rule his psyche."

Tom appreciated the Martel's choice. Mohammed Elison's barbarous activities warranted his talents. Tom was pleased he joined the Martels to give him opportunities to exact justice on the perpetrators of terrorism. Tom took satisfaction of his efforts to rid the world of such wretched characters.

Jackie continued, "This shoot differs from the others. First, it takes place in a Muslim country – Egypt. Second, where your other assignments were in urban settings, this target will be found in the desert, approximately a hundred miles south of Cairo. Third, you will work alongside the Martels on this shoot. I will be your spotter. We have another concern -- this will be a long shot – more than a thousand yards."

Tom asked why they couldn't kill the target with a drone. Jackie replied, "Collateral damage. Two of our assets will accompany him. We risk killing them by bombing Elison. I'm afraid we are required to do this the old-fashioned way."

Tom agreed.

Jackie explained the assignment. "Mohammed Elison takes a twice-monthly trip via camel caravan from his desert hideaway to the Bahariya Oasis to meet and instruct new jihadists. Fifteen miles outside the oasis is a valley lined by short hills and rocky outcroppings – a perfect locale for a shoot. Customarily, an additional business deal supplemented the assignment.

"This deal involves financing for a desalination plant in Egypt, a plant to be built by a Morgan firm. After your last meeting in Cairo we will arrange helicopter service from Cairo International Airport to the shoot and back. You should be well on your way to Rome within an hour of the shot being fired - long before the news reaches anyone. Our friends in Mukhabarat, the Egyptian intelligence agency, will help with the assignment. They have tried to eliminate Elison for years. I believe the mission would be easier if Martin Paxton were away from Cairo. J. Bailey will arrange a meeting for him to be in Rome concurrently with your Cairo meeting. Tell him you will meet him after your meeting. It shouldn't arouse any suspicion. Questions?"

Tom replied, "I'll need to practice the shot; the desert presents certain problems and challenges."

Jackie said, "I agree, you can compare the difficulty of this shot to a long putt on a huge two-tiered green,"

Tom understood the problems a desert shot presents -- strong winds, higher temperatures and the mirage effect all add difficulty to the shot. He needed to practice this shot. New Hampshire won't do. He must find a desert location for practice.

Tom recalled the region near Anthony Wayne's Ranger School. "I need to practice in a similar setting as Egypt. Remember that area around Ord Mountain? We should practice there. The topography resembles an oasis."

"Sounds good. We'll fly to San Bernardino and pick up my jeep."

Two days later, they were in the desert with Tom shooting and Jackie spotting for him -- Jackie maintained the important Ballistics Data Card. They experimented with various guns and cartridges for the shot but settled on the RPA .338 rifle and the .338 Lapua Magnum. Tom chose a Leupold 6.5x20x50 scope, boosted to 14x35.

Aside from the wind, the weather did not significantly affect any of Tom's previous assignments. The desert conditions present significant challenges on this shot.

Hence the Kestral 5500 Weather Meter. The handheld computer can track twenty separate weather parameters, all, of which affects the shot's accuracy. Tom and Jackie experimented with the Kestral and adjusted the sights accordingly. Tom and Jackie experimented with the Kestral and adjusted the sights accordingly.

They practiced for three days while boarding at Jackie's house for the night. They spoke a little about the Martels and Tom ascertained Jay Bailey Morgan III was the man behind the entire effort. The Martels were his idea; his effort and his money made it work. Tom always suspected this but it was good to hear it from Jackie.

****

Kat busied herself preparing for the gallery opening and her move to New York City. She spoke to Tom daily, yearning for the time they will again be together.

Kat established a Skype account when she learned of Tom's trip to Cairo. He already had one.

In two weeks, Kat will return to New York. She had never previously depended on a man, except her father during her early years. Her father raised her a strong, independent woman -- not the faux feminist man-hating virago, a vision of the 1970s women's liberationists, but a confident, feminine woman laboring earnestly to avoid the troublesome territory of the Sista Harpies.

Kat noted she was even more of a woman since she met Tom. Her love wasn't rooted in dependence. On the contrary, she had never felt more free to be herself. She had no fear of intimacy. She had no concern Tom would reject anything he discovered about her. Kat was happy before she met Tom, but her happiness had reached a new plateau where she was content to linger awhile.

She adored his old-fashioned, gallant gentlemanliness, which true women, free from feminist bias, only dream of. Feminists, Kat recognized, betrayed women. They weakened them, which gave a generation of angry women hatred of traditional gentleman, a man who dared to hold a door for them or offer other expressions of honor and respect. Tom, if anything, was a traditional gentleman.

Kat recalled Tom's observation of the male-female relationship: "Women want to admire the men they love, men want to be admired by the women they love." How sacrilegious to today's depraved sensibilities! But Kat appreciated such venerable principles.

Her friends and her boss noticed a change in Kat. Not that Kat previously had serious flaws of her personality or character. She didn't. It was simply that Kat's nature and qualities were enhanced, like saturating a photo with more color -- the same photo, but only more beautiful.

Tom returned to New York to complete plans for Cairo. He convinced Martin Paxton to take the Rome trip for business. It would allow him to go to Cairo alone. By this time, Martin trusted Tom Ford's skills to close a deal on his own and had no problem with the suggestion.

****

Kat's gallery was located on a side street off Worth Avenue in central Palm Beach. Their opening parties were popular with the locals, art lovers and shoppers. The gallery holds two hundred people and another fifty in the back garden. Although a caterer prepared the food, the owner decided to handle the bar in house. Kat took responsibility for the bar.

She purchased ten cases of wine, eight white and two red, which the liquor store delivered a half-hour before the party started. The two bartenders prepared the bar for the oncoming rush.

With the bar preparations completed, Kat had a some time to relax before the doors opened to the public at 5:00 P.M. She tried to call Tom, but he didn't answer. Curious, she thought. Tom is usually in his office at this time, unless he was on a trip, but his flight to Cairo isn't until tomorrow morning.

The first guests arrived promptly at five. Kat worked the room answering questions about the artwork. She enjoyed socializing at these parties, especially when the gallery featured an artist she admired. Today's artist was Dante Moore, perhaps America's finest wildlife artist. He specialized in Everglade's wildlife and scenery, a region Kat was thoroughly familiar, as she had lived her youth on its outskirts.

177

Rachel Lewis approached Kat, "Kat, I don't know how I'll manage when you leave."

"Oh, you'll do fine, Rachel. Rebecca is a good hard worker."

"She is, but she isn't nearly as organized as you."

Rebecca walked up and said, "Kat, here come your customers."

"That's Mr. and Mrs. Dunhill. I invited them last week and told them which artist will be featured at the party. We should soon have our first sale."

Kat walked up to the Dunhills, shook their hands and showed them the art.

At six-thirty, the party hit its crescendo. The sales were brisk. Kat was registering a credit card sale at the desk. Rebecca Latham stood beside her.

Rebecca, ever hunting for her next man, raised her eyebrows and gazed past Kat, "Ooh, my Lord, look at the Greek god who just walked in!" Kat turned to see the object of Rebecca's surprise. Kat bolted toward the man. She seized him in an embrace, forcing her head into his chest. After a few moments she looked up and they kissed.

Kat's performance impressed Rebecca. She wondered, *"Either he is her Tom or Kat is quite the aggressive young lady."*

"What are you doing here?" Kat asked.

"I am taking the roundabout way to Cairo: New York to Miami to Cairo. I'll leave tomorrow morning, if that's all right with you."

"Do you even have to ask?"

Kat introduced Tom around. The party had ended by eight. Her boss told her, "Kat, we'll handle everything from here. Go enjoy your time with Tom."

"Thanks, Mrs. Lewis. I'll finish my work tomorrow."

She led Tom to Worth Ave where they enjoyed a pleasant stroll, arm in arm, past the stores, the Everglades Club and a park by the Palm Beach docks. They sat for hours alongside the hundreds of yachts berthed at the marina.

"Three weeks is far too long for us to be apart. Thanks for coming, Tom."

Tom said, "We must never even consider such a separation again. I couldn't do it. I would miss you too much and try something crazy to be with you."

"Tom Ford try something crazy? Whatever has possessed you?" Kat loved his words.

They held hands, kissed and discussed their future. A cool breeze enveloped them when the wind abruptly shifted. Tom took off his jacket and wrapped it around Kat. They took a taxi to Kat's apartment in West Palm and made love that exceeded the passion they shared in New Hampshire.

****

Tom left early the next morning to catch his flight to Cairo, but he departed the country certain he will share his remaining life with Kathryn St. John.

Well, most of it.

Tom arrived in Cairo fifteen hours later at 3:00 A.M. Cairo time completely refreshed as he spent ten hours sleeping in First Class comfort.

He proceeded to the Four Seasons Hotel where he called Kat to assure her his flight was fine and he had already missed her. She thanked him again for his surprise visit telling him everyone at the gallery vented feigned jealousy of her good fortune to land such a catch.

They expected to see one another in New York City within ten days. Presently, Tom had considerable work in Cairo. He had a business meeting scheduled at 10:00 A.M. and a later dinner with Jackie Brandt to complete plans for the shoot in two days.

JBM Construction Inc., a Top 10 construction company with more than $10 billion annual revenue, sought financing for a water desalinization plant. SBT gave Tom a limit to issue a $100 million loan, but he knew they needed more since the project had expanded to three smaller desalinization plants instead of a single large plant. He called Martin to authorize the loan. Martin, in turn, required Jameson Lorimer's green light for such an appreciable increase.

As expected, the Egyptians asked for a more substantial loan: $250 million – more than double the original request. Tom set the deal. He was aware they encountered no competition here, but Morgan Holdings has been good to Tom, Martin and SBT Worldwide. He had no trouble convincing Martin. Cautious, old-school Jameson considered the risk too great.

"Egypt is hardly the world's most stable country," Lorimer Jameson argued.

Tom retorted, "No it isn't, but Egypt has been in existence for five thousand years. I believe we could give them a shelf life of another five years. Besides, I persuaded JBM to co-sign the loan." After reviewing the information, Jameson gave his authorization for the entire amount. Before long, they completed the deal.

Tom thought of his ex-girlfriend Carol who frequently disparaged his work. "You can do much more with your life than merely earn money. There are plenty of opportunities to do good in the world," she said frequently. Tom believed then, and more so now, that delivering money to the right places -- his job -- will benefit the people of the world than a few altruistic gestures. This latest deal is just another example. Many Egyptians would soon be drinking clean water by his efforts.

JBM Construction gave Tom a tour of the three sites that afternoon from a comfortable EC 155 helicopter. The sites were separated by fifty miles along the northern coast of Egypt along the Mediterranean. These plants will produce economic development, raising millions of Egyptians from poverty. How ironic, he reasoned, that these plants employ Israeli desalinization technology, the world's standard. He also reflected on the irony that he will shortly be flying in a helicopter for a completely different objective.

That day arrived quickly. Jackie informed him of a change of plans during the helicopter trip. "The latest intelligence from their spies in the terrorist cell indicated Mohammed Elison's lieutenant, Khalid Abedi, will travel with the group. The powers that be requested you take the two out," said Jackie. He added, "They seldom travel together for obvious reasons. Let's give their jihadist brothers motivation never to repeat it. Do you foresee a problem shooting two targets?"

Tom replied, "That depends on their reaction to the first shot. Sgt. York shot attacking Germans in WWI by shooting the last soldier of the charge. This way, the guy in front didn't see his comrade fall and continued his charge. At one thousand yards, no one will hear the shot because we'll be using a suppressor. However, they will see the body drop. I will need to hit the second man in line first to give me time to sight and dispatch the other. I can do two targets but you must be sure we have the correct targets."

Jackie said, "Don't worry. I etched those guys' faces into my mind. I know them better than their mothers."

On D-Day Tom met Jackie on the outskirts of Cairo. They drove to a private heliport (surely owned by J. Bailey Morgan III, guessed Tom) to collect their gear. From Cairo they took the half-hour trip to the shooting site. The helicopter dropped them near the hills that would provide cover for the helicopter and the shoot. Jackie's assets estimated the caravan would pass by within two hours of the helicopter's expected landing. Tom and Jackie secured a remote site in the desert and didn't expect any witnesses for the mission. Nevertheless, they wore the traditional Galabeya and kufiya to avoid unwanted attention should they be seen.

The helicopter landed on a rocky but level valley behind the hills they chose for the shoot. The hills, rocky outcrops barely covered with vegetation, were roughly a hundred feet high. Tom and Jackie found a perfect spot to provide ample cover, a great view of the trail the caravan will use and an easy egress for their escape. They had an hour or two before the caravan passed and used the time to calculate and recalculate the shot employing the Kestral 5500 Weather Meter.

They determined that unless the wind shifted they had the shot well sighted.

This pause allowed Tom an opportunity to thank Jackie for his help with Kat's legal problem.

"Jackie, I appreciate the leads you gave me with the media. Kat would be wasting away in prison today but for your help."

Jackie responded, "You are welcome Tom, but you should thank J. Bailey Morgan III. He did most of the work. I contacted Ken Randall, but the others were from Jay."

"What is it with that guy? Have you ever met him?"

"Oh yeah. He is quite the eccentric. You wouldn't forget him. I'll introduce you to him someday."

"I'd like to meet him to thank him for the help he gave Kat, the business leads and the Jaguar."

"Jay Bailey appreciates your efforts for his cause. He also thinks your business skills were a find. He previously used bankers who, and I quote, '… have no fuckin' imagination and are as boring as shit.' His language is colorful and vulgar, regardless to whom he speaks."

"No problem. I've heard all the words but prefer not to use them."

Jackie scoured the horizon with his Swarovski Spotting Scope. He found the camel caravan approaching in the distance. Tom determined the final calculations. He designated a rock by the side of the road to mark the target The actual distance measured 1,134.69 yards to the spot on the road where the caravan will pass when he took the shot. Tom had the magazine loaded with four Lapuas. He hoped to use only two.

The caravan comprising fourteen camels and twelve men advanced. Jackie continued to give a steady stream of wind velocity and direction. "Wind at eight from the north…wind at 11 from NNW…wind back to eight from the north." Tom discounted the mirage effect. He was ready to take the shot. He heard Jackie announce Target #1 (Elison) is number three in line, Target # 2 (Abedi) is number four. That will make it easier. He will first shoot Abedi, then Elison.

Jackie's chant continued…wind at seven NNW…wind at twelve NNW. The caravan reached the stone marker. Tom focused clearly on Abedi. He pulled the trigger. A second later Abedi fell off his camel. A definite kill shot. Tom manipulated the bolt and inserted another round into the breech. He focused his sights on Elison, who wasn't yet aware of his lieutenant's fate. But Elison turned as Tom pulled the trigger. The Lapua hit Elison's shoulder; the force hammered the jihadist to the ground. Tom searched for Elison, exploring the area through the scope. He found Elison flailing in pain behind his camel. Tom didn't have a shot…the animal screened Elison from another shot.

Tom had one chance to finish the mission. He took a shot to move the camel and grazed its ass. The camel bolted forward, giving Tom a clear shot at Elison. He aimed and fired -- his shot hits center chest, an instant conclusion to Elison's terrorist life.

"May the power of Christ compel you," whispered Tom.

"Amen," responded Jackie. He had heard Tom in the now quiet desert.

Tom and Jackie gathered their equipment and ran to the helicopter for their extraction. They were on their way back to Cairo within minutes: Mission accomplished!

****

Kat moved to New York during the Fourth of July weekend. She again booked a room at the Plaza to begin her apartment search. She preferred the Columbus Circle neighborhood, a short walk from the FOXc studios on Avenue of the Americas. She wouldn't admit it, but the apartment was also close to Tom's co-op on Central Park West.

On New York's quiet holiday weekend only a few real estate offices were open, but Kat found a perfect one bedroom with a magnificent southern view of the skyline. She couldn't believe her luck and took it. The agent, a twenty-something recent college graduate, thanked Kat for her courage to fight back against the thug who tried to rape her. Kat, ever gracious, thanked the woman but wondered whether that episode would ever be forgotten.

Kat plunged that Tuesday into her work as an assistant producer for Ted O'Hara. Head producer Roni Levine, her immediate supervisor, initially considered Kat another O'Hara chippy -- hired for the short term like numerous others. Ted had his fun with them and she never saw the girls again.

Kat's first day at FOXc proved a whirlwind of staff meetings and learning the system. The staff members were cordial, or as cordial as possible despite the stress inflicted by the daily deadline of producing an hour live show. The crew impressed her by their smooth coordination of the hectic pace.

Kat didn't see Ted O'Hara until late afternoon. She was fact-checking points of a story in Roni Levine's office. Roni was in the studio working with the teleprompter operator on the script for the opening monologue. O'Hara walked in, clearly familiar with Roni's schedule. He greeted Kat, welcoming her to the crew. Kat thanked him for the opportunity. They were discussing the show when O'Hara approached her and unexpectedly encircled his long arms around her, searching her lips with his.

Kat thought to herself, *"Does this guy know what I did to the last guy who tried something like this? Is he crazy?"*

Without further hesitation, Kat slammed her high heel into O'Hara's instep. He released her, suffering intense pain from her strike. She stepped back, grabbed his arm as he reached for his wounded foot. With a quashing motion Kat secured a hammerlock on her assailant.

She bent his hand against his forearm, thrust her left foot behind his leg, simultaneously pushing him and crashing her tall boss to the floor, his free arm preventing a broken nose or worse.

Kat shouted into his ear, "Is this how you greet your new employees?"

"Please let go. I'm sorry." Ted O'Hara realized his mistake dealing this forthrightly with Kat St. John.

Kat let go. He stood, lifted his injured foot to the desktop, nursing it to relieve the pain.

Kat defiantly stepped back, "So, I guess I'm fired."

O'Hara laughed, "Of course not. I was a pig and got what I deserved. How did you do that? I didn't see it coming."

Kat looked at him with hands now on hips, "Boxers say that about the knockout punch they received – they never saw it coming."

"Well, you're remarkable. Now I know what Griffin felt during those last seconds of his life."

Kat laughed, "For some reason, I feel merciful today. I'll let you live."

O'Hara laughed. He offered his hand, "Friends?"

She took his hand saying, "Friends…so long as you learned your lesson."

"Oh, I learned my lesson, all right."

Kat forgave him. She wanted the job. Besides, he helped with the DA encounter and she was confident she could repeat her disciplinary lesson on O'Hara…if needed.

O'Hara kept his word. He treated her respectfully throughout the next months. They developed an excellent working relationship. Soon after, Kat was promoted to associate producer. She assumed many on-air assignments to provide depth to stories she researched. O'Hara proved correct with his initial notion: Kat St. John gave his ratings a substantial boost.

At this time O'Hara asked her to investigate the recent strange assassinations of Muslim terrorist leaders. These differed from customary Muslim killings. These terrorists were killed by a long-range sniper, shooting a sophisticated rifle — not by the traditional scimitar.

Kat investigated these assassinations. Aided by an anonymous source at the NSA (her father's friend), Kat discovered rumors of suspected rogue elements in the intelligence community. Her source didn't reveal much beyond a rumor but suggested military, intelligence and law enforcement constituents were all elements of the conspiracy.

Each victim led a powerful Islamic terrorist organization and was killed by a long distance rifle shot. That is all anyone knows. Thus far, Kat found no suspects or leads in any of the shootings. Apparently, a mysterious ghost shooter took the shots. Kat generated a chart of the six assassinations during the last three years: The first, London 2012, Paris 2012, Berlin and London 2013, Detroit 2014 and finally Egypt, outside Cairo, three months ago.

A momentary panic assailed her. Her face flushed with fear and apprehension. She checked the timeline in her daybook: Tom was in Cairo for the latest shooting. She remembered his uncanny marksmanship -- shooting the cork off a bottle at five hundred yards. The evidence depressed Kat. Tom couldn't be a killer, she didn't believe it. He was an investment banker from New Hampshire. He never served in the military; except for the Ranger training he took. However, there was no connection to the military at that school. These were guys pretending to be soldiers - like fantasy baseball camps where you could play against ex-major leaguers for a fee. Tom can't be the shooter!

Nevertheless, she had to find the truth. Kat needed additional evidence before she proved Tom's involvement. She developed a plan. She would visit Tom that night, as she had almost every night for the last few months. His passport should render some clues. She had seen it on his home office desk and would search for it when possible -- away from Tom's scrutiny. Tom will be cooking dinner requiring him to spend considerable time in the kitchen. Tom usually turned the television off when he had guests, but he gave exception to the Ted O'Hara Show. Kat will hunt for the passport when Tom worked in the kitchen and Ted was on the TV.

She told Tom of her latest assignment for O'Hara. She hoped to elicit an unusual response to detect any involvement from his part. However, he remained as calm...or utterly innocent of her suspicions. She mentioned nothing about the timeline she found or her apprehension of his involvement, but kept the conversation to generalities. She changed the subject when it became clear Tom was not confessing to murdering seven men.

After dinner, Tom ambled to the kitchen, placed the dishes in the dishwasher to re-established the order from the chaos created by his cooking. Kat knew these chores generally took about five minutes. She turned on the television and found Ted's show. He finished his monologue, "...doubtless Ronald Trumbull fully intended to enter the presidential sweepstakes. He lacks political experience but certainly has name recognition. The odds are against him but he..."

Kat raised the volume slightly, leaving the room for Tom's office just feet away. She found his passport inside the top desk drawer, opened it to the full pages of stamps. She took out her iPhone and noticed the bedroom door still open. She quietly closed it not wanting the flash to alert Tom. Kat took photos of the seven pages and placed the passport exactly where she found it.

Kat left Tom's office with time to spare. He continued to work in the kitchen. Ted O'Hara interviewed a college professor who argued that all claims of Muslim terrorism were a right-wing plot to smear a great religion. Ted had no trouble humiliating the man. Good television, but Kat wondered whether he needed to embarrass such a moonbat on national television. She thought, *"Why not, it was good television."*

Kat, impatient to examine her new evidence, lied to Tom and told him she felt ill and had to go home. Kat hated the deceit – they had been completely honest with the other until now. Or had they? Kat had to know. Tom looked disappointed but showed concern. At that moment, nothing else mattered to Kat. Kat hastened a return to her apartment. Frantic, she downloaded the photos onto her computer. She took out her chart to compare the passport stamps with the dates of the shootings. Her alarm instantly overwhelmed her. A wave of distress and nausea punched her stomach. Her face flushed, the evidence told her a story she dreaded to contemplate -- Tom is a killer!

She again compared the passport data to the shooting dates.
London 2011: check
Paris 2012: check

Berlin 2013: check
London 2013: check
Detroit 2014: N/A
Cairo, Egypt: check

Tom clearly was the shooter! Her entire world turned upside down. The man she loved and trusted is a killer. The man to whom she committed her love betrayed her.

Nothing else mattered. Kat had to confront Tom about her evidence.

Now!

She ran from her apartment with her iPhone and hurried to Tom's apartment. He was still awake and surprised by her return. "Kat, feeling better now?"

"No. Take a look."

She opened her iPhone to show Tom her chart and the stamps. "We have far too many coincidences here. What is your explanation for this? Did you shoot these men? I want the absolute truth from you."

A protracted chilled moment passed between them. Tom turned around and headed to his bar. He calmly poured a couple of single malts into his Glencairn Scotch glasses, handing one to Kat.

"Kat, please sit down."

Tom realized she had discovered his secret. He looked at her obvious distress weighing his options. He promised Jackie he would tell nobody about his activities, except his parents. Four years since his first hit and he kept his word. The Martels had been extraordinarily successful lately, mainly by the complete dedication its members had for the cause -- there has never been a breach of secrecy by anyone. Tom Ford also embraced the Martel cause and took internal pride in all he had done for them. The lives he took by his marksmanship saved countless innocent lives. Conversely, he would do anything for the woman he loved. She was his life and he believed he was hers. His love for her led to an easy decision.

"Here's the story, Kat."

Tom iterated his meeting Jackie Brandt at the Ranger school, his later Israel meeting with Jackie and Reuven Berman, Jackie recruiting him in New York and Tom's tour of the DIA's facility. Tom described each assignment in detail, plus the deals arranged with J. Bailey Morgan's companies. Tom even told her about shooting the Lattimore brothers and the Jaguar appearing in his parent's driveway one morning. But more importantly, he explained his justification for the shootings.

Tom's revelations astounded Kat.

"We have a situation around the world where Islamic splinter groups wouldn't stop with anything less than the complete destruction of our civilization and everyone in it. These Muslims embrace their faith, but reject reason.

They want to destroy us and don't play by any rules. The West struggles to defend itself but adheres to the Marquess of Queensbury Rules – policies ineffective against terrorists."

Tom continued, "Furthermore, our governments are not only complacent about their duties to protect their citizens, they now assist the jihadist efforts. These open borders in Europe and the U.S. are a godsend to them. They recruit eager followers with no government interference. Numerous countries have legislated hate speech laws to expunge any mention of Islam from the growing terrorist threat. You know it's all true. You researched it for Ted O'Hara when you produced a show on our president who even feared mentioning the words "radical Islamic terrorism.""

Kat nodded, "Yes, I remember."

"Kat, I have been doing to terrorists what you did to Bill Griffin. You protected your life by a well-placed shot to his head. I do the same to protect our country and its people from the jihadists' murderous plans. We shoot the leaders, the brains of the organization. The intelligence is clear: these groups are in disarray after the shooting. Yes, the target can be replaced but not by someone as experienced and competent. Bottom line: their efforts are crippled and we save innocent lives."

Kat looked at Tom, her distress softened by his persuasive explanation. Her emotions abruptly flowed in the opposite direction, like tidewater after a high tide.

Tom took her hand, "What do you want to do now that you found your boyfriend is a killer?"

"I don't know."

Kat grabbed her bag and stormed out the door. She walked from Tom's building and turned onto Columbus Ave. After a long walk she stepped into a bar and took a seat. The pub was virtually empty, permitting the bartender to quickly greet her.

"What would you like?"

Kat responded, "Double Bulleit, neat."

The bartender placed a rocks glass in front of her on a napkin, reached behind for a bottle and poured her the drink. Kat immediately took a long swig and started crying.

The bartender walked over, "Are you all right, ma'am?"

"I will be. Please give me another."

The bartender poured another double and walked away. He knew when a customer wanted to be left alone. Kat stared at her image reflected in the back bar mirror as she sipped her drink. She observed a woman who needed to decide about her life-changing quandary. She looked down at the bar and pondered her predicament.

Within minutes, she finished the drink, paid the bill and walked from the bar.

Soon, she found her way back to Tom's building and knocking on Tom's door.

Her emotions stabilized, her thinking clear, Kat found the answer to Tom's last question. She was Mike St. John's daughter and she had one choice. Kat wrapped her arms around him when he opened the door. She looked straight into his eyes, "I want to join you."

Kat's words shocked Tom.

He proclaimed, "Impossible. I work by myself."

Kat replied, "Those days are over, buster, if you want to keep me around."

Tom's initial surprise by Kat's aspiration turned to understanding. Kat was, raised by her father, a father she adored and idolized. He also proudly fought hard for his country and taught her to respect guns and appreciate their effectiveness in equating power differences among nations and people. Kat understood the global terrorism problem and the seemingly endless murder of innocents. Most importantly, she had protected herself from death by killing her attacker with a gun. Kat was an excellent marksman.

He pulled Kat to his lap. Kat enfolded Tom in her arms. "I am serious, Tom. I want to volunteer for your group, whatever it may be. Originally, I was shocked when I discovered your secret, but you make sense. We must do something about terrorism and murders threatening the world. The governments dragged their feet doing their duty. I'd be dead today if I didn't struggle to protect myself against Griffin. I envision these barbarians ravaging our society and way of life, creating a river of blood with their efforts. My father volunteered to fight for his country. I can do the same. Besides, do you think I'd willingly trade my miniskirt for a burka?"

Tom knew he had lost the argument. He also knew she will be an excellent partner on these assignments. She shoots exceptionally well, is in tremendous physical condition, meticulous about her work, and killed her attacker in self-defense. She didn't panic or freeze – she did all she had to do to survive. Kat will be the perfect partner.

Tom's arm around her waist tightened ever so slightly. Gee, you are persuasive. O.K. I'll talk to Jackie Brandt. That is, if he doesn't kill me for telling you about the group."

Kat laughed, "Well, maybe he'll just take back the Jaguar."

Tom returned her laugh, "Anything but that!"

Kat pulled herself closer to Tom. She kissed him harder than she had ever before. They fell off the couch; their subsequent lovemaking reflected the passion they had for the objectives and danger they will soon confront.

Chapter 10: *Koranland*

The next morning, Tom caught the shuttle to Washington. He'd scheduled a midday lunch with Jackie at the Old Ebbit Grille after deciding they needed to talk about Kat's recruiting in person. Tom was apprehensive of talking to Jackie about Kat. On the one hand, he betrayed his friend, but he had a woman he loved who discovered his secret. Furthermore, she wanted to join him on these assignments. What a predicament.

Jackie handled the news unexpectedly well after Tom explained his dilemma.

"Tom, I trust your judgment. You were stuck in the corner with no options. Kat discovered your secret, but you kept her in your camp. Quite an accomplishment. Imagine if she became furious with you? Considering her position on O'Hara's show the Martels could have been all over the country by tonight. No, you did well."

Jackie added, "Besides, you'll need a partner for your next assignment and I prefer to keep my distance on this one."

Tom's interest piqued, "It must be a killer. No pun intended."

"Yes, your next mission will, indeed, be different. We have highly reliable intelligence that ISIS is planning a massive suicide bomber attack on New York City. These bombers will target dozens of tourist sites on a Friday night. Lincoln Center, Broadway plays, Madison Square Garden and other targets will become victims of these psychos. Thousands will die, many more injured."

Jackie pulled a New York State road map from his pocket and opened it. He pointed to Tom's new target, "Koranland is a Muslim retreat in upstate New York and has been a legitimate retreat for 30 years. It is located deep in the woods near small remote communities. There is a minimum police presence. The owners have an excellent reputation in the community and cultivated many friends. However, a Sheikh Ali Al-Badawi recently seized control of the commune. His resources from the Muslim Brotherhood and Hamas backed by the brutality of ISIS persuaded the Koranland residents to buckle to the radical's demands."

"We noticed peculiar activity on the premises. Satellite photos, bolstered by drones and on-the-ground informants, have indicated they are training men in more than the Koran. Our investigation has revealed that they assemble suicide vests in a barn on the property. The local police won't touch it, the state troopers won't touch it and the feds won't touch it. Whether political correctness or friends in the governor's office, we can't persuade anyone to investigate. The FBI strives to avoid the appearance of scrutinizing Muslim organizations too closely and infringing their religious freedom. Furthermore, despite overwhelming proof, Hillary Clinton's State Department declined to label Al-Badawi a terrorist. And, of course, our historic president is worthless fighting such terrorism."

Tom asked, "So this is a job for Superman?"

Jackie gave a serious smile, "...or Superman and Supergirl, as the case may be. Have you ever shot a grenade launcher?"

"Only at the Ranger school."

"Well, you need to become an expert with the grenade launcher. I'll give you a launcher for practice with some practice rounds. You'll employ an M203 grenade launcher on an M16. You will be required to shoot an incendiary grenade through a barn window. The grenade should ignite the Semtex explosives we suspect are in the barn. You will end their plans for jihad against thousands of innocents. A well-placed round should blow the place like Hiroshima. The explosion should also alert the locals and persuade them to investigate Koranland.

"The problem is that these launchers have an effective 150 yard range max. You should take the shot at around 100 yards to increase the probability of success. Naturally, this increases the danger of detection and capture. You won't benefit from your usual long-distance shot that gives you time for escape. This is why you will need someone to ride shotgun – to cover your back when you launch the grenade and help your escape. I guess you'll partner with Kat. We should do this in three weeks, a few days before their planned attack. One more thing: Don't shoot the guy with the bright orange Miami Dolphin hat if you see him – he's on our team. I will visit you in Orford to train you with the M203 and to finalize our plans."

Jackie's serious military face melted, replaced by his usual smiling countenance, "So when will you marry Kat?"

****

Tom returned to his office by 4:00 P.M. He called Kat. "You are on. Jackie had no problem with you. I will tell you about the mission tonight."

Tom had already started his research on Google Earth. He found Koranland in the Adirondack Mountains. He also noticed a stone wall winding its way through the woods where it passed approximately 100 yards from the barn. Perfect! He will launch the grenade from behind the wall. He would access the old logging road from the main highway. They needed to hike three miles to reach the target.

Tom told Kat about the plans at dinner. They intended to visit Orford that weekend as it was "leaf-peeping" season in northern New England. Amelia Briggs Ford also hosted her annual antique show benefit at the commodious town barn which doubles as a party space.

The proceeds were given to New Hampshire or Vermont soldiers, sailors or airmen who were seriously wounded in the recent Middle East wars. Each received a $10,000 gift to spend as they pleased. She had raised more than $250,000 annually, aided by a donation from the Briggs Family Foundation. Antique dealers from New England and New York attended to purchase the donated treasures found at the show. Tom and Kat volunteered to help organize the Friday night sale. Tom donated a Russian icon he purchased in Moscow. Kat gave Amelia one of her grandfather's paintings (with her father's blessing when he learned of the benefit).

Tom added another activity to the weekend's schedule: Jackie Brandt's visit with equipment for the Koranland assignment. Tom had considerable work to do before Jackie arrived later Saturday morning. He found a rusted 4' X 8' piece of quarter-inch plate left over from their gun safe project in the barn. He cut a 24" x 24" hole in the plate's center with an acetylene torch. He hauled the target to the 100-yard range with the Kubota. Now, he had his target window.

Jackie arrived at eleven bearing a vanload of goodies for the Koranland hit. He brought a hundred rounds of 40 X 46mm TP Training Rounds, also called chalk rounds for the orange chalk that dispersed when hitting the ground. Jackie included a pair of incendiary grenades among his inventory, white phosphorus rounds, painted red, for use on the barn.

"Don't be caught with these, ATF won't like you," Jackie joked. He continued adding further descriptions, "These two red-painted grenades are the only two in existence. Don't lose them. They splatter hot phosphorus in all directions; no metals are in the grenade, nor any markers or taggants. A fire and explosion should eliminate all traces of the grenade."

Tom looked confused, "I understand Semtex requires high heat and a powerful shockwave to detonate it. Will this grenade initiate detonation?"

Jackie Brandt replied, "Our brilliant technicians specifically designed this grenade to detonate Semtex. Hundreds of superhot magnesium pellets will be propelled at high speed into their explosives stockpile. We only need one pellet to ignite the Semtex."

Tom nodded. Jackie's explanation satisfied him.

Jackie instructed Tom and Kat about the launcher's proper operation. Tom had experience with it, Kat, of course, hadn't. Jackie thought that Kat must learn to operate the launcher -- should Tom be disabled before the mission is completed. They agreed. "It's crucial that you shoot the grenade through the window. These grenades won't penetrate barn boards. I like the target you built; it's perfect for our purposes. Operating the grenade launcher differs from shooting a rifle. You lob the grenade, similar to a forward pass -- think of Drew Brees throwing a 50-yard pass downfield."

Jackie adjusted the sight to one hundred yards, loaded the grenade and fired. A pop launched the round to the target. Because the grenade was a low-velocity round it maintained visibility as it zoomed along its path. The dummy grenade plunged through the iron cutout leaving an orange dust cloud behind the plate.

"That looks easy," Tom stated. He took the launcher. He took careful aim, pulled the trigger, but the round fell 10 feet short to the left. Kat laughed, "He may have been born with a rifle in his hand but our boy has a brand new toy he can't handle."

Quiet girl," Tom replied.

Kat stood at attention, "Sir, yes sir!"

Tom tried again. The shot hit the plate about a foot to the right of the open window. Five attempts later he still didn't breach the window.

Kat taunted him for his unaccustomed lack of marksmanship. He looked back at her and handed her the launcher. "Here, you try." Jackie gave her some quick pointers and she took aim. Her first attempt landed two feet to the right of the window. She reloaded, took aim and fired again: Bull's-eye - - right through the window. Kat placed three of her five shots through the window. She beamed, handing the launcher back to Jackie.

Jackie held the launcher pointing to the gunsight, "Tom, here's the problem. You are overthinking the shot. This isn't a thousand-yard desert shot that presents dozens of factors to gauge for an accurate shot. Here, you are a hundred yards away; let the sight do your work. Compensate for windage but not much more. Here, try again."

Tom took the launcher from Jackie, reloaded, aimed and pulled the trigger. Finally, he found his target and continued through the next four. He looked back at Kat and Jackie and grinned, "I think I got it."

He took five more, hitting them all.

Jackie nodded his approval. He opened the equipment bag to take out another launcher. "I pulled a few strings to secure this for you -- the H & K M320." Jackie displayed the launcher, "This is an upgrade from the M203 that you now are expert. H & K M320 is a standalone that doesn't need to be mounted on a rifle. It's also small and lightweight -- perfect for the hike to your target. Give it a try."

He gave Tom and Kat a quick lesson in the launcher and handed it to Tom. Tom loaded and aimed: straight through the window.

Tom offered his critique of the launcher, "I prefer the H & K to the M203. The flip-up sites provide a finer view of the target. The round has greater acceleration, giving a far more accurate shot and the forward grip helps stabilize the launcher" He launched ten more chalk grenades, breaching the target every time.

Jackie took out a rifle from the bag. "This is the M4, similar to the M16, but can hold a 30 round magazine. It also has a Picatinny rail system to accept a scope. I'll install it for you later. You could practice with it later. I'll leave you plenty of ammo."

"We'll give the M16 to Kat for the mission." Jackie looked at Kat, "Have you ever fired an M-16 rifle, Kat?"

"I am thoroughly familiar with the gun. My father kept his M-16A1 from Vietnam. When the Army asked him to return it, he preceded Charlton Heston by twenty years roaring a resolute 'From my cold, dead hands.' I guess they didn't want to challenge one of the few heroes at the time so they let him keep it."

Tom quipped, "They probably couldn't find any volunteers to take it from him."

Jackie laughed, "Knowing the Army as I do you are probably right."

He took several magazines of 5.56 NATO rounds from the bag. "Here, let's see you shoot, Kat. He handed the gun to her.

Kat gripped the rifle, deftly snapped in a magazine. She set the selector to semiauto and commenced firing at the various targets at the 100-yard range. She had no trouble hitting them all. Jackie smiled and remarked, "Tom, you recruited a great partner here."

The van also held several American Woodland Battle Dress Uniforms or BDUs.

"These are perfect for the conditions you will operate in -- here are two camouflage kits. Tom, do you recall that lesson at Camp? Well, you can teach Kat how to paint her face."

Kat said, "Don't worry about me guys; I've been using makeup for years, far longer than you two...I hope."

Finally, Jackie pulled out a couple of Multicam chest rigs , extra ammo, pistols, the two incendiary grenades and other gear for the mission.

Tom and Kat practiced with their new toys for the rest of the afternoon. Jackie was confident his new team had the skills to complete the mission. At 3:00 P.M. he told his students he had to leave to meet his son in Boston.

"Oh, by the way, my son, Todd, who you have met, will drive you to Koranland. He has access to a Toyota Land Cruiser."

After saying goodbye to Jackie, Tom and Kat visited Amelia's charity auction and antique show.

The booths of the one hundred antique and art dealers, plus a sizable public, packed the extensive barn as customary on the Saturday afternoon of that weekend. They found Amelia and Dr. Ford manning the silent auction table set in the center of the barn. Amelia warmly greeted Kat, "Kat, thank you for your generous donation. The painting is the hit of the show. The bids already exceed $100,000!"

Kat could never have imagined the painting's high value, but appreciated the benefits the money will give the veterans.

"Where did you find such a painting?"

Kat, aware of Mrs. Ford's proper upbringing, couldn't possibly tell her about her bootlegging grandfather and his WWII businesses. She replied, "The painting has been in the family awhile...long before I was born. My father gladly donated it when I told him about your charity. I'm delighted it will benefit the vets."

"Kat, you must give me your father's address. I'll send him a thank you card plus a charitable donation receipt from our organization."

Later, Tom told Kat she gave the perfect PR and lawyerly response. Kat said, "I guess I listened to these politicians at work too long. Besides, what would your mother think of my family if I divulged that grandpa bootlegged cigarettes and worked with the Mafia during the war?"

Tom agreed, "I see your point. Grandpa St. John would be a tough one to explain to a proper old Yankee like mom."

****

With two weeks remaining until the shoot Tom continued planning the mission's details. He evaluated every scenario that could go wrong and the viable remedies to maintain the objective. He had to...he was no longer responsible for his life; he now had Kat to protect.

They spent another day practicing the following weekend in Orford, mainly shooting the remaining practice grenades. Kat also practiced with the M-16. She had no problem hitting wine bottles at a hundred yards. Her shooting impressed Tom, his confidence in his new partner validated.

That Sunday, six days until the shoot, they took a drive to Koranland on the way to the city. It was rainy, damp and dreary. Tom installed the hardtop. He intended to check the logging road to determine whether it was still passable as indicated on Google Maps, which frequently displayed years-old photos. To his relief, he found the vegetation had grown since Google took the photos, but not enough undergrowth the Toyota Land Cruiser couldn't handle. The road was passable to the Koranland property border. That left Tom and Kat with a manageable three-mile hike to their target.

Tom drove to the entrance. The sign at the top of the long driveway looked welcoming. The compound appeared like a typical summer camp for kids -- a peaceful, innocuous-looking hamlet in the Adirondacks. They surveyed the driveway and noticed three well-armed guards standing at a small guardhouse a hundred yards from the entrance.

Tom said, "Friendly looking crew aren't they?"

Kat replied, "They don't look much like the local Welcome Wagon."

Tom said, "Next week, we will change the way the world regards Koranland."

The week flew by. Kat convinced O'Hara that, "…after serious investigation I determined nothing unusual regarding these deaths. These are nasty guys with plenty of enemies, especially within their camp. Chances are their people murdered them." O'Hara bought Kat's explanation and never mentioned the story again.

Tom continued to research the mission. He visited the NY Public Library, found topographical maps of the Koranland property and discovered the stone wall on a plateau 15 feet higher than is the barn. He would need to slightly change the grenade launcher's elevation. Otherwise, he saw no other obstacles.

The following week J. Bailey Morgan III made front-page news. His Gulfstream G5 crashed somewhere in the Atlantic between Bermuda and the Bahamas – the Bermuda Triangle. The plane instantly dropped off the radar. Coast Guard helicopters found debris from the jet. A Coast Guard cutter later recovered debris from the plane off South Carolina. They found no bodies. Morgan, and his pilot, Anthony Michael, were presumed dead.

The news shocked Tom. He immediately called Jackie. Yes, Jackie heard about the accident and had already spoken to Morgan's children, who were now managing the company. They were also well acquainted with Martel's activities and foresaw no changes regarding the Morgans' support of the cause.

Tom commented, "I regret never meeting Morgan, he sounded quite the maverick."

Jackie replied, "He certainly was. He would have enjoyed meeting you... and Kat. He always had an eye for the ladies. I read he had six wives throughout the years, each rather crazy in her own way. I am amazed that his two children are so well grounded."

Tom asked, "Can I assume plans won't change for the weekend?"

"No change in plans, whatsoever. Good luck. Call me with the dedicated phone when you are finished."

After the call, Tom wondered whether Morgan's death would have any impact on the Martels. He ended his musings by filing this concern for future consideration. He had a job on Saturday that demanded his full concentration.

Tom and Kat traveled to Orford, NH on Friday night for a Doubravka wonderful supper with his parents. They retired early that night; Todd Brandt will pick them up at 6:00 A.M. Their packed bags stood by the bed as their plans included a week's trip to Palm Beach after the assignment. Tom planned several business meetings with investors that week in nearby Hobe Sound. By now, Kat had O'Hara under her complete control and persuaded him to send her to Florida to research a story about illegal aliens and the Miami gangs. Tom and Kat reasoned it would be advantageous to be far from Koranland when the fallout from the explosion hit the media wires.

Todd arrived at six; they loaded the gear and headed west. Tom estimated the drive time to Koranland at three hours. The weather reminded him of his London hit, a light misty rain fell, the clouds were low. A light fog covered northern New England. The skies were dark, foreboding of even worse weather. It was a gloomy day for a mission...all Tom could ask for.

During the trip, Tom, Kat and Todd discussed J. Bailey Morgan's death. Todd mentioned he sometimes visited Morgan with his father and liked the man " –he had a potty mouth but was incredibly cordial and genuinely interested in the person he talked to. Morgan had an opinion about everything. He craved debate, but never became disagreeable with expressing his opinion. He challenged your opinions with his encyclopedic knowledge, but, generally, an all-around good guy."

Todd paused, "My father and Morgan were very close."

Tom and Kat discussed the plans again, thinking of possible complications or obstacles. Tom thought of a palpable concern. "Our goal is to frame the explosion to look like an accident. Have you ever heard about the Greenwich Village townhouse explosion forty years ago?"

Kat responded, "Yes, my father told me the story. According to dad, some hippy radicals blew themselves up making bombs."

"That's right. Members of the Weathermen, a radical SDS offshoot, assembled numerous dynamite and nail bombs. They planned to bring the war home and detonate their bombs at a Fort Dix Army base dance for returning Vietnam soldiers. Fortunately, the bombs detonated in the townhouse, killing three of the radicals. The enormous explosion obliterated the bomb makers' bodies and the entire front façade of the building blew onto West Eleventh Street in Greenwich Village. They identified one of the radicals by a finger – the only body part they found."

Kat replied, "I didn't know the story's details. Thank God they killed themselves by their incompetence."

"So the objective here is to prevent anyone from escaping the barn. We want no witnesses of the incendiary grenade bouncing inside the barn. The explosion should appear to be an accident. Kat, I want you to eliminate that particular problem."

"I understand. Any escapee from the barn will meet Mr. M16. I'll give a lead greeting to any escaping jihadist."

"Good. Oh, one more thing. Don't shoot the guy wearing an orange Miami Dolphin cap. Todd's father would be annoyed – he is a DIA asset. I assume you know what a Miami Dolphins cap looks like, having lived there for a while."

"Of course. I'm a big Dolphins fan. My father still has season tickets though I haven't been to a game for a few years. As a young girl I had a crush on Dan Marino – his poster still hangs on my bedroom wall."

"I guess that establishes your bona fides as a Dolphins fan."

They shortly found themselves in the vicinity of Koranland. Tom pointed to the logging road and Todd took the turn. He shifted the vehicle into Four-Wheel Drive to proceed over the rough road that previously accommodated a skidder. They arrived at a dead-end twenty minutes later – an old stone wall that marked the property's boundary.

Tom and Kat exited the vehicle to change into the BDUs and chest rigs. Kat packed her extra magazines into the pouches on the rig and a Ka-Bar into the shoulder loop designed for the wide blade. Tom did the same, adding his 9mm Beretta M9 to a holster on his right hip. Each of them meticulously applied the camo makeup to their faces, carefully painting their nose, chin and cheeks a darker shade than are their eyes and forehead.

Tom conducted a final inventory. "It looks like we didn't forget anything. Do you have your tolerance bracelet?"

"What is a tolerance bracelet?" asked Kat giving Tom a quizzical gaze.

"It's a bracelet that expresses one's inclusiveness preference -- a must for all virtuous social justice warriors. My bracelet is an anti-bullying awareness bracelet."

"You are kidding, aren't you?"

"Yes!"

Tom scrutinized Kat, his warrior girl, "You make a tempting soldier."

He wrapped his arms around her waist. They kissed hard and long. Kat pushed him away. "Let's go to work before I forget why I am here."

"You're right," said Tom.

Tom walked to Todd, "You should turn the Cruiser around so we can quickly getaway if necessary. I saw a turnoff a hundred yards down the road. We should be back by noon. I doubt anyone will see you here, but should you see someone tell them you were sleeping it off away from the main road. However, get out fast if you see anyone looking like Mohammed Atta running at you with a crazed look in his eyes."

Todd gave Tom a half laugh, "Will do. Good luck."

Tom and Kat snatched the M320 and M-16 from the vehicle, vaulted over the stone wall, and hiked their way to the barn. Tom found the woods consisted mainly of red spruce. Their needles produce an acidic soil that discourages undergrowth, making for a bramble-free easier hike. They had left Todd at 9:30 A.M. -- Tom aimed to be on the Interstate, mission accomplished, by one.

The couple hiked through the woods. Kat asked, "Do you think they patrol the property?"

"I doubt it. According to Jackie's intelligence they don't have the staffing to patrol such an extensive property. The police leave them alone and they have more than two thousand acres to cover. It's unlikely we will come across anyone."

"Are you nervous, Kat?"

"Not with you in the lead."

"You have that much confidence in me?"

"No, with you in front of me I realize you will draw the bullet if a sniper is ahead of us. Remember the Japanese couples after the war? The man had his wife walk in front of him when mines were reported in the area. Besides, I am holding the M16 with a 30 round magazine."

"Very funny."

They hiked through the woods for another hour and spotted the old red barn in the distance. Tom spotted the stone wall and motioned to Kat. They followed the wall to the barn and stopped at a spot a hundred yards from the barn. He noticed the barn window was considerably larger than his 2' X 2' practice window. Tom appreciated the larger target.

Tom and Kat settled behind the stone wall. They inserted their NRR foam earplugs, anticipating a deafening explosion. Kat took out the rangefinder and found the distance to be one hundred and five yards. Tom observed substantial activity in the barn through the binoculars -- perhaps a dozen men working inside. Tom adjusted the sights and compensated for the fifteen-foot decline in topography. He detected no wind. Kat scanned the barn with her scope, but she observed no one outside. Nor did she see anyone along the path leading to the barn. Kat aimed her rifle at the front door looking for any movement. Tom took a red-tipped grenade from its pouch and fitted it onto the launcher.

"Let's hope we won't need the second grenade," he whispered.

"Are you ready?"

Kat nodded affirmatively.

Tom took careful aim at the window. He pulled the trigger and a light pop propelled the grenade to the window. The grenade crashed through taking countless glass shards with it to the floor.

The jihadi bomb makers were initially surprised by the grenade. Then they detected the sparks. One man tried to pick it up and throw it out the window. The intense heat of the grenade forced him to immediately drop it. His fellow jihadists panicked and ran for the doors. The DIA asset with the Dolphins cap had purposely stationed himself near the door, knowing the grenade coming.

Tom counted, one, two, three -- already the first man crashed through the door. Jackie's asset. A second followed, close behind.

Kat recognized the bright orange Dolphin hat on the first man and focused her efforts to the second man. She caught the bomb maker in her sight and dropped him ten feet from the door with a perfect chest shot. Jackie's asset continued to run from the barn, but the men inside stopped their efforts to escape.

Kat had no remorse or guilt concerning her kill. She did everything she had to do. She volunteered for the mission knowing full well she could likely shoot and kill someone. Like her shooting Griffin, she considered it justified and essential for the mission's success.

Fearing the first grenade was a dud, Tom reached for the second. As he reached into the bag he caught a dazzling flash of light from inside the broken window. A split second later, the barn expanded like an inflating balloon. Then it happened. The barn exploded into a massive potpourri of wood, glass, body parts and considerable other miscellaneous debris in all directions. Tom and Kat gazed at the shockwave from the explosion heading their way.

Kat screamed, "Holy Shit!"

"Duck," Tom yelled over the din of the explosion.

They ducked and huddled tightly behind the stone wall as the high heat and blast from the explosion passed overhead.

The explosion quickly spent its energy but within seconds thousands of tiny ball bearings, the size of No. 1 shot, pummeled them as the steel balls filtered through the trees. Tom shielded Kat with his body, protecting his head with his arms. Tom looked around when the iron stopped raining. He gathered a handfuls of pellets for evidence. "Jackie will appreciate seeing these. Can you imagine setting those bombs at a Knicks game or the Metropolitan Opera? They would have killed or injured thousands."

Kat said, "Now I understand why you joined the Martels, those nuts packed enough TNT into that barn to create incredible havoc on our city. We stopped the barbarians at their gate."

They patrolled the grounds removing any evidence of their occupation. and embarked on their return trek, satisfied they left nothing behind.

"Let's get the hell out of here, Kat."

Kat gave a girlish giggle as she took his arm, "Tom Ford said 'Hell!'"

He looked at her with feigned annoyance, "Are you finished?"

Kat gave him a coy smile that he loved.

They jogged through the woods back to the Cruiser in under twenty minutes. Todd had turned the car around, leaving the engine running. Tom and Kat tumbled into the vehicle. Todd looked at the two panting bodies in the back seat, "I heard your handiwork. That was an incredible explosion. They must have had a ton of explosives in that barn. Dad will be glad to hear the news."

Kat replied, "Quite the explosion. Far greater than I imagined it would be."

Todd drove off in a hurry.

Tom called Jackie when he had cell phone reception. "Mission accomplished. Jay Bailey would have been satisfied with the results." They stopped on a bridge above a raging river and Tom tossed the phone into the water. "The phone should eventually find its way to the bottom of the Atlantic judging by the speed of those rapids."

Todd dropped them off at Westchester Airport where Morgan's G-7 awaited them for the planned flight to Palm Beach, Florida. They arrived on time for their flight.

For the next few weeks it became apparent Tom and Kat completed a perfect mission. Newspapers reported ATF, Fire Department arson investigators and the FBI found the explosion an accident caused by faulty handling of explosives during the assembly of the bombs. Roughly 24 suicide vests and the remains of twelve bodies were found amidst the rubble.

Kat's target was found partially burned and riddled with ball bearings. Fortunately, the bullet passed through the mangled body. No one ever questioned the true cause of his death.

The authorities closed Koranland and the leaders absconded. They arrested dozens of residents for harboring terrorists, possessing illegal weapons and other charges. The explosion was enormous and the resultant fire so hot they discovered no remains of Tom's special incendiary. The blast created a crater large enough to indicate a cache of more than two hundred pounds of Semtex explosives stored in the barn. According to all investigators, the explosives, coupled with the ball bearings, would have been catastrophic for New York City and the nation.

****

The warm, semi-tropical air welcomed Tom and Kat to Florida; a stark contrast to the chilly, damp weather they left in New England and New York. They had changed from their combat gear, removed the face camo during the trip to the airport and now looked like typical tourists wearing Bermuda shorts, polo shirts and sneakers.

William Bishop waited at the gate for the anonymous combat heroes. He detected Kat and waved his hand to attract her attention. She ran and hugged him. Kat had known Bill her entire life and considered him more of an uncle than her father's employee.

Kat introduced Tom to Bill. They shook hands, Bill commented, "We could use a strong-looking guy like you for my crew."

Kat looked at him disapprovingly, "No deal, Bill. He's all mine. Find your own men."

Bill laughed, "I am glad the city hasn't changed you one bit, Kat."

Bill looked at Tom, "You realize that Kat is the grove's real boss. Actually, she's considered the queen."

Kat asked, "You don't think I'm a bitch, do you Bill?"

"No Kat, but I enjoy ruffling your feathers."

Kat playfully punched his arm as they headed to the luggage carousel for their bags.

The thirty-minute ride to the grove in the restored red 1947 Ford F-1 pick-up was uneventful but loud. Bill ordered a new muffler but it wasn't expected until the following week. Meanwhile, the passengers suffered through the high decibel noise created by the exhaust.

Tom asked Bill whether he was concerned about receiving a ticket from the cops. Bill replied, "Nope. Did you see the sign painted on the doors ' —St. John's Groves, Wellington, Florida'? That's like a cross to a vampire. Nobody would dare challenge Mike, who regarded such tickets an affront. He'd take the ticket to the Supreme Court if he had to, regardless of whether he was at fault. It's the insult that counts to Mike, not the cases's merit. Right, Kat?"

"Oh so right, Bill," responded Kat. She twas well aware of her father's demeanor throughout the years.

"Well I guess I'll be on my best behavior during the visit," remarked Tom.

"Tom, you are always on your best behavior," Kat asserted, seizing his hand.

They turned off highway 98 onto a long driveway leading to the St. John home. Above the entrance a large sign spanned the driveway to greet visitors, "Welcome to St. John's Orange Groves." -- orange trees are painted to the left of the sign.

"Kat built the sign," said Bill.

"Yes, my senior high school art project. I wanted to do something special for dad."

"Oh, he loves the sign. We take it down each year, clean it, and apply another polyurethane layer for protection. That sign will last forever."

They drove along the dirt road through thousands of orange trees that surrounded the house situated precisely in the middle of the grove.

Mike exited the house to greet them. He gave Kat a big hug and Tom a handshake.

"Tom, good to see you again. Great timing. You're right on time for dinner."

Kat took her father's arm. "We know that Carmelita is a great cook but she is under great competition from the Ford's Polish cook, Panie Doubravka."

"Well, I hope one day you will invite me to the Ford home to sample her cuisine."

"I'm sure we can arrange that, Mike," Tom replied.

The trio walked into the living room. Tom was astounded by the four walls that were adorned with spectacular Renaissance paintings, all bounded by beautiful gold frames.

"So, these are the famous paintings I heard about? I haven't seen a collection like this since I visited the Pinacoteca Vaticana. Very impressive. Grandpa St. John was quite the art connoisseur."

Mike laughed, "Dad didn't know anything about art. He knew value though and traded hundreds of these for cash."

Kat interjected, "Talk about value, dad, that painting I took for the charity auction sold for $150,000!"

"Amazing, it decorated the guest bathroom for 50 years. You said the money benefits wounded New England vets? We'll give another away next year."

Carmelita walked in to announce that dinner will be served.

Dinner was excellent. Carmelita proved to be in league with Panie Doubrovka. After an indescribably delicious Tocinillo del Cielo, a favorite Cuban dessert, Mike asked Kat to help Carmelita do the dishes, "I want to show Tom my war museum."

Kat stared at him with feigned shock, "Oh No! You are taking Tom to your Sanctum Sanctorum - the Holy of Holies?"

She ran to Tom and hugged him. "It's been nice knowing you, partner. Many have entered but not one has returned from the Sanctum Santorum."

Mike and Tom laughed, but Kat maintained character and hugged Tom tighter continuing her merrymaking.

Mike took Tom's arm, separated him from Kat, then led him to his office. She screamed as they walked into the office, "I lose so many boyfriends down there."

Mike reached under his desk to activate a switch that unlocked a panel on the far wall inside the office. Tom appreciated the mystery it raised. Mike led Tom into the darkness. The lights automatically switched on illuminating a cavernous room crammed with war relics, souvenirs and various battle trophies. A wrought-iron spiral staircase led to the navy blue-carpeted floor below.

The room astonished Tom. Hundreds of objects comprised the collection. He recognized a Model 1841 10-inch Civil War era Siege Mortar that lie in the middle of the room and a WWI British Vickers machine gun against the wood-paneled wall. Tom asked, "How did you move everything into the basement? That spiral staircase is narrow. There is no way to carry those items down the steps."

We found a simple solution. This room is the cellar under the extension to the original house. I built a twenty-five hundred square foot addition in 1983. After we poured the foundation and floor, I lowered the heftiest objects, including the mortar, into the cellar and built the house above it. I'm not too worried about theft."

Tom thought, "*No thief would survive a minute in the St. John house and doubtless become natural organic fertilizer for Mike's orange trees.*"

Mike gave Tom a tour of his collection. I purchased some of the items, but vets gave me nearly all these items. Some no longer wanted them in their homes, others just wanted me to have them. Most appeared at the doorway after the president gave me the Medal of Honor at the White House. Dozens of news media interviewed me during the following weeks. I guess the vets liked what I said. I'm sure their wives were tired of looking at them or their kids didn't appreciate their value. I saved the letters that accompanied the gifts. Some were given anonymously. but nearly all were given to me."

They approached a glass case with a skull displayed inside. Mike opened the case taking out the skull. "This is a Japanese skull from Iwo Jima." Mike turned it around. Carved on the back, "Iwo Jima. 3/15/45. B. R. "The skull represents an untold story of WWII. The Marines were severely criticized for collecting war souvenirs, but the American soldier knew of the wretched treatment Japs gave American POWs...and it wasn't pretty. The Japs had no concern for any formal rules of war. The Marines merely reciprocated the treatment. Iwo Jima, the most brutal battle our country ever fought, generated twenty-seven Medals of Honor from the 30 day battle."

Tom pointed to a framed partially burnt Japanese flag. Mike explained this artifact, "The Japs hunkered deep in the cave system they dug and the Marines employed flame-throwers to clean them out. They found this burnt flag on the cave dweller. Read the letter that came with the flag."

Tom stepped up to read the letter below the flag framed by the matting, "*Mike, I've seen you on the news a few times and liked all you said. Please take this flag I took off a Jap soldier on Iwo. My hippy kids will never appreciate it, but, no doubt, you will.*" Signed, 'An Old Sergeant.'

Tom shook his head, "Amazing. All these guys seem to know and trust you."

Mike waved Tom to another item. Framed in a deep shadow box: a hangman's noose. Mike grabbed a letter from the top of the frame.

He opened the letter and handed it to Tom, "*This is the noose that hanged Lt. General Yoshio Tachibama in Guam. I was stationed there in 1947 and took the noose after his hanging. I stashed the noose in a box and stored it in the attic for over 30 years. I heard you collect war relics. This is an interesting one. Best, Cpl. Edward Malecki.*"

Tom read the letter, "Who was General Yoshio Tachibama and why did they hang him?"

"Tachibama was a war criminal responsible for murdering Australian, English, Indian and American POWs. But his savagery went far beyond mere murder and torture. He had the livers cut from downed American fliers and served them at a feast for his officers. The American hatred for the Japs wasn't built on racism, as is alleged today, but rooted in the reality of an enemy with a corrupted moral code. The Nips commonly practiced cannibalism during the war."

Mike said, "Take a seat. Let me explain something to you."

They walked to the far corner where four leather armchairs were placed in a circle around a coffee table fabricated from a wooden Civil War ammunition box, a round tempered glass piece attached to the top. "I understand you appreciate Single Malts, but you must sample my Bourbons."

Mike seized a Blanton's Single Barrel Bourbon bottle from his dry bar and poured two glasses. He handed one to Tom.

Mike proposed a toast to all Americans killed by war. They clanged glasses to the soldiers, sailors and airmen who died for their country.

Mike sat on the chair. Tom noticed a shadow box hanging on the wall behind him displaying bronze, silver, a Purple Heart and a cluster of other medals and ribbons surrounding the Medal of Honor. "We fought the commies and failed. Yes, we didn't lose a single battle and killed perhaps a million Vietcong and NVA regulars but we lost the war. I joined the Army unconditionally imbued with patriotic fervor. I believed patriotism would drive me in battle, but I was wrong.

"The demands for survival, not only for you, but also for your buddies, are all that drive you. You want to return home alive. There is an unspoken agreement among fellow soldiers -- they will help you get back home, and you reciprocate by helping them return home. That 'Band of Brothers' thing rings true. You don't think of the flag, country or other symbols of patriotism in battle. You hope to live through the mayhem and do everything you can to ensure that. That means killing the enemy before they kill you — winning the battle. I learned that a soldier has a better chance surviving the battle if he is more ruthless and brutal than is the enemy. Patton said it best, 'The object of war is not to die for your country but to make the other bastard die for his.' I can't tell you how spot on he was with his observation."

Mike took a long sip of bourbon, "Each of those guys sent me their war souvenirs saying, in their way, they would trust me in the foxholes with them. They know I'd have their backs…that I would die to save their lives, as they would to protect mine. It's the greatest compliment an old soldier can receive. And do you know what? I would die for every one of them. They are all great Americans. I love them all. This is a museum dedicated to their guts."

Mike shifted his posture on the chair to signal a change of topic.

"Tom, I asked you here for another reason than to show you my collection and to tell war stories. I was intrigued by you after you helped Kat with her legal problem. She appears devoted to you and, may I say, loves you.

I am pleased for her happiness, but I am still that protective father. I thought it prudent to learn more about you. I hired a detective to search your background."

"What is it with these St. Johns?" Tom wondered. *"They revel in their investigations."*

Tom responded only with a simple, "Oh?"

"He confirmed all you appear to be: A productive, law-abiding, tax-paying patriotic citizen. He found that you were adopted, but Kat knew of your adoption – you told her. You have a clean arrest record, an 800+ FICO score, no violations on your FINRA sheet. Furthermore, you're not a registered sex offender anywhere in the country."

Tom laughed hard at the last finding. "You certainly thoroughly investigated me. Were your concerns satisfied?"

"Well, the detective's investigation satisfied my concerns, but I also called my contacts in military intelligence. None of them found anything, but a DIA friend of mine told me of rumors that a shadow group in the intelligence community conducts assassinations around the world.

"He spoke glowingly of their top assassin, a civilian who can outshoot any military sniper. He is allegedly a mild-mannered banker who travels the world making business deals and killing a few jihadis along the way. Kat told me you shot the cork off a champagne bottle at 500 yards. I met the top snipers in Vietnam, including Carlos Hathcock, but none could do that -- perhaps they could hit the bottle, but not the cork. That's ridiculous shooting."

Tom remembered his reaction when Kat confronted him in his apartment. She had concrete evidence of his extracurricular activities, Mike was speculating. Tom decided to deny everything and change the conversation's direction.

"Mike, I'd be flattered to be identified as this assassin, but the only live targets I ever shot were animals while hunting. No humans. However, I will admit I love your daughter and adore her. I assure you I will give her the care and protection you gave her all these years. We have developed an incredible relationship and I hope to continue our growth together."

"Do you plan to marry my daughter?"

"We discussed marriage, but will, of course, ask your blessing before we make any decision."

"Tom, in that case, let's have another and give a toast to that."

Mike suspected Tom was the sniper but didn't want to pursue the matter at this time. Call it veteran's intuition, or a combat leader's objective evaluation of another man but he was proud of the boy and pleased his daughter loved such a man.

Unknown to Tom, Kat and Mike engaged in the following conversation earlier that day: "Kat, your life and well-being have been my most important concern since you were born, but I knew the day will come when I will no longer be the main man in your life. I have always been critical of your boyfriends; none ever approached the standards I believed you needed from a man to sustain your happiness. I warned you not to marry a wimp -- it would be the worst thing for you. I raised you to be strong. They were outclassed and overwhelmed by your toughness in any relationship with you. Your mother didn't tolerate the crap I sometimes gave her. She was tough, we had our arguments, but I loved her for it."

"You and I had some debates about this over the years, but once everything was settled, you assured me that I was correct about your boys. So, regarding Tom, I agree with you. I believe he is ideal for you. Unlike that Dave character you had a crush on a few years back, you two are strong and will complement each other wonderfully."

Kat wrapped her arms around her father. "Please don't remind me of Dave, but I'm glad you approve of Tom. I have never been happier with someone."

Mike gently pushed her away and looked her in the eyes, "So when will you marry him?"

****

Tom and Kat went their ways the next morning, both fulfilling the responsibilities of their jobs -- Tom to Hobe Sound, Kat to Miami. They planned to meet that evening at McCarthy's Steak House in Palm Beach.

McCarthy's was Mike's favorite restaurant in town. He had called Michael McCarthy to charge their meal to his house account. Kat had been to McCarthy's often with her father and appreciated the opportunity to share this slice of her childhood with Tom.

Kat arrived and warmly greeted by Michael McCarthy, "Kat, good to see you again. We were all rooting for you here and celebrated when you beat that bastard D.A." McCarthy was also a Vietnam vet and admired Mike St. John, their shared war experience propelled them to a loyal friendship. Their friendship extended to friendly competition on the golf course.

Tom soon walked in and Kat introduced him to Michael. He sat them at the best table with an ocean view -- a corner booth that offered the couple some privacy. A waiter delivers a bottle of Moet et Chandon champagne and three glasses. Michael opened the bottle and filled the three glasses. "I propose a toast to the toughest lady I know. Tom, you may not know it, but Kat's New York experience surprised no one around here. We know you can't bully Kat St. John – she's like her father." Tom supported Michael's toast, "I am beginning to appreciate Kat's iron will." He smiled a knowing and appreciative smile at Kat. They clinked their glasses and sipped the champagne.

Kat thanked Michael for the champagne and both for their kind words. "I appreciate your words but you two guys better not forget I'm still a girl and enjoy being one. I hope you see me as more than as a ruthless, hard-boiled bitch."

"Kat, no one regards you as anything but a woman. Right, Michael?"

"No disagreement from me. Kat, you have grown to be a beautiful woman, but your dad told me about your karate and judo lessons throughout the years. I'm wary where any St. John treads…(Michael quickly changing the subject)… we offer a Filet Mignon special today, served with mashed garlic potato, fresh garden vegetable and finished with a red wine Demi reduction. I guarantee the sauce won't overwhelm the the mignon but will subtly complement it. You will love it."

In addition to the special, Tom and Kat shared a bottle of Stag's Leap Cabernet Sauvignon.

Tom proposed another toast. He poured the wine and declared, "To the best partner I could ever have. Kat, I haven't told you but you were outstanding on the mission we successfully completed yesterday. I've worked with Jackie and others, but all were trained professionals. This was new to you. True, you had that experience in Central Park, but this was a planned mission. You didn't disappoint."

"Why, thank you, Tom. I virtually ordered you to include me in the Martels. I couldn't disappoint. I found it easy to work with you. We're a great team."

Tom responded, "Your shot at that bomb-maker attempting an escape was critical. The entire mission could have been ruined had you missed. Doubtless, he was running away from the inevitable when he noticed the grenade sparking on the barn floor. Clint Eastwood said, 'Nothing wrong with shootin' somebody if the right person gets shot.' You targeted the right person at the right time."

Kat commented, "I saw those ball bearings all around us strewn around the ground, imagining them tearing through the kids visiting a museum with their parents. I confess I felt pleased with that shot. I wish I could tell my father about it."

Tom looked at her and cupped her hands in his, "Perhaps one day we will tell him. He would be pleased with your marksmanship and courage. I'm betting few modern women have the strength and courage to accomplish what you did yesterday."

"I love all the praise you throw my way. When is the next job?"

"Nothing planned -- probably nothing for a few months. However, the assignments seem to be escalating. I wonder what repercussions J. Bailey Morgan's death will have on the Martels?"

Kat took a more serious tone, "Will we still be a team in six months?"

"We will if I can help it."

"I want that Tom. You are the first man I ever genuinely loved and don't want to lose you."

"Kat, you are stuck with me. I know it would be impossible to find another girl who handles an M16 like you."

"Keep thinking that way, buster, or you'll suffer the full wrath of a St. John."

Tom looked serious, "Kat, did Mike tell you about our conversation last night?"

"No. I had to leave early that morning before he woke."

"He told me he hired a detective to check into my background. I have no problem with that. His curiosity demonstrates his concern for your well-being. However, he spoke to his friends in the intelligence community and almost discovered my involvement with the Martels."

Kat said, "Dad always investigates my new boyfriends. He once found a two-time loser masquerading as a Palm Beach party boy. That guy fooled me for a couple of weeks, but dad wasn't. I dropped him and later read in the local paper Mr. Two-time Loser became Mr. Three-time Loser. The cops caught him in a smash-and-grab of a jewelry store on Worth Ave."

Tom replied, "As I said, I have no problem with the investigation but, you must ask him all he knows concerning the Martels. You must alleviate his suspicions about our recent activities...about us."

"You are right, Tom. I'll discuss it with him tomorrow to confirm you are nothing but a milquetoast investment banker who couldn't possibly be that ruthless killing machine he suspects you of being."

"Kat, go easy with that milquetoast remark with your father. I suspect your father wouldn't appreciate anything "milquetoast" for his daughter."

"You are right. I hear it from him anytime I introduced him to a boy demonstrating even the slightest hint of beta. He claims only a real man honors his responsibilities as a husband and father. And do you know what? I believe him."

"He and my mother should exchange notes. They would get along."

"Come to think about it, from all I know talking to your mother, you're right."

Tom thought it was the proper time to tell her of his thoughts that day, "Kat, I love you and could never leave you. I hope you believe it."

"I wanted to hear that from you." The repressed emotions of the last few days, the past months, the past year, generated tears in Kat's eyes. She tried to hide them from Tom but they continued to flow.

"Why are you crying?" Tom was surprised and perplexed.

"I love you so much, Tom. I love you so much." She looked down and continued crying.

Tom took her hands in his, saying nothing.

She looked at him. Consoled. Kat regained her composure. However, she remained bewildered by her emotional outburst. For her twenty-five years, Kat hadn't experienced these emotions; however, she had no regret for the tears shed. She realized at that moment Tom will always be her life's partner, lover and best friend. She needed the tears to confirm her feelings.

The waiter arrived to serve the meal.

As they ate Kat noticed an elderly couple sitting across the room from them. Kat said, "They don't even look at each other, nor exchange a word between them. I hope we don't become like that couple over there, Tom. They look sad together." Tom smiled and took Kat's hand, "Neither of us will allow that to happen. So it won't."

They finished their meal, thanked Michael McCarthy for his hospitality and took a leisurely stroll along the waterfront to Kat's car. It was a glorious, warm night, an utter contrast to the dreary rain and chill they encountered a day ago at Koranland.

That evening's tranquility was quickly shattered. Whether the wine and champagne, the dizzying conversation of their love and commitment to each other or simply complacency, but Tom didn't see the men hidden in the huge Kapok tree that canopied the path they walked.

Suddenly, six Ninja-like assailants, all dressed in black, dropped in unison on the couple, imprisoning them with an old sisal cargo net. Tom, angered by his failure to protect Kat, judged the circumstances helpless considering the sturdiness of the net and the circle of well-armed guards. Two black vans rolled behind them, and six more Ninjas carrying UZIs exited the second van. The crew bundled Tom and Kat in the net and tossed them through the side door of the first van. Tom noted the Uzis they carried and decided resistance was futile. Soon they were on their way: Destination Unknown. For now, escape was not possible.

Distressed, Kat asked Tom, "Who are these guys?"

"No idea, but they don't appear too friendly, do they?"

He spoke to Kat who was crushed against him in the cargo net bundle.

"Are you OK, Kat?"

"I'm fine. What happened?"

"We apparently have been kidnapped."

Tom took notice through the netting of an Uzi barrel pointed at his head, held by the obvious leader. He barked, "Shut up. Not another word from you two."

Those were the only words he heard spoken. The team performed their assignment wordlessly and effortlessly. Tom concluded resistance was futile and decided to comfort Kat the best he could under the circumstances. Judging by the van's speed over the pavement and the occasional sign advertising a Fort Lauderdale business Tom determined they were on the Interstate heading south. He wrapped his arms around Kat. He assured her all will be all well, though he wasn't sure himself of their fate.

Nearly an hour later, they sensed the truck slowly taking an exit from the highway. Minutes later, Tom observed hundreds of cargo containers stacked high as the truck continued to its destination.

"*Port of Miami,*" thought Tom.

The van stopped in front of an old rust-bucket of a ship -- an American single-screw tramp steamer. Tom remembered as a child building a plastic model of this class of ship. Tom looked through the netting, surprised such ships still existed. The Ninja crew dragged the restrained couple from the van, net and all, and carried them towards the steamer. The ship's crane boom lowered its hooked cable to within feet from the cargo net. A Ninja fastened the hook to the net and the boom lifted the couple 40 or 50 feet above the pavement.

The other boom of the ship was busy removing the hatch from the hold with the crew's aid. The hatch cleared from the hold's opening, the boom operator centered his human cargo above the hold and slowly lowered it into the darkness of TomKat's looming prison.

Kat looked at their black destination through the netting and quipped, "Mr. Ford, I'll say this about you: You sure know how to show a girl a good time."

CHAPTER 11: *Jay Bailey Morgan III*

Once on the hold's deck, Tom felt for his Swiss Army Knife. He reached into his pocket, pulled it out, manipulated his arm through the netting cords and opened the knife to cut the old sisal net. They were free, at least free to stand in near darkness; the glimmer from the red exit lights giving some illumination.

"Are you all right, Kat?"

"Yeah, I'm fine. What's going on here?"

"I have no idea, but don't worry, I assume they plan to keep us alive. Otherwise, they would have killed us in Palm Beach or in the van."

Suddenly, the lights turned on, revealing the hold's interior. Tom estimated the room to be about 20' x 30' and more than 20 feet high. The bright titanium-oxide white walls, ceiling and floor reflected the warm glow of the overhead incandescent lights. The room appeared perfectly clean, almost grand, but the atmosphere elicited an eerie feeling from Tom and Kat. They looked around and saw a green Parisian Bistro table flanked by two matching side chairs. The table and chairs were arranged on a red circular Heriz Persian Rug. Behind the chairs and tables stood a long antique mahogany sideboard, also fixed to a carpet. Everything was secured to the deck, as is customary on boats and ships.

A large silver champagne bucket, two fluted glasses and a chilled Jeroboam of Veuve Clicquot La Grande Dame resting in ice provided a centerpiece for the display. Dozens of red roses artfully arranged in two silver vases framed the impressive presentation. A generous cheese, pâté and crostini platter completed the sumptuous display.

Tom, amazed by the incongruity of such opulence in the old ship, said, "Someone gave considerable effort for us to be comfortable in our prison."

Kat said, "I hope they aren't fattening us for the eventual slaughter."

"This is weird," commented Kat. She walked to the sideboard. "There's a note."

She picked up the note and read it.

Dear Miss St. John and Mr. Ford,

I heartily apologize for any rough treatment you may have suffered by my men. I needed to meet and talk to you and doubt you would consent to talk to a dead man. Besides, it is far more fun this way. Enjoy the champagne and I hope to see you in a few hours.

I am,

Most respectfully yours,

J. Bailey Morgan III

Kat set the note back on the sideboard. "Is this all a joke, Tom?"

"I doubt it. I wouldn't be surprised if Morgan is alive. He probably faked his death to divert any scrutiny from himself. He may be planning something significant and needs our help."

"You think so? What if this is a kidnapping? Our parents have money. Why wouldn't we be targets?"

"Serious kidnappers don't provide their victims with such great champagne."

No believer in quiet desperation Tom continued, "Rudyard Kipling once wrote, 'There comes a night when the best get tight.' My suggestion is that we relax, enjoy the hospitality...for what it is...and start drinking."

The engine's rumble reverberated throughout the ancient rickety ship. Soon they were underway. The cowl vents refreshed the stale, hot air of the hold with the cooler salt-scented sea air.

Kat sat. Tom brought the bucket and the glasses to the table. He poured the first glass. "Let's do the Russian practice and give a toast with every glass we drink."

Kat initiated the tributes, "Well, I want to propose a toast to us. Do you realize all we have experienced together since you spotted me standing over Bill Griffin's worthless carcass? I could write a book about it already. Who'd ever believe Miss Tight Ass of Williams College falling for a killing machine like you?"

Tom laughed lifting his glass, "I'll drink to that." They clinked their glasses and sipped the champagne.

"My turn," said Tom. He raised his glass. "I propose a toast to our parents, who gave extraordinary efforts to raise us correctly, instill at least a modicum of patriotism, solid values and the skills to allow us to survive all challenges life throws at an individual."

"Amen to that." They repeated the routine.

The now happy couple proceeded through three more toasts to offer tribute to Jackie Brandt, Jay Bailey Morgan III and Western Civilization.

"Western Civilization?" Kat asked.

"Yep. What do you think our fight is all about? We are soldiers fighting to defend the Western Civilization heritage from barbarians."

They refilled the glasses and Kat mischievously looked at Tom, "Let's play "100 Questions.""

"OK, you first."

Kat asked, "Would you rather be less attractive and rich or extremely attractive and poor?"

"That's easy – extremely attractive and poor. You can change poor, it's not as simple to change looks...my turn."

Tom asked. "Here is a challenging question. Who was your favorite Jonas brother?"

"Tom, what makes you assume I was a fan of the Jonas Brothers?"

"I thought all teenyboppers were fans of the Jonas Brothers."

"Listen Buster, don't you ever call me a teenybopper."

Tom laughed at Kat's reaction. "Deal!. Now for a serious question. What was your greatest childhood fear?"

Kat didn't hesitate. "Losing my father. I lost my mother when I was five and I couldn't bear the thought of losing my father. I remember running to him and hugging him when I got scared. He'd hug me back, but I never told him what occasioned the panic."

Kat took another sip of the champagne and emptied the bottle to the half-way point. She looked through the glass. "Is the bottle half empty or half full?"

"I'm an optimist. It is half full but can be refilled until the bottle is full again."

Tom looked at Kat and smiled, "How many children do you want to have?"

"I reserve the right to answer that question at another time, another place."

"Coward!"

"I plead guilty, Tom."

Kat asked, "Have you ever thought of searching for your biological mother?"

"Never have and never will. Amelia Briggs Ford is my mother. When I learned to read, my mother gave me a note she found in the box dropped off at the front door. My biological mother clearly wanted to wash her hands of me. Nevertheless, she gave me life and refused to have an abortion. I'll respect her for that and honor her request. Amelia gave me love – I value all my parents gave me far more than any idle curiosity I may have about a Dartmouth student's indiscretions decades ago. However, not too long ago, my parents purchased a DNA test for a birthday gift. The results were intriguing. From the haplogroup sequence of genes we found that my ancestors began a multi-thousand-year journey from the Tigris-Euphrates to Mongolia, a millennium meander through Siberia ending their trip in Finland. My father called me a Viking."

Kat exclaimed, "A Viking. No wonder why you're so adept with all that fighting you do."

"Well, I don't know about that, but they taught Vikings to exercise a great deal of self-discipline. They insisted the warrior remain true to his principles -- he must develop self-discipline. A thorough recognition and development of this trait, I have determined, is far more powerful than is any external forces imposed on you."

"Tom, you truly are a Viking."

"Well, according to my mother, I am an English 19th Century country gentleman. She worked hard to inculcate me with those Victorian values of manners, etiquette, honesty and perseverance -- the old Stoic-Christian honor code. My father took me to 20th Century bourgeois capitalism. He taught me the virtues of hard work, entrepreneurship, risk-taking and, may I add, enjoyment of the good life."

"Tom, you are the kind of guy the feminist professors taught us to despise in college. Fortunately for you, none of it stuck."

They continued their banter for the next hours until they emptied the champagne bottle of its contents.

The couple looked at the empty bottle. Kat commented, "You know, Tom, that bottle will make an excellent target for your range."

"Let's take it with us. Perhaps we can shoot it one day."

The now peaceful and somewhat inebriated couple improvised a bed. They moved the table and chairs off the carpet and fashioned the cargo net into a pillow. They soon passed out in each other's arms.

Hours later, the sunlight flooded the hold through the open hatch. An UZI burst in the air awoke the prisoners.

They noticed the diminished noise and vibrations of the tired diesel engines.

"We must be nearing our destination," Tom said.

Kat asked, "Where do you think we are?"

"My guess: the Bahamas. We haven't sailed too long, less than twelve hours."

The engines were cut and the engine vibrations ceased to rattle the ship. A rope ladder tumbled from above stopping three feet from the floor.

Kat commented, "I guess this is their way of saying our party is over."

Tom grabbed the ladder, securing it for Kat. "Ladies first."

Kat climbed the ladder, followed by Tom. Tom took the empty bottle for more as a weapon than for a souvenir. A warm, gentle sea breeze greeted them when they reached the deck. They were emancipated from their captivity.

"Such a gorgeous morning," Kat exclaimed, "I'm going to identify as a Ze today."

Tom gave her a quizzical look, "What are you talking about?"

"Tom, if you attended college you would have learned to self-identify as anything you want. Why else would dad give $50,000 a year to Williams College?"

Tom rolled his eyes. He looked at his captors.

The Ninjas surrounded them. Again, they carried UZIS. The apparent leader approached. He was an imposing man, as tall as Tom and wearing a black du-rag and dark sunglasses to complement his ninja uniform. He carried a hefty knife in his right hand, using the knife for a pointer. The man spoke with a heavy accent. Tom speculated Russian or a former USSR satellite country. "There is a Zodiac inflatable over the starboard side. Take it to the island." He pointed his knife to a small island, perhaps a mile away. "You only have enough gas to reach it. Don't get the idea you can go anywhere else. You'll see a dock as you approach. Tie the raft to the dock. Someone will be waiting for you there. I hope your stay wasn't too unpleasant."

Tom smiled, "We had a great time, didn't we Kat?"

"The company superb, the champagne excellent, the ambiance passable but

I especially liked the Port-o-Potty in the corner -- a thoughtful touch. My compliments."

Blade, the humorless leader, grunted but said nothing. He led them to a break in the ship's gunwale. A crewman lowered a rope ladder to the raft bobbing on the water. Tom and Kat descended the ladder to the raft;Tom with champagne bottle in hand. Blade threw Tom the bowline who instinctively coiled and stowed the rope into an open compartment on the raft's bow. His Boy Scout training again proved handy.

He eyed the motor, a five hp Honda outboard. He checked the gas valves to assure they were open, set the choke and pulled the cord. The motor started. Tom adjusted the choke and navigated a course towards the dock. After a few minutes they looked back to see the old steamer already underway.

The inflatable skimmed over the calm blue-green Bahamian waters. Tom examined the island. A grand stone house dominated the island. Tom thought of Edmond Dantes' prison in *"The Count of Monte Cristo."* However, several antennas and satellite dishes arrayed along the roof diminished that image. Ahead, Tom spotted a wood dock extending well into the water, a powerful-looking speedboat tied to the other side.

They approached the island. A smiling black man walked to the end of the dock to greet them. He wore a white suit topped by a Raffia hat; all appropriate for the climate. Kat scrutinized the man and thought him the most beautiful man she had ever seen. The man, six feet tall, trim in his impeccably white tailored suit, exhibited a shaved head and a perfectly chiseled face -- his skin so black it displayed remarkable subtle shades of dark blue hues. She recalled Michelangelo who tried to portray the face of God in his works. *"God created mankind in his image, in the image of God he created them."* This man, Kat believed, would have inspired Renaissance sculptors by his Nubian perfection. Any trepidation she may have had by their grim circumstances dissipated by the man's cheerful appearance.

As they approached the dock he shouted above the motor's din, "Please toss me the line."

Kat grabbed the line and pitched the rope in his direction. The man pulled in the raft and tied the proper cleat hitch to secure the raft to the dock. Tom turned off the outboard.

The man gave the couple a wide, radiating smile and spoke with a fine deep voice in a strong Bahamian accent, "Hello, my name is Anthony Michael. Welcome to Morgan Island."

He offered Kat his hand to pull her onto the dock. She looked back, "Tom, don't forget the bottle."

Tom hopped onto the dock with the bottle.

"I hope your trip wasn't too distressing, " Anthony Michael said. "Mr. Morgan has a flair for the dramatic. He prefers to do everything…a little differently. Come, follow me. He eagerly awaits your arrival."

Tom and Kat followed Anthony Michael along the narrow path, leading to a stone stairway to the house. Red and white Bougainvillea lined the entire path to the house. They entered the stone house and ushered to a cozy library, the walls lined on all four sides with packed bookshelves of collectible leather-bound scientific journals. "The house was originally a British lookout post and prison for pirates -- a mini fort. Mr. Morgan purchased the island, renovated and expanded the prison into his home which he has used as his getaway for thirty years. Please take a seat. I'll notify Mr. Morgan that you've arrived. "

The couple sat on the long leather couch. Tom took Kat's hand. "This should be interesting."

Anthony Michael opened the doors, stood at near attention by the doorway and announced, "Miss Kathryn St. John and Mr. Thomas Ford, I introduce you to Mr. Jay Bailey Morgan III." With those words, a tall, good-looking and imposing man with a full, but neatly trimmed salt and pepper beard, barged into the room.

Morgan bellowed, "How the fuck are you two?" Tom heard Morgan had a Tourette's use of the English language. He walked straight to Kat, enveloping her with a hug.

"My, you are as exquisite as the television portrays you. Tom, this is a mighty fine wench you have here. She certainly rates a high millihelen score. Her face could launch a thousand jihads " Kat didn't know what to do or say. She said and did nothing.

Tom laughed. Kat playfully hit him in the ribs.

Morgan next focused his attention to Tom. "Tom, thank you for all the fuckin' great work you have brought to our cause. Jackie hit a god-damn home run finding you."

Tom replied, "Well, thank you, Mr. Morgan. I also want to thank you for your generous gifts throughout the years."

"Think nothing of it, Tom. You deserved them, but I'm glad you enjoyed them. Please sit."

Morgan's regal bearing, despite his language, nourished an appearance of a man younger than his 70 years. He assumed the character of a Scottish clan chief – an image he worked hard to maintain. A blue plaid tartan representing the Ancient Clan Morgan of Aberdeenshire comprised his full kilt outfit that included sporran, flashes, kilt pin and a properly sheathed sgian dubh. Although somewhat out of place for semi-tropical Bahamas, the kilt fit perfectly in his castle-like home.

"You must have wondered why I had myself killed in the public's eye? The fact is that the cocksucking feds had planned to investigate me and my various charities and donations. I wanted to stop them or at least slow them down before they discovered the Martels. We are at a critical point with the Martel's efforts, and federal meddling would have been very inconvenient. I rigged one of my G-5s as a drone. Everyone suggested I use my G-7 but they are too fuckin' hard to find. I decided to sacrifice my oldest G-5. We flew it over the deepest waters of the Atlantic, not far off Bermuda Island, ditched it, and, voilà, I am fuckin' dead!"

Morgan laughed, "Anthony, here, is my pilot. He's dead, too. I stole him from the Royal Bahamas Defence Force years ago – he was their best damn pilot. I paid to qualify him for twin-engine jets and he has been flying my Gulfstreams ever since."

Anthony Michael smiled and nodded.

Morgan asked them to sit. He sat on the leather wing chair opposite them. "I want to apologize for any shit you suffered from the kidnapping, but I did it for a reason. First, I hoped to introduce you to the ninjas and their capabilities."

"We train those little bastards more thoroughly than any special forces you will find. They are all victims of Muslim terrorism. Each lost their entire family by jihad and live for buggering revenge. Blade, their leader who you met, a Chechen, a rare Catholic Chechen, also lost his family. He lives to bitch-slap jihadists to hell."

Kat quipped, "You mean Mr. Personality."

Morgan laughed, "I'll admit he wouldn't make much of an escort at the International Ball and he is an asshole, but he is perfect for the job. He is also completely dedicated to our cause and to me. He was a fuckin' officer for the Russian Special Forces Unit called Zapad. I recruited him when the Russians disbanded that squad."

Tom asked, "Why do you call him Blade?"

"His real name is so damn unpronounceable and he is superior at handling a knife than can any fuckin' Mayo Clinic surgeon."

Tom could only speculate Jay Bailey Morgan's language in a boardroom composed of starched and stilted executives.

"Blade travels the Middle East and Africa looking for that special person to recruit. He especially likes Coptic Christians. The peckerheads have been persecuting Coptics for centuries. The Coptic hate for Islamists gives them an incredible incentive for revenge.

"As I mentioned, they must be victims of jihad, physically fit and be between 5' 6" and 5' 9" – the short wiry types develop to the best ninjas. They are the bollocks. We treat them well, train them and give them motivation to live, which all had lost.

"Shit, I also pay them well. Besides their full living expenses, I deposit $100,000 a year into a joint Cayman account for each of them. In return, I ask for ten kickass years. They all will leave with a million dollars plus interest – far more damn money than they could ever imagine acquiring in their country. I also teach them English and an equivalent of a G.E.D. Most are illiterate when they join us. I keep them away from the drugs and the knock shops so they focus on their training and studies. We never had to toss anyone out – they experienced the poverty and misery of their homelands. None want to go back."

"But none have joined strictly for the bloody money. They want to fuck-bugger their family's killers. We provide the opportunity. They consider all jihadis as their enemy, deserving the nastiest death. Our fuckin' ninjas are the perfect foot soldiers for the Martels. I trained three dozen little shitkickers in three separate units of twelve. Our best crew fuckin' kidnapped you."

Tom replied, "Well, they surprised us in Palm Beach and managed to drag us here without breaking our necks. Well done."

Morgan added, "And I brought you here for a reason. Tom, you have been with us for nearly five fuckin' years. You are acquainted with our goals, tactics and, probably, a bit of our structure. You have heard much of the "shadow government" and "deep state." The truth is that in a federal government as fuckin' massive as ours there are plenty obscure cliques in our bureaucratic bowels conducting policies nobody will ever know about. I call it the invisible government. I saw it years ago as a government contractor and filed it to the back of my mind for possible future consideration. Now, the escalation of that God-damned jihad terrorism and the irresponsible, meek pussy-footing response to it by those cowardly government slim dicks. I spoke to plenty of people, great patriots all, in the military and intelligence who understood the situation as well as I did. We needed extraordinary efforts to protect the fuckin' country from jihadists. Remember Clint Eastwood's quote, 'Sometimes if you want to see a change for the better, you need to take things into your own hands.'"

Kat interjected, "What is it with you alpha males and Clint Eastwood quotes?"

Morgan responded, "Clint's words are quite significant despite the few damn words he uses, Kat."

He resumed his monologue, "Perhaps you prefer a Winston Churchill quote: 'Islam is a militant and proselytizing faith. It has already spread throughout Central Africa, raising fearless warriors at every step, and were it not that Christianity is sheltered by the strong arms of science, the science against which Islam has vainly struggled, the civilization of modern Europe might fall, as fell the civilization of ancient Rome.'"

Morgan continued, "Churchill said that in 1899. It is as true today. Today's fuckin' terrorist won't stop at killing hundreds of people with suicide bombs or even thousands by attacks like 9/11. No, they want to destroy entire cities, perhaps nations, with biological, chemical and nuclear weapons. The open-border policies of recent administrations have made the jihadist's job a helluva a lot easier. We are engaged in an asymmetrical war fighting with fuckin' traditional weapons and tactics, and too often on defense. Until now that is. Our little group is fighting those cocksuckers far more effectively than the combined governments of the world. We took the offense by fighting fuckin' terrorism with terrorism. We maintain, and Jackie in the DIA has evidence, that our assassinations, bombings and other measures increased the difficulty of recruiting jihadis.

"The media speaks about the existential threat we face from radical Islam, well we throw the threat right back up fuckin' Mohammed's ass. Some fanatics would die for their religion but how many can there be?. I believe that our successes discouraged many away from terror…but not enough. We have fuckin' intelligence that the jihadists are combining forces with the pussy Left for a massive attack on our country; an attack far more sizable than the one you two stopped last week. We must stop them because the government tards are in denial and sitting on their collective asses with this info. Our fuckin' government's lack of resolve will get us all killed. I'll be damned to let that happen. Tom, you understand these terrorists aren't interested in debate? They only want to conquer.

"We're about to have a fucking election. Ronald Trumbull, a personal friend, has a great chance of winning. He unconditionally agrees with our goals and wholeheartedly supports the Martels. We faked my death to plan these needed assaults on our country's fuckin' enemies without scrutiny from the government, the media, our targets or other worthless dickheads. We will meet him soon after he wins the damn election. It may shock you by what he will tell you, but that is all I can fuckin' tell you for now."

Morgan moved to the couch to sit between his guests.

He took their hands, "I wanted to meet you two to ascertain whether you would care to continue with us. I have no doubt you fuckin' do, but we have some critical missions are coming up and I need to hear it directly from you."

Tom and Kat looked at the other and in unison stated, "We do."

"Tom, I'd like to know whether you have ever felt any fuckin' guilt or remorse shooting the cocksuckers."

Tom spoke without hesitation, "Never. I'd feel guilt and remorse had I missed a target who would have later killed by his terrorism. I am motivated to shoot straight by this prospect. Fortunately, I haven't missed."

Morgan laughed, "Damn straight you haven't missed -- which is why we value your talents – and yours too, Miss St. John. Jackie Brandt tells me you have a kill from that Koranland mission."

Morgan didn't give her time to respond. "I have a gift for you two." He reached into his pocket to pull out two gold pins. He showed them the 22 carat solid gold medieval war hammer pins, three-quarter of an inch long. Morgan explained pinning them on Kat and Tom, "The hammer, represented by this pin, was the weapon wielded by Charles Martel. A huge man, and a ferocious fighter, he swung a massive hammer to crush his enemies' skulls. Unlike most generals, he fought on the front lines alongside his men. At the Battle of Tours he stopped the advance of the Moslem horde. On that day he became a great Christian hero. Perhaps the greatest. Armor gave no protection against Charles the Hammer. He swung his massive hammer with such force that the sounds of crushing men's helmets and skulls were heard above the noise of battle. Tours became the high water-mark for Islam in Europe. Martel stopped their conquest. We named our group to honor him."

Tom and Kat thanked Jay Bailey for the gift they were honored to receive.

Morgan looked serious for a moment. "I have a favor I must ask you."

Tom replied, "Sure. What is it?"

"I have a friend, Annie Wright - I am sure you heard of her - a real fuckin' firebrand."

Kat said, "I pre-interviewed her for the Ted O' Hara Show. She was genial, until she entered the debate against a leftist feminist professor. She viciously destroyed the woman in front of three million people. I felt bad for the professor."

Morgan said, "Yes, I saw that. Annie was great. Well, the Antifa bastards have her in their sights and protest her speeches. No problem there, I'm all for free speech, but they act too aggressively against her for my taste. They want to shut her down, perhaps worse. At her latest speech two months ago some nasty cocksucker ran to her on stage to throw a pie toward her. She ducked and it missed but I am afraid they may try again -- next time, a little more seriously."

Morgan walked to the shelf pulled a newspaper and handed it to Tom and Kat. He had circled a story describing the attack on Annie Wright. Wright commented that like most liberals the attacker threw like a girl.

Morgan added, "Read the last paragraph."
Kat took the paper and read the paragraph, "The attorney general dropped all charges against the pie thrower which included two felony charges."

Morgan spoke, "Obviously, established law enforcement don't protect conservative speakers like Wright. Will you two do me the favor? Please attend her next speech at the University of Miami? She'll speak in next week? Keep an eye on things for me."

Kat and Tom nodded affirmatively, "We'd be happy to help."

"Great. I'll reserve a couple of front row seats for you under Mr. and Mrs. Michael Anthony's name."

Tom and Kat accepted their new assignment: Provide Annie protection. Simple.

Morgan said, "Should you catch any of the bastards give them beatdown for me."

Tom appreciated Morgan's concern for his friend, but doubted he would need to hit anyone.

Morgan walked to the door and with a grand flourish announced, "You two are fuckin' the greatest! Now get the fuck out of here. Anthony will give you a tour and take you to the dining room for lunch with my son. Tom, he has a business proposition for you -- the most lucrative one yet. Unfortunately, I can't join you, I have an important video conference we planned a week ago and I cannot change it. I hope to see you two again. Soon."

Morgan turned to Tom and Kat, "Anthony will take you back to Florida in the Skater. You'll be back in no time. He handles the boat like the goddamned jets he flies. He fancies himself a fighter pilot barreling down on his prey. Right, Anthony?"

"Yes, Mr. Morgan," replied a beaming Anthony Michael.

Kat and Tom gave their goodbyes and thanks to Jay Bailey Morgan III. They followed Anthony Michael from the room. Kat took Tom's arm and asked him,

"I know what a knock shop is, but what's a millihelen?"

Tom smiled, "A millihelen measures the beauty needed to launch a ship. The word rests on Christopher Marlowe's 1604 play *"The Tragical History of Doctor Faustus,"* when Faustus asks of Helen of Troy, 'Was this the face that launched a thousand ships?' He complimented you."

Anthony Michael, overheard the conversation, turned and gave them a warm, knowing smile.

Tom's explanation soothed and somewhat cooled Kat's annoyance at Morgan's comment.

Tom thought he would tease Kat a little, "Of course he may be referring to a negative millihelen."

Kat asked, "What's a negative millihelen?"

"…the amount of ugliness required to sink a battleship."

Anthony Michael, when hearing this, gave a loud laugh. Kat gave him an impish punch to the ribs, her personal gesture of affection to the recipient of her playfulness.

Anthony Michael took Kat and Tom on a tour of Morgan's castle. They stopped at a spacious room with a dozen men manning computer stations. Expansive screens lined the walls. The room reminded Tom of a smaller version of Jackie Brandt's DIA command center.

Michael explained, "Mr. Morgan monitors everything from this room – his business empire, the Martels, world news, his enemies, his friends, everything. Those men are recruits who couldn't pass the rigorous ninja training, but were bright and dedicated enough to train for these positions. We operate the room 24 hours a day."

Kat asked, "Where do all these men live?"

Anthony replied, "Mr. Morgan built a dormitory behind the castle for them. We house fifty men there. It is utterly impressive. They have their own cafeteria, workout room, gymnasium, classroom and library."

Next on the tour was the armory room. Anthony Michael explained, "Here is probably the greatest medieval weaponry and armor collection you will find."

Tom and Kat looked in amazement at the sizable room stocked with swords, shields, crossbows, daggers, flails, battleaxes and other exotic weapons. Three walls were lined with suits of armor.

Anthony Michael said, "Mr Morgan covered nearly every square inch of this four-thousand square feet room with his collection. Some items even hangs from the ceiling. The center of the room holds a colossal wood catapult."

Tom and Kat asked Anthony Michael about the apparatus.

Anthony explained, "It's a trebuchet, a type of catapult. Trebuchets use the force of gravity to propel an object. This is a scaled-down model, a reproduction. A typical trebuchets couldn't fit in this room."

Anthony Michael took them to the basement where a dozen jail cells were dug into the island's coral foundation.

Kat asked, "What were these cells used for?"

"The English used them to imprison the captured pirates before execution, usually by hanging. We now use them for storage, but here is an empty cell."

Tom walked into the cell past the rusted iron bars. He noticed the graffiti scratched into the begrimed limestone wall. One stood out: "Fuk the queen." He thought to himself: *"This guy was unquestionably defiant to the end."*

Anthony looked at his watch. "I have much more to show, but it's lunchtime. I'll take you to the dining room to meet Peter Morgan."

Within minutes he escorted Tom and Kat to the dining room where Peter Morgan waited. Peter Morgan did not resemble his father. He wore an IZOD shirt, khaki shorts and topsiders (without socks), a stark contrast to his eccentric father's kilt outfit. Peter was in his mid-thirties, clean-shaven, lean and of average height. He looked pleasant and rose to give Kat and Tom a warm smile and a handshake for each.

"So nice to meet you two. I heard a lot about you and appreciate it all. Kat, we were rooting for you during your New York adventure. Tom, I recognize your contributions to the Martel cause of which dad is supportive."
Peter continued, "Please sit down, care for a drink?"

Tom and Kat looked at each other and both declined the offer. Tom added, "Your father was very generous with his champagne last night."

"I understand. Care for some tea?"

Kat answered, "Tea would be perfect."

Peter looked at Anthony Michael, "Anthony, will you have Sabu deliver us a tea tray."

Leaving the room, Anthony went to the kitchen to order tea from Sabu. Sabu was a ninja recruit injured during training. He shattered his foot rappelling a thirty-foot cliff and suffered a compound fracture that became infected. Unfortunately, antibiotics failed to halt the infection and the doctors determined no alternative but to amputate the foot. Jay Bailey Morgan covered the medical bills and later had him fitted for a prosthetic.

Sabu's days as a ninja was finished, Morgan recognized that his intelligence and language skills would make him an excellent valet and butler. After the amputation, Morgan visited Sabu in the hospital to give him a box of P. G. Wodehouse books. "I want you to be like fuckin' Jeeves," he told the confused Sabu.

Named by Morgan because he resembled Sabu, the diminutive Indian actor from the 1940s. He was of Pakistani background, spoke perfect English and attended college before the Taliban arrived in his village. The Taliban Movement of Pakistan, also called the TTP, massacred his family amidst a raid on his village. These disasters could have destroyed his life but Blade rescued him and smuggled him from Pakistan.

Sabu humorously calls himself a "house ninja" – a reference to the bifurcation of social strata of antebellum Southern plantation life. He is completely loyal to Jay Bailey Moran III, accepts his eccentricities, and assumes

Jeeves' mannerisms to please Morgan; though he doesn't engage in any plots or maneuvers with his employer as did the fictional Jeeves.

Within minutes Sabu entered the dining room carrying a fully-stocked Edwardian Silver Tea Set. No tea bags here, Sabu prepared tea the traditional English method as custom in colonial India.

Kat sipped the tea, "This tea is amazing. Far more flavorful than any I've ever tasted."

"Dad wants the finest of everything," Paul said.. That includes his tea. He purchased an island off Thailand and built a sizable plantation on it. He had a special strain of tea leaves developed in India. It took years to develop into a viable crop. He was ecstatic when he found the soil saturated with bird guano. He believes the guano fertilizes the plants and gives the tea its distinct flavor."

Tom lifted his cup, closely examining the tea.

Kat exclaimed, "Tom, don't say it!"

Paul laughed, "Don't worry Kat, I've heard all the remarks when I tell the story of Morgan tea. Dad sells the tea to his friends and 4 or 5-star hotels worldwide. He eventually turned a profit three years ago."

Tom asked Paul, "So what was it like growing up as Jay Bailey Morgan III's son?"

"Always an adventure. I know that my father is a true eccentric, but he is a kind man and treats everyone well. He treated his children especially well, though we wished we saw him more often."

Kat asked, "Does he usually wear a kilt around the castle?"

"No, but he loves his costumes. He once addressed a ninja graduating class dressed like Field Marshal Horatio Kitchener in full dress uniform. They really got a kick out of him. It created a strong bond, which, I guess, was his intention.

"I realize my father is a unique individual. He prefers to do things with a trace of style and more than a hint of mischief, but never with any malice intended."

Paul continued, "Your kidnapping is an example of his elfish demeanor. But don't let his pranks cause you to underestimate him. He is absolutely brilliant. For example, he knows and understands more history than does the combined history faculty of Yale, Harvard and Princeton. And he once ventured to prove it. Twenty years ago, he invited the entire history faculty of those three Ivies to a luncheon at the Harvard Club in New York.

"He enticed them with an endowed history professorship for each school. I suspect all attended for the money. He highlighted his luncheon with a speech that challenged them on specific arcane points of history. Dad easily parried the many objections from the learned men during the question and answer period. He gave quite a performance. We filmed the entire event. I should upload the speech to YouTube one day."

Sabu returned with lunch: Broiled Black Grouper, wild rice and hydroponic asparagus. Peter continued, "We grow asparagus and other vegetables in a hydroponic greenhouse dad built on the southern side of the island. This Grouper swam the reefs this morning. Sabu fishes for lunch early every morning. There's nothing like fresh fish for lunch."

Paul said, "Tom, I want to talk business here. As you know, I'll be the nominal head of my father's businesses. Of course, dad will be involved but he has given me more responsibilities. I am now in charge of new acquisitions. We receive dozens of offers each year to purchase billion-dollar companies but seldom act on them. I plan to be far more aggressive with acquisitions and I plan to work with you about the financing."

Tom smiled, "I'll be glad to help, but I must work within SBT. They took a chance on me, and I'll remain loyal to them."

"That should be no problem. We welcome SBT. For decades dad feuded with Prescott Browning, but they eventually forgot what the bickering was all about and shared a few cognacs at the Brooks. They have been friends since then. Let's tea toast to future business."

They finished lunch exchanging stories of their experience with the Martels, Kat's television work, funny stories about Jay Bailey, Ronald Trumbull's presidential campaign and the Middle East situation. Kat even recounted her first day working for Ted O'Hara. Tom had never heard of Ted's aggression previously.

After two hours Anthony Michael entered, "We must leave now if we are to take you two back to Florida today. A storm is developing -- we have a two-hour window before the storm hits." Tom realized they were in for a rough ride back to Florida, and, indeed, it was quite a ride as they flew crashing from wave to wave — Anthony Michael enjoying every minute of it.

They arrived safely and an awaiting limo, obviously arranged by Morgan, took them back to the grove where her father was preparing to call the Missing Persons Bureau. Kat explained to her father that they took an overnight trip to a Freeport casino following dinner. Mike accepted the explanation. Kat knew they had been away for less than twenty-four hours, but their Bahamian adventure seemed far longer.

Two days later, Tom and Kat fought a crowd of barbarians to enter Storer Auditorium at The University of Miami. Annie Wright was scheduled to speak at the sold-out venue but Antifa and their allies intended to disrupt her speech. Tom and Kat attended to keep an eye on the place for Jay Bailey Morgan III.

They took their front row seats. Soon, the emcee introduced Annie Wright and she commenced her speech. All went well in front of a largely friendly audience. Annie presented her stand-up comedy routine; heavy on politics that targeted lefties who made easy targets. After the speech, questioners lined behind two microphones on each side of the auditorium.

The questioners were courteous, a few were contentious, but none were too impolite. Tom noticed, however, a questioner in the line looked too similar to the outside protestors. He also wore a heavy loose jacket – unusual for a warm Florida evening.

He also looked fidgety and nervous. When it was his turn to speak, he pulled something from his jacket pocket. Tom realized it was a Nalgene flask.

The flask appeared to contain a red liquid. The man ran towards the stage, directly towards Annie Wright. Tom didn't hesitate. Instantly, he bolted to intercept the man. He didn't want to tackle him, not knowing whether the liquid acid, paint, blood or simply tinted water. Accordingly, he decided a block his best option to stop the assailant. Tom hit Annie's attacker with overwhelming force; knocking the man five or six feet against the curtain and back wall. The man, stunned by Tom's attack, was not rendered speechless. He screamed, "What the fuck!"

Pandemonium erupted in the auditorium. Security led Annie Wright from the stage, unsure if the threat had passed.

Tom decided he needed to mete out some immediate justice as the authorities would likely go easy on this radical. He landed a powerful strike on the man's kidney. The radical emitted an audible "oomph" from the punch. Tom knew he had connected with his target. The man will piss blood for the next few days. Perhaps he will be deterred from such behavior in the future.

Kat, charged with protecting Tom's back, grabbed Tom's arm, "Let's go, Tom." Tom agreed and the couple melted into the frenzied crowd. They quickly exited the auditorium and drove back to St. John's Orange Groves.

On the drive home Kat asked Tom, "Why did you hit that guy so hard?"

Tom replied, "He needed it."

Kat laughed but never brought the topic to conversation again. She recalled her treatment of Gladys at her Williams College confrontation with the sisterhood and understood Tom's power punch.

The attack on Annie Wright and Tom's defense took seconds, agitating the crowd to chaos and total pandemonium. Fortunately, the security cameras did not catch Tom's thrashing of the radical. Nonetheless, Tom received a letter from Annie Wright the following week. He imagined Jay Bailey Morgan III told her about the arrangements to protect her.

Regardless, she thanked him for his protection that night and asked whether he would want a job giving security at her public appearances. Tom sent her a note politely declining her offer, but wished her the best and lauded her efforts to educate the American public of her views. He agreed with her fight for individual rights and the traditional American way. After all, he was doing the same, in his own uncommon way.

CHAPTER 12: *Abdul the Butcher*

Sayeed Farouk Abayaagoub was an enormous, imposing and intimidating man. Born in Ankara, September 1980.He was a monster of a baby weighing more than 11 pounds, he grew to a monster of a man – 6' 7," 330 pounds of bone and muscle with less than 10% body fat.

No one called him Sayed or Farouk. Long ago, he assumed the name Abdul the Butcher after his hero, a professional wrestler of the same name. As a young boy in Turkey, he watched muddy videos of the American wrestlers of the various professional circuits. He followed wrestlers from Bruno Sammartino to Hulk Hogan and Brock Lesnar, but Abdul the Butcher remained his favorite. Abdul portrayed the most brutal, violent and bloody wrestler of his time. His Sudanese piledriver broke a few wrestlers' necks prompting the wrestling promoters to ban the move.

The sport captivated Sayed, now called Abdul. He joined a local wrestling club and learned Greco-Roman, freestyle and Kurash – a Middle East type of wrestling. His size, conditioning and strength, together with considerable practice, took Abdul to the top of the Turkish wrestling world. At nineteen, he was undefeated after more than a hundred matches, he earned a spot on the Turkish Olympic Team as their Super-Heavyweight. However, Abdul's membership on the team lasted until his blood test came back. The test revealed a near overdose level of Dianabol. They dropped him from the team that prompted a rage which motivated his emigration to the United States in disgust of his native country.

Abdul settled in Syracuse, N.Y., helped by a Catholic Charities program. The program included a special English language class. Abdul never became proficient with this new language but he spoke English well enough to get by. He found a job as a wrestling coach at the local fitness club. He didn't last long. One night while drinking at the town watering hole, Abdul perceived an insult from a fellow patron and broke the man's jaw and zygomatic optic bone with a single punch. The judge would have handed him a light sentence if that was the extent of his crime, but Abdul attacked a few of the arresting cops. It took a dozen cops to slap the cuffs on him. He sent three cops to the hospital along with the original victim. Abdul faced a dozen felony aggravated assault charges plus a myriad of lesser crimes and misdemeanors. The judge didn't need much persuasion from the DA to send Abdul to Attica for six years.

Abdul wasn't the model prisoner at Attica, but he did find God, or at least Allah. It is called Prislam – the jailhouse conversion of prisoners to Islam. Muslim imams, paid by the state as chaplains, aggressively recruited apostate Muslims back into their faith. Although born of the Muslim faith Abdul never gave the faith much attention. He attended a madrasa when a boy, but soon lost interest in the religion. Wrestling and weightlifting were his religion.

The prison's imam considered Abdul a prime catch. They tutored him in the finer points of the Koran and the Hadith. These lessons included Jihad. The imams considered him an excellent candidate for enforcer and protector of the religion within the prison confines. Abdul proved an easy convert. He was comfortable among the Muslim prisoners and worshipped the prison imams. Besides, where else could he go? He hated the black and Hispanic prisoners and didn't fit in with the whites; some, of whom, were into White Power and Nazism. He rose in the prison hierarchy after some challengers were dispatched to the prison hospital ward. No one dared threaten his authority with the Muslim population during his remaining years at Attica.

The parole board released Abdul in 2014. They permitted him to work for an upstate Muslim community called Koranland, the headquarters of a radical imam named Yazid Umar. Yazid Umar had ambitious plans for jihad and needed a man like Abdul.

Within a couple of years, Abdul led the jihadi forces from Koranland. He was the master sergeant to the imam's generalship. He and the imam had plans against the infidels and now had an army for a spectacular attack. They longed for something to match Osama bin Laden's and Mohammed Atta's achievements on September 11, 2001.

Yazid and Abdul promptly developed a plan. A dozen suicide bombers would be dispatched to New York City landmarks on a busy Friday night to detonate their suicide vests crammed with high-powered explosives and ball bearings. These terrorists would shoot their way into a dozen venues like Madison Square Garden, Lincoln Center and the Convention Center, embed themselves into the large crowds and explode their vests. To increase the carnage and death a team of jihadis will stand near the doorways with fully automatic tec-9s to shoot anyone surviving the explosion -- a simple plan that could break Mohammed Atta's record deaths of three thousand infidels.

The planning, the recruiting, the training and the acquisition of supplies were completed; arming the vests with explosives and ball bearings was all that remained. Abdul grew excited about the expected death and mayhem his jihad would create among the Kafir.

However, their plans were foiled when the barn used to store supplies exploded, killing twelve suicide bombers. That explosion also brought substantial scrutiny from the FBI, DHS, the ATF and the New York State Police. They ruled the blast an accident but it was clear to law enforcement the imam and Abdul had planned a murderous terrorist attack. Abdul, Imam Umar, and the surviving terrorists departed to safe houses in Syracuse and Buffalo. The FBI placed Abdul and the imam on their Ten Most Wanted List.

Abdul didn't believe the barn explosion an accident. He trained his men too well, also the explosives they handled required more than a simple spark to ignite. He suspected sabotage and was determined to find the truth.

When the heat from the investigation cooled Abdul hurried back to Koranland to search for answers. He realized the risks involved but had to find the truth about the barn explosion. He wanted to find the half dozen motion-activated trail cameras he planted on trees around the property's perimeter. Abdul hoped the investigators hadn't found them. They were camouflaged and well hidden.

Two of his soldiers joined Abdul for the search. They arrived at the property, ironically at the same back road Tom and Kat had previously walked. Abdul and his crew hiked along the road towards the first camera marked on a simple map he had drawn. They soon found it. For the next hours they searched and found all six cameras. All were in excellent condition.

They brought back the cameras to the safe house for inspection. The short videos revealed deer, squirrels, foxes and wolves wandering through the camera's field of vision. Abdul was furious. He growled, "How many more of these videos do we have? This is all junk - nothing but animals walking around."

However, the last camera gave Abdul everything he wanted: the video displayed a well-armed camouflaged couple hiking directly towards the barn.

The man carried a grenade launcher, the woman, a rifle.

Abdul became enraged at these two and roared revenge against them. "There they are! I knew it was no accident. We will find these two Kafirs and give them revenge, just as the Prophet ordered us. Inshallah!!!

The jihadists rose and in chorus: "Inshallah! Inshallah! Inshallah!"

But first, he had to find the identities of these two. He inquired around his jihadi community and found a new method for face detection called enhanced facial detection that employed computer-calculated depth information. He learned the Iranians were thoroughly adept with this technology and asked Imam Umar to request their help.

The Iranians agreed to assist. Abdul had a copy of the photos hand-delivered to their embassy in Ottawa, Canada. He didn't want any NSA internet surveillance to discover these photos. He was sure the NSA scrutinized anything sent via any electronic means to Iran, its embassies, consulates or other offices.

Within a week they had a hit: a Tom Ford of Orford, NH visited Oman and was added to their database. Iran had complete access to that database, unknown to the techies in Oman. Tom Ford registered an 87% match with the photos Abdul found on the trail cameras. Close enough for Abdul.

They couldn't identify the woman, but that wasn't important. Abdul reasoned that if he found Tom Ford he would also find the woman. If she wasn't with Ford when Abdul found him, a little painful persuasion before Ford's death will provide Abdul the information he needed to find her.

Abdul the Butcher developed his plans for revenge against Tom Ford. He found the Ford house on Google Maps and devised a simple plan: surround the house with his soldiers and kill the inhabitants. The house's remoteness with no nearby neighbors decreased the chance of detection. He didn't want to waste time killing any witnesses. This attack was for revenge, not jihad.

Abdul sent a three-man scout team to surveil the property. The team was careful. Two were dropped off near Tom's home. They walked the property taking dozens of photos. No one detected them during their daytime incursions to Orford, making their job much easier. They didn't want to break into the house and alert Tom Ford of impending trouble, nor the police, had the doors been alarmed. Abdul's men took photos through the windows. Later, Abdul scrutinized the high-resolution photos and noticed the couple's framed portrait on the fireplace mantel — the same two he had found on the surveillance camera. He was now 100% sure Tom Ford was his man and he now had a photo of his accomplice.

Abdul's stakeout team took a motel room in West Lebanon, NH during their daily spy duties. They planned to discretely monitor the property each night to spotTom Ford's arrival.

It didn't take long. Within three days, they observed the cottage lights on. A closer check found that, indeed, Tom Ford and the woman have arrived.

Abdul thought when hearing good news, "Tomorrow night they will be dead." He called his team together to explain the simple plan.

Tom and Kat arrived in Orford with much work to do. His parents were enjoying a month-long African vacation. They were intrigued by the continent when on their world cruise and promised to return for a more extended trip.

Tom had chores his mother asked him to do while Kat had some research to conduct for Ted O'Hara. Ted O'Hara usually sent an email to Kat concerning an issue he needed to have researched. Kat was happy to oblige these requests from her boss, even during weekends.

On the second day, Tom and Kat prepared Amelia's numerous gardens for the approaching winter, adding some mulch here, pruning there, pulling out the dead vegetation, cutting dead flowers from the perennials and digging out the Dahlia tubers for winter storage in the basement. Tom had completed this chore annually with his parents through the years and now enjoyed sharing this aspect of gardening with Kat...as did Kat with him.

They finished their work before sundown and looked forward to a quiet evening together. Kat cooked a tremendous seafood risotto under a new showpiece: the Jeroboam champagne bottle signed by Jay Bailey Morgan III, Anthony Michael and Peter Morgan. They rescued the bottle from the practice range and assigned it the honor of permanent kitchen decoration. Tom had carried the bottle from Morgan's Island to Morgan's Skater 46 and the bracing nighttime trip back to Miami at 80 mph.

Tom found a perfect bottle in his wine cellar to complement the risotto: a 2013 Chimney Rock Sauvignon Blanc. Later, Tom planned to show Kat his favorite movie – *High Noon* with Gary Cooper. Kat commented on his choice of movies, "Why am I not surprised? It's also among my father's favorites, but I haven't seen the movie in fifteen years and would love to see it again."

A remarkably warm late fall evening allowed them to have dinner on the deck. Tom and Kat enjoyed a delightful night with every star giving their maximum luminosity and the new moon giving a perfect dark background for the celestial display. They finished dinner and Tom found another bottle of Chimney Rock to drink during the movie. Tom and Kat sank into the other's arms and the comfortable black leather Chesterfield sofa, an heirloom housewarming gift from his parents.

Marshall Kane and Amy Fowler were about to marry when shots rang out through the window behind them. The barrage of bullets continued, destroying the television screen and everything around it. Tom pulled Kat to the floor as the fusillade of automatic fire continued to ravage the room. He gathered his wits during the surprise attack and thanked his stone cottage for providing considerable protection from the gunfire...but for how much longer?

Tom crawled to the gun cabinet that was shot up along with most of the guns. Nevertheless, he noticed his 20 gauge Benelli Black Eagle was still intact. He grabbed the shotgun from the rack and slid it across the floor to Kat. He followed with a box of three inch #2 Buckshot. "It takes four shells. Shoot anyone who doesn't look like me crashing through the door or windows."

"No need to worry about that, Marshall." Kat was too focused to be alarmed, but she realized she must concentrate for her and Tom to survive this attack.

Tom took his Ka-bar and his 9mm Beretta pistol from the cabinet's bottom drawer. He kept the knife sharp in preparation for such circumstances as he now confronted. He also took a couple of loaded magazines and looked back at Kat, "I have more yard work to do, I'll be right back. Don't go anywhere."

Kat gave him a quizzical *"Where do you think I'd go."* But she said instead, "I promise I'll be right here when you return. I love you."

Tom smiled at her and crawled to the basement door. The shots continue pinging above him off the fieldstone fireplace. *"Just how much ammo do they have?"* he thought.

He opened the door, entered the basement and hurried straight to the escape tunnel. Tom feared years ago that his extra-curricular activities with the Martels may someday be discovered and his enemies seek revenge. He built a tunnel that took him from the cellar to an outbuilding a hundred feet from the house.

The tunnel was composed of a 48" corrugated culvert pipe he buried six feet deep one day with a backhoe. Tom planned to build a safe room in the basement but believed it could become a death trap should a home invader use explosives or poison gas. He thought of the safe room that didn't save Ambassador Stevens in Libya. Tom now thanked God for his foresight.

Tom traversed the tunnel in under a minute. He reached a short ladder leading to the exit, turned off the flashlight and pulled out his Beretta. He snapped off the safety. Tom emerged from the tunnel and forced open the trapdoor in the shed. He hoped no attackers were there. There weren't. He silently exited the shed. Tom gazed into the dim light. The stars gave enough light to evaluate the surroundings. He found himself beyond the attacker's perimeter. Their now sporadic bursts gave away their positions in the bushes. Tom assessed his options.

He employed the old Muslim practice of Dhakat – cut the esophagus, trachea and jugular with a single slice -- ironic, considering the targets, but effective.

The shooting had now ceased but for an occasional burst from an automatic followed by a shotgun blast. Kat performed well, but can she hold out any longer? Tom decided he must do the dirty swiftly before they overwhelmed her.

Tom spotted his first target crouched behind a rhododendron bush. He crept towards the man, so quietly that he soon stood directly behind the gunman without detection. He covered the shooter's mouth, pulled the head violently backward, exposing the throat. Tom forced his knee between the shoulder blades for added leverage and slashed horizontally across the throat and the jugular veins. The man exhaled a soft gurgle and fell limp on Tom's arm. The entire attack lasted a few short moments. Tom looked for his next mark.

He slinked counter-clockwise around their perimeter. Each attacker appeared to be separated by thirty to forty feet. They were crouched, armed with a Tec 9 and concealed from the house by the many trees and thick bushes. Tom had no problem finding and mechanically killing all the shooters by the same M.O.

He completed his circumnavigation around the house in less than ten minutes. None of his victims ever realized their fate. Tom thanked Mad Anthony Wayne for the skills he employed to produce such carnage.

He heard four shotgun rounds during his killings, but was confident Kat had blasted more brave souls attempting to breach the house's doors and windows.

With his Beretta in one hand and his now bloody knife in the other equally bloody hand, he carefully approached the house. Sure that no more threats remained from the outside, he looked into the house and observed Kat still crouched behind the now shot-up chesterfield, shotgun ready. She appeared unharmed. Tom also spotted four dead attackers, two on the floor and two hanging from the windowsills, which were now destroyed by the barrage of bullets. He smiled to himself, "My girl did OK."

Without warning, a colossal figure bounded from the kitchen heading directly for Kat.

Abdul recognized her as Tom Ford's woman. He will take tremendous pleasure in killing her, but despite what the imams teach about the evil of female infidel flesh, he will first rape her every which way.

Kat concentrated on the doors and windows. She didn't see Abdul approaching her from behind. Abdul lumbered forward, stomped her to the floor, kicked the dropped shotgun away, grabbed her like a rag doll and started choking her -- not to kill her, but to soften her for the rape. Kat fought back, clanging his ears with her open hands but the blows had little effect on the giant.

Through the window Tom saw an intruder strangling Kat. Tom had no time to lose. He raced to the front door and crashed through it. He found Abdul ten feet away, raising Kat off her feet, her back to Tom. Tom hesitated to take a shot with the pistol. Although trained for pistol shooting under duress, Tom realized he wasn't quite the sure shot with a handgun as with a rifle...and Abdul gave him a small target crouched behind Kat's limp body.

Tom yelled, "Yo Achmed, Allah considers such abuse of women as haram. Let her go."

Abdul laughed at Tom when he spotted the gun. Kat was nearly unconscious by this time but Abdul stopped choking her. He lowered Kat using her as a shield to bull rush Tom. Tom tossed the knife to the side, concerned he was of accidentally sticking Kat. Tom held on the gun as he was crushed against the wall from Kat's and Abdul's combined weight.

Abdul had Tom pinned against the wall. He grabbed for the gun with both hands, Kat remained between them.

As they wrestled for the gun Kat crumpled to the floor. With Kat on the floor Tom delivered a powerful punch with his free hand to Abdul's upper cheek. A long gash opened to the bone. Blood flowed down his face, but Abdul battled to maintain his grip on Tom's right hand that held the gun. Abdul then delivered a tremendous strike to Tom's ribs; the snap of his bones clearly audible. Stars danced about his eyes. He realized that Abdul injured him, but should he succumb to the pain he knew that he and Kat would soon be dead. His eyes blazed a virtual inhuman, intense blue fire. Like a shot, he dropped to his knees in front of the shocked Abdul, who now controlled the gun.

But he didn't have a chance to use it. Tom sprung with all the force his body could generate and slammed Abdul's lower jaw with an open palm so hard he thrust the jawbone into the temporal mandibular nerve causing a sensory overload that temporarily stopped Abdul's brain from functioning.

Tom recognized the Bambi Dance – the wobbly knees, eyes rolled into the head, and that paralyzed, contorted expression on the face. Tom saw a beaten Abdul. His stunned opponent collapsed to the floor. Tom caught him with a brutal right fist to the temple, smashing Abdul's cheekbone.

Abdul, battered and defeated, dropped the gun, falling heavily on top of it. Rapidly losing consciousness, he realized all was lost. The wounded giant instinctively used whatever energy remained in him to feel blindly for the gun. Tom grabbed the shotgun, aimed it at Abdul's head and pulled the trigger. The gun was out of ammo. *"Well, if one end doesn't work, the other end will."* Tom took the gun by the barrel and swung the butt into Abdul's skull, extinguishing any remaining life he had.

Tom, satisfied that the giant was dead, ran to Kat. He carried her to the ravaged couch.

She was barely conscious. Dark red contusions from Abdul's attack marked her neck. He raced to the kitchen for water and with a washcloth dabbed her face and neck with the cool water. She awakened and opened her eyes.

"How are you Kat?"

She tried to speak, and with a raspy voice quipped, "I'll survive but won't be singing La Traviata at the Met for awhile." She stood and enclosed Tom with her arms. He gently pushed her away. "We'll need to restrain the affection for a while. Achmed broke my ribs."

Kat backed off a step, "What was that all about, Tom?"

"I don't know. They appeared from nowhere and did a remarkable job on the house."

Kat looked at Tom, "What do we do now?"

"Better call Jackie."

Tom headed to his office to call Jackie Brandt.

Jackie was asleep but awoke by the phone call Tom explained all that transpired during the last half-hour.

"I'll see you in the morning. Be sure they all are dead."

Tom responded, "Bring along a doctor too, I may have broken ribs and Kat was nearly choked to death."

"Will do, Tom. See you soon. I'm glad you both survived the attack."

Tom rushed outside again to check the bodies. They were all in the same place and state of health as he left them. The four bodies inside had large gruesome chunks of their bodies blown off by the close-range shot from the shotgun. They were obviously dead. Tom rechecked Abdul but found no pulse. The deep bloody head wound assured Tom of his fate.

Tom walked to the dry bar to snag the remaining undamaged bottle. Fortunately, a single malt. Tom was annoyed his Glengoyne 35 Year Old, another generous gift from Jay Bailey Morgan III, was victim of the attack. His anger was only somewhat mitigated by the punishment the attackers received for their transgressions. He turned to Kat.

"Care for a drink?"

She whispered, "Make mine a double, plenty of ice."

Jackie Brandt appeared promptly at seven followed during the next two hours by his crew. An unmarked First Aid Ambulance with a doctor arrived soon afterward. The doctor checked on the damage to Kat and Tom. Kat had a bruised windpipe that should heal in a week or two. The doctor told Kat, "Drink milkshakes and you'll feel better, unless you want something a little stronger."

Kat politely declined. "Thanks, I'll stick with the milkshakes."

Tom had two broken ribs from Abdul's punch. The doctor taped them giving Tom some advice, "Your ribs should heal in six weeks. Stay away from any mortal combat in the meantime."

Tom felt fine so long as he didn't take too deep a breath. He decided to avoid jihadist giants for the foreseeable future.

A refrigerated truck, again unmarked, rolled in next. Jackie explained, "That is the meat wagon where we store the bodies until we dump them in the middle of the Atlantic from a C-17 Globemaster. Nobody will ever find them. We'll weigh them down and drop them into a deep site of the ocean. It will be like they never existed."

The crew lined the corpses along the walkway and photographed, fingerprinted, retinal scanned (for those who still had eyes) each body. Dental impressions were taken along with a DNA sample.

Kat gazed at the thirteen bodies – eight with cleanly slashed throats, a gruesome scene. Kat quipped with a quiet, hoarse voice, "Mr. Bellicose Ka-bar, you sure did a job on those poor souls. They look like discarded Pez dispensers. OJ would have admired your skill. Now I understand what they mean by toxic masculinity. Remind me to stay on your right side."

Tom said, "Your boys won't be attracting any virgins they died for. They are missing sizable pieces from their body -- not too appealing. We're a fantastic team, aren't we?"

Jackie walked up to Tom, "We'll have your house cleaned and repaired in a couple of days. A full sanitizing team should arrive by 10:00 A.M. You won't believe the work they do."

"Great, we'll stay at my parents' house until they finish the work."

Kat interjected, "I don't know. Tom likes that shabby chic look. Achmed did a greater job on his house than any New York decorator could have. I think he should keep it this way."

Tom gave Kat his best "Quiet Alice" expression.

He turned to Jackie. "So who were those guys?"
Jackie replied, "The monster you fought was Sayeed Farouk Abayaagoub, aka, Abdul the Butcher. He was an enforcer for the Koranland imam. I suspect he somehow discovered you sabotaged the plans for jihad and wanted revenge. You did a great job of staying alive, but killing 12 men armed with Tec-9s, was a helluva feat. They won't give a good impression on their dates with those 69 virgins."

"Kat did her part," Tom said with a smile. "She held the fort and killed four of the bastards with a 20 gauge." Tom inspected his attackers' weapons that were carefully arranged along the ground. "I hope you don't mind, I'd like to keep a couple of the Tec-9s and a few extra magazines for my collection."

Jackie laughed, "Not a bit. You earned them. I'll keep one for myself and give the rest to Blade. His crews can use them. These are fully automatic."

Tom continued, "Do you believe there are any more jihadists who'd seek revenge on us for killing these losers?"

"I doubt it, at least not immediately. I doubt Abdul told anyone about his plans. This was personal to him. He was out for revenge and was clearly unrelated to any organized jihad. That's not their modus operandi. Nonetheless, I authorized DHS and the NY State Police to raid the suspect Muslim enclaves and a dozen known safe houses today. Additionally, our Martel snipers will discretely take out a some selected targets about the state this week. It's housecleaning time for the State of New York."

Jackie added, "You and Kat should go back to work as though nothing happened. We'll have this cleaned quickly. I'm surprised no locals heard the shots last night."

Tom explained, "No noise escapes this property, the lofty ridgelines surrounding us prevent that. What's more, our nearest neighbor, Jim Scott, is half deaf. He couldn't hear a 12 gauge blast at 50 feet."

"That's great. We don't want to complicate matters."

Jackie left by noon but, true to his word, the sanitizing crew, a mini-army of craftsmen, did their jobs and three days later they finished repairs on the house. They replaced all windows, patched all walls, reupholstered the damaged furniture, washed the blood and smoothed the bullet dings in the fieldstone.

The foreman counted more than a thousand rounds found in the walls, ceiling and floor. "I've sanitized plenty of sites for Jackie, but nothing like this. This was a massacre."

Tom smiled and thanked them for their excellent work. As his custom, Tom tipped them well.

He had already thought what to tell his parents about the invasion. They would never appreciate the true carnage that night, judging by the restored condition of his house.

Unfortunately, most of his paintings and prints in the living room were damaged beyond repair, but, all told, Tom was satisfied with the outcome. Kat won't deliver any on-air presentations for the next few weeks and Tom would suspend his jogs with Martin for a month but both realized all could have been far worse after their battle with Abdul the Butcher.

The next day, Tom and Kat were back to the city at their jobs, only slightly damaged from their recent experience.

They enjoyed their drive back, concocting excuses for their injuries. Tom's excuse was easy: "I fell off a ladder from 20 feet, removing a bird's nest under the eave. I guess I was lucky to only suffer some broken ribs."

Kat's story proved more difficult to contrive; they believed that some will automatically assume Tom responsible for her bruised neck and raspy voice. They spun a narrative that Kat fought an amateur MMA contest during the weekend and lost by a rear-naked chokehold. The story was silly, but no one in the office questioned her story, certainly not Ted O'Hara. She was soon back giving her analysis of her research for the show.

Chapter 13: *Allahlaberg*

Tom again settled into a routine following the Abdul the Butcher ambush. He told his parents of the attack, omitting the more gory details. He gave his father one of the Tec-9s and two full clips. Robert Ford took the gun and kept it loaded under the bed. Just in case.

Amelia, though hardly alarmed, thought it prudent to improve her marksmanship. Dr. Ford and, on weekends, Tom and Kat, gave her lessons. After a couple of weeks her confidence with a gun grew. She believed she could help her husband defend their home, as Kat St. John helped Tom defend his.

Amelia remembered a story from Briggs family lore. In 1729, Hannah Briggs shot and killed two Indians intending to kidnap her children. This incident occurred three centuries ago, but she realized the dangers to her family remained, even in the 21st Century. She recognized she must be ready to help her husband and son should they experience an attack.

Jay Bailey, true to his word, gave Tom his largest deal yet. Tom and Martin spent months with the mega multi-billion dollar deal to finance a purchase of Aerolyft, a company that builds drones for video surveillance and tactical purposes. The company ventured into the commercial market, especially for agricultural and energy applications. Morgan wanted Aerolyft under his control. Tom, Martin and SBT pulled extraordinary political and financial strings to assure it happens. Tom, satisfied with the progress of the deal, expected to close that month.

Kat found herself busy as ever at FOXc Communications. She covered the 2016 presidential campaign with Ted O'Hara. Ronald Trumbull spun the news cycle at maximum speed. The new president promised substantial change, and many opposed those changes – it made for great politics and incredible ratings. Ted O'Hara increased his reliance on Kat for basic research, and she shared airtime with him virtually daily.

Kat wondered about Trumbull's presidency impact to the Martels and their battle against jihad. Her brief relationship with them through Tom has been exciting and created a new aspect to their relationship -- a relationship that has grown since their latest encounter with jihad. Each encountered death, relied on the other for survival and succeeded with their missions. Nothing could ever separate TomKat, an appellation taken from the gossip pages, and assigned to them by Roni Levine at the company Christmas party. Tom liked the name, Kat was skeptical, but the label seemed to have stuck around the studio.

Jackie Brandt kept Tom informed about the changes the new administration intended to fighting terrorism. Trumbull took the jihadi threat far more seriously than did the previous administration. Jackie learned that Trumbull had already contacted Jay Bailey, who had publicly resurfaced following the election, regarding a developing terrorist plot in southern California.

On his first day in office, an informer, through VP Jack Larsen, submitted evidence that a major terrorist attack was planned in Southern California. An alliance of radical Muslims and social warriors from Californian universities coordinated the attack, financed by Silicon Valley billionaires, who, for some inexplicable reason loathed the country that allowed them to amass their wealth. It was a new development that alarmed the Trumbull administration.

Captured coyotes told investigators that serious money, ranging from thirty to forty-thousand dollars, were paid for each of the dozens of Middle Eastern men trafficked from Mexico to Southern California. Asked why the former president didn't act a week ago when he received this information, he was informed that he and his advisors were skeptical of any intelligence involving Muslims. The historical president had no reliable military advisors in his inner circle. He relied on academic types deeply ensconced in Cultural Marxism. His advisers opposed deploying a military or police force under any circumstances, particularly when minorities were involved.

However, the intelligence immediately alarmed the newly inaugurated Trumbull. One of his offices and thirteen of his employees fell victim to the 9/11 attack on the World Trade Center, and he pledged during his campaign, not only to take all terrorist threats seriously, but to destroy, whenever possible, all terrorists.

Trumbull was very aware of the dangers radical Islam presents the country. "I won't wait until after the body count to fight terrorism. I will judge all threats as urgent and use all available resources to prevent the deaths we suffered on 9/11. Believe me."

Trumbull quickly discovered he had another problem. Few in government shared his concern for this problem. The "deep state" holdovers from the previous administration: FBI, Homeland Security and CIA gave the same answer to his inquiries, "We are on top of the problem, but we receive dozens of these reports daily, and must allocate our resources wisely." Not good enough for Trumbull. The new president was livid these bureaucrats were sandbagging his young administration. He realized government bureaucracies worked harder to protect their institution than they have an interest of doing the work their job requires. Trumbull resolved to end this dangerous mindset.

He called his attorney general to explain the situation. Trumbull gave the AG the names of those he had spoken to. "I want these people immediately terminated. I know firing government workers is more difficult than is firing workers in the private sector, but find a plan I can support. So far as I'm concerned these people are traitors and we need to set an example for everyone. They are supposed to serve my administration and the country. They should leave government employment if this doesn't suit them."

The president knew he had to install his loyal followers in these agencies quickly or these roadblocks will continue. However, there was something about this particular intelligence, given to him by a supporter in homeland security that seemed too real -- too much of a potentially catastrophic threat to the country. The new president knew that until he could install his people in law enforcement and intelligence he must rely on extraordinary means to verify and eliminate these threats. He called his old friend Jay Bailey Morgan III.

"Jay, how's life on the other side?"

"Ron, I've been busier than I ever have since I died. By the way, congratulations on your victory over the darkness -- quite a feat. You did well."

"Thanks Jay, but I already have a problem."

Trumbull explained the intelligence he received, and the bureaucracy's muted response to his inquiries about it. "Jay, I heard talk and have seen serious evidence that a secret society exists in the F.B.I. bureaucracy. This group is planning to make my life miserable; perhaps, to lead a coup.

Who'd ever believe something like this could ever happen in this country?"

Morgan replied, "Mr. President, your secret society is bigger and better than is their secret society." Trumbull was well acquainted with the Martels. He covertly gave financial and other support to their activities for the last years.

"I'm worried Jay. I won't stand by while terrorists plot to kill Americans. I need your help."

"You know I'll do anything you ask."

"Good, I have a man who gave me the information. He's an FBI veteran and a true patriot. He's also a close friend of Jack Larson, my VP. Jack, a twenty-five-year FBI agent is concerned about the direction law enforcement has lately taken, as I am."

Morgan replied, "I'll have my man talk to him about this intelligence. What's his contact information?"

Trumbull replied, "I'll send that to you and tell him to expect a call. By the way, I didn't hear a single curse or swear word from you Jay. Have you found religion?"

"Hell no, but you are president now. I can't swear to an American president."

After his phone call to the president Jay Bailey contacted Jackie Brandt, "Jackie I want you to look into this possible fuckin' terrorist attack developing in California. The president told me of some damn shit he received of a buildup in Los Angeles. An FBI agent gave him a few troubling facts. Call me after you talk to him. I'll give you his phone number when I receive it."

****

Praise Allah! Hasan Al-Tamini asked Allah to reveal a path of retribution for all the blasphemy and indignity America imposed on world Islam. He found the revelation during an Anaheim traffic jam. The traffic stopped him for a half hour on I-5 adjacent to Disneyland. Since it was time for evening prayers what else could he conclude but that he received a signal from The Merciful One. The more he thought of Disneyland the more excited he became. Disneyland, an icon of American culture, presents a per-

257

fect target for retaliation against the infidel's country that had killed thousands of his brother and sister Ummah.

The huge crowds of infidels, packed together, presented an opportunity to strike a mighty blow for Islam. Hasan Al-Tamini, the Imam of Allahlaberg was eager to plan the attack. The idea was to kill as many Americans as possible on their home turf. If it was Allah's will, he, too, must die in the attack.

Ten martyrs with vests could kill thousands at a crowded Disneyland; he will become famous for a successful attack against America.

These words from ISIS leader Abu Mohammad al-Adnani (Peace be upon Him) inspired Hassan to jihad:

"How can you enjoy life and sleep while not aiding your brothers, not casting fear into the hearts of the cross worshippers, and not responding to their strikes with multitudes more? If you cannot find an IED or a bullet, then single out the disbelieving American, Frenchman, or any of their allies. Smash his head with a rock, or slaughter him with a knife, or run him over with your car, or throw him from a high place, or choke him, or poison him. If you are unable to do so, then burn his home, car, or business. Or destroy his crops. Do not lack. Do not be contemptible. Let your slogan be, "May I not be saved if the cross worshipper and taghūt patron survives."'

Hasan returned to Allahlaberg to explain to his followers that Disneyland could become Islam's greatest triumph against the infidel. After considerable discussion, he decided to commit ten men to attack with suicide vests, accompanied by 30 additional men carrying automatic weapons. They will kill those who were not killed by the bomb. Forty beautiful Soldiers of Allah. This plan was comparable to that of Koranland, but it focused on a single large target instead of a dozen smaller venues. He added more men armed with Tec-9s to increase the carnage than did the Koranland plan.

"May Allah liberate us from the aggressor's hands and the occupiers. May Allah destroy everyone who craves evil for Islam and Muslims," Hasan proclaimed at his recent pep rally. He proudly looked out to his newly imported terrorist army as he finished with a loud, forceful, "Inshallah" -- If Allah so wills. The men returned his call: "Inshallah...Inshallah...Inshallah!"

Allahlaberg was companion to Koranland. Saudi money funded the purchase of the property a dozen years ago. A group of pious Muslims purchased a dying date grove near the edge of California's Mojave Desert and nursed it back to health. They raised families and devoutly worshipped Allah. With the money earned from the sale of their dates they built a mosque to accommodate the 35 families living on the 400-acre compound. Allahlaberg earned the respect from the outside community for turning the business around. The prosperity lasted until the radical Hasan Al-Tamini became their imam. He soon took Allahlaberg from a family-friendly religious enclave to a training ground for jihad. Hasan had an arrangement with ISIS to assist in training their jihadists. They paid him well for the use of Allahlaberg and Hasan continually planned new ways to kill the Jew-Christian American Crusaders.

Hasan couldn't forget his latest contact with the American military a few years ago. He had planned an ambush in Iraq that went terribly wrong. He didn't know whether a timely drone pass or an informant had warned the Special Forces, but he and his brothers in jihad had been ambushed. They had retreated as best they could, dragging and carrying the wounded. Hasan remembered his cousin's head exploding when they stopped a mile away to catch their breath. He later learned Americans had a new sniper rifle called the .50-caliber Barrett with a kill range of up to two miles.

Hasan never again underestimated the American soldier. Though he considered the typical American soft and spoiled, he respected their military a well-trained machine of war. The Navy SEALS and Delta Forces were positively intimidating. Hasan and his fellow jihadists had lost family and friends to them. During one day, he had seen the loss of more than a hundred men to the U.S. military. On that day his brother and two cousins were killed. They had vastly outnumbered the Americans, but the troop's marksmanship coupled with the Apache helicopter's rapid-fire chain guns and hellfire missiles overwhelmed them. A strafing run by an A-10 Warthog finished them off.

Hasan Al-Tamini was not the product of a madrassa but of Afghanistan's mujahedeen -- his religion more pragmatic. He didn't develop much love for humanity. No, he hated all things Western, Christian and Jewish. They must be destroyed.

This will be the first major attack on the United States since 9-11, and he will plan the assault with military precision. Nor will it suffer from the same fate as Koranland. He strictly controlled all plans and disseminated the information discretely. Total surprise was essential for a successful attack. He expected that this would be the first of many strikes within the U.S.

Hasan believed his success will inspire and mobilize the entire Muslim world. ISIS leaders decided Hasan Al-Tamini and his men drill for the next month at Allahlaberg, located in a remote region bordering the Mohave Desert.

Most of Hasan's men had been in operations throughout the Middle East, recently in Syria. They were battle-hardened veterans who had fought the infidels for years. All would gladly die for Allah.

Hasan first had six of his jihadists from Allahlaberg, months before the planned attack, to apply for employment at Disneyland as security guards. These were thoroughly Americanized Muslims, recent college graduates from nearby universities who would not attract undue attention. They were to monopolize the evening shifts, open the gates for the forty jihadists after the park closed and hide them in remote storage rooms of the various attractions of Disneyland until the time for attack.

Hasan will give all efforts to assure the success of his personal jihad. He aspired to strike a mighty blow for Allah, and he will target the United States. The entire Muslim revolution would be jeopardized if he did not attack. He prayed, "praise Allah and please let us succeed."

****

Jackie Brandt spoke to the FBI agent who convinced him, by the man's apparent sincerity and his considerable experience in the bureau, that the Southern California situation had reached a critical point and immediate action was needed.

Apparently, significant suspicious activity at Allahlaberg required further attention. Brandt had an informer inside Allahlaberg, but had no contact with him in over a month.

He hoped his man was still viable.

He had no time to waste on permissions, planning or training but had to initiate efforts today – thousands of lives depended on it.

He called Tom Ford, Alvin Haney (chief of the special ops and sniper vets) and Blade to gather at his San Bernardino house in twenty-four hours. A Morgan G-7 waited at Westchester Airport to fly Tom, Kat and Haney to California. Blade was onboard the cargo ship in New Orleans. He took a G-5 from Lakefront Airport, but only after arranging for twelve of his best

Ninjas to take the 1900-mile, twenty-eight hour trip in a specially outfitted, fully equipped Neoplan Skyliner bus.

The bus compares to the president's "Ground Force 1" but included a special suspension and a larger engine to accommodate the extra weight of the exotic military equipment hidden in the luggage holds. The bus was utterly luxurious at the insistence of Blade, who argued that his ninjas deserved the best. Jay Bailey Morgan agreed.

The Martel leaders met Thursday night at Brandt's house. They formed six squads of four men. Each squad consisted of two Special Forces men armed with rifles paired with two ninjas bearing shotguns. Jackie coordinated the effort from the bus at the entrance to Allahlaberg – his squad also protected the gates from any escapees. There were to be no prisoners and no escapees. All jihadists must be killed.

The Martels finished their plans early. They had twenty hours before the bus arrived with the equipment. Jackie recommended dinner and drinks at the local hangout, "Great food, good drinks, a somewhat rough crowd, but we can handle it."

Two of the special ops guys lived in Los Angeles and had their vehicles with them. They all hopped into the two vehicles and headed to the restaurant. The twelve Martels took a substantial table in the dining room corner. The crew enjoyed the new friendships, the drinks and the food. A four-foot divider separated the restaurant from the gaming room but all patrons were visible to each other. Tom noticed that a biker club congregated around the pool tables in the back of the room. They looked like trouble. Tom kept his eye on them.

Kat visited the Ladies Room, which, unfortunately, required her to wade through the game room. Tom told her he'd escort her to the bathroom. He waited for her, leaning against the room divider watching the biker's antics.

Minutes later, Kat emerged from the Ladies Room when a biker -- a hulking, ugly brute displaying an eye patch -- grabbed her as she walked by the pool table. Kat poked him hard in his good eye, which sent him to his knees in pain. She followed with a knee to his chin, driving him hard to the floor, flat on his back. Seeing his friend writhing on the floor, one of his friends attacked Kat, but Tom caught him then slammed him against the wall before he reached her. The biker created his outline on the now broken drywall.

Within seconds the Martels pitched in to assist their new partners. The altercation didn't last long. Although the bikers were accomplished brawlers, they were no match for the well-trained Martel fighters. Within minutes, the bikers were tossed out the door with a minimum of bloodshed. The Martels received a standing ovation from the patrons. A free round of drinks arrived at the table followed by the manager who thanked them for bouncing the bikers. The Martels continued with their meal as if nothing had happened. Jackie Brandt was pleased with their teamwork; efficiently ejecting the bikers from the restaurant.

****

Jackie Brandt's plans against Allahlaberg included the use of night vision sights by the snipers. He hoped they will provide them an advantage over the probable jihadis superior numbers. His twenty-four well-armed and trained fighters should be an adequate force to overwhelm the estimated 30 to 50 terrorists training at Allahlaberg.

Two riflemen and two ninjas manned each squad. The two riflemen carried M-4 assault rifles topped by EOTech Holographic Red Dot Sights. The sight projects a red dot onto the sight plane -- the bullet strikes wherever the red dot is placed. The combination was designed for quick, close engagements less than 100 yards -- the type of combat the Martels will likely engage that night.

Tom liked the speed with which he could strike multiple targets. Employing the old sights, a shooter had to align the rear sight to the target's front sight. The EOTech quickened the procedure: the shooter spotted the red dot on the target and fired. Point and shoot. It allowed a quicker, more accurate shot from the hip – crucial in close combat. Tom could engage several targets in mere seconds. He and Kat had practiced for hours in Orford with an M4 carbine rigged with the sight. Both developed complete confidence in the equipment.

The Ninjas were armed with the short-barreled DP-12 pump-action and double-barrel shotguns. Two shots are semi-auto that are fired by successive trigger pulls. A quick pump reloads the two barrels simultaneously for two more quick shots. The short gun, ideal for close-in combat, holds sixteen $2^{3}/_{4}$" shells. It was a devastating weapon. Jackie considered each squad perfectly armed for the adversary they will encounter and convinced they would prevail in any engagement.

They waited for the bus the next day, exchanging war stories until Jackie received a call from the bus driver. Jackie spoke on the phone awhile to give the driver his orders. He placed the phone in his pocket to talk to his crew.

"Listen up now. The bus passed the California border. We'll leave to meet them off I-15 west of Barstow."

TomKat sat in the back of the SUV with Kat on the way to their rendezvous. As they entered the highway he took her hand and asked, "Can I persuade you to stay with Jackie to coordinate the attack from the driveway?"

Kat's displayed her anger and gave him a serious look. "You will have a greater chance of restoring my virginity than of persuading me not to partner you on this assignment. Don't you trust me? How could you even think of such silliness after all we've been through?"

Tom replied, "I trust you, but you know enough about me to know I don't fear much. Yet I fear losing you. This will be an exceedingly dangerous mission. You could be killed."

"Tom, are you getting soft on me? What happened to the guy who slid that shotgun to me across the room when we were under attack in your house?"

Tom knew the answer but judged it would be best to tell her over drinks after the fighting. He managed a weak, "Forget I asked."

Two hours later, the convoy of the two SUVs rendezvoused with the bus off I-15 to Yermo Road. Jackie's vehicle led the caravan up the hills on an old unpaved and rutted mining road. Kat looked down at the long lines of gamblers heading to and from Las Vegas along the interstate from her vantage point high on the hill. The quiet darkness swallowed them as they approached the ridgeline that marked the compound's boundary.

Time was now 2:00 A.M. A three-quarter moon will provide more than adequate illumination for the upcoming activities.

A few minutes later, Jackie Brandt stood next to the bus driver and addressed his crew, "I received a text from Mr. Morgan. He wrote, 'I want you to hit them so hard their teeth fly out their asses.'"

Tom and Kat looked at each other and smiled. No words were needed. They knew everything Jay Bailey Morgan III expected from them.

The caravan stopped a hundred feet from the ridgeline; the crew exited the vehicles and gathered by the cargo door. Blade, the Ninja leader, opened the cargo doors to distribute the weapons. Jackie ordered the two snipers, both equipped with EOTech M963/PVS7 Nightvision Goggles, to hike past the ridgeline and scout the terrain.

Blade distributed the remaining weapons. He gave a rare smile as he handed Kat an M4 and four magazines. Kat noticed under the door's lights that someone had sprayed painted the barrel and stock of her rifle a bright pink. Blade snickered. Kat laughed, "…and here I thought you had no sense of humor. Thank you, Blade. I'll put it to good use."

Within twenty minutes, the two scouts returned with a report. Anthony Marino, one of the scouts, gave Jackie his appraisal, "We observed a small guardhouse manned by two guards near the entrance. They looked bored and weren't giving any attention to anything except the computer games on their iPads. We should have no problem taking the guardhouse. The compound looked quiet. The bunkhouse lights were on but otherwise, all looked quiet."

The men in the bunkhouse were preparing for their trip to Disneyland… and they weren't going to enjoy the Disney rides. The jihadists were planning to leave that morning and all were thinking, "Death to America."

Jackie gave his final orders, "We march the last mile double time to the compound. Blade and An Li (his most experienced Ninja) will run ahead, subdue and disarm the guards. The two snipers will circle around to take their positions on hills a hundred yards away from the target farmhouse and bunkhouses. The remaining squads will fan out to surround the two bunkhouses. Tom Ford and Paul Hill (the ex-SEAL) will run to the bunkhouse and toss grenades through the windows. We open fire when they return to our lines. The targets should be confused by then. And for the last time: We take no prisoners but don't harm the women, children and non-jihadi men.

It is important we confirm that their leader, Hasan Al-Tamini, is dead. After we secure the property, we search for the suicide vests and other weapons . We will then destroy those weapons. The bus driver will meet us when he hears the exploding vests. We board the bus and get the hell out of here. Any questions?"

Tom asked, "I understand that the men in the bunkhouses are jihadis. How do we determine which men are residents or terrorists?"

"We'll question the women. I believe that they will be pleased to rid themselves of the vermin that infected their community."

Kat raised her hand, "Can I keep my gun afterward. I kind of like the pink accents?"

Jackie gave her a serious look, "No, you will return all weapons. We will later jettison them into the deep ocean. We want no evidence of the massacre we are all about to commit. Let's go."

Jackie turned to the crew, "Blade, take An Li and secure the two guards in the lookout hut. Don't kill them. I want to question them."

"Yes, Col. Brandt. Will do."

Blade pulled out his infamous knife – an oversized Bowie knife -- that gave him his name. "Are you sure you don't want me to kill them?"

"No. I'll need to question them."

Blade, looked disappointed but motioned to An Li to follow him. The Martels, except for the two snipers, followed a hundred yards behind them. The snipers took positions, one to the left, the other to the right, to establish cover and backup positions.

These snipers carried standard Remington 700 sniper rifles. Attached were Armasight Drone Pro Night Vision scopes. The snipers would cover the operation and take out any escaping stragglers. Anthony Marino, the lead sniper, was as skilled as it gets. He had served three Iraq tours and was credited with more than 100 confirmed kills. His actual kills probably exceeded 150 but for a kill to count there had to be second party confirmation, often impossible in battle. He joined the Martels after his retirement at the urging of Alvin Haney, his first instructor and a great sniper from the Iraq war. Neither ever regretted their new part-time activity.

Within five minutes, Brandt received an all-clear from Blade – they secured the lookout hut. The Martels approached the guardhouse and the entrance to Allahlaberg. The guardhouse was a cheaply built shack built on ten-foot stilts. Jackie climbed the aluminum ladder and accessed the shack through a circular cutout in the floor. He saw Blade holding his knife and An Li carrying a shotgun standing over a slightly bloodied pair of guards.

Jackie approached them and noticed they were kids -- one had a scraggly beard, the other, clean-shaven. These weren't jihadists; they were kids from the compound. They couldn't be more than eighteen and didn't bear the hate in their eyes that he observed in jihadists he interrogated in Iraq and Afghanistan. These kids simply looked scared. Understandable, Blade can be intimidating.

"Take it easy, we won't harm you."

The two young guards said nothing.

Jackie asked, "How many jihadists are there in the camp?"

The older guard replied, "There are forty -- thirty trained with guns, ten with suicide vests. Most sleep in the bunkhouses but some are with our women. Those guys are nuts. They took over Allahlaberg more than a month ago, raped our mothers and sisters, beat the men and boys and stole our money. These are bad Muslims. Are you here to arrest them?"

Lt. Col. Jackie Brandt looked at them, "No son, we are here to kill them."

Jackie continued his interrogation, "Where do they store the explosives and vests?"

The guard, eager to cooperate and help the strangers' efforts responded, "They store everything in a pump house about fifty yards past the mosque. ...are you going to kill the imam?"

"Yes."

The two young guards smiled.

Jackie said, "Blade, bind their hands and gag them...and don't hurt them."

Blade took out a couple of nylon zip ties to secure the two guards. He fastened rags over their mouths and around their necks to keep them quiet.

Jackie found the guardhouse gave him a great view of the entire compound. He will use it for command central. Through his binoculars, he could see the activity in the long bunkhouse. He exited the guardhouse to address his crew to explain the situation, "You must take out the bunkhouses first but other jihadists could be interspersed with the civilians. After the bunkhouse is taken, clear every house and building. I want to see forty-one bodies – the forty jihadists and their leader, the imam. Are your radios working?"

Jackie counted quietly into his wrist radio, everyone heard him with their earplugs and nodded affirmatively. They were ready to rumble.

Five squads dispersed to their pre-assigned location. The sixth, led by Jackie, secured the entrance – there will be no escape via Allahlaberg's main gate. Jackie climbed the ladder into the guardhouse, this time he carried a Remington sniper rifle. He looked at the two guards, "You'll be free of the vermin in an hour."

Jackie looked out the landscape with his ATN NVG7 night vision goggles. They gave him a great view and perspective of the battlefield. He lifted his wrist, "Tom, are you ready with the grenade?"

Tom whispered back, "Ready." He repeated the question, "Paul, are you ready with the grenade?"

"Ready."

Jackie gave the order, "Grenadiers attack."

Tom and Paul sprinted thirty yards to their assigned wood bunkhouses. They reached their objective and tossed their grenades through the windows.

Paul, thrilled to be back in combat, yelled, "Wake up call!"

They sprinted back to the fire line and hit the ground when the grenades detonated. The grenades did their job and created pandemonium in the bunkhouse. The flash signaled the start of an incredible fusillade of M4 5.56 mm bullets from the riflemen and 12 gauge slugs from the ninjas. The three-quarter-inch board sheathing offered little protection to the inhabitants from the high-powered rounds and rapidly turned to Swiss cheese. The snipers searched for anyone exiting the houses and outbuildings.

The volley lasted about two minutes when Jackie ordered the squads to proceed into the bunkhouses. They poured enough lead into the bunkhouse to fill a 12-meter's keel.

Kat remembered a video her father showed her as a kid: the intense shelling of Iwo Jima followed by the Marines invasion. Her father would be proud of her. She had been subject to attack a few times in her life. She was satisfied to be an attacker for a change.

Tom believed that some would judge their raid as cruel, vicious murder. But the Martels were at war – all was fair but the most unspeakable cruelties. Kill before you are killed. Kill before you give the enemy a chance to kill you. These jihadis must never be given a chance to kill innocents...all the better for civilization.

The ninjas reloaded their shotguns with nasty 00 buckshot for the expected close-in combat. Ten yards away now, the riflemen, each, of whom, carried an M67 fragmentation grenade, ran to the now broken windows, and tossed their grenades into the bunkhouses. The grenades exploded and the Ninjas poured into the bunkhouses from the two side entrances.

Tom heard shotgun blasts, interspersed with return fire, but all was quiet within 30 seconds. He entered the bunkhouse, followed by the other riflemen. He ordered Kat to stay outside to cover them. Inside, he noticed the Ninjas checking the bodies. To his surprise, they were shoving hot dogs down the throats of the dead jihadis."What are they doing?" Tom asked Blade, realizing that now was not the time to teach the ninjas about respect for the dead."

"They are giving revenge. By stuffing pork into a dead jihadi body they believe Allah stopped them from entering heaven. You don't understand the hatred the ninjas have for them. They lost family and friends to jihad. They live for revenge. They used to stick the hotdogs elsewhere, but Jackie convinced them that Allah will keep them from heaven if they simply shoved the hot dogs down their throats."

Tom walked through the bunkhouse inspecting the blood, the bodies and the carnage. Reminded of a Milton quote appropriate for the occasion, "Sin opens the gates of hell, which now can never be shut, and they gaze at the abyss of Night and Chaos," Tom understood these men chose their fate, as did the Lattimore brothers years previously.

From the guardhouse Jackie observed two men emerging from the main house. He aimed and shot one of them not too far from the door. The other escaped by running around the house. But his escape was brief. A sniper on the ridge shot him through the heart as he ran toward the grove.

Tom received a call from Jackie, "Drag out the bodies and count them, we need forty-one."

The crew pulled out the bodies from the bunkhouse. They counted thirty-eight. Add the two sniper victims and they were one short -- the imam.

Jackie Brandt arrived to survey the scene. "Any casualties?" Tom quipped, "Yes, Kat broke a nail flipping off the safety of her M4." The crew laughed and Kat hit Tom in the ribs. She yelled, "Such a chauvinist pig!"

The Martels suffered no other casualties – the element of surprise combined with over-whelming firepower created little danger to the attackers -- the targeted jihadists had no time to prepare a counterattack.

Jackie continued, "We have 40 stiffs, but we are missing the imam. Go find him. He is the brains of this operation. We must kill him before he plans another attack elsewhere. Paul, I want you to search for the explosives and the vests. The guards said they stored them in the pump house down that path. Take your squad, find the stash and prepare them for detonation. If you see the imam – shoot him."

"Yes sir." Paul Hill led his squad to the pump house.

"The rest of you follow me to the main house, barns and mosque. We must find the bastard."

****

Hasan Al-Tamini anticipated his impending big day in his basement apartment below the mosque. With jihad filling his mind he gave his final prayers. He thought of the infidels his brilliant plan will eliminate from this filthy country -- a country in desperate need of a strong Caliphate. His plans had proceeded satisfactorily last month. The explosives arrived and the jihadis will construct their suicide vests next week. Forty men, thirty shooters and ten shahids were nearly finished with their training. The shahids volunteered to walk among the infidels, find the largest crowds and blow themselves up along with thousands of kafirs. The shooters would perfect his jihad masterpiece by spraying thousands of rounds of lead at the survivors of the blast. Hasan believed the Muslim world will celebrate him much as they acclaimed Osama bin Laden (Peace be upon him), and he will secure an exalted place in paradise under Allah for eternity.

Hasan's reverie ended with a deafening stream of gunshots.Perhaps the men decided they needed more practice or were celebrating their duties to Allah. He reached under his pillow for his decrepit, half-rusted revolver -- a snub-nosed .38. He wished he had one of those Tec-9s his men practiced with this morning.

The imam walked upstairs to see the cause of the disturbance. He looked out the window and watched the bunkhouses under attack by a horde of commandos. Hasan had no idea whether they were the FBI, the police, the Army – it didn't matter. His plans were ruined. They will certainly search for him after their attack. He must not panic and had to escape.

The imam opened the door only to see one of his men fall from a gunshot as he emerged from the main house. Hasan slammed the door, now panicked. He had to hide. He looked around the mosque. A sizable stage fronted the room -- he could hide below it.

Hasan ran to the stage, opened the trap door and lowered himself to under the stage. A pile of prayer rugs filled the corner. He felt his way throughout the blackened space to the rugs and assembled a makeshift rampart. He completed this task, crawled behind the rugs, pulled out his revolver and waited for any assailant.

 Jackie Brandt assigned Tom's squad to clean out the mosque. Tom, Kat and two ninjas carefully approached the front door, the moon providing sufficient light for their assault. Not knowing what lie inside Tom took no chances. "Kat, you secure a position ten feet in front of the door and cover us when we enter. Give them a full magazine if anyone fires any shots at us."

Kat stepped back following his orders. Tom looked at the two ninjas, pointed one to the left, the other to the right. He pointed to himself indicating he will sprint straight up the middle. He approached the door, grabbed the doorknob. Without delay the trio crashed the room, tumbled to a prone position, weapons ready to return fire. No fire came their way. They saw nothing in the muted light. Tom looked back motioning for Kat to join them.

Tom noticed a stairway that led to the basement. He told the ninjas to check out the basement. They found the light switches and turned on the lights. The ninjas took the steps to the basement as Tom looked about the room. Prayer rugs covered the entire floor. He walked towards the stage at the far end of the room. "Kat, cover me." Tom ascended the four steps to the stage. He scrutinized the area but detected nothing unusual. He walked around again, this time concentrating his gaze to the floor. He noticed a hatch cut into the floor. Footprints disturbed the noticeable dust that covered the hatch. Tom thought, *"He's down there."*

Tom checked his M4 to assure the safety off. He lowered himself to one knee and stuck his finger through the small brass pulled the hatch. Abandoning all fear, he tore open the hatch and jumped into the darkness. As he hit the ground four shots whizzed by him, one grazing his tactical vest. Tom pointed the laser sight in the direction of the shots. The laser caught the eye of Hasan Al-Tamini. Tom pulled the trigger. A strobe-like three-shot burst brightened the space by its muzzle flash. His aim true, the bullets found the target, and snapped the imam's head back forcing a large fragment of bone to fly off his skull. The imam fell over the prayer rugs, his fate not in doubt. Quiet returned to the mosque.

Tom heard Kat yell, "Tom, are you OK?"

"Couldn't be better. All is well here." Tom pulled out his flashlight and crawled to the pile of rugs. Illuminating his kill, he inspected the imam.

Tom was always astonished of the damage a modest-sized piece of lead and brass inflicted on flesh and bone.

He seized the old snub nose speculating, *"What did he expect to hit with this? Then again, those shots almost hit me. "*

Tom stuffed the gun into his vest pocket intending to keep it as a souvenir. Jackie sent a squad to the mosque when he heard the shots. Tom greeted them as he emerged from below stage, "He's dead."

Kat noticed that Tom had blood on his sleeve. "Tom, you're bleeding."

Tom looked at his sleeve and the blood — he realized that the imam didn't miss his shot but grazed his arm. He smiled at Kat, "Not to worry. A fifteen cent washer will fix that."

Kat, confused by the reference, quizzically looked at him.

All walked out to join the their teammates, Tom's two ninjas carried the imam's computer and other assets they found in the basement. Jackie's techies will examine the booty for possible intelligence. The Martels again proved uncommonly professional and adept at their assignments.

By this time, Jackie had secured the main house. All the residents of Al-lahlaberg were corralled outside, the Ninjas guarding them. Composed mainly of women and children, only a few men were among the residents. Jackie questioned each to determine whether any more jihadis were hiding on the grounds. The residents were all cooperative. All said no. Jackie believed them – they were extremely grateful to Jackie for clearing their home and farm of the imam and his dreaded jihadis. He noticed it in Iraq when his squad cleared a village of ISIS jihadists – the women were thankful. They suffered incredible misery from Islamist occupation. This imam imposed his own peculiar version of Sharia Law on the community.

The imam kept his men sexually satisfied by forcing the women of the grove to regularly service them. They forced most of the grove's men to leave -- one severely beaten to send a message. A few were allowed to stay -- they were needed to keep the grove operating.

Kat watched Jackie walk to one of the remaining men in the group and started an animated conversation. The two were laughing. Kat noticed that the man wore a Miami Dolphins hat. All became clear to Kat. She tugged on Tom's vest: "Tom, remember Jackie warned us before the Koranland mission not to shoot anyone wearing a Dolphin's hat?"

"I remember," replied Tom

"Well take a look." She pointed at Jackie and the man with the hat.

"That makes sense."

A woman presented herself to Kat and gave her a basket of dates as a gift for her efforts.

Kat thanked the woman and gave her a warm hug with her free arm. Kat backed off and held the woman's hand as she told her, "I hope you all live in peace here from now on. You have a wonderful grove. I wish you all the best."

The woman smiled and thanked her again.

Tom approached Jackie, "The imam is dead. Do you want the body?"

"No, leave him where he lies. Let the cops take care of him. We'll be leaving soon. We have one more job to do."

Jackie turned to address the crowd of Allahlaberg residents. "You are safe now. Call your men to return; they won't be harmed. And do yourself a favor – be careful of your next imam. Be sure he isn't a radical jihadist. Peace be upon you."

Next, Jackie led the Martels to the pump house where Paul Hill had found the terrorists' cache. He and his squad had finished amassing a six-foot-high pile of explosives, vests and other jihadist paraphernalia, ready for detonation. Jackie asked Blade, "Where's the time bomb?" Blade reached into his vest and pulled out a powerful incendiary bomb with an electronic timer. Jackie looked at it, "Set the timer for three minutes and place it under the pile."

The Martels turned away from the pile and jogged back to the bus that had now arrived. They had all gathered in front of the main house, when the explosion illuminated the sky. Seconds later, scraps of vests and other debris rained on the crowd. Kat recalled the ball bearings from the Koranland mission.

Tom reached and gathered some pieces and showed Kat, "More souvenirs."

"Tom, you are such a packrat!" Tom smiled in affirmation. He didn't tell her about the imam's gun he saved and now stored in his vest pocket.

Jackie Brandt ordered everyone into the bus. He looked at Blade, "…free those two kids in the guardhouse. Put a smile to their faces. Tell them all the jihadis are dead. Tell them the imam is dead."

"Let's go to the bus, I have been cooling a case of Cristal to celebrate our victory. We had an outstanding day…mission accomplished. No casualties suffered. I couldn't be happier. Let's go, we need to leave before the authorities arrive -- they will have too many questions that I'd rather not answer."

Jackie Brandt realized the police would be ordered to stand down and he will never be required to answer any of those questions -- especially now that Ronald Trumbull sits in the Oval Office of the White House. Nonetheless, he and his crew should promptly depart. Why complicate matters?

Inside the bus the driver had prepared the celebratory party for the short trip to San Bernardino. A sumptuous spread of Asian food accompanied with the Cristal Champagne.

Tom and Kat sat in back, relaxing after the Allahlaberg operation. Tom looked at Kat, "Remember when we shared champagne on the boat?"

Kat replied, "Sure. On the boat after they kidnapped us."

I asked you a question that you refused to answer. Do you remember?"

Kat asked, curious where the conversation was leading, "You asked me how many children I wanted to have."

"...and you refused to answer."

Kat laughed, "You called me a coward."
"Let me show you something."

Tom jabbed his hand into his pocket, reached out for Kat's left hand and slipped a ring to her fourth finger, "Will you marry me?"

At first, stunned by the proposal, Kat jumped on Tom, wrapping her arms around him, "Of course, I will marry you. I love you so much...I love you so much." She felt tears welling from within her but succeeded in suppressing them.

She stood and shouted, "Hey everyone, Tom and I are getting married." Kat exuberantly waved her hand for all to see the ring. Tom gave her Grandma Briggs' wedding ring, a one-of-a-kind Victorian-era diamond ring in a gold setting. Its beauty and understatement impressed even Tom as he was not much of a jewelry aficionado. His mother gave him the ring when he told her of his engagement plan.

The Martels all turned to give them an ovation; even Blade and the ninjas, who acknowledged the courage and fighting skills TomKat had exhibited alongside them, stood and joined the ovation.

Jackie approached them, "Congratulations kids, I am happy for you."

Tom and Kat acknowledged their friend's approval. Kat gave a big hug to the soldier.

Tom took Kat's hand, "Do you remember I asked you a question on the boat that you refused to answer?"

Kat smiled, "I certainly do."

"Can you answer that question now?"

Kat, beaming with joy, gave her answer, "As many as you want, Tom."
Tom smiled and embraced her as the bus entered the highway heading to their headquarters at Jackie Brandt's house.

Unknown to the Martels, the leaders of ISIS, remembering the Koranland debacle, trained another team, a backup in the mountains north of Los Angeles. ISIS took no chances this time.

By the end of the day, no terrorism materialized at Disneyland. The imam, leading the jihadist reserve force, suspected that someone compromised the Allahlaberg force. He tried to call his counterpart of Allahlaberg, Hasan Al-Tamini, on his cell phone. No answer.

He had his orders: send his force to Disneyland to fulfill the duties of the Allahlaberg contingency should they not complete their assignment. The following morning, his crew found themselves on their way to Disneyland. He prayed to Allah that he would not fail. They trained hard and were ready to serve. His crew of thirty terrorists -- ten bombers and twenty gunners boarded the white vans for the final trip of their lives. Allah commanded them to jihad and none of them intended to disappoint.

The Martels were soon to embark on another chapter in their defense of country and civilization. TomKat's next encounter will be the most crucial and perilous of their short time together.

The End.

We will soon continue this story. If you enjoyed the book please give us a great review on Amazon. We will appreciate it.

Also watch for news of the movie production of this story.

What will the movie be about?

Jack Reacher meets Hanna with a touch of Thin Man savoir vivre tossed in.